Introducing Discworld®

The Discworld is a world not totally unlike our own, except that it is flat, sits on the backs of four elephants who hurtle through space balanced on a giant turtle, and magic is as integral as gravity to the way it works. Though some of its inhabitants are witches, dwarfs, wizards and even policemen, their stories are fundamentally about people being people.

The Discworld novels can be read in any order, but the City Watch series can be a good place to start.

Discworld Novels in the City Watch Series

Guards! Guards!
Men at Arms
Feet of Clay
Jingo
The Fifth Elephant
Night Watch
Thud!
Snuff

A full list of the Discworld novels can be found at the end of this book.

BOOKS BY TERRY PRATCHETT

THE DISCWORLD® SERIES

OTHER BOOKS ABOUT DISCWORLD®

Non-Discworld Books
Good Omens (with Neil Gaiman)

Shorter Writing

A Stroke of the Pen
A Blink of the Screen
A Slip of the Keyboard

The Long Earth Series (with Stephen Baxter)

The Long Earth
The Long War
The Long Mars

The Long Utopia
The Long Cosmos

Books for Young Readers

The Carpet People
Nation
Dodger
Dragons at Crumbling Castle
The Witch's Vacuum Cleaner

THE BROMELIAD TRILOGY
Truckers
Diggers
Wings

THE JOHNNY MAXWELL TRILOGY
Only You Can Save Mankind
Johnny and the Dead
Johnny and the Bomb

A complete list of Terry Pratchett books can be
found at WWW.TERRYPRATCHETT.COM.

THE
FIFTH
ELEPHANT

A Discworld® Novel

TERRY PRATCHETT

HARPER

NEW YORK • LONDON • TORONTO • SYDNEY

HARPER

A hardcover edition of this book was published in 2000 by HarperCollins Publishers.

FIRST HARPER PAPERBACKS EDITION PUBLISHED 2024.

Designed by Jen Overstreet

Library of Congress Cataloging-in-Publication Data
Names: Pratchett, Terry, author.
Title: The fifth elephant / Terry Pratchett.
Description: First Harper Paperbacks Edition | New York : Harper, 2024. |
Series: The Discworld Series | "A Discworld Novel"
Identifiers: LCCN 2024006590 | ISBN 9780063374232 (trade paperback)
Subjects: LCSH: Vimes, Samuel (Fictitious character)--Fiction. | Discworld
(Imaginary place)--Fiction. | LCGFT: Fantasy fiction. | Novels.
Classification: LCC PR6066.R34 F54 2024 | DDC 823/.914--dc23/eng/20240216
LC record available at https://lccn.loc.gov/2024006590

ISBN 978-0-06337423-2 (pbk.)

24 25 26 27 28 LBC 5 4 3 2 1

THE
FIFTH
ELEPHANT

THEY SAY THE WORLD is flat and supported on the backs of four elephants who themselves stand on the back of a giant turtle.

They *say* that the elephants, being such huge beasts, have bones of rock and iron, and nerves of gold for better conductivity over long distances.*

They *say* that the fifth elephant came screaming and trumpeting through the atmosphere of the young world all those years ago and landed hard enough to split continents and raise mountains.

No one actually saw it land, which raised the interesting philosophical point: When millions of tons of angry elephant come spinning through the sky, but there is no one to hear it, does it—philosophically speaking—make a noise?

And if there was no one to see it hit, did it *actually* hit?

In other words, wasn't it just a story for children, to explain away some interesting natural occurrences?

As for the dwarfs, whose legend it is, and who mine a lot deeper than other people, *they* say that there is a grain of truth in it.

On a clear day, from the right vantage point on the Ramtops, a watcher could see a very long way across the plains. If it was high summer, they could count the columns of dust as the ox trains plodded on at a top speed of two miles an hour, each two pulling

---

* Not rock and iron in their dead form, as they are now, but *living* rock and iron. The dwarfs have quite an inventive mythology about minerals.

1

a train of two wagons carrying four tons each. Things took a long time to get anywhere, but when they did, there was certainly a lot of them.

To the cities of the Circle Sea they carried raw material, and sometimes people who were off to seek their fortune and a fistful of diamonds.

To the mountains they brought manufactured goods, rare things from across the oceans, and people who had found wisdom and a few scars.

There was usually a day's traveling between each convoy. They turned the landscape into an unrolled time machine. On a clear day, you could see last Tuesday.

Heliographs twinkled in the distant air as the columns flashed messages back and forth about bandit presence, cargoes and the best place to get double egg, treble chips and a steak that overhung the plate all around.

Lots of people traveled on the carts. It was cheap, it beat walking and you got there eventually.

Some people traveled for free.

The driver of one wagon was having problems with his team. They were skittish. He'd expect this in the mountains, where all sorts of wild creatures might regard the oxen as a traveling meal. Here there was nothing more dangerous than cabbages, wasn't there?

Behind him, down in a narrow space between the loads of cut lumber, something slept.

It was just another day in Ankh-Morpork . . .

Sergeant Colon balanced on a shaky ladder at one end of the Brass Bridge, one of the city's busiest thoroughfares. He clung by

2

one hand to the tall pole with the box on top of it, and with the other he held a homemade picture book up to the slot in the front of the box.

"And this is *another* sort of cart," he said. "Got it?"

"'S," said a very small voice from within the box.

"O-kay," said Colon, apparently satisfied. He dropped the book and pointed down the length of the bridge.

"Now, you see those two markers what has been painted across the cobbles?"

"'S."

"And they mean . . . ?"

"If-a-cart-g's-tween-dem-in-less'na-minute-'s-goin-too-fas'," the little voice parroted.

"Well done. And then you . . . ?"

"Painta pic-cher."

"Taking care to show . . . ?"

"Drivr's-face-or-cart-lisens."

"And if it's nighttime you . . . ?"

"Use-der-sal'mander-to-make-it-brite . . ."

"Well done, Rodney. And one of us will come along every day and collect your pictures. Got everything you want?"

"'S."

"What's that, Sergeant?"

Colon looked down at the very large, brown upturned face, and smiled.

"Afternoon, All," he said, climbing ponderously down the ladder. "What you're looking at, Mister Jolson, is the modern Watch for the new millenienienum . . . num."

"'S a bit big, Fred," said All Jolson, looking at it critically. "I've seen lots of smaller ones."

"Watch as in City Watch, All."

"Ah, right."

"Anyone goes too fast around here and Lord Vetinari'll be looking at his picture next morning. The iconographs do not lie, All."

"Right, Fred. 'Cos they're too stupid."

"His Lordship's got fed up with carts speeding over the bridge, see, and asked us to do something about it. I'm Head of Traffic now, you know."

"Is that good, Fred?"

"I should just think so!" said Sergeant Colon expansively. "It's up to me to keep the, er, arteries of the city from clogging up, leadin' to a complete breakdown of commerce and ruination for us all. Most vital job there is, you could say."

"And it's just you doing it, is it?"

"Well, mainly. Mainly. Corporal Nobbs and the other lads help, of course."

All Jolson scratched his nose.

"It was on a similar subject that I wanted to talk to you, Fred," said Jolson.

"No problem, All."

"Something very odd's turned up outside my restaurant, Fred."

Sergeant Colon followed the huge man around the corner. Fred usually liked All's company because, next to All, he was very skinny indeed. All Jolson was a man who'd show up on an atlas and change the orbit of smaller planets. Paving stones cracked under his feet. He combined in one body—and there was plenty of room left over—Ankh-Morpork's best chef and its keenest eater, a circumstance made in mashed potato heaven. Sergeant Colon couldn't remember what the man's real first name had been; he'd picked up the nickname by general acclaim, since no one seeing him in the street for the first time could believe that it was *all* Jolson.

There was a big cart on Broad Way. Other traffic was backed up trying to maneuver around it.

"Had my meat delivered at lunchtime, Fred, and when my carter came out . . ."

All Jolson pointed to the large triangular construction locked around one wheel of the cart. It had been made of oak and steel, and then someone had sloshed some yellow paint over it.

Fred tapped it carefully.

"I can see where your problem is, right here," he said. "So how long was your carter in there?"

"Well. I gave him lunch . . ."

"And very good lunches you do, All, I've always said. What was the special today?"

"Smitten steak with cream sauce and slumpie, and Black Death meringue to follow," said All Jolson.

There was a moment of silence as they both pictured this meal. Fred Colon gave a little sigh.

"Butter on the slumpie?"

"You wouldn't insult me by suggesting I'd leave it off, would you?"

"A man could linger a long time over a meal like that," said Fred. "The trouble is, the Patrician, All, gets very short about carts parking on the street for more than ten minutes. He reckons that's a sort of crime."

"Taking ten minutes to eat one of *my* lunches isn't a crime, Fred, it's a tragedy," said All. "It says here 'City Watch—fifteen-dollar removal,' Fred. That's a couple of days' profits, Fred."

"Thing is," said Fred Colon, "it'll be paperwork, see? I can't just wave that away. I only wish I could. There's all them counterfoils on

5

the spike in my office. If it was me running the Watch, of course . . . but my hands are tied, see . . ."

The two men stood some way apart, hands in pockets, apparently paying little attention to one another. Sergeant Colon began to whistle under his breath.

"I know a thing or two," said All, carefully. "People think waiters ain't got ears."

"I know lots of stuff, All," said Colon, jingling his pocket change.

Both men stared at the sky for a while.

"I may have some honey ice cream left over from yesterday—"

Sergeant Colon looked down at the cart.

"Here, Mister Jolson," he said, in a voice of absolute surprise, "some complete bastard's put some sort of clamp on your wheel! Well, we'll soon see about *that*."

Colon pulled a couple of round, white-painted paddles from his belt, sighted on the Watch House semaphore tower peeking over the top of the old lemonade factory, waited until the watching gargoyle signaled him, and with a certain amount of verve and flair ripped off an impression of a man with stiff arms playing two games of table tennis at once.

"The team'll be along any minute—ah, watch this . . ."

A little farther along the street two trolls were carefully clamping a hay wagon. After a minute or two one of them happened to glance at the Watch House tower, nudged his colleague, produced two bats of his own and, with rather less élan than Sergeant Colon, sent a signal. When it was answered the trolls looked around, spotted Colon, and lumbered toward him.

"Ta-da," said Colon, proudly.

"Amazing, this new technology," said All Jolson, admiringly. "And they must've been, what, forty or fifty yards away?"

"'S'right, All. In the old days I'd've had to blow a whistle. And they'll arrive here knowin' it was *me* who wanted 'em, too."

"Instead of having to look and see it was you," said Jolson.

"Well, yeah," said Colon, aware that what had transpired might not be the brightest ray of light in the new dawn of the communications revolution. "Of course, it'd have worked just as well if they'd been streets away. On the other side of the city, even. And if I told the gargoyle to, as we say, 'put' it on the 'big' tower over on the Tump they'd have got it in Sto Lat within minutes, see?"

"And that's twenty miles."

"At least."

"Amazing, Fred."

"Time moves on, All," said Colon, as the trolls reached them. "Constable Chert, who told you to clamp my friend's cart?" he demanded.

"Well, Sarge, dis morning you said we was to clamp every—"

"Not *this* cart," said Colon. "Unlock it right now, and we'll say no more about it, eh?"

Constable Chert seemed to reach the conclusion that he wasn't being paid to think, and this was just as well, because Sergeant Colon did not believe trolls gave value for money in that department. "If you say so, Sarge . . ."

"While you're doing that, me and All here will have a little chat, right, All?" said Fred Colon.

"That's right, Fred."

"Well, I *say* chat, but I'll be mostly listenin', on account of having my mouth full."

* * *

Snow cascaded from the fir branches. The man forced his way through, stood fighting for breath for a moment and then set off across the clearing at a fast jog.

Across the valley he heard the first blast on the horn.

He had an hour, then, if he could trust them. He might not make it to the tower, but there were other ways out.

He had plans. He could outwit them. Keep off the snow as much as you can, double back, make use of the streams . . . it was possible, it *had* been done before.

He was sure of that.

A few miles away sleek bodies set out through the forest. The hunt was on.

And elsewhere in Ankh-Morpork, the Fools' Guild was on fire.

This was a problem, because the Guild's fire brigade largely consisted of clowns.

And *this* was a problem because, if you show a clown a bucket of water and a ladder, he knows only one way to act. Years of training take over. It's something in the red nose speaking to him. He can't help himself.

Sam Vimes of the Ankh-Morpork City Watch leaned against a wall and watched the show.

"We really must put that proposal for a civic fire service to the Patrician again," he said. Across the street, a clown picked up a ladder, turned, knocked the clown *behind* him into a bucket of water, then turned *again* to see what the commotion was, thus sending his rising victim into the bucket again with a surprising parping noise. The crowd watched silently. If it were funny, clowns wouldn't be doing it.

"The guilds are all against it," said Captain Carrot Iron-foundersson, his second in command, as the clown with the ladder had a bucket of water poured down his trousers. "They say it'd be trespass."

The fire had taken hold in a first-floor room.

"If we let it burn it'd be a blow for entertainment in this city," said Carrot earnestly.

Vimes looked sideways at him. That was a true Carrot comment. It sounded as innocent as hell, but you *could* take it a different way.

"It certainly would," he said. "Nevertheless, I *suppose* we'd better do something." He stepped forward and cupped his hands.

"All right, this is the Watch! Bucket chain!" he shouted.

"Aw, *must* we?" said someone in the crowd.

"Yes, you must," said Captain Carrot. "Come on, everyone, if we form two lines we'll have this done in no time at all! What d'you say, eh? It might even be fun!"

And they did it, Vimes noted. Carrot treated everyone as if they were jolly good chaps and somehow, in some inexplicable way, they couldn't resist the urge not to prove him wrong.

And to the disappointment of the crowd the fire was soon put out, once the clowns were disarmed and led away by kind people.

Carrot reappeared, wiping his forehead, as Vimes lit a cigar.

"Apparently the fire eater was sick," he said.

"It's just possible we might never be forgiven," said Vimes, as they set off on patrol again. "Oh no . . . what now?"

Carrot was staring upward, toward the nearest clacks tower.

"Riot in Cable Street," he said. "It's All Officers, sir."

They broke into a run. You always did for an All Officers. The people in trouble might well be you.

There were more dwarfs on the streets as they got nearer, and Vimes recognized the signs. The dwarfs all wore preoccupied looks and were walking in the same direction.

"It's over," he said, as they rounded a corner. "You can tell by the sudden increase in suspiciously innocent bystanders."

Whatever else the emergency had been, it had been a big one. The street was strewn with debris, and a fair amount of dwarfs. Vimes slowed down.

"Third time this week," he said. "What's gotten into them?"

"Hard to say, sir," said Carrot. Vimes shot him a glance. Carrot had been raised by dwarfs. He also, if he could possibly avoid it, never told a lie.

"That isn't the same as *I don't know*, is it," he said.

The captain looked awkward.

"I think it's . . . sort of political," he said.

Vimes noted a throwing ax buried in a wall.

"Yes, I can see that," he said.

Someone was coming along the street, and was probably the reason why the riot had broken up. Lance-Constable Bluejohn was the biggest troll Vimes had ever met. He *loomed*. He was so big that he didn't stand out in a crowd because he *was* the crowd; people failed to see him because he was in the way. And, like many overgrown people, he was instinctively gentle and rather shy and inclined to let others tell him what to do. If fate had led him to join a gang, he'd be the muscle. In the Watch, he was the riot shield. Other watchmen were peering around him.

"Looks like it started in Gimlet's Delicatessen," said Vimes, as the rest of the Watch moved in. "Get a statement off Gimlet."

"Not a good idea, sir," said Carrot firmly. "He didn't see anything."

"How do you know he didn't see anything? You haven't asked him."

"I know, sir. He didn't see anything. He didn't hear anything, either."

"With a mob trashing his restaurant and scrapping in the street outside?"

"That's right, sir."

"Ah. I get it. There's none so deaf as those that won't hear, are you saying?"

"Something like that, sir, yes. Look, it's all over, sir. I don't think anyone's seriously hurt. It'll be for the best, sir. Please?"

"Is this one of those private dwarf things, Captain?"

"Yes, sir—"

"Well, this is Ankh-Morpork, Captain, not some mine in the mountains, and it's my job to keep the peace, and *this*, Captain, doesn't look like it. What're people going to say about rioting in the streets?"

"They'll say it's another day in the life of the big city, sir," said Carrot woodenly.

"Yes, I suppose they would, at that. However—" Vimes picked up a groaning dwarf. "Who did this?" he demanded. "I'm not in the mood for being messed around. Come on, I want a name!"

"Agi Hammerthief," muttered the dwarf, struggling.

"All right," said Vimes, letting him go. "Write that down, Carrot."

"No, sir," said Carrot.

"Excuse me?"

"There is no Agi Hammerthief in the city, sir."

"You know every dwarf?"

"A lot of them, sir. But Agi Hammerthief is only found down mines, sir. He's a sort of mischievous spirit, sir. For example, 'put it where Agi puts the coal,' sir, means—"

11

"Yes, I can guess," said Vimes. "You're telling me that dwarf just said this riot was started by Sweet Fanny Adams?" The dwarf had disappeared smartly around a corner.

"More or less, sir. Excuse me a moment, sir." Carrot stepped across the street, pulling two white painted paddles out of his belt. "I'll just get a line of sight on a tower," he said. "I'd better send a clacks."

"Why?"

"Well, we've kept the Patrician waiting, sir, so it'd be good manners to let him know we're late."

Vimes pulled out his watch and stared at it. It was turning out to be one of those days . . . the sort that you got every day.

It is in the nature of the universe that the person who always keeps you waiting ten minutes will, on the day you are ten minutes tardy, have been ready ten minutes early and will make a point of *not mentioning this.*

"Sorry we're late, sir," said Vimes, as they entered the Oblong Office.

"Oh, *are* you late?" said Lord Vetinari, looking up from his paperwork. "I really hadn't noticed. Nothing serious, I trust."

"The Fools' Guild caught fire, sir," said Carrot.

"Many casualties?"

"No, sir."

"Well, that is a blessing," said Lord Vetinari carefully. He put down his pen.

"Now . . . what do we have to discuss?" He pulled another document toward him and read it swiftly.

"Ah . . . I see that the new traffic division is having the desired effect." He indicated a large pile of paper. "I am getting any amount of complaints from the Carters' and Drovers' Guild. Well done. Do pass on my thanks to Sergeant Colon and his team."

"I will, sir."

"I see in one day they clamped seventeen carts, ten horses, eighteen oxen and one duck."

"It was parked illegally, sir."

"Indeed. However, a strange pattern seems to emerge."

"Sir?"

"Many of the carters say that they were not in fact parked but had merely halted while an extremely old and extremely ugly lady crossed the road extremely slowly."

"That's their story, sir."

"They know she was an old lady by her constant litany on the lines of 'oh deary me, my poor old feet' and similar expressions."

"Certainly sounds like an old lady to me, sir," said Vimes, his face still wooden.

"Quite so. What is rather strange is that several of them then report seeing the old lady subsequently legging it away along an alley rather fast. I'd discount this, of course, were it not for the fact that the lady has apparently been seen crossing another street, very slowly, some distance away shortly afterward. Something of a mystery, Vimes."

Vimes put his hand over his eyes. "It's one I intend to solve quite quickly, sir."

The Patrician nodded, and made a short note on the list in front of him.

As he went to move it aside he uncovered a much grubbier, much folded scrap of paper. He picked up two letter knives and, using them fastidiously, unfolded the paper and inched it across the desk toward Vimes.

"Do you know anything about this?" he said.

Vimes read, in large, round, crayoned letters:

**DeEr Cur, The CruELt to HOMLIss DoGs In thIs
CITy Is A DIssGrays, Wat arE The WaTCH
Do Ing A BouT IT¿
SiNeD The LeAK AgyANsct CrUle T To DoGs.**

"Not a thing," he said.

"My clerks say that one like it is pushed under the door most nights," said the Patrician. "Apparently no one is seen."

"Do you want me to investigate?" said Vimes. "It shouldn't be hard to find someone in this city who dribbles when he writes and spells even worse than Carrot."

"Thank you, sir," said Carrot.

"None of the guards report noticing anyone," said the Patrician. "Is there any group in Ankh-Morpork particularly interested in the welfare of dogs?"

"I doubt it, sir."

"Then I shall ignore it pro tem," said Vetinari. He let the soggy letter splash into the wastepaper basket.

"On to more pressing matters," he said briskly. "Now, then . . . what do you know about Bonk?"

Vimes stared.

There was a polite cough from Carrot.

"The river or the town, sir?" he said.

The Patrician smiled. "Ah, Captain, you have long ago ceased to surprise me. Yes, I was referring to the town."

"It's one of the major towns in Überwald, sir," said Carrot, balancing the umlaut perfectly. "Exports: precious metals, leather, timber and of course fat from the deep fat mines at Shmaltzberg—"

"There's a *place* called Bonk?" said Vimes, still marveling at the speed with which they'd got here from a damp letter about dogs.

"Strictly speaking, sir, it's more correctly pronounced Beyonk," said Carrot.

"Even so—"

"And in Beyonk, sir, 'morpork' sounds exactly like their words for an item of ladies' underwear," said Carrot. "There's only so many syllables in the world, when you think about it."

"How do you *know* all this stuff, Carrot?"

"Oh, you pick it up, sir. Here and there."

"Really? So exactly *which* item of—"

"Something extremely important will be taking place there in a few weeks," said Lord Vetinari. "Something which, I have to add, is vital to the future prosperity of Ankh-Morpork."

"The crowning of the Low King," said Carrot.

Vimes stared from Carrot to the Patrician, and back again.

"Is there some kind of circular that goes around that doesn't get as far as me?" he said.

"The dwarf community has been talking about little else for months, sir."

"Really?" said Vimes. "You mean the riots? Those fights every night in the dwarf bars?"

"Captain Carrot is correct, Vimes. It will be a grand occasion, attended by representatives of many governments. And from various Uberwald principalities, of course, because the Low King only rules those areas of Uberwald that are below ground. His favor is valuable. Borogravia and Genua will be there, without a doubt, and probably even Klatch."

15

"Klatch? But they're even farther from Uberwald than we are! What are they bothering to go for?"

He paused for a moment, and then added: "Hah. I'm being stupid. Where's the money?"

"I beg your pardon, Commander?"

"That's what my old sergeant used to say when he was puzzled, sir. Find out where the money is and you've got it half-solved."

Vetinari stood up and walked over to the big window, with his back to them.

"A large country, Uberwald," he said, apparently addressing the glass. "Dark. Mysterious. Ancient . . ."

"Huge untapped reserves of coal and iron ore," said Carrot. "And fat, of course. The best candles, lamp oils and soap come ultimately from the Shmaltzberg deposits."

"Why? We've got our own slaughterhouse, haven't we?"

"Ankh-Morpork uses a great many candles, sir."

"It certainly doesn't use much soap," said Vimes.

"There are so many uses for fats and tallows, sir. We couldn't possibly supply ourselves."

"*Ah*," said Vimes.

The Patrician sighed.

"Obviously I hope that we may strengthen our trading links with the various nations within Uberwald," he said. "The situation there is volatile in the extreme. Do you *know* much about Uberwald, Commander Vimes?"

Vimes, whose knowledge of geography was microscopically detailed within five miles of Ankh-Morpork and merely microscopic beyond that, nodded uncertainly.

"Only that it's not really a country," said Vetinari. "It's—"

"It's rather more what you get *before* you get countries," said Carrot. "It's mainly fortified towns and fiefdoms with no real boundaries and lots of forest in between. There's always some sort of feud going on. There's no law apart from whatever the local lords enforce, and banditry of all kinds is rife."

"So unlike the home life of our own dear city," said Vimes, not quite under his breath. The Patrician gave him an impassive glance.

"In Uberwald the dwarfs and trolls haven't settled their old grievances, there are large areas controlled by feudal vampire or werewolf clans, and there are also tracts with much higher than normal background magic. It is a chaotic place, indeed, and you'd hardly think you were in the Century of the Fruitbat. It is to be hoped that things will improve, however, and Uberwald will, happily, be joining the community of nations."

Vimes and Vetinari exchanged looks. Sometimes Carrot sounded like a civics essay written by a stunned choirboy.

"Well put," said the Patrician, at last. "But until that joysome day, Uberwald remains a mystery inside a riddle wrapped in an enigma."

"Let me see if I've got this right," said Vimes. "Uberwald is like this big suet pudding that everyone's suddenly noticed, and now with this coronation as an excuse we've all got to rush there with knife, fork and spoon to shovel as much on our plates as possible?"

"Your grasp of political reality is masterly, Vimes. You lack only the appropriate vocabulary. Ankh-Morpork must send a representative, obviously. An ambassador, as it were."

"You're not suggesting I should go to this affair, are you?" said Vimes.

"Oh, I couldn't send the Commander of the City Watch," said Lord Vetinari. "Most of the Uberwald countries have no concept of a modern civil peacekeeping authority."

Vimes relaxed.

"I'm sending the Duke of Ankh-Morpork, instead."

Vimes sat bolt upright.

"They are mostly feudal systems," Vetinari went on. "They set great score by rank—"

"I'm not being ordered to go to Uberwald!"

"Ordered, Your Grace?" Vetinari looked shocked and concerned. "Good heavens, I must have misunderstood Lady Sybil . . . She told me yesterday that a holiday a long way from Ankh-Morpork would do you the world of good . . ."

"You *spoke* to Sybil?"

"At the reception for the new president of the Tailors' Guild, yes. I believe you left early. You were called away. Some emergency, I understand. Lady Sybil happened to mention how you seemed to be, as she put it, constantly on the job, and one thing led to another. Oh dear, I do hope I haven't caused some marital misunderstanding . . ."

"I can't leave the city *now* of all times!" said Vimes desperately. "There's so much to do!"

"That is exactly why Sybil says you ought to leave the city," said Vetinari.

"But there's the new training school—"

"Ticking over nicely now, sir," said Carrot.

"The whole carrier pigeon network is a complete mess—"

"More or less sorted out, sir, now that we've changed their feed. Besides, the clacks seems to be functioning very well."

"We've got to get the River Watch set up—"

"Can't do much for a week or two, sir, until we've dredged up the boat."

"The drains at the Chitterling Street station are—"

"I've got the plumbers working on it, sir."

Vimes knew that he had lost. He had lost as soon as Sybil was involved, because she was always a reliable siege engine against the walls of his defenses. But there was such a thing as going down fighting.

"You *know* I'm no good at diplomatic talk," he said.

"On the contrary, Vimes, you appear to have amazed the diplomatic corps here in Ankh-Morpork," said Lord Vetinari. "They're not used to plain speech. It confuses them. What was it you said to the Istanzian ambassador last month?" He riffled through the papers on his desk. "Let me see, the complaint is here somewhere . . . Oh yes, on the matter of military incursions across the Slipnir River, you indicated that further transgressions would involve him, personally, that is to say the ambassador, and I quote 'going home in an ambulance.'"

"I'm sorry about that, sir, but it had been a long day and he was really getting on my—"

"Since when their armed forces have pulled back so far that they are nearly in the next country," said Lord Vetinari, moving the paper aside. "I have to say that your observation complied only with the general *thrust* of my view in this matter but was, at least, succinct. Apparently you also looked at the ambassador in a very threatening way."

"It was only the way I usually look."

"To be sure. Happily, in Uberwald you will only need to look friendly."

"Ah, but you don't want me saying things like 'how about selling us all your fat really cheap?' do you?" said Vimes, desperately.

19

"You will not be required to do *any* negotiating, Vimes. That will be dealt with by one of my clerks, who will set up the temporary embassy and discuss such matters with his opposite numbers among the courts of Uberwald. All clerks speak the same language. *You* will simply be as ducal as you can. And, of course, you will take a retinue. A staff," Vetinari added, seeing Vimes's blank look. He sighed. "People to go with you. I suggest Sergeant Angua, Sergeant Detritus and Corporal Littlebottom."

"Ah," said Carrot, nodding encouragingly.

"Sorry?" said Vimes. "I think there must have been a whole piece of conversation just then that I must have missed."

"A werewolf, a troll and a dwarf," said Carrot. "Ethnic minorities, sir."

". . . but, in Uberwald, they are ethnic *majorities*," said Lord Vetinari. "All three officers come from there originally, I believe. Their presence will speak volumes."

"So far it hasn't sent me a postcard," said Vimes. "I'd rather take—"

"Sir, it will show people in Uberwald that Ankh-Morpork is a multicultural society, you see?" said Carrot.

"Oh, I see. 'People like us.' People you can do business with," said Vimes, glumly.

"Sometimes," Vetinari said, testily, "it really does seem to me that the culture of cynicism in the Watch is . . . is . . ."

"Insufficient?" said Vimes. There was silence. "All right," he sighed, "I'd better go off and polish the knobs on my coronet, hadn't I?"

"The ducal coronet, if I remember my heraldry, does not have knobs on it. It is decidedly . . . spiky," said the Patrician, pushing across the desk a small pile of papers topped by a gold-edged invitation card. "Good. I will have a . . . a clacks sent immediately. You

20

will be more fully briefed later. Do give my regards to the duchess. And now, please do not let me detain you further . . ."

"He always says that," muttered Vimes, as the two men hurried down the stairs. "He knows I don't like being married to a duchess."

"I thought you and Lady Sybil—"

"Oh, being married to Sybil is fine, fine," said Vimes hurriedly. "It's just the duchess bit I don't like. Where is everyone tonight?"

"Corporal Littlebottom's on pigeon duty, Detritus is on night patrol with Swires, and Angua's on special duty in the Shades, sir. You remember? With Nobby?"

"Oh gods, yes. Well, when they come in tomorrow you'd better get them to report to me. Incidentally, get that bloody wig off Nobby and hide it, will you?" Vimes leafed through the paperwork. "I've never heard of the Low King of the Dwarfs. I thought that 'king' in Dwarfish just meant a sort of senior engineer."

"Ah, well, the Low King is rather special," said Carrot.

"Why?"

"Well, it all starts with the Scone of Stone, sir."

"The what?"

"Would you mind a little detour on the way back to the Yard, sir? It'll make things clearer."

The young woman stood on a corner of the Shades. Her general stance indicated that she was, in the specialized patois of the area, a lady in waiting. To be more precise a lady in waiting for Mr. Right, or at least Mr. Right Amount.

She idly swung her handbag.

This was a very recognizable signal, for anyone with the brains of a pigeon. A member of the Thieves' Guild would have passed carefully by on the other side of the lane, giving her nothing more than a gentlemanly and above all nonaggressive nod. Even the less-polite freelance thieves that lurked in this area would have thought twice before eyeing the handbag. The Seamstresses' Guild operated a very swift and nonreversible kind of justice.

The skinny body of Done It Duncan however, did *not* have the brains of a pigeon. The little man had been watching the bag like a cat for fully five minutes, and now the very thought of its contents had hypnotized him. He could practically taste the money. He rose on his toes, lowered his head, dashed out of the alley, grabbed the bag and got several inches before the world exploded behind him and he ended up flat in the mud.

Something right by his ear started to drool. And there was a long, very long drawn out growl, not changing in tone at all, just unrolling a deep promise of what would happen if he tried to move.

He heard footsteps, and out of the corner of his eyes saw a swirl of lace.

"Oh, *Done It*," said a voice. "Bag snatching? That's a bit low, isn't it? Even for you? You could've got really hurt. It's only Duncan, miss. He'll be no trouble. You can let him up."

The weight was removed from Duncan's back. He heard something pad off into the gloom of an alley.

"I done it, I done it," said the little thief desperately, as Corporal Nobbs helped him to his feet.

"Yes, I know you did. I *saw* you," said Nobby. "And you know what'd happen to you if the Thieves' Guild spotted you? You'd be dead in the river with no time off for good behavior."

"They hate me 'cos I'm so good," said Duncan, through his matted beard. " 'Ere, you know the robbery at All Jolson's last month? I done that."

"That's right, Duncan. You done that."

"An' that haul at the gold vaults last week, I done that, too. It wasn't Coalface and his boys."

"No, it was you, wasn't it, Duncan."

"An' that job at the goldsmith's that everyone says Crunchie Ron done—"

"You done it, did you?"

"'S'right," said Duncan.

"And it was you what stole fire from the gods, too, wasn't it, Duncan?" said Nobby, grinning evilly under his wig.

"Yeah, that was me." Duncan nodded. He sniffed. "I was a bit younger then, of course." Duncan peered shortsightedly at Nobby Nobbs.

"Why've you got a dress on, Nobby?"

"It's hush hush, Duncan."

"Ah, right." Duncan shifted uneasily. "You couldn't spare me a bob or two, could you, Nobby? I ain't eaten for two days."

Small coins gleamed in the dark.

"Now push off," said Corporal Nobbs.

"Thanks, Nobby. You got any unsolved crimes, you know where to find me."

Duncan lurched off into the night.

Sergeant Angua appeared behind Nobby, buckling on her breastplate.

"Poor old devil," she said.

"He was a good thief in his day," said Nobby, taking a notebook out of his handbag and jotting down a few lines.

"Kind of you to help him," said Angua.

"Well, I can get the money back out of petty cash," said Nobby. "An' now we know who did the bullion job, don't we. That'll be a feather in my cap with Mister Vimes."

"Bonnet, Nobby."

"What?"

"Your bonnet, Nobby. It's got a rather fetching band of flowers around it."

"Oh . . . yeah . . ."

"It's not that I'm complaining," said Angua, "but when we were assigned this job I thought it was *me* who was going to be the decoy and you who was going to be the backup, Nobby."

"Yeah, but what with you bein' . . ." Nobby's expression creased as he edged his way into unfamiliar linguistic territory. ". . . mor . . . phor . . . log . . . ic . . . ally gifted . . ."

"A werewolf, Nobby. I know the word."

"Right . . . well, obviously, you'd be a lot better at lurkin', an' . . . an' obviously it's not right, women havin' to act as decoys in police work . . ."

Angua hesitated, as she so often did when attempting to talk to Nobby on difficult matters, and waved her hands in front of her as if trying to shape the invisible dough of her thoughts.

"It's just that . . . I mean, people might . . ." she began. "I mean . . . well, you know what people call men who wear wigs and gowns, don't you?"

"Yes, miss."

"You do?"

"Yes, miss. Lawyers, miss."

"Good. Yes. Good," said Angua slowly. "Now try another one . . ."

"Er . . . actors, miss?"

Angua gave up. "You look good in taffeta, Nobby," she said.

"You don't think it makes me look too fat?"

Angua sniffed.

"Oh no . . ." she said, quietly.

"I thought I'd better put scent on for verysillymitude," said Nobby quickly.

"What? Oh . . ." Angua shook her head, took another breath. "I can smell . . . some . . . thing . . . else . . ."

"That's surprising, 'cos this stuff's a bit on the pungent side and frankly I don't think lily of the valley is supposed to smell like this . . ."

". . . it's not perfume . . ."

". . . but the lavender stuff they had you could clean brass with . . ."

"Can you get back to the Chitterling station by yourself, Nobby?" said Angua. Despite her rising panic, she mentally added: *After all, what could happen? I mean, really?*

"Yes, miss."

"There's something I'd better . . . sort out . . ."

Angua hurried away, the new scent filling her nostrils. It would have to be powerful to combat Eau de Nobbs, and it was. Oh, it *was*.

Not here, she thought. Not now.

Not him.

The running man swung along a branch wet with snow, and managed at last to lower himself onto a branch belonging to the next tree. That took him a long way from the stream. How good was their sense of smell? Pretty damn good, he knew. But this good?

He'd gotten out of the stream onto another overhanging branch. If they followed the banks, and they'd be bright enough to do that, they'd surely never know he'd left the stream.

There was a howl, away to the left.

He headed right, into the gloom of the forest.

Vimes heard Carrot scrabble around in the gloom, and the sound of a key in the lock.

"I thought the Campaign for Equal Heights was running this place now," he said.

"It's so hard to find volunteers," said Carrot, ushering him through the low door and lighting a candle. "I come in every day just to keep an eye on things, but no one else seems very interested."

"I can't imagine why," said Vimes, looking around the Dwarf Bread Museum.

The one positive thing you could say about the bread products around him was that they were probably as edible now as they were on the day they were baked. "Forged" was a better term. Dwarf bread was made as a meal of last resort and also as a weapon and a currency. Dwarfs were not, as far as Vimes knew, religious in any way, but the way they thought about bread came close.

There was a tinkle and a scrabbling noise somewhere in the gloom.

"Rats," said Carrot. "They never stop trying to eat dwarf bread, poor things . . . Ah, here we are. The Scone of Stone. A replica, of course."

Vimes stared at the misshaped thing on its dusty display stand. It *was* vaguely sconelike, but only if someone pointed this out to you beforehand. Otherwise, the term "a lump of rock" was pretty accurate. It was about the size, and shape, of a well sat-on cushion. There were a few fossilized currants visible.

"My wife rests her feet on something like that when she's had a long day," he said.

"It's fifteen hundred years old," said Carrot, with something like awe in his voice.

"I thought this was the replica."

"Well, yes . . . but it's a replica of a very important thing, sir," said Carrot.

Vimes sniffed. The air had a certain pungent quality.

"Smells strongly of cats in here, doesn't it?"

"I'm afraid they get in after the rats, sir. A rat who's nibbled on dwarf bread tends not to be able to run very fast."

Vimes lit a cigar. Carrot gave it a look of uncertain disapproval.

"We do thank people for not smoking in here, sir," he said.

"Why? You don't know they're not going to," said Vimes. He leaned against the display cabinet. "All right, Captain. Why am I *really* going to . . . Bonk? I don't know a lot about diplomacy, but I do know it's never just about one thing. What's the Low King? Why're our dwarfs scrapping?"

"Well, sir . . . have you heard of *kruk*?"

"Dwarf mining law?" said Vimes.

"Well done, sir. But it's a lot more than that. It's about . . . how you live. Laws of ownership, marriage laws, inheritance, rules for dealing with disputes of all kinds, that sort of thing. Everything, really. And the Low King . . . well, you could call him the final court of appeal. He's advised, of course, but he's got the last word. Still with me?"

"Makes sense so far."

"And he is crowned on the Scone of Stone and sits on it to give his judgments because all the Low Kings have done that ever since B'hrian Bloodaxe, fifteen hundred years ago. It . . . gives authority."

Vimes nodded, dourly. That made sense, too. You did something because it had always been done, and the explanation was "but we've *always* done it this way." A million dead people can't have been wrong, can they?

"Does he get elected, or born or what?" he said.

"I suppose you could say he's elected," said Carrot. "But really a lot of senior dwarfs arrange it among themselves. After listening to other dwarfs, of course. Taking soundings, it's called. Traditionally he's from one of the big families. But . . . er . . ."

"Yes?"

"Things are a little different this year. Tempers are a bit . . . stretched."

Ah, thought Vimes.

"Wrong dwarf won?" he said.

"Some dwarfs would say so. But it's more that the whole process has been called into question," said Carrot. "By the dwarfs in the biggest dwarf city outside Uberwald."

"Don't tell me, that must be that place hubward of—"

"It's Ankh-Morpork, sir."

"What? We're not a dwarf city!"

"Fifty thousand dwarfs now, sir."

"Really?"

"Yes, sir."

"Are you *sure*?"

"Yes, sir."

Of course he is, Vimes thought. He probably knows them all by name.

"You have to understand, sir, that there's a sort of big debate going on," said Carrot. "On how you define a dwarf."

"Well, *some* people might say that they're called dwarfs because—"

"No, sir. Not size. Nobby Nobbs is shorter than many dwarfs, and we don't call *him* a dwarf."

"We don't call him a human, either," said Vimes.

"And, of course, I am also a dwarf."

"You know, Carrot, I keep meaning to talk to you about that—"

"Adopted by dwarfs, brought up by dwarfs . . . to dwarfs, I'm a dwarf, sir. I can do the rite of *k'zakra*, I know the secrets of *h'ragna*, I can *ha'lk* my *g'rakha* correctly . . . I am a dwarf."

"What do those things mean?"

"I'm not allowed to tell non-dwarfs." Carrot tactfully tried to stand out of the way of the cigar smoke. "Unfortunately, some of the mountain dwarfs think that dwarfs who have moved away aren't proper dwarfs, either. But this time, the kingship has been swung by the views of the Ankh-Morpork dwarfs, and a lot of dwarfs back home don't like it. There's been a lot of bad feeling all round. Families falling out, that sort of thing. Much pulling of beards."

"Really?" Vimes tried not to smile.

"It's not funny if you're a dwarf."

"Sorry."

"And I'm afraid this new Low King is only going to make matters worse, although of course I wish him well."

"Tough, is he?"

"Er . . . I think you can assume, sir, that any dwarf who rises sufficiently in dwarf society to even be *considered* as a candidate for the kingship did not get there by singing the hi-ho song and bandaging wounded animals in the forest. But by dwarf standards, King Rhys Rhysson is a modern thinker, although I hear he doesn't like Ankh-Morpork very much."

"Sounds like a very clear thinker, too."

"Anyway, this has upset a lot of the more, er, traditional mountain dwarfs who thought the next king would be Albrecht Albrechtson."

"Who is *not* a modern thinker?"

"He thinks even coming up above ground is dangerously non-dwarfish."

Vimes sighed. "Well, I can see there's a problem, Carrot, but the thing about this problem, the key point, is that it's not mine. Or yours, dwarf or not." He tapped the Scone's case.

"Replica, eh?" he said. "Sure it's not the real one?"

"Sir! There is only one real Scone. We call it the 'thing and the whole of the thing.'"

"Well, if it's a good replica, who'd know?"

"Any dwarf would, sir."

"Only joking."

There was a hamlet down there, where two rivers met. There would be boats.

This was *working*. The slopes behind him were white and free of dark shapes. No matter how good they were, let them try to out-swim a boat . . .

Hard-packed snow crunched under his feet. He staggered past the few rough hovels, saw the jetty, saw the boats, fought with the frozen rope that moored the nearest one, grabbed an oar and pushed himself out into the current.

There was still no movement on the hills.

Now, at last, he could take stock. It was a bigger boat than one man could handle, but all he had to do was fend off the banks. That'd do for tonight. In the morning he could leave it somewhere, perhaps ask someone to get a message through to the tower, and then he'd buy a horse and . . .

Behind him, under the tarpaulin in the bows, something started to growl.

They really were *very* clever.

* * *

In a castle not far away, the vampire Lady Margolotta sat quietly, leafing through *Twurp's Peerage*.

It wasn't a very good reference book for the countries on this side of the Ramtops, where the standard work was *The Almanac de Gothick*, in which she herself occupied almost four pages,* but if you needed to know who thought they were who in Ankh-Morpork it was invaluable.

Her copy was now bristling with bookmarks. She sighed and pushed it away.

Beside her was a fluted glass containing a red liquid. She took a sip, and made a face. Then she stared at the candlelight, and tried to think like Lord Vetinari.

How much did he suspect? How much news got back? The clacks tower had only been up for a month, and was being roundly denounced throughout Bonk as an intrusion. But it seemed to be doing a good if stealthy local traffic.

Who would he send?

His choice would tell her everything, she was sure. Someone like Lord Rust or Lord Selachii . . . well, she'd think a lot less of him if he sent someone like those. All that she had heard, and Lady Margolotta heard a lot of things, the Ankh-Morpork diplomatic corps as a whole could not find its backside with a map. Of course, it was good business for a diplomat to appear stupid, right up to the moment when he'd stolen your socks, but Lady Margolotta had met some of Ankh-Morpork's finest and no one could act *that* well.

The growing howling outside began to get on her nerves. She rang for her butler.

---

* Vampires evolve long names. It's something to do to pass the long years.

"Yeth, mithtreth?" said Igor, materializing out of the shadows.

"Go and tell the children of the night to make wonderful music somewhere else, will you? I have a headache."

"Indeed, mithtreth."

Lady Margolotta yawned. It had been a long night. She'd think better after a good day's sleep.

As she went to blow out the candle, she glanced at the book again. There was a marker in the Vs.

But . . . surely even the Patrician couldn't know *that* much . . .

She hesitated, and then pulled the bellpull above the coffin. Igor reappeared, in the way of Igors.

"Those keen young men at the clacks tower will be awake, won't they?"

"Yeth, mithtreth."

"Send a clacks to our agent asking for *everything* about Commander Vimes of the Watch, will you?"

"Ith he a diplomat, mithtreth?"

Lady Margolotta lay back. "No, Igor. He's the *reason* for diplomats. Close the lid, will you?"

Sam Vimes could parallel process. Most husbands can. They learn to follow their own line of thought while *at the same time* listening to what their wives say. And the listening is important, because at any time they could be challenged and must be ready to quote the last sentence in full. A vital additional skill is being able to scan the dialogue for telltale phrases, such as "and they can deliver it tomorrow" or "so I've invited them for dinner" or "they can do it in blue, really quite cheaply."

Lady Sybil was aware of this. Sam could coherently carry on an entire conversation while thinking about something completely different.

"I will tell Willikins to pack winter clothes," she said, watching him. "It'll be pretty cold up there at this time of year."

"Yes. That's a good idea." Vimes continued to stare at a point just above the fireplace.

"We'll have to host a party ourselves, I expect, so we ought to take a cartload of typical Ankh-Morpork food. Show the flag, you know. Do you think I should take a cook along?"

"Yes, dear. That would be a good idea. No one outside the city knows how to make a knuckle sandwich properly."

Sybil was impressed. Ears operating entirely on automatic had nevertheless triggered the mouth into making a small but coherent contribution.

She said, "Do you think we ought to take the alligator with us?"

"Yes, that might be advisable."

She watched his face. Small furrows formed on Vimes's brow as the ears nudged the brain. He blinked.

"What alligator?"

"You were miles away, Sam. In Uberwald, I expect."

"Sorry."

"Is there a problem?"

"Why's he sending *me*, Sybil?"

"I'm sure Havelock shares with me a conviction that you have hidden depths, Sam."

Vimes sank gloomily into his armchair. It was, he felt, a persistent flaw in his wife's otherwise practical and sensible character that she believed, against all evidence, that he was a man of many talents. He *knew* he had hidden depths. There was nothing in them that he'd like to see float to the surface. They contained things that should be left to lie.

There was also a nagging worry that he couldn't quite pin down. Had he been able to, he might have expressed it like this:

Policemen didn't go on holiday. Where you got policemen, as Lord Vetinari was wont to remark, you got crime. So if he went to Bonk, however you pronounced the damn place, there *would* be a crime. It was something the world always laid on for policemen.

"It'll be nice to see Serafine again," said Sybil.

"Yes, indeed," said Vimes.

In Bonk he would not, officially, *be* a policeman. He did not like this at all. He liked this even less than all the other things.

On the few occasions he'd been outside Ankh-Morpork and its surrounding fiefdom he'd either been going to other local cities where the Ankh-Morpork badge carried some weight, or he had been in hot pursuit, that most ancient and honorable of police procedures. From the way Carrot talked, in Bonk his badge would merely figure as extra roughage on someone's menu.

His brow wrinkled again.

"Serafine?"

"Lady Serafine von Uberwald," said Sybil. "Sergeant Angua's mother? You remember me telling you last year? We were at finishing school together. Of course, we all knew she was a werewolf, but nobody would ever dream of talking about that sort of thing in those days. Well, you just *didn't*. There was all that business over the ski instructor, of course, but I'm certain in my own mind that he must have fallen down some crevasse or other. She married the baron, and they live just outside Beyonk. I write to her with a little news every Hogswatch. A very old werewolf family."

"A good pedigree," said Vimes, absently.

"You know you wouldn't like Angua to hear you say that, Sam. Don't *worry* so. You'll have a chance to relax, I'm sure. It will be good for you."

"Yes, dear."

"It'll be like a second honeymoon," said Sybil.

"Yes indeed," said Vimes, remembering that what with one thing and another they'd never really had a first one.

"On that, er, subject," said Sybil, a little more hesitantly, "you remember I told you I was going to see old Mrs. Content?"

"Oh yes, how is she?" Vimes was staring at the fireplace again. It wasn't just old school friends, sometimes it seemed Sybil kept in touch with anyone she'd ever met.

Her Hogswatch card list ran to a second volume.

"Quite well, I believe. Anyway, she agrees that—"

There was a knocking at the door.

She sighed. "It's Willikins's evening off," she said. "You'd better answer it, Sam. I know you want to . . ."

"I've told them *not* to disturb me unless it's serious," said Vimes, getting up.

"Yes, but you think all crime is serious, Sam."

Carrot was on the doorstep.

"It's a bit . . . political, sir," he said.

"What's so political at a quarter to ten at night, Captain?"

"The Dwarf Bread Museum's been broken into, sir," said Carrot.

Vimes looked into his honest blue eyes.

"A thought occurs to me, Captain," he said, slowly. "And the thought is: A certain item has gone missing."

"That's right, sir."

"And it's the replica Scone."

"Yes, sir. Either they broke in just after we left, or"—Carrot licked his lips nervously—"they were hiding while we were there."

"Not rats, then."

"No, sir. Sorry, sir."

Vimes fastened his cloak and took his helmet off its peg.

35

"So someone has stolen a replica of the Scone of Stone a few weeks before the real one is due to be used in a very important ceremony," he said. "I find this intriguing."

"That's what I thought, too, sir."

Vimes sighed. "I *hate* the political ones."

When they'd gone, Lady Sybil sat for a while staring at her hands. Then she took a lamp into the library and pulled down a slim volume, bound in white leather on which had been embossed in gold the words OUR WEDDING.

It had been a strange event. Ankh-Morpork's high society—so high that it's stinking, Sam always said—had turned up mostly out of curiosity. She was Ankh-Morpork's most eligible spinster who'd never thought she'd be married, and he was a mere captain of the guard who tended to annoy a lot of people.

And here were the iconographs of the event. There she was, looking rather more expansive than radiant, and there Sam was, scowling at the camera with his hair hastily smoothed down. There was Sergeant Colon with his chest inflated so much his feet had almost left the ground, and Nobby grinning widely or perhaps just making a face, it was so hard to tell with Nobby.

Sybil turned over the pages with care. She had put a sheet of tissue between each one, to protect them.

In many ways, she told herself, she *was* very lucky. She was very proud of Sam. He worked hard for a lot of people. He cared about people who weren't important. He always had far more to cope with than was good for him. He was the most *civilized* man she'd ever met. Not a gentleman, thank goodness, but a gentle man.

She never really knew what it was he *did*. Oh, she knew what the *job* was, but by all accounts he didn't spend much time behind his desk. He tended to drop his clothes into the laundry basket before he eventually came to bed, so she'd only hear later from the laundry girl about the bloodstains and the mud. There were rumors of chases over rooftops, hand-to-hand and knee-to-groin fights with men who had names like Harry "The Boltcutter" Weems . . .

There was a Sam Vimes she knew, who went out and came home again, and out there was another Sam Vimes who hardly belonged to her and lived in the same world as all those men with the dreadful names . . .

Sybil Ramkin had been brought up to be thrifty, thoughtful, genteel in an outdoor sort of way, and to think kindly of people.

She looked at the pictures again, in the silence of the house.

Then she blew her nose loudly and went off to do the packing and other sensible things.

Corporal Cheery Littlebottom pronounced her name "Cheri." She was a she, and therefore a rare bloom in Ankh-Morpork.

It wasn't that dwarfs weren't interested in sex. They saw the vital need for fresh dwarfs to leave their goods to and continue the mining work after they had gone. It was simply that they also saw no point in distinguishing between the sexes anywhere but in private. There was no such thing as a Dwarfish female pronoun or, once the children were on solids, any such thing as women's work.

Then Cheery Littlebottom had arrived in Ankh-Morpork, and had seen that there were men out there who did *not* wear chain mail or leather underwear,* but *did* wear interesting colors and exciting makeup, and these men were called "women."**

---

* At least, of the sort *she* normally wore.

** And, just lately, Corporal Nobbs.

And in the little bullet head the thought had arisen: "Why not me?"

Now she was being denounced in cellars and dwarf bars across the city as the first dwarf in Ankh-Morpork to wear a skirt. It was hard-wearing brown leather and as objectively erotic as a piece of wood but, as some older dwarfs would point out, somewhere under there were his *knees*.*

Worse, they were now finding that among their sons were some—they choked on the word—"daughters." Cheery was only the frothy bit on the tip of the wave. Some younger dwarfs were shyly wearing eye shadow and declaring that, as a matter of fact, they *didn't* like beer. A current was running through dwarf society.

Dwarf society was not against a few well-thrown rocks in the direction of those bobbing on the current, but Captain Carrot had put the word on the street that this would be assault on an officer, a subject on which the Watch held *views*, and however short the miscreants, their feet really would *not* touch the ground.

Cheery had retained her beard and round iron helmet, of course. It was one thing to declare that you were female, but quite unthinkable to declare that you weren't a dwarf.

"Open and shut case, sir," she said, when she saw Vimes come in. "They opened the window in the back room to get in, a very neat job, and didn't shut the front door after they left. Smashed the Scone's case; there's the glass all round the stand. Didn't take anything else that I can see. Left a lot of footprints in the dust. I took a few pictures, but they're scuffed up and weren't much good in the first place. That's about it, really."

"No dropped cigarette butts, wallets or bits of paper with an address on them?" said Vimes.

---

* They couldn't bring themselves to utter the word "her."

"No, sir. They were inconsiderate thieves."

"They certainly were," said Carrot grimly.

"A question that springs to mind," said Vimes, "is: Why does it reek even worse of cat's piss now?"

"It *is* rather sharp, isn't it," said Cheery. "With a hint of sulfur, too. Constable Ping said it was like this when he arrived, but there's no cat prints."

Vimes crouched down and looked at the broken glass.

"How did we find out about this?" he said, prodding a few fragments.

"Constable Ping heard the tinkle, sir. He went around the back and saw the window was opened. Then the crooks got out through the front door."

"Sorry about that, sir," said Ping, stepping forward and saluting. He was a cautious-looking young man, who appeared permanently poised to answer a question.

"We all make mistakes," said Vimes. "You heard glass break?"

"Yessir. And someone swore."

"Really? What did they say?"

"Er . . . 'bugger,' sir?"

"And you went around the back and saw the broken window and you . . . ?"

"I called out 'is there anyone there?,' sir."

"Really? And what would you have done if a voice had said 'no'? No, don't answer that. What happened next?"

"Er . . . I heard a lot more glass break and when I got around to the front the door was open and they were gone. So I legged it back to the Yard and told Captain Carrot, sir, knowing he sets a lot of store by this place . . ."

"Thank you . . . Ping, is it?"

"Yessir." Entirely unasked, but obviously prepared to answer, Ping said, "It's a dialect word meaning 'watermeadow,' sir."

"Off you go, then."

The lance-constable visibly sagged with relief, and left.

Vimes let his mind unfocus a little. He enjoyed moments like these, the little bowl of time when the crime lay before him and he believed that the world was capable of being solved. This was the time you really *looked* to see what was there, and sometimes the things that weren't there were the most interesting things of all.

The Scone had been kept on a plinth about three feet high, inside a case made of five sheets of glass, forming a box that was screwed down on the plinth.

"They smashed the glass by accident," he said, eventually.

"Really, sir?"

"Look here, see?" Vimes pointed to three loose screws, neatly lined up. "They were trying to take the box apart carefully. It must have slipped."

"But what's the *point*?" said Carrot. "It's just a replica, sir! Even if you could find a buyer, it's not worth more than a few dollars."

"If it's a good one, you could swap it with the real thing," said Vimes.

"Well, yes, I suppose you could try," said Carrot. "There would be a bit of a problem, though."

"What is it?"

"Dwarfs aren't stupid, sir. The replica has got a big cross carved into the underside. And it's only made of plaster in any case."

"Oh."

"But it was a good idea, sir," Carrot said encouragingly. "You weren't to know."

"I wonder if the thieves knew."

"Even if they didn't, they wouldn't have a hope of getting away with it, sir."

"The real Scone is very well guarded," said Cheery. "It's very rare that most dwarfs get a chance to see it."

"And other people would notice if you had a great lump of rock up your sweater," said Vimes, more or less to himself. "So . . . this was a stupid crime. But it doesn't *feel* stupid. I mean, why go to all this trouble? The lock on that door is a joke, you could kick it right out of the woodwork. If *I* was going to pinch this thing, I could be in here and out again before the glass had stopped tinkling. What would be the point of being quiet at this time of night?"

The dwarf had been rummaging under a nearby display cabinet. She drew her hand out. Drying blood glistened on the blade of a screwdriver.

"See?" said Vimes. "Something slipped, and someone cut their hand. What's the *point* of all this, Carrot? Cat's piss and sulfur and screwdrivers . . . I hate it when you get too many clues, it makes it so damn hard to solve anything."

He threw the screwdriver down. By sheer luck it hit the floorboards tip first and stood there shuddering.

"I'm going home," he said. "We'll find out what this is all about when it starts to smell."

Vimes spent the following morning trying to learn about two foreign countries. One of them turned out to be called Ankh-Morpork.

Uberwald was easy. It was five or six times bigger than the whole of the Sto Plains, and stretched all the way up to the Hub. It was mostly so thickly forested, so creased by little mountain ranges and beset by rivers, that it was largely unmapped. It was mostly unexplored, too.* The people who lived there had other things on their mind, and the people from outside who came to explore went into the forests and never came out again. And for centuries no one had bothered about the place. You couldn't sell things to people hidden by too many trees.

It was probably the coach road that had changed everything, a few years back, when they drove it all the way through to Genua. A road is built to follow. Mountain people had always gravitated to the plains, and in recent years Uberwald folk had joined them. The news got back home: There's money to be made in Ankh-Morpork, bring the kids. You don't need to bring the garlic though, because all the vampires work down at the kosher butchers'. And if you're pushed in Ankh-Morpork, you are allowed to push back. No one cares enough about you to want to kill you.

Vimes could just about tell the difference between the Uber-wald dwarfs and the ones from Copperhead, who were shorter, noisier and rather more at home among humans. The Uberwald dwarfs were quiet, tended to scuttle around corners and often didn't speak Morporkian. In some of the alleys off Treacle Mine Road you could believe you were in another country. But they were what every copper desires in a citizen. They were *no trouble*. They mostly had jobs working for one another, they paid their taxes rather more readily than humans did, although to be honest there were small piles of mouse droppings that yielded more money than most Ankh-Morpork citizens, and generally any problems they had they sorted out among themselves. If such people ever come to the attention of the police, it's usually only as a chalk outline.

* At least, by proper explorers. Just living there doesn't count.

It turned out, though, that within the community, behind the grubby facades of all those tenements and workshops in Cable Street and Whalebone Lane, there were vendettas and feuds that had their origins in two adjoining mine shafts five hundred miles away and a thousand years ago. There were pubs you only drank in if you were from a particular mountain. There were streets you didn't walk down if your clan mined a particular lode. The way you wore your helmet, the way you parted your beard, spoke complicated volumes to other dwarfs. They didn't even hand a piece of paper to Vimes.

"Then there's the way you *krazak* your *G'ardrgh*," said Corporal Littlebottom.

"I won't even ask," said Vimes.

"I'm afraid I can't explain in any case," said Cheery.

"Have I got a Gaadrerghuh?" said Vimes. Cheery winced at the mispronunciation.

"Yes, sir. Everyone has. But only a dwarf can *krazak* his properly," she said. "Or hers," she added.

Vimes sighed, and looked down at the pages of scrawl in his notebook, under the heading: UBERWALD. He wasn't strictly aware of it, but he treated even geography as if he was investigating a crime (Did you see who carved out the valley? Would you recognize that glacier if you saw it again?).

"I'm going to make a lot of mistakes, Cheery," he said.

"I shouldn't worry about that, sir. Humans always do. But most dwarfs can spot if you're trying not to make them."

"Are you sure you don't mind coming?"

"Got to face it sooner or later, sir."

Vimes shook his head sadly.

"I don't get it, Cheery. There's all this fuss about a female dwarf trying to act like, like—"

"A lady, sir?"

"Right, and yet no one says anything about Carrot being called a dwarf, but he's a human—"

"No, sir. Like he says, he's a dwarf. He was adopted by dwarfs, he's performed the *Y'grad*, he observes the *j'kargra* insofar as that's possible in a city. He's a dwarf."

"He's six foot high!"

"He's a tall dwarf, sir. We don't mind if he wants to be a human as well. Not even the *drudak'ak* would have a problem with that."

"I'm running out of cough drops here, Cheery. What was that?"

"Look, sir, most of the dwarfs here are . . . well, I suppose you'd call them liberal, sir. They're mainly from the mountains behind Copperhead, you know? They get along with humans. Some of them even acknowledge that . . . they've got daughters, sir. But some of the more . . . old-fashioned . . . Uberwald dwarfs haven't gotten out so much. They still act as if B'hrian Bloodaxe were still alive. That's why we call them *drudak'ak*."

Vimes had a go, but he knew that to really speak Dwarfish you needed a lifetime's study and, if at all possible, a serious throat infection.

". . . 'above ground' . . . 'they negatively' . . ." he faltered.

" 'They do not get out in the fresh air enough,' " Cheery supplied.

"Ah, right. And everyone thought the new king was going to be one of these?"

"They say Albrecht's never seen sunlight in his life. His clan never goes above ground in daylight. Everyone was certain it'd be him. "

And as it turned out it wasn't, thought Vimes. Some of the Uberwald dwarfs hadn't supported him. And the world had moved on. There were plenty of dwarfs around now who had been *born* in Ankh-Morpork. Their kids went around with their helmets on back to front and spoke Dwarfish only at home. Many of them wouldn't know a pick-ax if you hit them with it.* They weren't about to be told how to run their lives by an old dwarf sitting on a stale bun under some distant mountain.

He tapped his pencil on his notebook thoughtfully. And because of this, he thought, dwarfs are punching one another on *my* streets.

"I've seen more of those dwarf sedan chair things around lately," he said. "You know, the ones carried by a couple of trolls. They have thick leather curtains..."

"*Drudak'ak,*" said Cheery. "Very... *traditional* dwarfs. If they *have* to go out in daylight, they don't look at it."

"I don't recall them a year ago..."

Cheery shrugged. "There's lots of dwarfs here now, sir. The *drudak'ak* feel they're among dwarfs now. They don't have to deal with humans for anything."

"They don't like us?"

"They won't even talk to a human. They're fairly choosy about talking to most dwarfs, to tell you the truth."

"That is daft!" said Vimes. "How do they get food? You can't live on fungi! How do they trade ore, dam streams, get wood for shoring up their shafts?"

"Well, either other dwarfs are paid to do it, or humans are employed," said Cheery. "They can afford it. They're *very* good miners. Well... they own very good mines, in any case."

"Sounds to me they're a bunch of..." Vimes stopped himself. He was aware that a wise man should always respect the folkways of others, to use Carrot's happy phrase, but Vimes often had difficulty with this idea. For one thing, there were people in the world

---

* At least, if you hit them hard enough.

whose folkways consisted of gutting other people like clams and this was not a procedure that commanded, in Vimes, any kind of respect at all.

"I'm not thinking diplomatically, am I?" he said. Cheery watched him with a carefully blank expression.

"Oh, I don't know about that, sir," she said. "You didn't actually finish the sentence. And . . . well, a lot of dwarfs respect them. You know . . . feel better for seeing them."

Vimes looked puzzled. Then understanding dawned.

"Oh, I get it," he said. "I bet they say things like 'thank goodness people are keeping up the old ways,' eh?"

"That's right, sir. I suppose that inside every dwarf in Ankh-Morpork is a little part of him—or her—that knows real dwarfs live underground."

Vimes doodled on his notepad. "Back home," he thought. Carrot had innocently talked about dwarfs "back home." To all dwarfs far away, the mountains were "back home." It was funny how people were people everywhere you went, even if the people concerned weren't the people the people who made up the phrase "people are people everywhere" had traditionally thought of as people. And even if you weren't virtuous, as you had been brought up to understand the term, you did like to see virtue in other people, provided it did not cost you anything.

"*Why* have these *d'r* . . . these traditional dwarfs come here, though? Ankh-Morpork's full of humans. They must have their work cut out avoiding humans."

"They're . . . needed, sir. Dwarf law is complicated, and there's often disputes. And they conduct marriages and that sort of thing."

"You make them sound more like priests."

"Dwarfs aren't religious, sir."

"Of course. Oh well. Thank you, Corporal. Off you go. Any fallout from last night? No sulfurous incontinent cats have come forward to confess?"

"No, sir. The Campaign for Equal Heights has put out a pamphlet saying it was another example of the second-class treatment of dwarfs in the city, but it was the same one they always put out. You know, the one with blanks to fill in the details."

"Nothing changes, Cheery. See you tomorrow morning, then. Send Detritus up."

Why *him*? Vimes thought. Ankh-Morpork was lousy with diplomats. It was practically what the upper classes were *for*, and it was easy for them because half the foreign bigwigs they'd meet were old chums they'd played Wet Towel Tag with back at school. They tended to be on first-name terms, even with people whose names were Ahmed or Fong. They knew which forks to use. They hunted, shot and fished. They moved in circles that more or less overlapped the circles of their foreign hosts, and were a long way from the rather grubby circles that people like Vimes went around in every working day. They knew all the right nods and winks. What chance had he got against a tie and a crest?

Vetinari was throwing him among the wolves. And the dwarfs. And the vampires. Vimes shuddered. And Vetinari never did anything without a reason.

"Come in, Detritus."

It always amazed Sergeant Detritus that Vimes knew he was at the door. Vimes had never mentioned that the office wall creaked and bent inward as the big troll made his way along the corridor.

"You want to see me, sir."

"Yes. Sit down, man. It's this Uberwald business."

"Yessir."

47

"How do *you* feel about visiting the old country?"

Detritus's face remained impassive, as it always did when he was waiting patiently for things to make sense.

"Uberwald, I mean," Vimes prompted.

"Dunno, sir. I was a just a pebble when we left dere. Dad wanted a better life in der big city."

"There'll be a lot of dwarfs, Detritus." Vimes didn't bother to mention vampires and werewolves. Either of those who attacked a troll was making the last big mistake of its career in any case. Detritus carried a two-thousand-pound–draw crossbow as a hand weapon.

"Dat's okay, sir. I'm very modern 'bout dwarfs."

"These might be a bit old-fashioned about you, though."

"Dem deep-down dwarfs?"

"That's right."

"I heard about dem."

"There's still wars with trolls up near the Hub, I hear. Tact and diplomacy will be called for."

"You have come to der right troll for that, sir," said Detritus.

"You did push that man through that wall last week, Detritus."

"It was done with tact, sir. Quite a *fin* wall."

Vimes let it go at that. The man in question had just laid out three watchmen with a club, which Detritus had broken in one hand before selecting the suitably tactful wall.

"See you tomorrow, then. Best dress armor, remember. Send Angua now, please."

"She's not here, sir."

"Blast. Put out some messages for her, will you?"

Igor lurched through the castle corridors, dragging one foot after the other in the approved fashion.

He was Igor, son of Igor, nephew of several Igors, brother of Igors and cousin of more Igors than he could remember without checking up in his diary. Igors did not change a winning formula.*

And, as a clan, Igors liked working for vampires. They kept regular hours, were generally polite to their servants and, an important extra, didn't require much work in the bed-making and cookery department, and tended to have cool, roomy cellars where an Igor could pursue his true calling. This more than made up for those occasions when you had to sweep up their ashes.

He entered Lady Margolotta's crypt and knocked politely on the coffin lid. It moved aside a fraction.

"Yes?"

"Thorry to wake you in the middle of the afternoon, Your Lady-thip, but you did *thay*—"

"All right. And—?"

"It's going to be Vimeth, Ladythip. You were right."

A dainty hand came out of the partly opened coffin and punched the air.

"Yes!"

"Well thpotted, Ladythip."

"Well, well. Samuel Vimes. Poor devil. Do the doggies know?"

Igor nodded. "The baron'th Igor was altho collecting a meth-age, Ladythip."

"And the dwarfs?"

"It *ith* an official appointment, Ladythip. Everyone knows. Hith Grace the Duke of Ankh-Morpork, Thir Thamuel Vimeth, Commander of the Ankh-Morpork Thity Watch."

"Then the midden has hit the windmill, Igor."

---

* Especially if it was green, and bubbled.

"Very well put, Ladythip. No one liketh a thort thower of thit."

"I imagine, Igor, that he'll leave *them* behind."

Let us consider a castle from the point of view of its furniture.

This one has chairs, yes, but they don't look very lived in. There *is* a huge sofa near the fire, and that is ragged with use, but other furnishings look as if they're there merely for show.

There is a long oak table, well polished and looking curiously unused for such an old piece of furniture. Possibly the reason for this is that on the floor around it are a large number of white earthenware bowls.

One of them has FATHER written on it.

The Baroness Serafine von Uberwald slammed shut *Twurp's Peerage*, irritably.

"The man is a . . . a nothing," she said. "A paper man. A man of straw. An *insult*."

"The name Vimes goes back a long time," said Wolfgang von Uberwald, who was doing one-handed push-ups in front of the fire.

"So does the name Smith. What of it?"

Wolf changed to the other hand, in midair. He was naked. He liked his muscles to get an airing. They shone. Someone with an anatomical chart could have picked out every one. They might also have remarked on the unusual way his blond hair grew not only on his head but down and across his shoulders as well.

"He *is* a duke, Mother."

"Hah! Ankh-Morpork hasn't even got a king!"

". . . nineteen, twenty . . . I hear stories about that, Mother . . ."

"Oh, *stories*. Sybil writes a silly little letter to me every year! Sam this, Sam that. Of course, she had to be grateful for what she could get, but . . . the man is just a thief-taker, after all. I shall refuse to see him."

"You will not do that, Mother," Wolf grunted. "That would be . . . twenty-nine, thirty . . . dangerous. What do you tell Lady Sybil about us?"

"Nothing! I don't write *back*, of course. A rather sad and foolish woman."

"And she still writes every year? . . . thirty-six, thirty-seven . . ."

"Yes. Four pages, usually. And that tells you everything about her you need to know. Where *is* your father?"

A flap in the bottom of a nearby door swung back and a large, heavyset wolf trotted in. It glanced around the room, and then shook itself vigorously. The baroness bridled.

"Guye! You *know* what I said! It's after six! *Change* when you come in from the garden!"

The wolf gave her a look, and strolled behind a massive oak screen at the far end of the room. There was a . . . noise, soft and rather strange, not so much an actual *sound* as a change in the texture of the air.

The baron walked around from behind the screen, doing up the cord of a tattered dressing gown. The baroness sniffed.

"At least your father wears clothes," she said.

"Clothes are unhealthy, mother," said Wolf, calmly. "Nakedness is purity."

The baron sat down. He was a large, red-faced man, insofar as a face could be seen under the beard, hair, mustache and eyebrows which were engaged in a bitter four-way war over the remaining areas of bare skin.

"Well?" he growled.

"Vimes the thief-taker from Ankh-Morpork is going to be the *alleged* ambassador," snapped the baroness.

"Dwarfs?"

"Of course they'll be told."

The baron sat staring at nothing, with the same expression Detritus used when a new thought was being assembled.

"Bad?" he ventured, at last.

"Ruston, I've *told* you about this a thousand times!" said the baroness. "You're spending far too much time Changed! You *know* what you're like afterward. Supposing we had official visitors?"

"Bite 'em!"

"You see? Go on off to bed and don't come down until you're fit to be human!"

"Vimes *could* ruin everything, Father," said Wolfgang. He was now doing handstands, using one hand.

"Ruston! *Down!*"

The baron stopped trying to scratch his ear with his leg.

"Do?" he said.

Wolfgang's gleaming body dipped a moment as he changed hands again.

"City life makes men weak. Vimes will be . . . fun. They do say he likes running, though." He gave a little laugh. "We shall have to see how fast he is."

"His wife says he's very softhearted— *Ruston! Don't you dare do that! If you going to do that sort of thing, do it upstairs!*"

The baron looked only moderately ashamed, but readjusted his clothing anyway.

"Bandits!" he said.

"Yes, they could be a problem at this time of year," said Wolfgang.

"At least a dozen," said the baroness. "Yes, that should—"

Wolf grunted, upside down.

"*No*, mother. You are being stupid. His coach must get here safely. You understand? *When* he is here . . . that is a different matter."

The baron's massive eyebrows tangled with a thought.

"Plan! King!"

"Exactly."

The baroness sighed. "I don't trust that little dwarf."

Wolf somersaulted onto his feet.

"No. But trustworthy or not, he's all we've got. Vimes must get here, with his soft heart. He may even be useful. Perhaps we should . . . assist matters."

"Why?" snapped the baroness. "Let Ankh-Morpork look after their own!"

There was a knock on the door while Vimes was having breakfast. Willikins ushered in a small thin man in neat but threadbare black clothes, whose overlarge head gave him the appearance of a lollypop nearing the last suck. He was carrying a black bowler hat like a soldier carries his helmet and walked like a man who had something wrong with his knees.

"I am so sorry to disturb Your Grace . . ."

Vimes laid down his knife. He'd been peeling an orange. Sybil insisted he eat fruit.

"Not Your Grace," he said. "Just Vimes. Sir Samuel if you must. Are you Vetinari's man?"

"Inigo Skimmer, sir. Mhm, mhm. I am to travel with you to Uberwald."

"Ah, you're the clerk who's going to do all the whispering and winking while I hand around the cucumber sandwiches, are you?"

"I will try to be of service, sir, although I'm not much of a winker. Mhm, mhm."

"Would you like some breakfast?"

"I ate already, sir. Mhm-mhm."

Vimes looked the clerk up and down. It wasn't so much that his head was big, it was simply that someone appeared to have squeezed the bottom half of it and forced everything up into the top. He was going bald, too, and had carefully teased the remaining strands of hair across the pink dome. It was hard to tell his age. He could be twenty-five and a big worrier, or a fresh-faced forty. Vimes inclined to the former—the man had the look of someone who had spent his life watching the world over the top of a book. And there was that . . . well, was it a nervous laugh? A giggle? An unfortunate way of clearing his throat?

And that strange way he walked . . .

"Not even some toast? A piece of fruit? These oranges are fresh from Klatch, I really can recommend them . . ."

Vimes tossed one at the man. It bounced off his arm, and Skimmer took a step backward, mildly appalled at the upper class's habit of fruit hurling.

"Are you all right, sir? Mhm-mhm?"

"Sorry about that," said Vimes. "I was carried away by fruit."

He laid aside his napkin and came around the table, putting his arm around Skimmer's shoulders.

"I'll just take you into the Mildly Yellow drawing room where you can wait," he said, walking him toward the door and patting him on the arm in a friendly way. "The coaches are loaded up. Sybil is re-grouting the bathroom, learning Ancient Klatchian and doing all those other little last minute things women always do. You're with us in the big coach."

Skimmer recoiled. "Oh, I couldn't do that, sir! I'll travel with your retinue. Mhm-mhm. Mhm-mhm."

"If you mean Cheery and Detritus, they're in there with us," said Vimes, noting the look of horror deepen slightly. "You need four for a decent game of cards and the road's as boring as hell for most of the way."

"And, er, your servants?"

"Willikins and the cook and Sybil's maid are in the other coach."

"Oh."

Vimes smiled inwardly. He remembered the saying from his childhood: too poor to paint, but too proud to whitewash . . .

"Bit of a tough choice, is it?" he said. "I'll tell you what, you can come in our coach but we'll give you a hard seat and patronize you from time to time, how about that?"

"I am afraid you are making a mockery of me, Sir Samuel. Mhm-mhm."

"No, but I may be assisting. And now, if you'll excuse me, I've got to nip down to the Yard to sort out a few last minute things."

A quarter of an hour later Vimes walked into the charge room at the Yard. Sergeant Stronginthearm looked up, saluted, and then ducked to avoid the orange that was tossed at his head.

"Sir?" he said, bewildered.

"Just testing, Stronginthearm."

"Did I pass, sir?"

"Oh yes. Keep the orange. It's full of vitamins."

"My mother always told me those things could kill you, sir."

Carrot was waiting patiently in Vimes's office. Vimes shook his head. He knew *all* the places to tread in the corridor and he *knew* he didn't make a sound, and he'd never once caught Carrot reading his paperwork, not even upside down. Just once it'd be nice to catch him out at something. If the man was any straighter you could use him as a plank.

Carrot stood up and saluted.

"Yes, yes, we haven't got a lot of time for that now," said Vimes, sitting behind his desk. "Anything new overnight?"

"An unattributed murder, sir. A tradesman called Wallace Sonky. Found in one of his own vats with his throat cut. No guild seal or note or anything. We are treating it as suspicious."

"Yes, I think that sounds *fairly* suspicious," said Vimes. "Unless he has a record as a very careless shaver. What kind of vat?"

"Er . . . rubber, sir."

"Rubber comes in vats? Wouldn't he bounce out?"

"No, sir. It's a liquid in the vat, sir. Mister Sonky makes . . . rubber things . . ."

"Hang on, I remember seeing something once . . . Don't they make things by dipping them in the rubber? You made sort of . . . the right shapes and dip them in to get gloves, boots . . . that sort of thing?"

"Er . . . that . . . er . . . *sort* of thing, sir."

Something about Carrot's uneasy manner got through to Vimes. And the little file at the back of his brain eventually waved a card.

"Sonky, Sonky . . . Carrot, we're not talking about Sonky as in 'a packet of Sonkies,' are we?"

Now Carrot was bright red with embarrassment. "Yes, sir!"

"My gods, what was he dipping in the vat?"

"He'd been thrown in, sir. Apparently."

"But he's practically a national hero!"

"Sir?"

"Captain, the housing shortage in Ankh-Morpork would be a good deal worse if it wasn't for old man Sonky and his penny-a-packet preventatives. Who'd want to do away with him?"

"People do have Views, sir," said Carrot coldly.

Yes, you do, don't you, Vimes thought. Dwarfs don't hold with that sort of thing.

"Well, put some men on it. Anything else?"

"A carter assaulted Constable Swires last night for clamping his cart."

"Assault?"

"Tried to stamp on him, sir."

Vimes had a mental picture of Constable Swires, a gnome six inches tall but a mile high in pent-up aggression.

"How is he?"

"Well, the man can speak, but it'll be a little while before he can climb back on a cart again. Apart from that, it's all run-of-the-mill stuff."

"Nothing more about the Scone theft?"

"Not really. Lots of accusations in the dwarf community, but no one really knows anything. Like you say, sir, we'll probably know more when it goes bad."

"Any word on the street?"

"Yes, sir. It's 'Halt,' sir. Sergeant Colon painted it at the top of Lower Broadway. The carters are a lot more careful now. Of course, someone has to shovel the manure off every hour or so."

"This whole traffic thing is not making us very popular, Captain."

"No, sir. But we aren't popular anyway. And at least it's bring-ing in money for the city treasury. Er . . . there is another thing, sir."

"Yes?"

"Have you seen Sergeant Angua, sir?"

"Me? No. I was expecting her to be here." Then Vimes noticed just the very edge of concern in Carrot's voice. "Something wrong?"

"She didn't turn up for duty last night. It wasn't full moon, so it's a bit . . . odd. Nobby said she was rather concerned about something when they were on duty the other day."

Vimes nodded. Of course, most people were concerned about something if they were on duty with Nobby. They tended to look at clocks a lot.

"Have you been to her lodgings?"

"Her bed hadn't been slept in," said Carrot. "Or her basket, either," he added.

"Well, I can't help you there, Carrot. She's your girlfriend."

"She's been a bit . . . worried about the future, I think," said Carrot.

"Um . . . you . . . she . . . the, er, werewolf thing . . . ?" Vimes stopped, acutely embarrassed.

"It preys on her mind," said Carrot.

"Perhaps she's just gone somewhere to think about things?" Like how on earth could she go out with a young man who, magnificent though he was, blushed at the idea of a packet of Sonkies.

"That's what I hope, sir," Carrot said. "She does that sometimes. It's really quite stressful, being a werewolf in a big city. I *know* we'd have heard if she'd run into any trouble—"

There was the sound of a harness outside, and the rattle of a coach. Vimes was relieved. Seeing Carrot worried was so unusual that it had the shock of the unfamiliar.

"Well, we'll have to go without her," he said. "I want to be kept in touch about everything, Captain. A fake Scone going missing a week or two before a big dwarf coronation—that sounds like another shoe is about to drop and it might just hit me. And while you're about it, put the word out that I'm to be sent anything about Sonky, will you? I don't like mysteries. The clacks do a skeleton service as far as Uberwald now, don't they?"

Carrot brightened up. "It's wonderful, sir, isn't it? In a few months they say we'll be able to send messages all the way from Ankh-Morpork to Genua in less than a day!"

"Yes, indeed. I wonder if by then we'll have anything sensible to say to each other?"

Lord Vetinari stood at his window, watching the semaphore tower on the other side of the river. All eight of the big shutters facing him were blinking furiously—black, white, white, black, white . . .

Information was flying into the air. Twenty miles behind him, on another tower in Sto Lat, someone was looking through a telescope and shouting out numbers . . .

How quickly the future comes upon us, he thought.

He always suspected the poetic description of Time like an ever-rolling stream. Time, in his experience, moved more like rocks . . . sliding, pressing, building up force underground and then, with one jerk that shakes the crockery, a whole field of turnips has mysteriously slipped sideways by six feet.

Semaphore had been around for centuries, and everyone knew that knowledge had a value, and everyone knew that exporting goods was a way of making money. And then, suddenly, someone realized how *much* money you could make by exporting to Genua by tonight things known in Ankh-Morpork today. And some bright young man in the Street of Cunning Artificers had been unusually cunning.

Knowledge, information, power, words . . . flying through the air, invisible . . .

And suddenly the world was tap dancing on quicksand.

In that case, the prize went to the best dancer.

Lord Vetinari turned away, took some papers from a desk drawer, walked to a wall, touched a certain area and stepped quickly through the hidden door that noiselessly swung open.

Beyond was a corridor, lit by borrowed light from high windows and paved with small flagstones. He walked forward, hesitated, said ". . . no, this is Tuesday . . ." and moved his descending foot so that it landed on a stone that in every respect appeared to be exactly the same as its fellows.*

Anyone overhearing his progress along the passages and stairs may have caught muttered phrases on the lines of ". . . the moon is . . . waxing . . ." and "yes, it is before noon." A really *keen* listener would have heard the faint whirring and ticking inside the walls.

A really keen and *paranoid* listener would have reflected that anything the Lord Vetinari said aloud even while he was alone might not be *totally* worth believing. Not, certainly, if your life depended on it.

Eventually he reached a door, which he unlocked.

There was a large attic room beyond, suddenly airy and bright and cheerful with sunlight from the windows in the roof. It seemed to be a cross between a workshop and a storeroom. Several bird skeletons hung from the ceiling and there were a few other bones on the worktables, along with coils of wire and metal springs and tubes of paint and more tools, many of them probably unique, than you normally saw in any one place. Only a narrow bed, wedged between a thing like a loom with wings and a large bronze statue,

---

* Except that the ones around it were not good stones to tread on if it was a Tuesday.

suggested that someone actually lived here. They were clearly someone who was obsessively interested in *everything*.

What interested Lord Vetinari right now was the device all by itself on a table in the middle of the room. It looked like a collection of copper balls balanced on one another. Steam was hissing gently from a few rivets, and occasionally the device went *blup*—

"Your Lordship!"

Vetinari looked around. A hand was waving desperately at him from behind an upturned bench.

And something made him look up as well. The ceiling above him was crusted with some brownish substance, which hung from it like stalactites . . .

Blup

With quite surprising speed the Patrician was behind the bench. Leonard of Quirm smiled at him from underneath his homemade protective helmet.

"I *do* apologize," he said. "I'm afraid I wasn't expecting anyone to come in. I'm sure it will work this time, however."

Blup

"What is it?" said Vetinari.

Blup

"I'm not *quite* sure, but I *hope* it is a—"

And then it was, suddenly, too noisy to talk.

Leonard of Quirm never dreamed that he was a prisoner. If anything, he was grateful to Vetinari for giving him this airy work space, and regular meals, and laundry, and protecting him from those people who for some reason always wanted to take his perfectly innocent inventions, designed for the betterment of mankind, and use them for despicable purposes. It was amazing how many of them there were—both the people and the inventions. It was as if all the genius of a civilization had funneled into one head which was, therefore, in a constant state of highly inventive spin. Vetinari often speculated upon the fate of mankind should Leonard keep his mind on one thing for more than an hour or so.

The rushing noise died away. *Blup.*

Leonard peered cautiously over the bench and smiled broadly.

"Ah! Happily, we appear to have achieved coffee," he said.

"Coffee?"

Leonard walked over to the table and pulled a small lever on the device. A light brown foam cascaded into a waiting cup with a noise like a clogged drain.

"*Different* coffee," he said. "Very *fast* coffee. I rather think you will like it. I'm calling this the Very-Fast-Coffee machine."

"And that's today's invention, is it?" said Vetinari.

"Well, yes. It would have been a scale model of a device for reaching the moon and other celestial bodies, but I was thirsty."

"How fortunate." Lord Vetinari carefully removed an experimental pedal-powered shoe polishing machine from a chair and sat down. "And I have brought you some more little . . . messages."

Leonard almost clapped his hands.

"Oh, good! And I have finished the other ones you gave me last night."

Lord Vetinari carefully removed a mustache of frothy coffee from his upper lip. "I beg your . . . ? *All* of them? You broke the ciphers on *all* those messages from Uberwald?"

"Oh, they were quite easy after I had finished the new device," said Leonard, rummaging through the piles of paper on a bench and handing the Patrician several closely written sheets. "But once you realize that there are only a limited number of birth dates a person can have, and that people do tend to think the same way, ciphers are really not very hard."

"You mentioned a new device?" said the Patrician.

"Oh yes. The . . . thingy. It is all very crude at the moment, but it suffices for these simple codes."

Leonard pulled a sheet off something vaguely rectangular. It seemed to Vetinari to be all wooden wheels and long thin spars which, he saw when he moved closer, were inscribed thickly with letters and numbers. A number of the wheels were not round but oval or heart shaped or some other curious curve. When Leonard turned a handle, the whole thing moved with a complex oiliness quite disquieting in something merely mechanical.

"And what are you calling it?"

"Oh, you know me and names, my lord. I think of it as the Engine for the Neutralizing of Information by the Generation of Miasmic Alphabets, but I appreciate that it does not exactly roll off the tongue. Er . . ."

"Yes, Leonard?"

"Er . . . it's not . . . *wrong*, is it, reading other people's messages?"

Vetinari sighed. The worried man in front of him, who was so considerate of life that he carefully dusted around spiders, had once invented a device that fired lead pellets with tremendous speed and force. He thought it would be useful against dangerous animals. He'd designed a thing that could destroy whole mountains. He thought it would be useful in the mining industries. Here was a man who, *in his tea break*, would doodle an instrument for unthinkable mass destruction in the blank spaces around an exquisite drawing of the fragile beauty of the human smile. With a list of numbered parts. And if you taxed him with it, he'd say: Ah, but such a thing would make war completely impossible, you see? *Because no one would dare use it.*

Leonard brightened up as a thought apparently struck him. "But, on the other hand, the more we know about one another, the more we will learn to understand. Now . . . you asked me to construct some more ciphers for *you*. I am sorry, my lord, but I must have misunderstood your requirements. What was wrong with the first ones I did?"

Vetinari sighed. "I am afraid they were unbreakable, Leonard."

"But surely—"

"It is hard to explain," said Vetinari, aware that what to him were the lucid waters of politics was so much mud to Leonard. "These new ones you have are . . . merely devilishly difficult?"

"You specified *fiendishly*, sir," said Leonard, looking worried.

"Oh yes."

"There does not appear to be a common standard for fiends, my lord, but I did some research in the more accessible occult texts and I believe these ciphers will be considered 'difficult' by more than ninety-six percent of fiends."

"Good."

"They may perhaps verge on the diabolically difficult in places—"

"That is not a problem. I shall use them forthwith."

Leonard still seemed to have something on his mind.

"It would be so easy to make them archdemonically diff—"

"But these will suffice, Leonard," said Vetinari.

"My lord," Leonard almost wailed, "I really cannot guarantee that sufficiently clever people will be unable to read your messages!"

"Good."

"But, my lord, they will know what you are thinking!"

64

Vetinari patted him on the shoulder.

"No, Leonard. They will merely know what is in my messages."

"I really do *not* understand, my lord."

"No, but on the other hand, I cannot make exploding coffee. What would the world be like if we were all alike?"

Leonard's face clouded for a moment.

"I'm not sure," he said, "but if you would like me to work on the problem, I may be able to devise a—"

"It was merely a figure of speech, Leonard."

Vetinari shook his head ruefully. It often seemed to him that Leonard, who had pushed intellect into hitherto undiscovered uplands, had discovered there large and specialized pockets of stupidity. What would be the point of ciphering messages that very clever enemies couldn't break? You'd end up not knowing what they thought you thought they were thinking . . .

"There was one rather strange message from Uberwald, my lord," said Leonard. "It arrived yesterday morning, apparently."

"Strange?"

"It was not ciphered."

"Not at *all*? I thought everyone used codes."

"Oh, the sender and recipient are code names, but the message is quite plain. It was a request for information about Commander Vimes, of whom you have often spoken."

Lord Vetinari went quite still.

"The return message was mostly clear, too. A certain amount of . . . gossip."

"All about Vimes? Sent yesterday *morning*? *Before* I—?"

"My lord?"

"Tell me," said the Patrician, "this . . . message from Uberwald . . . it yields no clue at all to the sender?"

Sometimes, like a ray of light through clouds, Leonard could be quite perceptive.

"You think you might know the originator, my lord?"

"Oh, in my younger days I spent some time in Uberwald," said the Patrician. "In those days rich young men from Ankh-Morpork used to go on what we called the Grand Sneer, visiting far-flung countries and cities in order to see at first hand how inferior they were. Or so it seemed, at any rate. Oh yes . . . I spent some time in Uberwald . . ."

It was not often Leonard of Quirm paid attention to what people around him were doing, but he saw the faraway look in Lord Vetinari's eye.

"You have fond memories, my lord?" he ventured.

"Hmm? Oh . . . she was a very . . . *unusual* lady but, alas, rather . . . *older* than me," said Vetinari. "Much older, I have to say. But . . . it was a long time ago. Life teaches us its small lessons, and we move on. The world changes." There was the distant look again. "Well, well, well . . ."

"And no doubt the lady is now dead," said Leonard. He was not much good at this sort of conversation.

"Oh, I very much doubt that," said Vetinari, coming back to the present. "I have no doubt she thrives." He smiled. The world was becoming more . . . *interesting*. "Tell me, Leonard," he said, "has it ever occurred to you that one day wars will be fought with brains?"

Leonard picked up his coffee cup.

"Oh dear. Won't that be rather messy?" he said.

Vetinari sighed again.

"Not perhaps as messy as the other sort," he said, trying the coffee. It really was rather good.

* * *

The ducal coach rolled past the last of the outlying buildings and onto the vast, flat Sto Plains. Cheery and Detritus had tactfully decided to ride on the top for the morning, and leave the duke and duchess alone inside. Skimmer was indulging in some uneasy class solidarity and riding with the servants for a while.

"Angua seems to have gone into hiding," said Vimes, watching the cabbage fields pass by.

"Poor girl," said Sybil. "The city's not really the place for her."

"Well, you couldn't winkle Carrot out of it with a big pin," said Vimes. "And that's the problem, I suppose."

"Part of the problem," said Sybil.

Vimes nodded. The other part, which no one talked about, was children.

Sometimes it seemed to Vimes that everyone knew that Carrot was the true heir to the redundant throne of the city. It just so happened that he didn't want to be. He wanted to be a copper, and everyone went along with the idea. But kingship was a bit like a grand piano—you could put a cover over it, but you could still see what shape it was underneath.

Vimes wasn't sure what the result was if a human and a werewolf had kids. Maybe you just got someone who had to shave twice a day around full moon and occasionally felt like chasing carts. And when you remembered what *some* of the city's rulers had been like, a known werewolf as ruler ought to hold no terrors. It was the buggers who looked human all the time that were the problem. That was just his view, though. Other people might see things differently. No wonder she'd gone off to think about things.

He realized he was looking, unseeing, out of the window.

To take his mind off this he opened the package of papers that Skimmer had handed him just as he got on the coach. It was called "briefing material." The man seemed to be an expert on Uberwald, and Vimes wondered how many other clerks there were in the Patrician's palace, beavering away, becoming *experts*. He settled down glumly and began to read.

The first page showed the crest of the Unholy Empire that had once ruled most of the huge country. Vimes couldn't recall much about it, except that one of the emperors once had a man's hat nailed to his head for a joke. Uberwald seemed to be a big, cold, depressing place, so perhaps people would do *anything* for a laugh.

The crest was altogether too florid for Vimes's taste and was dominated by a double-headed bat.

The first document was entitled: THE FAT-BEARING STRATA OF THE SHMALTZBERG REGION ("THE LAND OF THE FIFTH ELEPHANT").

He knew the legend, of course. There had once been five elephants, not four, standing on the back of Great A'Tuin, but one had lost its footing or had been shaken loose and had drifted off into a curved orbit before eventually crashing down, a billion tons of enraged pachyderm, with a force that had rocked the entire world and split it up into the continents people knew today. The rocks that fell back had covered and compressed the corpse and the rest, after millennia of underground cooking and rendering, was fat history. According to legend, gold and iron and all the other metals were also part of the carcass. After all, an elephant big enough to support the world on its back wasn't going to have ordinary bones, was it?

The notes in front of him were a little more believable, talking about some unknown catastrophe that had killed millions of the mammoths, bison and giant shrews and then covered them over, pretty much like the fifth elephant in the story. There were notes about old troll sagas and legends of the dwarfs. Possibly ice had been involved. Or a flood. In the case of the trolls, who were believed to be the first species in the world, maybe they'd *been* there and seen the elephant trumpeting across the sky.

The result, anyway, was the same. Everyone—well, everyone except Vimes—knew the best fat came from the Shmaltzberg wells and mines. It made the whitest, brightest candles, the creamiest soap, the hottest, cleanest lamp oil. The yellow tallow from Ankh-Morpork's boilers didn't come close.

Vimes didn't see the point. Gold . . . now *that* was important. People died for it. And iron—Ankh-Morpork needed iron. Timber, too. Stone, even. Silver, now, was very . . .

He flocked back to a page headed NATURAL RESOURCES, and under SILVER read: "No silver has been mined in Uberwald since the Diet of Bugs in AM1880, and the possession of the metal is technically illegal."

There was no explanation. He made a note to ask Inigo. After all, where you got werewolves, didn't you need silver? And things must have been pretty bad if everyone had to eat insects.

Anyway . . . silver was useful, too, but fat was just . . . fat. It was like biscuits, or tea, or sugar. It was just something that turned up in the cupboard. There was no *style* to it, no *romance*. It was stuff in tubs.

A note was clipped to the next page. He read: "The Fifth Elephant as a metaphor also appears in the Uberwald languages. Depending on context it can mean 'a thing which does not exist' (as we would say 'Klatchian mist'), 'a thing which is other than it seems' and 'a thing which, while unseen, controls events' (in the same way that we would use the term *eminence gris*)."

I wouldn't, thought Vimes. I don't use words like that.

"Constable Shoe," said Constable Shoe, when the door of the boot-maker's factory was opened. "Homicide."

"You come 'bout Mister Sonky?" said the troll who'd opened the door. Warm damp air blew out into the street, smelling of incontinent cats and sulfur.

"I meant I'm a zombie," said Reg Shoe. "I find that telling people right away saves embarrassing misunderstandings later on. But *coincidentally*, yes, we've come about the alleged deceased."

"We?" said the troll, making no comment about Reg's gray skin and stitch marks.

"Doon here, bigjobs!"

The troll looked down, not a usual direction in Ankh-Morpork, where people preferred not to see what they were standing in.

"Oh," he said, and took a few steps backward.

Some people said that gnomes were no more belligerent than any other race, and this was true. However, the belligerence was compressed down into a body six inches high and, like many things when they are compressed, had an inclination to explode. Constable Swires had been on the force only for a few months, but news had gone around and already he inspired respect, or at least the bladder-trembling terror that can pass for respect on these occasions.

"Don't ye just stand there gawpin', where's yon stiff?" said Swire, striding into the factory.

"We put him in der cellar," said the troll. "And now we got half a ton of liquid rubber running to waste. He'd be livid 'bout that . . . if he was alive, o'course."

"Why's it wasted?" said Reg.

"Gone all thick and manky, hasn't it. I'm gonna have to dump it later on, and dat's not easy. We was supposed to be dipping a load of Ribbed Magical Delights today, too, but all der ladies felt faint when I hauls him outa der vat and dey went off home."

Reg Shoe looked shocked. He was not, for various reasons, a patron of Mr. Sonky's wares, romance not being a regular feature of the life of the dead, but surely the world of the living had *some* standards, didn't it?

"You employ *ladies* here?" he said.

The troll looked surprised.

"Yeah. Sure. It's good steady work. Dey're good workers, too. Always laughing and tellin' jokes while dey're doin' the dippin' and packin', 'specially when we're doin' der Big Boys." The troll sniffed. "Pers'nally, I don't unnerstan der jokes."

"Dem Big Boys are bludy good value for a penny," said Buggy Swires.

Reg Shoe stared at his tiny partner. There was just *no way* that he was going to ask the question. But Swires must have seen his expression.

"After a bit of work wi' yon scissors, ye won't find a better mackintosh in the whole city," said the gnome, and laughed nastily.

Constable Shoe sighed. He knew that Mr. Vimes had an unofficial policy of getting ethnic minorities into the Watch,* but he wasn't sure this was wise in the case of gnomes, even though there was, admittedly, no ethnic group that was more minor. They had a built-in resistance to rules. This didn't just apply to the law, but to all the invisible rules that most people obeyed unthinkingly, like "Do not attempt to eat this giraffe" or "Do not head-butt people in the ankle just because they won't give you a chip." It was best to think of Constable Swires simply as a small independent weapon.

---

* As a member of the dead community, Reg Shoes naturally thought of himself as an ethnic majority.

71

"You'd better show us the d— the person who is currently vitally challenged," he said.

They were led downstairs. What was hanging from a beam in the cellar would have frightened the life out of anyone who wasn't already a zombie.

"Sorry 'bout dat," said the troll, pulling it down and tossing it into a corner, where it coiled into a rubbery heap.

"What d'heel wazzit?" said Constable Swires.

"We had to pull der rubber off'f him," said the troll. "Sets quick, see? Once you get it out in der air."

"Hey, dat's a' biggest Sonky I ever saw," chuckled Buggy. "A whole-body Sonky! Reckon that's the way he wanted to go?"

Reg looked at the corpse. He didn't mind being sent out on murders, even messy ones. The way he saw it, dying was really just a career change. Been there, done that, worn the shroud . . . And then you got over it and got on with your life. Of course, he knew that many people didn't, for some reason, but he thought of them as not prepared to make the effort.

There was a ragged wound in the neck.

"Any next of kin?" he said.

"He got a brother in Uberwald. We've sent word," the troll added. "On der clacks. It cost twenty dollars! Dat's murder!"

"Can you think of any reason why someone would kill him?"

The troll scratched his head.

"Well, 'cos dey wanted him dead, I reckon. Dat's a good reason."

"And why would anyone want him dead, do you think?" Reg Shoe could be very, very patient. "Has there been any trouble?"

"Business ain't been so good, I know dat."

"Really? I'd have thought you'd be coining money here."

"Oh *yeah*, dat's what you'd fink, but not everyfing people calls a Sonky is made by us, see? It's to do wid us becomin'"—the troll's face screwed up with cerebral effort—"jer-nair-rick. Lots of other buggers are jumping up and down on the bandwagon, and dey got better plant and new ideas like makin' 'em in cheese-and-onion flavor an' wid bells on an' stuff like dat. Mister Sonky won't have nothin' to do wid dat kind of fing and dat's been costin' us sales."

"I can see this would worry him," said Reg, in a keep-on-talking tone of voice.

"He's been locking himself in his office a lot."

"Oh? Why's that?" said Reg.

"He's der boss. You don't ask der boss. But he did say dat dere was a special job comin' up and dat'd put us back on our feets."

"Really?" said Reg, making a mental note. "What kind of job?"

"Dunno. You don't—"

"—ask the boss," said Reg. "Right. I suppose no one saw the murder, did they?"

Once again the troll screwed up its enormous face in thought.

"Der murderer, yeah, an' prob'ly Mister Sonky."

"Was there a third party?"

"I dunno, I never get invited to dem things."

"Apart from Mister Sonky and the murderer," said Shoe, still as patient as the grave, "was there anyone else here last night?"

"Dunno," said the troll.

"Thank you, you've been very helpful," said Shoe. "We'll have a look around, if you don't mind."

"Sure."

The troll went back to his vat.

Reg Shoe hadn't expected to find anything and was not disappointed. But he was thorough. Zombies usually are. Mr. Vimes had told him never to get too excited about clues, because clues could lead you on a dismal dance. They could become a habit. You ended up finding a wooden leg, a silk slipper and a feather at the scene of a crime and constructing an elegant theory involving a one-legged ballet dancer and a production of *Chicken Lake*.

The door to the office was open. It was hard to tell if things had been disturbed; Shoe got the impression that the mess was normal. A desk was awash with paperwork, Mr. Sonky having followed the usual "put it down somewhere" method of filing. A bench was covered with samples of rubber, bits of sacking, large bottles of chemicals and some wooden molds that Reg refrained from looking at too closely.

"Did you hear Corporal Littlebottom talking about that museum theft when we came on duty today, Buggy?" he said, opening a jar of yellow powder and sniffing it.

"No."

"I did," said Reg.

He put the lid on the sulfur again and sniffed the air of the factory. It smelled of liquid rubber, which is very much like the smell of incontinent cats.

"And some things stick in the mind," he said. "Special job, eh?"

It was Constable Visit-The-Infidel-With-Explanatory-Pamphlets's week as Communications Officer, which largely meant looking after the pigeons and keeping an eye on the clacks, with of course the assistance of Constable Downspout. Constable Downspout was a gargoyle. When it came to staring fixedly at one thing, you couldn't beat a gargoyle. The gargoyles were getting a lot of employment in the clacks industry.

Constable Visit quite enjoyed the pigeons. He sang them hymns. They listened to short homilies, cocking their heads from side to side. After all, he reasoned, had not Bishop Horn preached to the mollusks of the sea? And there was no record of them actually listening, whereas he was certain that the pigeons were taking it in. And they seemed to be interested in his pamphlets on the virtues of Omnianism, admittedly as nesting material at the moment, but this was certainly a good start.

A pigeon fluttered in as he was scraping the perches.

"Ah, Zebedinah," he said, lifting her up and removing the message capsule from her leg. "Well done. This is from Constable Shoe. And you shall have some corn, provided locally by Josiah Frument and Sons, Seed Merchants, but ultimately by the grace of Om."

There was a whir of wings and another pigeon settled on the perch. Constable Visit recognized it as Wilhelmina, one of Sergeant Angua's pigeons.

He removed the message capsule. The thin paper inside was tightly folded and on it someone had written CPT. CARROT, PERSONAL.

He hesitated, then put the message from Reg Shoe into the pneumatic tube and heard the whoosh of the suction as it headed off to the main office. The other one, he decided, required a more careful delivery.

Carrot was working in Vimes's office but, Visit noticed, not at the Commander's desk. Instead, he'd set up a folding table in the corner. The tottering piles of paperwork on the desk were slightly less alpine than yesterday. There were even occasional patches of desktop.

"Personal message for you, Captain."

"Thank you."

"And Constable Shoe wants a sergeant down at Sonky's boot factory."

"Did you send the message down to the office?"

"Yes, sir. The pneumatic tube is very useful," Visit added dutifully.

"Commander Vimes isn't very keen on it, but I'm sure it will eventually save us time," said Carrot. He unfolded the note.

Visit watched him. Carrot's lips moved slightly as he read.

"Where did the pigeon come from?" he said at last, screwing up the note.

"It looks pretty worn out, sir. Not from inside the city, I'm sure."

"Ah. Right. Thank you."

"Bad news, sir?" Visit angled.

"Just news, Constable. Don't let me detain you."

"Right, sir."

When the disappointed Visit had gone, Carrot went and looked out of the window.

There was a typical Ankh-Morpork street scene outside, although people were trying to separate them.

After a few minutes he went back to his table, wrote a short note, put it into one of the little carriers and sent it away with a hiss of air.

A few minutes later, Sergeant Colon came panting along the corridor. Carrot was very keen on modernizing the Watch, and in some strange way sending a message via the tube was so much more *modern* than simply opening the door and shouting, which is what Mr. Vimes did.

Carrot gave Fred Colon a bright smile.

"Ah, Fred. Everything going well?"

"Yessir?" said Fred Colon, uncertainly.

"Good. I am off to see the Patrician, Fred. As senior sergeant you are in charge of the Watch until Mister Vimes gets back."

"Yessir. Er . . . until you get back, you mean . . ."

"I shall not be coming back, Fred. I am resigning."

The Patrician looked at the badge on the desk.

". . . and well-trained men," Carrot was saying, somewhere in front of him. "After all, a few years ago there were only four of us in the Watch. Now it's functioning just like a machine."

"Yes, although bits of it do go *boing* occasionally," said Lord Vetinari, still staring at the badge. "Could I invite you to reconsider, Captain?"

"I've reconsidered several times, sir. And it's not Captain, sir."

"The Watch *needs* you, Mister Ironfoundersson."

"The Watch is bigger than one man, sir," said Carrot, still looking straight ahead.

"I'm not sure if it's bigger than Sergeant Colon, though."

"People get mistaken about old Fred, sir. He's a man with a solid bottom to his character."

"He's got a solid bottom to his bottom, Ca— Mister Ironfoundersson."

"I mean he doesn't flap in an emergency, sir."

"He doesn't do *anything* in an emergency," said the Patrician. "Except possibly hide. I might go so far as to say that the man appears to consist of an emergency in his own right."

"My mind is made up, sir."

Lord Vetinari sighed, sat back and stared up at the ceiling for a moment.

"Then all I can do is thank you for your services, *Captain*, and wish you good luck in your future endeavor. Do you have enough money?"

"I've saved quite a lot, sir."

"Nevertheless, it is a long way to Uberwald."

There was silence.

"Sir?"

"Yes?"

"How did you *know*?"

"Oh, people measured it years ago. Surveyors and so forth."

"Sir!"

Vetinari sighed. "I think the term is . . . deduction. Be that as it may . . . Captain, I am choosing to believe that you are merely taking an extended leave of absence. I understand that you've never taken a holiday while you have been here. I am sure you are owed a few weeks."

Carrot said nothing.

"And if I were you, I'd begin my search for Sergeant Angua at the Shambling Gate," Vetinari added.

After a while, Carrot said quietly: "Is that as a result of information received, my lord?"

Vetinari smiled a thin little smile. "No. But Uberwald is going through some troubling times, and of course she is from one of the aristocratic families. I surmise that she has been called away. Beyond that, I cannot be of much help. You will have to follow, as they say, your nose."

"No, I think I can find a much more reliable nose than mine," said Carrot.

"Good." Lord Vetinari went back to his desk and sat down. "I wish you well in your . . . search. Nevertheless, I'm sure we will be seeing you again. A lot of people here . . . depend on you."

"Yes, sir."

"Good day to you."

When Carrot had gone Lord Vetinari got up and walked across to the other side of the room, where a map of Uberwald was unrolled on a table. It was quite old, but in recent years any mapmakers who had wandered off the beaten track in that country had spent all their time trying to find it again. There were a few rivers, their courses mostly guesswork, and the occasional town or at least the *name* of a town, probably put in to save the cartographer the embarrassment of filling his chart with, as they said in the trade, *MMBU.**

The door opened and Vetinari's head clerk, Drumknott, eased his way in with the silence of a feather falling in a cathedral.

"A somewhat unexpected development, my lord," he said quietly.

"An uncharacteristic one, certainly," said Vetinari.

"Do you wish me to send a clacks to Vimes, sir? He could be back in a day or so."

Vetinari was looking intently at the blind, blank map. It was, he felt, very much like the future; a few things were outlined, there were some rough guesses, but everything else was waiting to be created . . .

"Hmm?" he said.

"Do you wish me to recall Vimes, sir?"

"Good heavens, no. Vimes in Uberwald will be more amusing than an amorous armadillo in a bowling alley. And who else could I send? Only Vimes could go to Uberwald."

"But surely this is an emergency, sir?"

"Hmm?"

* Miles and Miles of Bloody Uberwald.

"What else are we to call it, sir, when a young man of such promise throws away his career for the pursuit of a girl?"

The Patrician stroked his beard and smiled at something.

There was a line across the map: the progress of the semaphore towers. It was mathematically straight, a statement of intellect in the crowding darkness of miles and miles of bloody Uberwald.

"*Possibly* . . . a bonus," he said. "Uberwald has much to teach us. Fetch me the papers on the werewolf clans, will you? Oh . . . and although I swore I would never ever do this . . . please prepare a message for Sergeant Colon, too. Promotion, alas, beckons."

A grubby cloth cap lay on the pavement.

On the pavement beside the cap, someone had written in damp chalk:

Plese HelP This LiTTle doGGie

Beside it sat a small dog.

It was not cut out by nature to be a friendly little waggy-tailed dog, but was making the effort. Whenever someone walked by it sat up on its hind legs and whined pitifully.

Something landed in the cap. It was a washer.

The charitable pedestrian had gone only a few steps farther along the road when he heard: "And I hope your legs falls off, mister."

He turned. The dog was watching him intently.

"Woof?" it said.

He looked puzzled, shrugged, and then turned and walked on.

"Yeah . . . bloody woof woof," said the strange voice, as he was about to turn the corner.

A hand reached down and picked up the dog by the scruff of its neck.

"Hello, Gaspode. I believe I've solved a little mystery."

"Oh *no* . . ." the dog moaned.

"That's not being a good dog, Gaspode," said Carrot, lifting the dog so they could meet eye to eye.

"All right, all right, put me down, will you? This hurts, you know."

"I need your help, Gaspode."

"Not me. I don't help the Watch. Nothing personal, but it doesn't do anything for my street cred."

"I'm not talking about helping the Watch, Gaspode. This *is* personal. I need your nose." Carrot lowered the dog to the pavement, and rubbed his hand on his shirt. "Unfortunately, this means I need the rest of you as well, although of course I am aware that under that itchy exterior beats a heart of gold."

"Really," said Gaspode. "*Nothing* good starts with 'I need your help.'"

"It's Angua."

"Oh dear."

"I want you to track her."

"Huh, not many dogs could track a werewolf, mister. They're *cunning*."

"Always go to the best, I always say," said Carrot.

"Finest nose known to man or beast," said Gaspode, wrinkling it. "Where's she gone, then?"

"To Uberwald, I think."

Carrot moved fast. Gaspode's flight was hindered by the hand gripping his tail.

"That's hundreds of miles away! And dog miles is seven times longer! Not a chance!"

"Oh? All right, then. Silly of me to suggest it," said Carrot, letting go. "You're right. It's ridiculous."

Gaspode turned, suddenly full of suspicion.

"No, I didn't say it was ridiculous," he said. "I just said it was hundreds of miles away . . ."

"Yes, but you said you had no chance."

"No, I *said* that you had no chance of getting *me* to do it."

"Yes, but winter's coming on and, as you say, a werewolf is very hard to track and on top of that Angua's a copper. She'll work out that I'd use you, so she'll be covering her trail."

Gaspode whined. "Look, mister, respect is hard to earn in this dog's town. If I'm not smelled around the lampposts for a couple of weeks my stock is definitely in the gutter, right?"

"Yes, yes, I understand. I'll make some other arrangements. Nervous Nigel's still around, isn't he?"

"What? That spaniel? He couldn't smell his own bottom if you put it in front of him!"

"They say he's pretty good, nasally."

"And he widdles every time anyone looks at him!" snapped Gaspode.

"I heard he can smell a dead rat two miles away."

"Yeah? Well, I can smell what *color* it is!"

Carrot sighed. "Well, I've got no choice, I'm afraid. You can't do it, so I'll—"

"I didn't say—" Gaspode stopped, and then went on. "I'm going to do it, aren't I? I'm bloody well going to do it. You're going to trick me or blackmail me or whatever it takes, aren't you . . ."

"Yes. How do you manage to write, Gaspode?"

"I holds the chalk in me mouth. Easy."

"You're a smart dog. I've always said so. The world's only talking dog, too."

"Lower your voice, lower your voice!" said Gaspode, looking around. "Here, Uberwald's wolf country, isn't it?"

"Oh yes."

"I could've *bin* a wolf, you know. With diff'rent parents, of course."

Gaspode sniffed, and looked furtively up and down the street again.

"Steak?"

"Every night."

"Right."

Sergeant Colon was a picture of misery, drawn on a lumpy pavement in bad crayon on a wet day. He sat on a chair and occasionally glanced at the message which had just been delivered, as if hoping that the words would somehow fade away.

"Bloody hell, Nobby," he moaned.

"There, there, Fred . . ." said Nobby, currently a vision in organdy.

"I can't be promoted! I'm not an officer! I am base, common and popular!"

"I've always said that about you, Fred. You got common off to a treat."

"But it's writ down, Nobby! Look, His Lordship's signed it!"

"We-ell, the way I see it, you've got three choices," said Nobby.

"Yeah?"

"You can go and tell him you're not doing it . . ."

The panic in Colon's face was replaced by glazed gray terror.

"Thank you very much, Nobby," he said bitterly. "Let me know if you've got any more suggestions like that, 'cos I'll need to go and change my underwear."

"Or you could accept it and make such a screw-up of it that he takes it away from you . . ."

"You're doing this on purpose, Nobby!"

"Might be worth a try, Fred."

"Yeah, but the thing about screw-ups, Nobby, is that it's hard for you to be, you know, *precise*. You might think you're making a little screw-up and then it blows up in your face and it turns out to be in fact a big screw-up, and in those circumstances, Nobby, I'm sort of worried that what His Lordship might take away from me wouldn't just be the job. I hope I don't have to draw you a picture?"

"Good point, Fred."

"What I'm saying is, screw-ups is like . . . well, screw-ups is . . . well, the thing about screw-ups is you never know what size they're going to be."

"Well, Fred, the *third* choice is you putting up with it."

"That's not helpful, Nobby."

"It'll only be for a couple of weeks, then Mister Vimes'll be back."

"Yeah, but supposing he isn't? Nasty place, Uberwald. I heard where it's a misery wrapped in an enema. That doesn't sound too good. You can fall down things. Then I'm stuck, right? I don't know how to *do* officering."

"*No one* knows how to do officering, Fred. That's why they're officers. If they *knew* anything, they'd be sergeants."

Now Colon's face screwed up again in desperate thought. As a lifelong uniformed man, a three-striped peg that had found a three-striped hole very early in its career, he subscribed automatically and unthinkingly to the belief that officers as a class could not put their own trousers on without a map. He conscientiously excluded Vimes and Carrot from the list, automatically elevating them to the rank of honorary sergeant.

Nobby was watching him with an expression of combined concern, friendliness and predatory intent.

"What shall I *do*, Nobby?"

"Well, 'Captain,'" said Nobby, and then he gave a little cough, "what officers *mainly* have to do, as you know, is sign things—"

The door was knocked on and opened at the same time, by a flustered constable.

"Sarge, Constable Shoe says he really *does* need an officer down at Sonky's factory."

"What, the rubber wally man?" said Colon. "Right. An officer. Right. We'll be along."

"And that's *Captain* Colon," said Nobby quickly.

"Er . . . er . . . yes, and that's *Captain* Colon, thank you very much," said Colon, adding as his resolve stiffened, "and I'll thank you not to forget it!"

The constable stared at them, and then stopped trying to understand.

"And there's a troll downstairs who insists on speaking to whoever's in charge—"

"Can't Stronginthearm deal with it?"

"Er . . . is Sergeant Stronginthearm still a sergeant?" said the constable.

"Yes!"

"Even unconscious?"

"What?"

"He's flat on the floor right now, Sa— Captain."

"What's the troll want?"

"Right now he wants to kill someone, but mainly I think he wants someone to take the clamp off'f his foot."

Gaspode ran up and down, nose barely an inch from the ground. Carrot waited, holding his horse. It was a good one. Carrot hadn't spent a lot of his wages, up until now.

Finally the dog sat down and looked depressed.

"So tell me about this wonderful nose the Patrician has got, then," he said.

"Not a trace?"

"You better get Vetinari down here, if he's so good," said Gaspode. "What's the *point* of starting here? Worst place in the whole city! It's the gate to the cattle market, am I right? Trying *not* to smell stuff is the trick here, is the point I'm makin'. There's *ground-in* stink. If you wanted to get on the trail of somebody, this is the last place I'd start."

"Very good point," said Carrot, carefully. "So . . . what's the strongest smell heading hubward?"

"Dung carts, o'course. Yesterday. Always a big clear-out of the pens first thing Friday morning."

"You can follow the smell?"

Gaspode rolled his eyes. "With my head in a bucket."

"Good. Let's go."

"So," said Gaspode, as they began to leave the gate's bustle behind, "we're chasing this girl, right?"

"Yes."

"Just you?"

"Yes."

"Not like with dogs, then, where there might be twenty or thirty?"

"No."

"So we're not looking at a bucket of cold water here?"

"No."

Constable Shoe saluted, but a little testily. He'd been waiting rather a long time.

"Afternoon, Sergeant—"

"That's Captain," said Captain Colon. "See the pip on my shoulder, Reg?"

Reg looked closely. "I thought it was bird doings, Sarge."

"That's Captain," said Colon automatically. "It's only chalk now because I ain't got time to get it done properly," he said. "So don't be cheeky."

"What's up with Nobby?" said Reg. Corporal Nobbs was holding a damp cloth over one eye.

"Bit of a contry tomps with an illegally parked troll," said Captain Colon.

"Shows what kind of troll *he* was, striking a lady," muttered Nobby.

"But you ain't a lady, Nobby. You're just wearing your traffic-calming disguise."

"He wasn't to know."

"You'd got your helmet on. Anyway, you shouldn't have clamped him."

"He *was* parked, Fred."

"He'd been knocked down by a cart," said Captain Colon. "And that's Captain."

"Well, they always have excuses," said Nobby sullenly.

"You'd better show us the corpus, Reg," said Colon.

The body in the cellar was duly inspected.

". . . and I remember Cheery saying there was a smell of cat's pee and sulfur at the Dwarf Bread Museum," said Reg.

"Certainly hangs about," said Colon. "You wouldn't have blocked sinuses if you worked here for a day."

"And I thought, 'I wonder if someone'd tried to make a mold of the replica Stone,' sir," said Reg.

"Now that *is* clever," said Fred Colon. "You'd get the real one back then, wouldn't you?"

"Er . . . no, Sarge— Captain. But you'd get a copy of the replica."

"Would that be legal?"

"Can't say, sir. I wouldn't think so. It wouldn't fool a dwarf for five minutes."

"Then who'd want to kill him?"

"A father of thirteen kids, maybe?" said Nobby. "Haha."

"Nobby, will you stop pinching the merchandise?" said Colon. "And don't argue, I just saw you put a couple of dozen in your handbag."

"Dat don't matter," rumbled the troll. "Mister Sonky always said dey was free to the Watch."

"That was very . . . civic of him," said Captain Colon.

"Yeah, he said der last fing we wanted was more bloody coppers around the city."

A pigeon chose that diplomatic moment to flutter into the factory and land on Colon's shoulder, where it promoted him. He reached up, removed the message capsule and unfolded the contents.

"It's from Visit," he said. "There's a clue, he says."

"What to?" said Nobby.

"Not *to* anything, Nobby. Just a clue." He took off his helmet and wiped his brow. *This* was what he'd hoped to avoid. In his heart of battered hearts, he suspected that Vimes and Carrot were good at putting clues next to other clues and thinking about them. That was their talent. He had other . . . well, he was good with people, and he had a shiny breastplate, and he could sergeant in his sleep.

"All right, write up your report," he said. "Well done. We're going back to the Yard.

"I can see this is going to get on top of me," said Colon, as they walked away. "There's paperwork, too. You know me and paperwork, Nobby."

"You're a very thorough reader, that's all, Fred," said Nobby. "I've seen you take *ages* over just one page. Digesting it magisterially, I thought."

Colon brightened a little. "Yes, that's what I do," he said.

"Even if it's only the menu down at the Klatchian take-out, I've seen you staring at one line for a minute at a time."

"Well, obviously you can't let people put one over on you," said Colon, sticking out his chest, or at least sticking it further up.

"What you need is an aide de camp," said Nobby, lifting his dress to step over a puddle.

"I do?"

"Oh yes. 'Cos of you being a figurehead and setting an example to your men," said Nobby.

"Ah. Right. Yes," said Colon, grasping the idea with relief. "A man can't be expected to do all that *and* read long words, am I right?"

"Exactly. And, of course, we're down one sergeant at the Yard now," said Nobby.

"Good point, Nobby. It's going to be busy."

They walked on for a while.

"You could promote someone," Nobby prompted.

"Could I?"

"What good's being the boss if you can't?"

"That's true. And it's sort of an emergency . . . Hmm . . . any thoughts, Nobby?"

Nobby sighed inwardly. A penny could drop through wet cement faster than it could drop for Fred Colon.

"A name springs to mind," he said.

"Ah, right. Yes. Reg Shoe, right? Good at writing, a keen thinker, and of course he's coolheaded," said Colon. "Icy, practically."

"But a bit on the dead side," said Nobby.

"Yes, I suppose that counts against him."

"And he goes to pieces unpredictably," said Nobby.

"That's true," said Captain Colon. "No one likes shaking hands and ending up with more fingers than they started with."

"So p'raps it might be better to consider someone who has been unreasonably overlooked," said Nobby, going for broke. "Someone who's face dunt fit, p'raps. Someone who's experience in the Watch gen'rally and in Traffic in particular could be great service to the city if people wouldn't go on about one or two lapses which didn't happen in any case."

The dawn of intelligence rose across the vistas of Colon's face.

"*Ah*," he said. "I *see*. Well, why didn't you come right out with that at the start, Nobby."

"Well, it's *your* decision, Fred . . . I mean, *Captain*," said Nobby earnestly.

"But 'sposing Mister Vimes doesn't agree? He'll be back in a couple of weeks."

"That'll be long enough," said Nobby.

"And you don't mind?"

"Me? Mind? Not me. You know me, Fred, always ready to do my bit."

"Nobby?"

"Yes, Fred?"

"The dress . . ."

"Yes, Fred?"

"I thought we weren't doing the . . . traffic calming any more?"

"Yes, Fred. But I thought I'd keep it on ready to swing into action just in case you decided that we should."

A chilly wind blew across the cabbage fields.

To Gaspode it brought, beside the overpowering fumes of the cabbage and the dark red smell of the dung carts, hints of pine, mountains, snow, sweat and stale cigar smoke. The last came from the cart men's habit of smoking large, cheap cigars. They kept the flies off.

It was better than vision. The world of smell stretched before Gaspode.

"My paws hurt," he said.

"There's a good dog," said Carrot.

The road forked. Gaspode stopped, and snuffled around.

"Well, here's an int'resting fing," he said. "Some of the dung's jumped down off'f the cart and headed away across the fields here. You were right."

"Can you smell water anywhere around?" said Carrot, scanning the flat plain.

Gaspode's mottled nose wrinkled up in effort.

"Pond," he said. "Not very big. 'Bout a mile away."

"She'll be heading toward it. Very meticulous about cleanliness, Angua. That's not usual in werewolves."

"Never been one for water myself," said Gaspode.

"Is that a fact?"

"Here, no need for that! I had a B . . . A . . . T . . . H once, you know, it's not as if I don't know what it's like."

The pond was in a clump of windblown trees. Dry grass rustled in the breeze. A single coot scuttled into the reeds as Carrot and Gaspode approached.

"Yeah, here we are," said Gaspode. "A lot of muck goes in, and . . ." He sniffed at the stirred-up mud. "Er . . . yeah, she comes out. Um."

"Is there a problem?" said Carrot.

"What? Oh, no. Clear scent. Headin' for the mountains, just like you said. Um." Gaspode sat down and scratched himself with a hind leg.

"There is a problem, isn't there . . ." said Carrot.

"Well . . . supposin' there was something really bad that you wouldn't really want to know, and I knew what it was . . . how'd you feel about me tellin' you? I mean, some people'd rather not know. It's a pers'nal thing."

"Gaspode!"

"She's not alone. There's another wolf."

"Ah."

Carrot's mild, uninformative smile did not change.

"Er . . . of the male persuasion," said Gaspode. "A boy wolf. Er. Very much so."

"Thank you, Gaspode."

"Extremely male. Um. In a very def'nite way. Unmistakably."

"Yes, I think I understand."

"And this is just Words. In Smell, it's a lot more, well, emphatic."

"Thank you for that, Gaspode. And they're heading . . ."

"Still straight for the mountains, boss," said Gaspode, as kindly as he could. He wasn't certain of the details of human sexual relationships, and the ones he was certain of he still couldn't quite believe, but he knew that they were a lot more complicated than those enjoyed by the doggy fraternity.

"This smell . . ."

"The extremely male one I was talkin' about?"

"The very one, yes," said Carrot levelly. "You could still smell it if you were on the horse, could you?"

"I could smell it with my nose in a sack of onions."

"Good. Because I think we should move a little faster now . . ."

"Yes, I thought you'd think that."

Constable Visit saluted when Nobby and Colon entered Pseudopolis Yard.

"I thought you ought to know about this right away, sir," he said, flourishing a square of paper. "I just got it off Ronald."

"Who?"

"The imp on the bridge, sir. He paints pictures of carts going too fast? No one had been feeding him," Visit added, in a mildly accusing tone.

"Oh. Someone speeding," said Colon. "So?" He looked again. "That's one of those sedan chairs the deep-down dwarfs use, isn't it? Them trolls must've been moving!"

"It was just after the Scone was stolen," said Visit. "Ronald writes the time in the corner, see? A bit odd, I thought. Like a kind of getaway vehicle, sir?"

"What'd a dwarf want to steal a worthless lump of rock for?" said Colon. "Especially them dark dwarfs. They give me the creeps in those stupid clothes they wear."

Angry silence rang like a dropped girder in a temple. There were three dwarfs in the room.

"You two! You ought to be out on patrol!" barked Sergeant

Stronginthearm. "*I've* got business down at Chitterling Street!"

All three dwarfs marched out, somehow contriving even to walk angrily.

"Well, what was that about?" said Fred Colon. "Bit touchy, aren't they? Mister Vimes says that sort of thing all the time and no one minds."

"Yes, but that's because he's Sam Vimes," said Nobby.

"Oh? And are you inferring I'm not?" said Captain Colon.

"Well . . . *yes*, Fred. You're Fred Colon," said Nobby patiently.

"Oh, I *am*, am I?"

"Yes, Captain Colon."

"And they'd better bloody remember it!" Colon snapped. "I'm not a soft touch, me. I'm not going to take insubordination like that! I've always said Vimes was a bit too soft on those dwarfs! They gets the same pay as us and they're only half the size!"

"Yes, yes," said Nobby, waving his hands placatingly in a desperate attempt to calm things down. "But, Fred, trolls are twice as *big* as us and they get paid the same, so it—"

"But they've only got a quarter of the brains, so it's just the same like I said—"

The noise they heard was long and drawn out and menacing. It was the sound of Lance-Constable Bluejohn's chair being pushed back.

The floor creaked as he shambled past Colon, removed his helmet from its peg with one enormous hand and headed for the door.

"'M goin' on patrol," he mumbled.

"You're not on patrol for another hour," said Constable Visit.

"'M goin' now," said Bluejohn. The room was darkened for a moment as he eclipsed the doorway, and then he was gone.

"Why's everyone so tetchy all of a sudden?" said Colon. The remaining constables tried not to catch his eye.

"Did I hear someone snigger?" he demanded.

"I didn't hear anyone snigger, Sarge," said Nobby.

"Oh? Oh? You think I'm a sergeant, do you, Corporal Nobbs?"

"No, Fred, I—oh gawds . . ."

"I can see things have got pretty *slack* around here," said Captain Colon, an evil little gleam in his eye. "I bet you were all thinking, oh, it's only fat old Fred Colon, it's all going to be gravy from now on, eh?"

"Oh, Fred, no one thinks you're old—oh gawds . . ."

"Just fat, eh?" Fred glowered around the room. Suddenly, and against all previous evidence, everyone was vitally interested in their paperwork.

"Right! Well, from now on things are going to be *different,*" said Captain Colon. "Oh yes. I'm up to all your little tricks— Who said that?"

"Said what, Captain?" said Nobby, who'd also heard the little whispered "We learned 'em all from you, Sarge" but at this moment would eat live coals rather than admit it.

"Someone said something blotto voice," said Captain Colon.

"I'm sure they didn't, Captain," said Nobby.

"And I won't be eyeballed like that, neither!"

"No one's looking at you!" wailed Nobby.

"Aha, you think I don't know that one?" Colon shouted. "There's plenty of ways to eyeball someone without lookin' at 'em, Corporal. That man over there is earlobing me!"

"I think Constable Ping is just really interested in the report he's writing, Fre— Sar— Captain."

Colon's ruffled feathers settled a little. "Well . . . all right. And now I'm going up to my office, all right? There'll be some *changes* around here. And someone bring me a cup of tea."

They watched him go up the stairs, enter the office and slam the door.

"Well, the—" Constable Ping began, but Nobby, who had a lot more experience with the Colon personality, waved one hand frantically for silence while he held the other one to his ear, very theatrically.

Then they all heard the door click open again, quietly.

"A change is as good as a rest, I suppose," said Constable Ping.

"As the prophet Ossory says, better an oxen in the potters' fields of Hersheba than a sandal in the wine presses of Gash," said Constable Visit.

"Yeah, so I've heard," said Nobby. "Well, I'll just make him his tea. Everyone feels better after a cup of tea."

A couple of minutes later the constables heard Colon shouting, even through the door.

"What is wrong with this mug, Corporal?"

"Nothing, Sa— sir. It's yer mug. You always have your tea in it."

"Ah, but, you see, it is a *sergeant's* mug, Corporal. And what is it that officers drink out of?"

"Well, Carrot and Mister Vimes have got their own mugs—"

"No, they may *choose* to drink out of mugs, Corporal, but Watch regulations say officers have a cup and saucer. Says so right here, regulation three-oh-one, subsection C. Do you understand me?"

"I don't think we've got any—"

"You know where the petty cash is. Usually, you're the only person that does. You're dismissed, Corporal."

Nobby came down the stairs white-faced, holding the offending receptacle.

The door opened again.

"And none of you are to gob in it, neither!" shouted Colon. "I know that one! And it's to be stirred with a *spoon*, understand? I know *that* one, too." The door slammed.

Constable Visit took the mug from Nobby's shaking hand and patted him on the shoulder.

"Chalky the troll does some very good seconds, I understand—" he began.

The door opened.

"Bloody china, too!"

The door slammed.

"Anyone *seen* the petty cash lately?" said Constable Ping.

Nobby reached mournfully into his pocket and pulled out some dollars. He handed them to Visit.

"Better go to that posh shop in Kings Way," he said. "Get one of those cups and saucers thin enough to see through. You know, with gold around the rim." He looked around the other constables. "What're you lot doing here? You won't catch many criminals in *here*!"

"Does the petty cash count, Nobby?" said Ping.

"Don't you Nobby me, Ping! You just get out there! And the rest of you!"

Days rolled by. More accurately, they rattled by. It was a comfortable coach, as coaches went, and as coaches on this road went over continual potholes, it swayed and rocked like a cradle. Initially, the motion was soothing. After a day or two, it palled. So did the scenery.

Vimes stared glumly out of the window.

There was another clacking tower on the horizon. They were putting them near the road, he recalled, even though that wasn't the direct route. Only a fool would build them across the badlands. You had to remember, sometimes, that within a few hundred miles of Ankh-Morpork there were still trolls who hadn't caught on to the fact that humans weren't digestible. Besides, most of the settlements were near the road.

The new guild must be coining money. Even from here he could see the scaffolding, as workers feverishly attached still more gantries and paddles to the main tower. The whole thing would likely be matchsticks after the next hurricane, but by then the owners would probably have earned enough to build another five. Or fifty.

It had all happened so fast. Who'd have believed it? But all the components had been there for years. Semaphore was ancient—a century ago the Watch had used a few towers to relay messages to patrolling officers. And gargoyles had nothing to *do* all day but sit and watch things, and usually were too unimaginative to make mistakes.

What *had* happened was that people thought differently about news now. Once upon a time they'd have used something like this to relay information about troop movements and the death of kings. True, that was something that people need to know, but they didn't need to know it every day. No, what they needed to know every day were things like *How much are cattle selling for in Ankh-Morpork today?* Because, if they weren't fetching much, maybe it was better to drive them to Quirm instead. People needed to know these little things. Lots and lots of little things. Little things like *Did my ship get there safely?* That's why the Guild was driving hell-bent across the mountains on to Genua, four thousand miles away. It took many months for a ship to round Cape Terror. How much, exactly, would a trader pay to know, within a day, when it had arrived? And how much the cargo was worth? Has it been sold? Is there credit to my name in Ankh-Morpork?

Coining money? Oh yes!

And it had caught on as fast as every other craze did in the big city. It seemed as though everybody who could put together a pole, a couple of gargoyles and some secondhand windmill machinery was in on the business. You couldn't go out to dinner these days without seeing people nip out of the restaurant every five minutes to check that there weren't any messages for them on the nearest pole. As for those who cut out the middleman and signaled directly to their friends across a crowded room, causing mild contusions to those nearby . . .

Vimes shook his head. *That* was messages without meaning: telepathy without brains.

But . . . it *had* been good, hadn't it, last week? When Don't Know Jack had pinched that silver in Sto Lat and then galloped at speed to the sanctuary of the Shades in Ankh-Morpork? And Sergeant Edge of the Sto Lat Watch, who'd trained under Vimes, had put a message on the clacks that arrived on Vimes's desk more than an hour before Jack sauntered through the city gates and into the waiting embrace of Sergeant Detritus? Legally it had been a bit tricky, since the offense hadn't been committed on Ankh-Morpork soil and a semaphore message did not, strictly speaking, come under the heading of "hot pursuit," but Jack had kindly solved that one by taking a wild swing at the troll, resulting in his arrest for Assault on a Watch Officer and treatment for a broken wrist . . .

There was a gentle snore from Lady Sybil. A marriage is always made up of two people who are prepared to swear that only the *other* one snores.

Inigo Skimmer was hunched in a corner, reading a book. Vimes watched him for some time.

"I'm just going up top for some air," he said at last, opening the door. The clattering of the wheels filled the tiny, hot space, and dust blew in.

"Your Grace—" Inigo began, standing up. Vimes, already clambering up the side of the coach, stuck his head back in.

"You're not making any friends with that attitude," he said, and kicked the door shut with his foot.

Cheery and Detritus had made themselves comfortable on the roof. It was a lot less stuffy and at least there was a view, if vegetables were your idea of a panorama.

Vimes worked himself into a niche between two bundles and leaned toward Cheery.

"You know about the clacks, right?" he said.

"Well, sort of, sir . . ."

"Good." Vimes passed her a piece of paper. "There's bound to be a tower near where we stop tonight. Cipher this and send it to the Watch, will you? They ought to be able to turn it around in an hour, if they ask the right people. Tell them to try Washable Topsy, she does the laundry there. Or Gilbert Gilbert, he always seems to know what's going on."

Cheery read the message, and then stared at Vimes.

"Are you *sure*, sir?" she said.

"Maybe. Make sure you send the *description*. Names don't mean much."

"May I ask what makes you think—"

"His walk. And he didn't catch an orange," said Vimes. "Mhm. Mhm."

* * *

100

Constable Visit was cleaning out the old pigeon loft when the message arrived on the clacks.

He had been spending more and more time with the pigeons these days. It wasn't a popular job, so no one had tried to take it away from him, and at least up here the shouts and door-slammings were muffled.

The perches *gleamed*.

Constable Visit enjoyed his job. He didn't have many friends in the city. Truth to tell, he didn't have many friends in the Watch, either. But at least there were people to talk to, and he was making headway with the religious instruction of the pigeons.

But now there was this . . .

It was addressed to Captain Carrot. That meant it probably ought to be delivered to Captain Colon now, and *personally*, because Captain Colon thought that people were spying on his messages sent via the suction tube.

Constable Visit had been fairly safe up until now. Omnians were good at not questioning orders, even ones that made no sense. Visit instinctively respected authority, no matter how crazy, because he'd been brought up properly. And he had plenty of time to keep his armor bright. Brightly polished armor had suddenly become very important in the Watch, for some reason.

Even so, going into Colon's office needed all the courage that the legendary Bishop Horn had shown when entering the city of the Oolites, and everyone knew what *they* did to strangers.

Visit climbed down from the loft and made his nervous way to the main building, taking care to walk smartly.

The main office was more or less empty. There seemed to be fewer watchmen around these days. Usually people preferred to loaf indoors in this chilly weather, but suddenly everyone was keen to be out of Captain Colon's view.

Visit went up to the office and knocked on the door.

He knocked again.

When there was no reply he pushed open the door, walked carefully over to the sparkling clean desk and went to tuck the flimsy message under the ink bottle in case it blew away—

"Aha!"

The ink soared up as Visit's hand jerked. He had a vision of the blue-black shower passing his ear, and heard the *splat* as it hit something behind him.

He turned like an automaton, to see a Captain Colon who would have been white-faced if it weren't for the ink.

"I *see*," said Colon. "Assault on a superior officer, eh?"

"It was an accident, Captain!"

"Oh, was it? And why, pray, were you sneaking into my office?"

"I didn't think you were in here, Captain!" Visit gabbled.

"Aha!"

"Sorry?"

"Sneaking a look at my private papers, eh?"

"No, Captain!" Visit rallied a little bit. "Why were you standing behind the door, Captain?"

"Oh? I'm not allowed to stand behind my own door, is that it?"

It was then that Constable Visit made his next mistake. He tried to smile.

"Well, it *is* a bit odd, sir—"

"Are you suggesting there is anything *odd* about me, Constable?" said Captain Colon. "Is there anything about me that you find *funny*?"

Visit stared at the mottled face, speckled with ink.

"Not a thing, sir."

"You've been working acceptably, Constable," said Colon, standing slightly too close to Visit, "and therefore I don't intend to be harsh with you. No one could call me an unfair man. You is demoted to lance-constable, understand? Your pay will be adjusted and backdated to the beginning of the month."

Visit saluted. It was probably the only way to get out of there alive. One of Colon's eyes was twitching.

"However, you could redeem yourself," said Colon, "if you was to tell me who has been stealing, I said *stealing*, the sugar lumps."

"Sir?"

"I *knows* there was forty-three last night. I counted 'em very thoroughly. There's forty-one this morning, Constable. And they're *locked* in the cupboard. Can you explain that?"

If Visit had been suicidal and honest, he'd have said: Well, Captain, while of course I think you have many worthy qualities, I *have* known you to count your fingers twice and come up with different answers.

"Er . . . mice?" he said, weakly.

"Hah! Off you go, Lance-Constable, and just you think about what I said!"

When the dejected Visit had gone, Captain Colon sat down at his big, clean desk.

The little flickering part of his brain that was still sparking coherent thought through the fog of mind-numbing terror that filled Colon's head was telling him that he was so far out of his depth that the fish had lights on their noses.

Yes, he did have a clean desk. But that was because he was throwing all the paperwork away.

It wasn't that he was illiterate, but Fred Colon did need a bit of a think and a run-up to tackle anything much longer than a list and he tended to get lost in any word that had more than three syllables. He was, in fact, *functionally* literate. That is, he thought of reading and writing like he thought about boots—you needed them, but they weren't supposed to be fun, and you got suspicious about people who got a kick out of them.

Of course, Mr. Vimes had kept his desk piled high with paperwork, but it occurred to Colon that maybe Vimes and Carrot between them had developed a way of keeping just ahead of the piles, by knowing what was *important* and what wasn't. To Colon, it was all gut-wrenchingly mysterious. There were complaints, and memos, and invitations, and letters requesting "a few minutes of your time" and forms to fill in, and reports to read, and sentences containing words like "iniquitous" and "immediate action" and they tottered in his mind like a great big wave, poised to fall on him.

The sane core of Colon was wondering if the purpose of officers wasn't to stand between the sergeants and all this sh—this slush, so that they could get on with sergeanting.

Captain Colon took a deep, wobbly breath.

On the other hand, if people were nicking the sugar lumps, no wonder things weren't working properly! Get the sugar lumps right, and everything else would work out!

That made sense!

He turned, and his eye caught the huge accusing heap of paperwork in the corner.

And the empty fireplace, too.

That was what officering was all about, wasn't it? Making *decisions*!

Lance-Constable Visit walked dejectedly back down to the main office, which had filled up for a watch change.

Everyone was clustered around one of the desks on which lay, looking slightly muddy, the Scone of Stone.

"Constable Thighbiter found it in Zephire Street, just lying there," said Sergeant Stronginthearm. "The thief must've gotten scared."

"A long way from the museum, though," said Reg Shoe. "Why lug it all the way across the city and leave it in a posh part of town where someone's bound to trip over it?"

"Oh woe is me, for I am undone," said Lance-Constable Visit, who felt he was playing a poor second fiddle to what he would call, if he had no use for his legs, a pagan image.

"Could be drafty," said Corporal Nobbs, a man of little sympathy.

"I mean I have been reduced to Lance-Constable," said Visit.

"What? Why?" said Sergeant Stronginthearm.

"I'm . . . not sure," said Visit.

"That just about does it!" said the dwarf. "He sacked three of the officers up at Dolly Sisters yesterday. Well, I'm not waiting for it to happen to me. I'm off to Sto Lat. They're always looking for trained watchmen. I'm a sergeant. I could name my price."

"But, look, Vimesy used to say that sort of thing, too, I heard him," said Nobby.

"Yeah, but that was different."

"How?"

"*That* was Mister Vimes," said Stronginthearm. "Remember that riot in Easy Street last year? Bloke came after me with a club when I was on the ground, and Mister Vimes caught it on his arm and punched the man right in the head."

"Yeah," said Constable Hacknee, another dwarf. "When your back's against the wall, Mister Vimes is right behind you."

"But old Fred . . . you all know old Fred Colon, boys," Nobby wheedled, taking a kettle off the office stove and pouring the boiling water into a teapot. "He knows coppering inside and out."

"His kind of coppering, yeah," said Hacknee.

"I mean, he's been a copper longer than anyone in the Watch," said Nobby.

One of the dwarfs said something in Dwarfish. There were a few smiles from the shorter watchmen.

"What was that?" said Nobby.

"Well, roughly translated," said Stronginthearm, "'My bum has been a bum for a very long time but I don't have to listen to anything it says.'"

"He fined me half a dollar for mumping," said Hacknee. "Fred Colon! He practically goes on patrol with a shopping bag! And all I had was a free pint at the Bunch of Grapes *and* I found out that Posh Wally is suddenly flashing a lot of money lately. That's worth knowing. I remember going out on patrol with Fred Colon when I started and you could practically see him tucking his napkin under his chin whenever we walked past a café. 'Oh *no*, Sergeant Colon, wouldn't *dream* of seeing you pay.' They used to lay the table when they saw him turn the corner."

"Everyone does it," said Stronginthearm.

"Captain Carrot never did," said Nobby.

"Captain Carrot was . . . special."

"But what am I supposed to do with this?" said Visit, waving the ink-speckled message. "Mister Vimes wants some information urgently, he says!"

Stronginthearm took the paper and read it.

"Well, this shouldn't be hard," he said. "Old Wussie Staid in Kicklebury Street was a janitor there for *years* and he owes me a favor."

"If we're going to send a clacks to Mister Vimes then we ought to tell him about the Scone and Sonky," said Reg Shoe. "You know he left a message about that. I've done a report."

"Why? He's hundreds of miles away."

"I'd just feel happier if he knew," said Reg. " 'Cos it worries me."

"What good will it do sending it to him, then?"

"Because then it'll worry *him*, and I can stop worrying," said Reg. *"Corporal Nobbs!"*

"He listens at the door, I'll swear he does," said Stronginthearm. "I'm off."

"Coming, Captain!" shouted Nobby. He pulled open the bottom drawer of his battered and stained desk and took out a packet of chocolate biscuits, some of which he arranged daintily on a plate.

"Does me no good at all to see you acting like this," Stronginthearm went on, winking at the other dwarfs. "You've got it in you to be a really bad copper, Nobby. Breaks my heart to see you throwin' it all away to become a really bad waitress."

"Ha ha ha," said Nobby. "Just you wait, that's all I'm saying." He raised his voice. "Coming right now, Captain!"

There was a sharp smell of burned paper in the captain's room when Nobby entered.

"Nothing cheers up the day like a good fire, I always say," he said, putting the tray on the desk.

But Captain Colon wasn't paying any attention. He'd removed the sugar bowl from the locked drawer of his desk and had laid the cubes out in rows.

"Do you see anything wrong with these lumps, Corporal?" he said quietly.

"Well, they're a bit manky where you've been handling them every—"

"There's thirty-seven, Corporal."

"Sorry about that, Captain."

"Visit must've pinched them when he was in here. He must've used some fancy foreign trick. They can do that, you know. Climb ropes and disappear up the top of 'em, that sort of thing."

"Did he have a rope?" said Nobby.

"Are you making fun of me, Corporal?"

Nobby saluted. "Nossir! Maybe it was a *invisible* one, sir. After all, if they can disappear up a rope, they can make the rope disappear, too. Obviously."

"Good thinking, Corporal."

"On the subject of thinking, sir," said Nobby, plunging in, "have you had time in your busy schedule to give some thought to the promotion of the new sergeant?"

"I have, as a matter of fact, put that very thing in hand, Corporal."

"Good, sir."

"I've borne in mind everything you said, and the choice was starin' me in the face."

"Yessir!" said Nobby, sticking out his chest and saluting.

"I just hope it don't cause loss of morals. It can do that, when people are promoted. So if there's any trouble like that, I want the sugar-stealing person reported to me right away, understand?"

"Yessir!" Nobby's feet had almost left the ground.

"And I shall rely on you, Corporal, to let me know if Sergeant Flint has any trouble."

"Sergeant Flint," said Nobby, in a little voice.

"I know he's a troll, but I won't have it said I'm an unfair man."

"Sergeant *Flint*."

"I know I can rely on you, Corporal."

"*Sergeant* Flint."

"That will be all. I've got to go and see His Lordship in an hour and I want some time to think for. That's what my job is, thinking."

"*Sergeant Flint.*"

"Yes. I should go and report to him if I was you."

White chicken feathers were scattered across the field. The farmer stood at the door of his henhouse, shaking his head. He glanced up as a horseman approached.

"Good morrow, sir! Are you experiencing trouble?"

The farmer opened his mouth for a witty or at least snappy response, but something stopped him. Perhaps it was the sword the horseman had slung across his back. Perhaps it was the man's faint smile. The smile was somehow more frightening.

"Er . . . somethin's been at my fowls," he ventured. "Fox, I reckon."

"Wolf, I suspect," said the rider.

The man opened his mouth to say "Don't be daft, we don't get wolves down here this time of the year," but again the confident smile made him hesitate.

"Got many hens, did they?"

"Six," said the farmer.

"And they got in by . . ."

"Well, that's the strange th— Here, keep the dog away!"

A small mongrel had leapt down from the saddle and was sniffing around the henhouses.

"He won't be any trouble," said the rider.

"I shouldn't push your luck, mate. He's in a funny mood," said a voice behind the farmer. He turned around quickly.

The dog looked up at him innocently. Everyone knew that dogs didn't talk.

"Woof? Bark? Whine?" it said.

"He's highly trained," said the rider.

"Yeah, right," said the voice behind the farmer. He felt an overpowering desire to see the back of the horseman. The smile was getting on his nerves, and now he was hearing things.

"I can't see how they got in," he said. "The door's latched . . ."

"And wolves don't usually leave payment, right?" said the rider.

"How the hell did you know that?"

"Well . . . several reasons, sir, but I couldn't help noticing that you clenched your fist tightly as soon as you heard me, and I surmise therefore that you found . . . let me see . . . three dollars left in the chicken house. Three dollars would buy six fine birds in Ankh-Morpork."

The man opened his fist, wordlessly. The coins glinted in the sunlight.

"But . . . but I sells 'em at the gate for ten pence!" he wailed. "They only had to *arsk*!"

"Probably didn't want to bother you," said the horseman. "Since I am here, sir, I would be grateful if you could sell *me* a chicken—"

Behind the farmer the dog *said,* "Woof woof!"

"—*two* chickens, and I will not trespass further upon your time."

"Woof woof woof."

"*Three* chickens," said the rider, wearily. "And if you have them dressed and cooked while I tend to my horse, I will gladly pay a dollar apiece."

"Woof, woof."

"Without garlic or any seasoning on two of the chickens, please," said the rider.

The farmer nodded wordlessly. A dollar a chicken wasn't chicken feed. You didn't turn up your nose at an offer like that. But most importantly, you didn't disobey a man with that faint little smile on his face. It didn't seem to move, or change. As smiles went, you wanted this one to go as far away as possible.

He hurried off to the yard that held his best fowls, reached down to select the fattest . . . and paused. A man who was fool enough to pay a dollar for a *good* chicken might be quite content with just a *reasonable* chicken, after all . . . He stood up.

"Only the best, mister."

He spun around. No one was there except the little scruffy dog, which had followed him and was now raising a cloud of dust as it scratched itself.

"Woof?" it said.

He threw a stone at it, and it trotted off. Then he selected three of the very best chickens.

Carrot was lying down under a tree, trying to make his head comfortable on a saddlebag.

"Did you see in the dust where she'd almost rubbed out her footprints?" said Gaspode.

"Yes," said Carrot, closing his eyes.

"Does she *always* pay for chickens?"

"Yes."

"Why?"

Carrot turned over.

"Because animals don't."

Gaspode looked at the back of Carrot's head. On the whole he enjoyed the unusual gift of speech, but something about the reddening of Carrot's ears told him that this was the time to employ the even rarer gift of silence.

He settled down in the position he almost unconsciously categorized as Faithful Companion Keeping Watch, got bored, scratched himself absentmindedly, curled up in the pose known as Faithful Companion Curled Up With His Nose Pressed On His Bottom,* and fell asleep.

He awoke shortly afterward, to the sound of voices. There was also a faint smell of roast chicken coming from the direction of the farmhouse.

Gaspode rolled over, and saw the farmer talking to another man on a cart. He listened for a moment and then sat up, locked in a metaphysical conundrum.

Finally he awoke Carrot by licking his ear.

"Fzwl . . . what?"

"You got to promise to collect the roast chicken first, all right?" said Gaspode urgently.

"What?" Carrot sat up.

"Get the chickens and then we gotta go, right? You gotta promise."

"All right, all right, I promise. What's *happening*?"

"You ever heard of a town called Scant Cullot?"

"I think it's about ten miles from here . . ."

"One of Mister Farmer's neighbors has just told him that they've caught a wolf there."

"*Killed it?*"

"No, no, no . . . but the wolf hunters . . . there's wolf hunters in these parts, see, 'cos of the sheep up on the hills and . . . they have to train their dogs first *remember you promised about the chickens!*"

At precisely eleven o'clock there was a smart rap on Lord Vetinari's door.

The Patrician gave the woodwork a puzzled frown. At last he said: "Come."

---

* One that *no* other creature in the world would ever adopt.

Fred Colon entered with difficulty. Vetinari watched him for a few moments until pity overcame even him.

"Acting Captain, it is not necessary to remain at attention at *all* times," he said, kindly. "You are allowed to unbend enough for the satisfactory manipulation of a doorknob.

"Yes, sah!"

Lord Vetinari raised a hand to his ear protectively.

"You may be seated."

"Yes, sah!"

"You may be quieter, too."

"Yes, sah!"

Lord Vetinari retreated to the protection of his desk.

"May I commend you on the gleam of your armor, Acting Captain—"

"Spit and polish, sah! No substitute for it, sah!" Sweat was streaming down Colon's face.

"Oh, good. Clearly you have been purchasing extra supplies of spit. Now then, let me see . . ."

Lord Vetinari drew a sheet of paper from one of the small stacks in front of him.

"Now then, Acti—"

"Sah!"

"To be sure. I have here another complaint of over-enthusiastic clamping . . . I'm sure you know to what I refer."

"It was causing serious traffic congestion, sah!"

"Quite so. It is well known for it. But it is, in fact, the opera house."

"Sah!"

"The owner feels that big yellow clamps at each corner detract from what I might call the *tone* of the building. And, of course, they do prevent him from driving it away."

"Sah!"

"Indeed. I think that this is a case where discretion might be advisable, Acting Captain!"

"Got to make an example to the others, sah!"

"Ah. Yes." The Patrician held another piece of paper delicately between thumb and forefinger, as though it were some rare and strange creature. "The others being . . . let me see if I can recall, some things do stick in the mind so . . . ah, yes . . . three other buildings, six fountains, three statues and the gibbet in Nonesuch Street. Oh, and my own palace."

"I fully understand you're parked on business, sah!"

Lord Vetinari paused. He found it difficult to talk to Frederick Colon. He dealt on a daily basis with people who treated conversation as a complex game, and with Colon he had to keep on adjusting his mind in case he overshot.

"Pursuing the business of your recent career with, I have to admit, some considerable and growing fascination, I am moved to ask you why the Watch now appears to have a staff of twenty."

"Sah?"

"You had around sixty a little while ago, I'm sure."

Colon mopped his face.

"Cutting out the dead wood, sah! Making the Watch leaner an' fitter, sah!"

"I see. The number of internal disciplinary charges you have laid against your men"—and here the Patrician picked up a much thicker document—"seems somewhat excessive. I see no fewer than one hundred and seventy three offenses of eyeballing, earlobing and nostrilling, for example."

"Sah!"

"Nostrilling, Acting Captain?"

114

"Sah!"

"Oh. And I see, ah yes, one charge of 'making his arm fall off in an insubordinate way' laid against Constable Shoe. Commander Vimes has always given me glowing reports about this officer."

" 'E's a nasty piece of work, sah! You can't trust the dead ones!"

"Nor, it would seem, most of the live ones."

"Sah!" Colon leaned forward, his face twisted in a ghastly grimace of conspiratoriality. "Between you and me, sir, Commander Vimes was a good deal too soft on them. He let them get away with too much. No sugar is safe, sah!"

Vetinari's eyes narrowed, but the telescopes on Planet Colon were far too unsophisticated to detect his mood.

"I certainly recall him mentioning a couple of officers whose timekeeping, demeanor, and all around uselessness were a dreadful example to the rest of the men," said the Patrician.

"There's my point," said Colon triumphantly. "One bad apple ruins the whole barrel!"

"I think there's only a basket now," said the Patrician. "A punnet, possibly."

"Don't you worry about a thing, Your Lordship! I'll turn things around. I'll soon get them smartened up!"

"I am sure you have it in you to surprise me even further," said Vetinari, leaning back. "I shall definitely keep my eye on you as the man to watch. And now, Acting Captain, do you have anything else to report?"

"All nice and quiet, sah!"

"I would that it was," said Vetinari. "I was just wondering if there was anything going on involving any person in this city called . . ." He looked down at another sheet of paper. "Sonky?"

Captain Colon almost swallowed his tongue.

"Minor matter, sah!" he managed.

"So . . . Sonky is alive?"

"Er . . . found dead, sah!"

"Murdered?"

"Sah!"

"Dear me. Many people would not consider that a minor matter, Acting Captain. Sonky, for one."

"Well, sah, not everyone agrees with what he does, sah."

"Are we by any chance talking about *Wallace* Sonky? The manufacturer of rubber goods?"

"Sah!"

"Boots and gloves seem noncontroversial to *me*, Acting Captain."

"It's . . . er . . . the other stuff, sah!" Colon coughed nervously. "He makes them rubber wallies, sah."

"Ah. The preventatives."

"Lot of people don't agree with that sort of thing, sah."

"So I understand."

Colon drew himself up to attention again.

"Not natural, in my view, sah. Not in favor of unnatural things."

Vetinari looked perplexed.

"You mean . . . you eat your meat raw and sleep in a tree?"

"Sah?"

"Oh, nothing, nothing. Someone in Uberwald seems to be taking an interest in him lately. And now he's dead. I would not dream of telling the Watch their job, of course."

He watched Colon carefully to see if this had sunk in.

"I said that it is entirely up to you to choose what to investigate in this bustling city," he prompted.

Colon was lost in unfamiliar country without a map.

"Thank you, sah!" he barked.

Vetinari sighed. "And now, Acting Captain, I'm sure there's much that needs your attention."

"Sah! I've got plans to—"

"I meant, do not let me detain you."

"Oh, that's all right, sir, I've got plenty of time—"

"*Goodbye*, Acting Captain Colon."

Out in the anteroom, Fred Colon stood very still for a while, until his heartbeat wound down from a whine to at least a purr.

It had, on the whole, gone quite well. Very well. Amazingly well, really. His Lordship had practically taken him into his confidence. He'd called him "a man to watch."

Fred wondered why he'd been so scared of officering all these years. There was nothing to it, really, once you got the bull between your teeth. If only he'd started years ago! Of course, he wouldn't hear a word said about Mr. Vimes, who should certainly be looking after himself in those dangerous foreign parts . . . but . . . well, Fred Colon had been a sergeant when Sam Vimes was a rookie, hadn't he? It was only his nat'ral deference that'd held him back all these years. When Sam Vimes came back, and with the Patrician there to put in a good word for him, Fred Colon would definitely be on the promotion ladder.

Only to full captain, of course, he thought as he strutted down the stairs—with great care, because strutting is usually impossible while walking downward. He wouldn't want to outrank Captain Carrot. That would be . . . wrong.

This fact shows that, however crazed with power someone may become, a tiny instinct for self-preservation always remains.

He got the chickens first, thought Gaspode, winding his way through the legs of the crowd. Amazin'.

They hadn't stopped to eat them, though. Gaspode had been stuffed into the other saddlebag and would not like to have to go through ten miles like that again, especially so close to the smell of roast chicken.

It looked as though there was a market going on, and the wolf-baiting had been saved as a sort of closing ceremony. Hurdles had been arranged on a rough circle. Men were holding the collars of dogs—big, heavy, unpleasant looking dogs, which were already wild with excitement and deranged stupidity.

There was a coop by the hurdles. Gaspode made his way to it, and peered through the wooden bars at the heap of matted gray fur in the shadows.

"Looks like you're in a spot of strife, friend," he said.

Contrary to legend—and there are so many legends about wolves, although mostly they are legends about the way men think about wolves—a trapped wolf is more likely to whine and fawn than go wild with rage.

But this one must have felt it had nothing to lose. Foam-flecked jaws snapped at the bars.

"Where's the rest of your pack, then?" said Gaspode.

"No pack, shorty!"

"Ah. A lone wolf, eh?" The worst kind, Gaspode thought.

"Roast chicken isn't worth this," he muttered. Out loud, he growled, "You seen any other wolves around here?"

"Yes!"

"Good. You want to get out of here alive?"

"I'll kill them all!"

"Right, right . . . but there's dozens of 'em, see. You won't stand a chance. They'll tear you to bits. Dogs're a lot nastier than wolves."

In the shade, the eyes narrowed.

"Why're you telling me, dog?"

"'Cos I am here to help you, see? You do what I tell you, you could be out of here in half an hour. Otherwise you're a rug on someone's floor tomorrow. Your choice. O'course, there might not be enough of you left to make a rug."

The wolf listened to the baying of the dogs. There was no mistaking their intent.

"What did you have in mind?" it said.

A few minutes later the crowd was gently nudged aside as Carrot edged his horse toward the pen. The hubbub died. A sword on a horse always commands respect; the rider is often a mere courtesy detail, but in this case it was not so. The Watch had put the final swell and polish on Carrot's muscles.

And there was that faint smile. It was the sort you backed away from.

"Good day. Who is in charge here?" he said.

There was a certain amount of comparison of status, and a man cautiously raised his hand.

"I'm the deputy mayor, y'honor," he said.

"And what is this event?"

"We'm about to bait a wolf, y'honor."

"Really? I myself own a wolfhound of unusual strength and prowess. May I test it against the creature?"

There was more mumbling among the bystanders, the general consensus being: Why not? Anyway, there was that smile . . .

"Go ahead, y'honor," said the deputy mayor.

Carrot stuck his fingers in his mouth and whistled.

The townspeople watched in astonishment as Gaspode walked out from between their legs and sat down. Then the laughter started.

It died away after a while, because the faint smile didn't.

"Is there a problem?" said Carrot.

"It'll get torn limb from limb!"

"Well? Do you *care* what happens to a wolf?"

Laughter broke out again. The deputy mayor had a feeling he was being got at.

"It's your dog, mister," he said, shrugging.

The little dog barked.

"And to make it interesting, we'll wager a pound of steak," said Carrot.

The dog barked again.

"Two pounds of steak," Carrot corrected himself.

"Oh, I reckon it's going to be interesting enough as it is," said the deputy mayor. The smile was beginning to prey on his nerves. "All right, boys—fetch the wolf!"

The creature was dragged into the ring of hurdles, slavering and snarling.

"No, don't tie it up," said Carrot, as a man went to wrap the halter around a post.

"It'll get away if we don't."

"It won't have a chance, believe me."

They looked at the smile, dragged the muzzle from the wolf and leapt to safety.

"Now, just in case you were havin' second thoughts about our agreement," said Gaspode to the wolf, "I suggest you look at the face of the bloke on the horse, right?"

The wolf glanced up. It saw the wolverine smile of the face of the rider.

Gaspode barked. The wolf yelped and rolled over.

The crowd waited. And then—

"Is that *it*?"

"Yes, that's how it normally goes," said Carrot. "It's a special bark, you see. All the blood in the victim congeals in an instant, out of sheer terror."

"It hasn't even worried the body!"

"What," said Carrot, "would be the point of that?"

He got down from the horse, pushed his way into the ring, picked up the body of the wolf and flung it across the saddle.

"It grunted! I heard it—" someone began.

"That was probably air being expressed from the corpse," said Carrot. The smile still hadn't gone, and at that point it suggested very subtly that Carrot had heard the last gasp of *hundreds* of corpses.

"Yeah, that's right," said a voice in the crowd. "Everyone knows that. And now what about the steak for the brave little doggie?"

The people looked around to see who had said this. None of them looked down, because dogs can't talk.

"We can forgo the steak," said Carrot, mounting up.

"No, w— No, you can't," said the voice. "A deal's a deal. Who was risking their life here, that's what I'd like to know?"

"Come, Gaspode," said Carrot.

Whining and grumbling, the little dog emerged from the crowd and trailed after the horse.

It wasn't until they were at the edge of the town square that one of the people said, "Oi, what the hell happened there?" and the spell broke. But by then both horse and dog were traveling really, really fast.

Vimes hated and despised the privileges of rank, but they had this to be said for them: At least they meant that you could hate and despise them in comfort.

Willikins would arrive at an inn an hour before Vimes's coach and, with an arrogance that Vimes would never dare employ, take over several rooms and install Vimes's own cook in the kitchen. Vimes complained about this to Inigo.

"But you see, Your Grace, you're not here as an individual but as Ankh-Morpork. When people look at you, they *see* the city, mhm, mhm."

"They do? Should I stop washing?"

"That is very droll, sir. But you see, sir, you and the city are one. Mhm, mhm. If you are insulted, Ankh-Morpork is insulted. If you befriend, Ankh-Morpork befriends."

"Really? What happens when I go to the lavatory?"

"That's up to you, sir. Mhm, mph."

At breakfast next morning Vimes sliced the top off a boiled egg, thinking: This is Ankh-Morpork slicing the top off a boiled egg. If I cut my toast into soldiers, we're probably at war.

Constable Littlebottom entered, carefully, and saluted.

"Your message came back, sir," she said, handing him a scrap of paper. "From Sergeant Strongintharm. I've deciphered it for you. Er . . . the Scone from the museum's been found, sir."

"Well, that's the other shoe dropped," said Vimes. "I was worried there for a moment."

"Er, in fact Constable Shoe is bothered about it," said Cheery. "It's a bit hard to follow what he says, but he seems to think someone made a copy of it."

"What, a fake of a fake? What good's that?"

"I really couldn't say, sir. Your other . . . surmise was correct."

Vimes glanced at the paper.

"Hah. Thanks, Cheery. We'll be down shortly."

"You're humming, Sam," said Sybil, after a while. "That means that something awful is going to happen to somebody."

"Wonderful thing, technology," said Vimes, buttering a slice of toast. "I can see it has its uses."

"And when you grin in that shiny sort of way it means that someone's playing silly buggers and doesn't know you've just thrown a six."

"I don't know what you mean, dear. It's probably the country air agreeing with me."

Lady Sybil put down her teacup.

"Sam?"

"Yes, dear?"

"This is probably not the best time to mention it, but you know I told you I went to see old Mrs. Content? Well, she says—"

There was another knock at the door. Lady Sybil sighed.

This time it was Inigo who entered.

"We should be leaving, Your Grace, if you don't mind. I would like us to be at Slake by lunchtime and through the pass at Wilinus before dark, mhm, mhm."

"Do we have to *rush* so?" sighed Sybil.

"The pass is . . . slightly dangerous," said Inigo. "Somewhat lawless. Mhm, mhm."

"Only somewhat?" said Vimes.

"I will just feel happier when it is behind us," said Inigo. "It would be a good idea if the second coach follows us closely and your men stay alert, Your Grace."

"They teach you tactics in Lord Vetinari's political office, do they, Inigo?" said Vimes.

"Just common sense, mhm, mhm, sir."

"Why don't we wait until tomorrow before attempting the pass?"

"With respect, Your Grace, I suggest not. For one thing, the weather is worsening. And I'm sure we are being watched. We must demonstrate that there is no yellow in the Ankh-Morpork flag, mhm, mhm."

"There is," said Vimes. "It's on the owl and the collars of the hippos."

"I mean," said Inigo, "that the colors of Ankh-Morpork do not run."

"Only since we got the new dyes," said Vimes. "All right, all right. I know what you mean. But, look, I'm not risking the servants if there's any danger. And there's to be no arguing, understand? They can stay here and take the mail coach tomorrow. No one attacks the mail coaches anymore."

"I suggest Lady Sybil remains here, too, sir. Mhm."

"Absolutely *not*," said Sybil. "I wouldn't hear of it! If it's not too dangerous for Sam, it's not too dangerous for me."

"I wouldn't argue with her, if I were you," said Vimes to Inigo. "I really wouldn't."

The wolf was not very happy about being tethered to a tree but, as Gaspode said, never trust nobody.

They'd paused awhile in a wood about five miles from the town. It'd be a brief stop, Carrot had said. Some of the people in the square looked the sort who treasured their lack of a sense of humor.

After some barking and growling, Gaspode said: "You got to understand that matey here is pers'naly non gratis in local wolf society, being a bit of a, haha, lone wolf . . ."

"Yes?" Carrot was taking the roast chickens out of their sack. Gaspode's eyes fixed on them.

"But he hears the howlin' at night."

"Ah . . . wolves communicate?"

"Basic'ly your wolf howl is just another way of pissin' against a tree to say it's your damn tree, but there's always a bit of news, too. Something nasty's happenin' in Uberwald. He doesn't know what." Gaspode lowered his voice. "Between you and me, our friend here was well behind the door when the brains was handed out. If wolves was people, he'd be like Foul Ole Ron."

"What is his name?" said Carrot, thoughtfully.

Gaspode gave Carrot a Look. Who cared what a wolf was called?

"Wolf names is difficult," he said. "More like a description, see? It's not like callin' yourself Mister Snuggles or Bonzo, you understand . . ."

"Yes, I know. So what is *his* name?"

"You want to know what his name is, then?"

"Yes, Gaspode."

"So, in fact, it's the name of this wolf you want to know?"

"That is correct."

Gaspode shifted uneasily.

"Asshole," he said.

"Oh." To the dog's frank astonishment, Carrot blushed.

"That's basic'ly a *summary*, but it's a pretty good translation," he said. "I wouldn't have mentioned it, but you *did* ask . . ."

Gaspode stopped and whined for a moment, trying to convey the message that he was losing his voice due to lack of chicken.

"Er . . . there's been a lot on the howl about Angua," he went on, when Carrot seemed unable to take the hint. "Er . . . they think she's bad news."

"Why? She's traveling as a wolf, after all."

"Wolves hate werewolves."

"What? That can't be right! When she's wolf-shaped she's just like a wolf!"

"So? When she's human-shaped she's just like a human. And what's that got to do with anything? Humans don't like were-wolves. *Wolves* don't like werewolves. People don't like wolves that can think like people, an' people don't like people who can act like wolves. Which just shows you that people are the same every-where," said Gaspode. He assessed this sentence and added, "Even when they're wolves."

"I never thought of it like that."

"And she smells wrong. Wolves are very sensitive to that sort of thing."

"Tell me more about the howl."

"Oh, it's like the clacky thing. News gets spread for hundreds of miles."

"Do the howls . . . mention her . . . companion?"

"No. If you like, I'd ask Ass—"

"I'd prefer a different name, if it's all the same to you," said Carrot. "Words like that aren't clever."

Gaspode rolled his eyes.

"There nothing wrong with the word among us pedestically gifted species," he said. "We're very smell-orientated." He sighed. "How about 'bum'? In the sense of, er, migratory worker? He's a freelance chicken-throttler, style of fing?"

He turned to the wolf, and spoke in canine.

"Now then, Bum, this human is insane and believe me, I know a mad human when I see one. He's frothing at the mouth inside and he'll rip your hide off and nail it to a tree if you aren't straight with us, understand?"

"What was that you just told him?" said Carrot.

"Just explainin' we're friends," said Gaspode. To the cowering wolf he barked: "Okay, he's prob'ly going to do that anyway, but I can talk to him, so your only chance is to tell us everything—"

"Know nothing!" the wolf whined. "She was with a big he-wolf from Uberwald! From the Clan That Smells Like This!"

Gaspode sniffed. "He's a long way from home, then."

"He's a bad news wolf!"

"Tell it there'll be roast chicken for its trouble," said Carrot.

Gaspode sighed. It was a hard life, being an interpreter.

"All right," he growled. "I'll persuade him to untie you. It'll take some doing, mark you. If he offers you a chicken, don't take it 'cos it'll be poisoned. Humans, eh?"

Carrot watched the wolf flee.

"Odd," he said. "You've have thought it'd be hungry, wouldn't you?"

Gaspode looked up from the roast chicken. "Wolves, eh?" he said, indistinctly.

That night, when they heard the wolves howling in the distant mountains, Gaspode picked up one solitary, lonely howl behind them.

The towers followed them up into the mountains although, Vimes noticed, there were some differences in construction. Down on the plains they were more or less just a high wooden gantry with a shed at the bottom but here, although the design was the same, it was clearly temporary. Next to it men were at work on a heavy stone base—fortifications, he realized, which meant that he really was beyond the law. Of course, technically he'd been beyond *his* law since leaving Ankh-Morpork, but laws were where you could make it stick and these days a City Watch badge would at least earn respect, if not actual cooperation, everywhere on the plains. Up here, it was just an ugly brooch.

Slake turned out to be a stone-walled coaching inn and not much else. It had, Vimes noticed, very heavy shutters on the window. It also had what he thought was a strange iron griddle over the fireplace until he recognized it for what it was, a sort of portcullis that could block off the chimney. This place expected to withstand the occasional siege that might include enemies who could fly.

It was sleeting when they went out to the coaches.

"A storm's closing in, mmm, mhm," said Inigo. "We shall have to hurry."

"Why?" said Sybil.

"The pass will probably be closed for several days, Your Ladyship. If we wait, we may even miss the coronation. And . . . er . . . there may be slight bandit activity . . ."

"*Slight* bandit activity?" said Vimes.

"Yes, sir."

"You mean they wake up and decide to go back to bed? Or they just steal enough for a cup of coffee?"

"Very droll, sir. They do, notoriously, take hostages—"

"Bandits don't frighten me," said Sybil.

"If I may—" Inigo began.

"Mister Skimmer," said Lady Sybil, drawing herself up to her full width, "I did in fact just tell you what we are going to do. See to it, please. There are servants at the consulate, aren't there?"

"There is one, I believe—"

"Then we shall happily make do as best we can. Won't we, Sam?"

"Certainly, dear."

It was seriously snowing by the time they left, in great feather lumps which fell with a faint damp hiss, muffling all other sound. Vimes wouldn't have known that they'd reached the pass if the coaches hadn't stopped.

"The coach with your . . . men on it should go in front," said Inigo, as they stood in the snow beside the steaming horses. "We should follow close behind. I'll ride with our driver, just in case."

"So that if we are attacked by anyone you can give them a potted summary of the political situation?" said Vimes. "No, *you* will ride inside with Lady Sybil, and *I'll* ride on the box. Got to protect the civilians, eh?"

"Your Grace, I—"

"However, your suggestion is appreciated," Vimes went on. "You get inside, Mister Skimmer."

The man opened his mouth. Vimes raised an eyebrow.

"Very well, Your Grace, but it is extremely—"

"Good man."

"I should like my leather case down from the roof, though."

"Certainly. A bit of fact-finding will take your mind off things."

Vimes walked forward to the other carriage, poked his head inside and said, "We're going to be ambushed, lads."

"Dat's interestin'," said Detritus. He grunted slightly as he wound the windlass of his crossbow.

"Oh," said Cheery.

"I don't *think* they'll try to kill us," Vimes went on.

"Does dat mean we don't try to kill dem?"

"Use your own judgment."

Detritus sighted along a thick bundle of arrows. They were his idea. Since his giant crossbow was capable of sending an iron bolt through the gates of a city under siege, he had felt it rather a waste to use it on just one person, so he had adapted it to fire a sheaf of several dozen arrows all at once. The threads holding them together were supposed to snap under acceleration. They did so. Quite often the arrows also shattered in midair as they failed to withstand the enormous pressure.

He called it the Piecemaker. He'd only tried it once, down at the butts; Vimes had seen a target vanish. So had the targets on either side of it, the earth bank behind it, and a spiraling cloud of feathers floating down had been all that remained of a couple of seagulls who had been in the wrong place at the wrong time. In this instance, the wrong place had been vertically above Detritus.

Now no other watchmen would go on patrol with the troll unless they could stay at least a hundred yards directly behind him. But the test had the desired effect, because someone saw everything in Ankh-Morpork and news about the targets had got around. Now just the knowledge that Detritus was on his way cleared a street much faster than any weapon.

"I got lots of judgment," he said.

"You be careful with that thing," said Vimes. "You could hurt someone."

The party started out again, through the swirls of snow. Vimes made himself comfortable among the luggage, lit a cigar and then, when he was sure that the rattling of the coach would mask the sounds, rummaged farther under the tarpaulin and drew out Inigo's cheap, scarred leather case.

From his pocket he took a small roll of black cloth, and unrolled it on his knee. Intricate little lockpicks glinted for a moment in the light of the coach lamps.

A good copper has to be able to think like a criminal. Vimes was a very good copper.

He was also a very *alive* copper and intended to remain that way. That was why, when the case's lock went *click*, he laid it down on the shaking roof with its lid opening away from him and, leaning back, carefully lifted the lid with his boot.

A long blade flicked out. It would have terminally ruined the digestion of a casual thief. Someone obviously expected very bad hotel security on this journey.

Vimes carefully eased it back into its spring-loaded sheath, looked upon the contents of the case, smiled in a not very happy way, and carefully lifted out something that gleamed with the silvery light of carefully designed, beautifully engineered and very compact evil.

He thought: Sometimes it would be nice to be wrong about people.

Gaspode knew they were in the high foothills now. Places to buy food were getting scarce. However carefully Carrot knocked at the door of some isolated farmstead, he'd end up having to talk to people who were hiding under the bed. People here were not used to the idea of muscular men with swords who were actually anxious to *buy* things.

In the end it generally worked out quicker to walk in, go through the contents of the pantry, and leave some money on the table for when the people came up out of the cellar.

It had been two days since the last cottage, and there was so little there that Carrot, to Gaspode's disgust, had just left some money.

The forest thickened. Alder became pine. There were snow showers every night. The stars were pinpoints of frost.

And, colder and harder, rising with the sunset, was the howl.

It went up on every side, a great mournful ululation across the freezing forests.

"They're so close I can smell 'em," said Gaspode. "They've been shadowing us for days."

"There has never been an authenticated case of an unprovoked wolf attacking an adult human being," said Carrot. They were both huddling under his cloak.

After a while Gaspode said, "An' that's good, is it?"

"What do you mean?"

"We-ell, o'course us dogs only has *little* brains, but it seems to *me* that what you just said was pretty much the same as sayin' 'no unprovokin' adult human bein' has ever returned to tell the tale,' right? I mean, your wolf has just got to make sure they kill people in quiet places where no one'll ever know, yes?"

More snow settled on the cloak. It was large, and heavy, and a relic of many a long night in the Ankh-Morpork rain. In front of it, a fire flickered and hissed.

"I wish you hadn't said that, Gaspode."

These were big, serious flakes of snow. Winter was moving fast down the mountains.

"*You* wish I hadn't said it?"

"But . . . no, I'm sure there's nothing to be afraid of."

A drift had nearly covered the cloak.

"You shouldn't've traded the horse for those snowshoes back at the last place," said Gaspode.

"The poor thing was done in. Anyway, it wasn't exactly a trade. The people wouldn't come down out of the chimney. They *did* say to take anything we wanted."

"They *said* to take everything, only spare their lives."

"Yes. I don't know why. I smiled at them."

There was a doggy sigh.

"Trouble is, see, you could carry me on the horse, but this is deep snow and I am a little doggie. My problems are closer to the ground. I hope I don't have to draw you a picture."

"I've got some spare clothes in my pack. I might be able to make you a . . . coat—"

"A coat wouldn't do the trick."

Another howl began, quite close this time.

The snow was falling a lot faster. The hissing of the fire turned into a sizzle. Then it went out.

Gaspode was not good at snow. It was not a precipitation he normally had to face. In the city, there was always somewhere warm if you knew where to look. Anyway, snow only stayed snow for an hour or two, and then it became brown slush and was trodden into the general slurry of the streets.

Streets. Gaspode really *missed* streets. He could be wise on streets. Out here, he was dumb on mud.

"Fire's gone out," he said.

There was no answer from Carrot.

"*Fire's gone out*, I said . . ."

This time there was a snore.

"Hey, you can't go to sleep!" Gaspode whined. "Not *now*. We'll *freeze* to death."

The next voice in the howl seemed only a few trees away. Gaspode thought he could see dark shapes in the endless curtain of snow.

". . . if we're lucky," he mumbled. He licked Carrot's face, a move that usually resulted in the lickee chasing Gaspode down the street with a broom. There was merely another snore.

Gaspode's mind raced.

Of course, he was a dog, and dogs and wolves . . . well, they were the same, right? Everyone knew that. So-oo, said a treacherous inner voice . . . maybe it wasn't exactly Gaspode and Carrot in trouble. Maybe it was only Carrot. Yeah, right on, brothers! Let us join together in wild runs in the moonlight! But first, let us eat this monkey!

On the other paw . . .

He'd got hard pad, soft pad, the swinge, licky end, scroff, mange and something rather strange on the back of his neck that he couldn't quite reach. Gaspode somehow couldn't imagine the wolves saying *Hey, he's one of us!*

Besides . . . while he'd begged, fought, tricked and stolen, he'd never actually been a Bad Dog.

You needed to be a moderate good theological disputant to accept this, especially since a fair number of sausages and prime cuts had disappeared from butchers' slabs in a blur of gray and a lingering odor of lavatory carpet, but nevertheless Gaspode was clear in his own mind that he'd never crossed the boundary from merely being a Naughty Boy. He'd never bitten a hand that fed him.* He'd never done It on the carpet. He'd never shirked a Duty. It was a bugger, but there you were. It was a dog thing.

He whined when the ring of dark shapes closed in.

Eyes gleamed.

He whined again, and then growled as unseen fanged death surrounded him.

This was clearly impressing no one, not even Gaspode.

He wagged his tail nervously.

"Just passin' through!" he said, in a strangulatedly cheerful voice. "No trouble to anyone!"

---

* After all, this made it so much harder for the hand to feed you tomorrow.

There was a definite feeling that the shadows beyond the snow-flakes were getting more crowded.

"So . . . have you had your holidays yet?" he squeaked.

This also did not appear to be well received.

Well, this was it, then. Famous Last Stand. Plucky Dog Defends His Master. What a Good Dog. Shame there'd be no one left to tell anyone . . .

He barked "Mine! Mine!" and leapt snarling toward the nearest shape.

A huge paw swatted him out of the air and then pinned him down, spread-eagled, in the snow.

He looked up past white fangs and a long muzzle into eyes that seemed familiar . . .

"*Hmine,*" growled the wolf. It was Angua.

The coaches slowed to a walk on a road that was rough with pot-holes under the unbroken snow, every one a wheel-breaking trap in the dark.

Vimes nodded to himself when he saw lights flickering beside the road a few miles into the pass. On either side, old landslides had formed banks of scree, down which the forests had spilled.

He dropped quietly off the back of the coach and vanished into the shadows.

The leading coach stopped at a log which had been dropped across the road. There was some movement, and then the driver swung himself down into the mud and set off at a dead run back down the pass.

Figures moved out of the trees. One of them stopped at the door of the first coach and tried the handle.

There was a moment when the world held its breath. The figure must have sensed it, because he was already leaping aside when there was a click and the whole door and its surrounding frame blew outward in a cloud of splinters.

The thing about fires, Vimes had once observed, was that only an idiot got between them and a troll holding a two-thousand-pound crossbow. All hell hadn't been let loose. It was merely Detritus. But from a few feet away you couldn't tell the difference.

Another figure reached for the door of the second coach just before Vimes fired out of the darkness and hit his shoulder with a butcher's sound. Then Inigo dived through the window, rolled with unclerklike grace as he hit the ground, rose in front of one of the bandits and brought his hand around, edge first, on the man's neck.

Vimes had seen this trick done before. Usually, it just made people angry. Occasionally, it managed an incapacitating blow.

He'd never seen it remove a head.

"Everybody stop!"

Sybil was pushed out of the coach. Behind her, a man stepped out. He was holding a crossbow.

"Your Grace Vimes!" he shouted. The word bounced back and forth between the cliffs.

"I know you're here, Your Grace Vimes! And here is your lady! And there are many of us! Come *out*, Your Grace Vimes!"

Flakes of snow hissed over the fires.

Then there was a whisper in the air followed by a second smack of steel into muscle. One of the hooded figures collapsed into the mud, clutching at its leg.

Inigo slowly got to his feet. The man holding the crossbow appeared not to notice.

"It is like chess, Your Grace Vimes! We have disarmed the troll and the dwarf! And I have the queen! And if you shoot at me, can you be sure I won't have time to fire?"

Firelight glowed on the twisted trees bordering the road.

Several seconds passed.

Then the sound of Vimes's crossbow landing in the circle of light was very loud.

"Well done, Your Grace Vimes! And now yourself, if you please!"

Inigo made out the shape that appeared at the very edge of the light, with both hands up.

"Are you all right, Sybil?" said Vimes.

"A bit cold, Sam."

"You're not hurt?"

"No, Sam."

"Keep your hands where I can see them, Your Grace Vimes!"

"And are you going to promise me you'll let her go?" said Vimes.

A flame flickered near Vimes's face, a bright pool in the darkness, as he lit a cigar.

"Now, Your Grace Vimes, why ever should I do that? But I am sure Ankh-Morpork will pay a lot for you!"

"Ah. I thought so," said Vimes. He shook the match out, and the cigar end glowed for a moment. "Sybil?"

"Yes, Sam?"

"Duck."

There was a second filled only with the indrawing of breath, and then, as Lady Sybil dived forward, Vimes's hand came around from behind him in an arc, there was a silken sound and the man's head was flung back.

Inigo leapt and caught his crossbow as it was dropped, then rolled and came up firing. Another figure staggered.

Vimes was aware of a commotion elsewhere as he grabbed Sybil and helped her back into the coach. Inigo had vanished, but a scream in the dark didn't sound like anyone that Vimes knew.

And then . . . only the hiss of snow in the fire.

"I . . . think they're gone, sir," said Cheery's voice.

"Not as fast as us! Detritus?"

"Sir?"

"Are you okay?"

"Feelin' very tactful, sir."

"You two take that coach, I'll take this, and let's get the hell out of here, shall we?"

"Where's Mister Skimmer?" said Sybil.

There was another scream from the woods.

"Forget him!"

"But he's—"

"Forget him!"

The snow was falling thicker as they climbed the pass. The deep snow dragged at the wheels, and all Vimes could see were the darker shapes of the horses against the whiteness. Then the clouds parted briefly, and he wished they hadn't, because here they revealed that the darkness on the left of him wasn't rock any more but a sheer drop.

At the top of the pass the lights of an inn glowed out onto the thickening snow. Vimes drove the carriage into the yard.

"Detritus?"

"Sir?"

"I'll watch our backs. Make sure this place is okay, will you?"

"Yessir."

The troll jumped down, slotting a fresh bundle of arrows into the Piecemaker. Vimes spotted his intention just in time.

"Just *knock*, Sergeant."

"Right you are, sir."

The troll knocked and entered. The buzz of sound from inside suddenly ceased. Vimes heard, muffled by the door, "Der Duke of Ankh-Morpork is coming in. Anyone have a problem with dis? Just say der word." And in the background, the little humming, singing noise the Piecemaker made under tension.

Vimes helped Sybil down from the coach.

"How do you feel now?" he said.

She smiled faintly. "I think this dress will have to go for dusters," she said. She smiled a little more when she saw his expression.

"I knew you'd come up with something, Sam. You go all slow and cold and that means something really dreadful's going to happen. I wasn't frightened."

"Really? I was scared shi—stiff," said Vimes.

"What happened to Mister Skimmer? I remember him rummaging in his case and cursing—"

"I suspect Inigo Skimmer is alive and well," said Vimes grimly. "Which is more than can be said for those around him."

There was silence in the main room of the inn. A man and a woman, presumably the landlord and his wife, were standing flat against the back of the bar. The dozen or so other occupants lined the walls, hands in the air. Beer dribbled from a couple of spilled mugs.

"Everyt'ing normal an' peaceful," said Detritus, turning around.

Vimes realized that everyone was staring at him. He looked down. His shirt was torn. Mud and blood caked his clothes. Melted snow dripped off him. In his right hand, unregarded, he was still holding his crossbow.

"Bit of trouble on the road," he said. "Er . . . you know how it is."

No one moved.

"Oh, good gods . . . Detritus, put that damn thing *down*, will you?"

139

"Right, sir."

The troll lowered his crossbow. Two dozen people all began to breathe again.

Then the skinny woman stepped around from behind the bar, nodded at Vimes, carefully took Lady Sybil's hand from his and pointed toward the wide wooden stairs. The black look she gave Vimes puzzled him.

Only then did he realize that Lady Sybil was shaking. Tears were running down her face.

"And ... er ... my wife is a bit shaken up," he said weakly. "Corporal Littlebottom!" he yelled, to cover his confusion.

Cheery stepped through the doorway.

"Go with Lady Syb—"

He stopped because of the rising hubbub. One or two people pointed. Someone laughed. Cheery stopped, looking down.

"What's up?" Vimes hissed.

"Er . . . It's me, sir. Ankh-Morpork dwarf fashions haven't really caught on here, sir," said Cheery.

"The skirt?" said Vimes.

"Yes, sir."

Vimes looked around at the faces. They seemed more shocked than angry, although he spotted a couple of dwarfs in one corner who were definitely unhappy.

"Go with Lady Sybil," he repeated.

"It might not be a very good id—" Cheery began.

"Godsdammit!" shouted Vimes, unable to stop himself. The crowd went silent. A ragged bloodstained madman holding a crossbow can command a rapt audience.

Then he shuddered. What he wanted now was a bed, but what he wanted, before bed, more than anything, was a drink. And he couldn't have one. He'd learned that long ago. One drink was one too many.

"All right, tell me," he said.

"All dwarfs are men, sir," said Cheery. "I mean . . . traditionally. That's how everyone thinks of it up here."

"Well . . . stand outside the door, or . . . or shut your eyes or something, okay?"

Vimes lifted Lady Sybil's chin.

"Are you all right, dear?" he said.

"Sorry to let you down, Sam," she whispered. "It was just so *awful*."

Vimes, designed by Nature to be one of those men unable to kiss their own wives in public, patted her helplessly on the shoulder. She thought *she'd* let *him* down. It was unbearable.

"You just . . . I mean, Cheery will . . . and I'll . . . sort things out and be along right away," he said. "We'll get a good bedroom, I suspect."

She nodded, still looking down.

"And . . . I'm just going out for some fresh air."

Vimes stepped outside.

The snow had stopped for now. The moon was half hidden by clouds, and the air smelled of frost.

When the figure dropped down from the eaves it was amazed at the way Vimes spun and rushed it bodily against the wall.

Vimes looked through a red mist at the moonlit face of Inigo Skimmer.

"I'll damn well—" he began.

"Look down, Your Grace," said Skimmer. "Mhm, mhm."

Vimes realized he could feel the faintest prick of the knife blade on his stomach.

"Look down farther," he said.

Inigo looked down. He swallowed. Vimes had a knife, too.

"You really *are* no gentleman, then," he said.

"Make a sudden move and neither are you," said Vimes. "And now it appears that we have reached what Sergeant Colon persists in referring to as an *imp arse.*"

"I assure you I will not kill you," said Inigo.

"I *know* that," said Vimes. "But will you *try*?"

"No. I am here for your protection, mhm, mhm."

"Vetinari sent you, did he?"

"You know we never divulge the name of—"

"That's true. You people are very *honorable*," Vimes spat the word, "in that respect."

Both men relaxed a little.

"You left me alone surrounded by enemies," said Inigo, but without much accusation in his tone.

"Why should I care what happens to a bunch of bandits?" said Vimes. "You are an Assassin."

"How did you find out? Mmm?"

"A copper watches the way people walk. The Klatchians say a man's leg is his second face, did you know that? And that little clerky, I'm-so-harmless walk of yours is too good to be true."

"You mean that just from my *walk* you—"

"No. You didn't catch the orange," said Vimes.

"Come now—"

"No, people either catch or flinch. *You* saw it wasn't a danger. And when I took your arm I felt metal under your clothes. Then I just sent a clacks back with your description."

He let go of Inigo and walked over to the coach, leaving his back exposed. He took something down from the box and came back and waved it at the man.

"I know this is yours," he said. "I pinched it out of your luggage. If I *ever* catch anyone with one of these in Ankh-Morpork, I will make their life a complete misery as only a copper knows how. Is that understood?"

"If you ever catch anyone with one of these in Ankh-Morpork, Your Grace, mhm, they will *still* be lucky that the Assassins' Guild didn't find them first, mmm. They are on our forbidden list, within the city. But we are a long way from Ankh-Morpork now. Mmm, mmm."

Vimes turned the thing over and over in his hands. It looked vaguely like a long-handled hammer, or perhaps a strangely made telescope. What it was, basically, was a spring. That's all a crossbow was, after all.

"It's a devil to load," he said. "I nearly ruptured myself cocking it against a rock. You'd only get one shot."

"But it's the shot no one expects, mhm, mhm."

Vimes nodded. You could even conceal this thing down your pants, although the thought of all that coiled power that close would require nerves of steel and other parts of steel, too, if it came to it.

"This is not a weapon. This is for killing people," he said.

"Uh . . . most weapons are," said Inigo.

"No, they're not. They're so you *don't* have to kill people. They're for . . . for *having*. For being *seen*. For *warning*. This isn't one of those. It's for hiding away until you bring it out and kill people in the dark. And where's that other thing?"

"Your Grace?"

"The palm dagger. Don't try to lie to me."

Inigo shrugged. The movement shot something silver out of his sleeve; it was a carefully shaped blade, padded on one side, that slid along the edge of his hand. There was a click from somewhere inside his jacket.

"Good gods," breathed Vimes. "Do you know how often people have tried to assassinate me, man?"

"Yes, Your Grace. Nine times. The Guild has set your fee at six-hundred-thousand dollars. The last time an approach was made, no Guild member volunteered. Mhm, mhm."

"Hah!"

"Incidentally, and very informally of course, we would appreciate knowing the whereabouts of the body of the Honorable Eustace Bassingly-Gore, mhm, mhm."

Vimes scratched his nose.

"Was he the one who tried poisoning my shaving cream?"

"Yes, Your Grace."

"Well, unless his body is an extremely strong swimmer, it's still on a ship bound for Ghat via Cape Terror," said Vimes. "I paid the captain a thousand dollars not to take the chains off before Zambingo, too. That'll give it a nice long walk home through the jungles of Klatch where I'm sure its knowledge of rare poisons will come in very handy, although not as handy perhaps as a knowledge of antidotes."

"A thousand dollars!"

"Well, he had twelve hundred dollars on him. I donated the rest to the Sunshine Sanctuary for Sick Dragons. I got a receipt, by the way. You chaps are keen on receipts, I think."

"You stole his money? Mhm, mhm."

Vimes took a deep breath. His voice, when it emerged, was flat calm. "I wasn't going to waste any of my own. And he *had* just tried to kill me. Think of it as an investment, for the good of his health. Of course, if in due course he cares to come and see me, I shall make sure he gets what's coming to him."

"I'm . . . astounded, Your Grace. Mhm, mhm. Bassingly-Gore was an extremely competent swordsman."

"Really? I generally never wait to find out about that sort of thing."

Inigo smiled his thin little smile.

"And two months ago Sir Richard Liddleley was found tied to a fountain in Sator Square, painted pink and with a flag stuck—"

"I was feeling generous," said Vimes. "I'm sorry, I don't play your games."

"Assassination is not a game, Your Grace."

"It is the way you people play it."

"There have to be rules. Otherwise there would just be anarchy. Mhm, mhm. You have your code, and we have ours."

"And you've been sent here to protect me?"

"I have other skills, but . . . yes."

"What makes you think I'll need you?"

"Well, Your Grace . . . here they *don't* have rules. Mhm, mhm."

"I've spent most of my life dealing with people who don't have rules!"

"Yes, of course. But when you kill *them*, they don't get up again."

"I've never killed anyone!" said Vimes.

"You shot that bandit in the throat."

"I was *aiming* for the shoulder."

"Yes, the thing does pull to the left," said Inigo. "You mean that you have never *tried* to kill anyone. I have, on the other hand. And here, hesitation may not be an option. Mmm."

"I didn't hesitate!"

Inigo sighed. "In the Guild, Your Grace, we don't . . . grandstand."

"Grandstand?"

"That business with the cigar . . ."

"You mean, when I shut my eyes and they had to look at a flame in the darkness?"

"Ah . . ." Inigo hesitated. "But they might have shot you there and then."

"No. I wasn't a threat. And you heard his voice. I hear that sort of voice a lot. He's not going to shoot people too soon and spoil the fun. I can assume that you have not got a contract on me?"

"That is correct."

"And you'd still swear to that?"

"On my honor as an Assassin."

"Yes," said Vimes. "That's where I hit a difficulty, of course. And . . . I don't know how to put this, Inigo, but you don't act like a typical assassin. Lord this, Sir that . . . the Guild *is* the school for gentlemen but you . . . and gods know I don't mean any offense here—are not exactly—"

Inigo touched his forelock.

"Scholarship boy, sir," he said.

My gods *yes*, thought Vimes. You can find your average, amateur killers on every street. They're mostly deranged or drunk or some poor woman who's had a hard day and the husband has raised his hand once too often and suddenly twenty years of frustration takes over. Killing a *stranger* without malice or satisfaction, other than the craftsman's pride in a job well done, is such a rare talent that armies spend months trying to instill it into their young soldiers. Most people will shy away from killing people they haven't been introduced to.

The Guild had to have one or two people like Inigo. Didn't some philosophical bastard once say that a government needed butchers as well as shepherds?

He indicated the little crossbow.

"All right, take it," he said. "But you can put the word about that if I ever, *ever* see one on the street the owner will find it put where the sun does not shine."

"Ah," said Inigo, "that's the rather amusingly named place in Lancre, isn't it? Only about fifty miles from here, I believe. Mhm, mhm."

"Rest assured that I can find a shortcut."

Gaspode tried blowing in Carrot's ear again.

"Time to wake *up*," he growled.

Carrot opened his eyes, blinked the snow out of them and then tried to move.

"You just lie still, right?" said Gaspode. "If it helps, just try to think of them as a very heavy eiderdown."

Carrot struggled feebly. The wolves piled on top of his shifted position.

"Warming you up a treat," said Gaspode, grinning nervously. "A wolf blanket, see? O'course, you're going to be a bit whiffy on the nose for a while, but better to be itchy than dead, eh?" He scratched an ear industriously with a hind leg. One of the wolves growled at him. "Sorry. Grub'll be up in a moment."

"*Food?*" muttered Carrot.

Angua appeared in Carrot's vision, dressed in a leather shirt and leggings. She stood looking down at him, hands on her hips. To Gaspode's amazement, Carrot actually managed to push himself up on his elbows, dislodging several wolves.

"*You* were tracking us?" he said.

"No, they were," said Angua. "They thought you were a bloody fool. I heard it on the howl. And they were right! You haven't eaten anything for three days! And up here, winter doesn't drop a few hints over a month or so. It turns up in one night! Why were you so *stupid*?"

Gaspode looked around the clearing. Angua had rekindled the fire; Gaspode wouldn't have believed it if he hadn't seen it, but actual wolves had dragged in actual fallen wood for her. And then another had turned up with a small deer, still fat after the autumn. He dribbled at the smell of it roasting.

Something human and complicated was going on between Carrot and Angua. It sounded like an argument but it didn't *smell* like one. Anyway, recent events all made perfect sense to Gaspode. The female ran away and the male chased her. That's how it went. Actually, it was usually about twenty males of all sizes, but obviously, Gaspode conceded, things were a bit different for humans.

Pretty soon, he reckoned, Carrot would notice the big male wolf sitting by the fire. And *then* the fur would fly. Humans, eh?

Gaspode wasn't sure of his own ancestry. There was some terrier, and a touch of spaniel, and probably someone's leg, and an awful lot of mongrel. But he took it as an article of faith that there was in all dogs a tiny bit of wolf, and his was urgently sending messages that the wolf by the fire was one you didn't even stare directly at.

It wasn't that the wolf was obviously vicious. He didn't need to be. Even sitting still, he radiated the assurance of competent power. Gaspode was, if not the victor, then at least the survivor of many a street fight, and as such would not have gone up against this animal even if backed up by a couple of lions and a man with an ax.

Instead, he sidled over to a female wolf who was watching the fire haughtily.

"Yo, bitch," he said.

"*Vot* vas that?"

Gaspode reconsidered his strategy.

"Hi, foxy . . . er . . . wolf lady," he tried.

A certain lowering of the temperature suggested that this one hadn't worked, either.

"'Ullo, miss," he said, hopefully.

Her muzzle turned to point at him. Her eyes narrowed.

"Vot *har* you?" Ice slithered off every syllable.

"Gaspode's the name," barked Gaspode, with insane cheerfulness. "'M a *dog*. That's a kind of wolf, sort of thing. So . . . what's your name, then?"

"Go avay."

"No offense meant. 'Ere, I heard tell wolves mate for life, right?"

"Vell?"

"Wish *I* could."

Gaspode froze as the she-wolf's muzzle snapped an inch from his nose.

"Vere I come from, ve *eat* things like you," she said.

"Fair enough, fair enough," muttered Gaspode, backing away. "I don't know, you try to be friendly and this is what you get . . ."

Nearer the fire, the humans were getting complicated. Gaspode slunk back and lay down.

"You could have told me," Carrot was saying.

"It would've taken too long. You always want to *understand* things. Anyway, it's none of your business. This is *family*."

Carrot waved a hand toward the wolf.

"He's a relative?" he said.

"No. He's a . . . friend."

Gaspode's ears waggled. He thought: Whoops . . .

"He's very big for a wolf," said Carrot slowly, as if filing new information.

"He's a very big wolf," said Angua, shrugging.

"Another werewolf?"

"No."

"Just a wolf?"

"Yes," said Angua sarcastically, "*just* a wolf."

"And his name is . . . ?"

"He would not object to being called Gavin."

"Gavin?"

"He once ate someone called Gavin."

"What, all of him?"

"Of course not. Just enough to make certain that the man set no more wolf traps." Angua smiled. "Gavin is . . . quite unusual."

Carrot looked at the wolf and smiled. He picked up a piece of wood and tossed it gently toward him. The wolf snapped it, doglike, out of the air.

"I'm sure we will be friends," he said.

Angua sighed. "Wait."

Gaspode, the unheeded spectator, watched as Gavin, without taking his eyes off Carrot, very slowly bit the wood in two.

"Carrot?" said Angua, sweetly. "Don't do that again. Gavin isn't even in the same clan as these wolves, and he took over the pack without anyone even whining. He's *not* a dog. And he's a killer, Carrot. Oh, don't look like that. I don't mean he pounces on wandering kids or eats up the odd grandmother. I mean that if he thinks a human ought to die, that human is dead. He will always, always fight. He's very uncomplicated like that."

"He's an *old* friend?" said Carrot.

"Yes."

"A . . . friend."

"Yes." Angua rolled her eyes and said, in a voice of singsong sarcasm, "I was out in the woods one day and I fell into some old pit trap under the snow and some wolves found me and would have killed me but Gavin turned up and faced them down. Don't ask me why. People do things sometimes. So do wolves. End of story."

"Gaspode said wolves and werewolves didn't get on," said Carrot patiently.

"He's right. If Gavin wasn't here they'd have torn me to pieces. I can look like a wolf, but I'm not a wolf. I'm a werewolf! I'm not a human, either. I'm a werewolf! Get it? You know some of the remarks people make? Well, wolves don't make remarks. They go for the throat. Wolves have got a very good sense of smell. You can't fool it. I can pass for human, but I can't pass for wolf."

"I never thought of it like that . . . I mean, you would just think that wolves and werewolves—"

"That's how it is," sighed Angua.

"You said this was family," said Carrot, as if working down a mental checklist.

"I meant it's personal. Gavin came all the way *into Ankh-Morpork* to warn me. He even slept on the timber wagons during the day so that he'd keep moving. Can you imagine how much nerve that took? It's got nothing to do with the Watch. It's got nothing to do with you."

Carrot looked around. The snow was falling again, turning into rain above the fire.

"I'm here now."

"Go away. Please. I can sort this out."

"And then you'll come back to Ankh-Morpork? Afterward?"

"I . . ." Angua hesitated.

"I think I should stay," said Carrot.

"Look, the city needs you," said Angua. "You know Vimes relies on—"

"I've resigned."

For a moment, Gaspode thought he could hear the sound of every settling snowflake.

"Not really?"

"Yes."

"And what did old Stoneface say?"

"Er, nothing. He'd already left for Uberwald."

"*Vimes* is coming to Uberwald?"

"Yes. For the coronation."

"He's got mixed up in this?" said Angua.

"Mixed up in what?"

"Oh . . . my family's been . . . stupid. I'm not quite sure I know everything, but the wolves are worried. When werewolves make trouble, it's the *real* wolves that always suffer. People'll kill anything with fur." Angua stared at the fire for a moment and then said, with forced brightness, "So who's been left in charge?"

"I don't know. Fred Colon's got seniority."

"Ha, yes. In his nightmares." Angua hesitated. "You really left?"

"Yes."

"Oh."

Gaspode listened to some more snowflakes.

"Well, you won't get far by yourselves now," said Angua, standing up. "Rest for another hour. And then we'll be going through the deep forest. Not too much snow there yet. We've got a lot of ground to cover. I hope you can keep up."

At breakfast early next morning Vimes noticed that the other guests were keeping so far away from him that they were holding on to the walls.

"The men who went out came back around midnight, sir," said Cheery quietly.

"Did they catch anyone?"

"Um . . . sort of, sir. They found seven dead bodies."

"Seven?"

"They think some others might have got away where there's a path up the rocks."

"But . . . seven? Detritus got one, and . . . I got one, and a couple were wounded, and Inigo got . . . one . . ." Vimes's voice tailed off.

He stared at Inigo Skimmer, who was sitting on the other side of the room at a crowded public table. The ones around Vimes and Lady Sybil were deserted; Sybil had put it down to deference. The little man was eating soup in a little neat self-contained world among the waving arms and intrusive elbows. He'd even tucked a napkin under his chin.

"They were . . . *very* dead, sir," Cheery whispered.

"Well, that was . . . interesting," said Sybil, wiping her mouth delicately. "I've never had soup with sausages in it for breakfast before. What is it called, Cheery?"

"Fatsup, Your Ladyship," said Cheery. "It means 'fat soup.' We're close to the Shmaltzberg fat layers now, and . . . well, it's nourishing and keeps out the cold."

"How very . . . interesting."

Lady Sybil looked at her husband. He hadn't taken his eyes off Inigo.

The door opened and Detritus ducked inside, banging snow off his knuckles.

"It's not too bad," he said. "Dey say it'd be a good idea to make an early start, sir."

153

"I bet they do," said Vimes, and thought: They don't want someone like *me* hanging around, there's no knowing who'll die next.

Several faces he vaguely recalled from last night were missing now. Presumably some travelers had started off even earlier, which meant that the news was probably running ahead of him. He'd staggered in, covered in blood and mud, carrying a crossbow and, d'you know, when they went back to look there were *seven* dead men. By the time that sort of story had gone ten miles he'd be carrying an ax as well, and make that thirty dead men and a dog.

The diplomatic career had certainly got off to a good start, eh?

As they got into the coach he saw the little dart stuck in the door jamb. It was metallic, with metal fins, and had overall a look of speed, as if, when you touched it, you'd burn your fingers.

He walked around to the back of the coach. There was another, much larger arrow high in the woodwork.

"They tried to catch up with you on the upgrade," said Inigo, behind him.

"You killed them."

"Some got away."

"I'm surprised."

"I've only got one pair of hands, Your Grace."

Vimes glanced up at the inn sign. Crudely painted on the boards was a large red head, complete with trunk and tusks.

"This is the Inn of the Fifth Elephant," said Inigo. "You left the law behind when we passed Lancre, Your Grace. Here it's the *lore*. What you keep is what you can. What's yours is what you fight for. The fittest survive."

"Ankh-Morpork is pretty lawless, too, Mister Skimmer."

"Ankh-Morpork has many laws. It's just that people don't obey them. And that, Your Grace, is quite a different bowl of fat, mhm, mmm."

They set off in convoy. Detritus sat on the roof on the leading coach, which lacked a door and most of one side. The view was flat and white, a featureless expanse of snow.

After a while they passed a clacks tower. Burn marks on one side of the stone base suggested that someone had thought that no news was good news, but the semaphore shutters were clacking and twinkling in the light.

"The whole world is watching," said Vimes.

"But it's never cared," said Skimmer. "Up until now. And now it wants to rip the top off the country and take what's underneath, mph, mhm."

Ah, thought Vimes, our killer clerk *does* have more than one emotion.

"Ankh-Morpork has always tried to get on well with other nations," said Sybil. "Well . . . these days, at least."

"I don't think we exactly *try*, dear," said Vimes. "It's just that we found that— Why're we stopping?"

He pulled down the window.

"What happening, Sergeant?"

"Waiting for dese dwarfs, sir," the troll called down.

Several hundred dwarfs, four abreast, were trotting across the white plain toward them. There was, Vimes thought, something very determined about them.

"Detritus?"

"Yessir?"

"Try not to look too troll-like, will you?"

"Tryin' like hell, sir."

The column was abreast of them before someone barked the command to halt. A dwarf detached himself from the rest and walked over to the coach.

"*Ta'grdzk?*" he bellowed.

"Would you like me to take care of this, Your Grace?" said Inigo.

"I'm the damn ambassador," said Vimes. He stepped down. "*Good morning, dwarf*"—indicating miscreant—"*I am Overseer Vimes of the Look.*"

Lady Sybil heard Inigo give a little groan.

"*Krz? Gr'dazak yad?*"

"Hang on, hang on, I know this one . . . *I am sure you are a dwarf of no convictions. Let us shake our business, dwarf*"—indicating miscreant.

"Yes, that will just about do it, I think," said Inigo. "Mmm, mhm."

The senior dwarf had gone red in those areas of his face that could be seen behind the hair. The rest of the squad were taking a renewed interest in the coach.

The leader took a deep breath.

"*D'kraha?*"

Cheery dropped down from the coach. Her leather skirt flapped in the wind.

As one dwarf, the column swiveled to stare at her. Their leader went pop-eyed.

"*B'dan? K'raa! D'kraga 'ha'ak'!*"

Vimes saw the expression that appeared on Cheery's small round face.

Above him there was a clunk as Detritus rested the loaded Piecemaker on the edge of the coach.

"I know dat word he said to her," he announced to the world. "It is not a good word. I do not want to hear dat word again."

"Well, this is all very jolly, mph, mhm," said Inigo, getting down. "And now if everyone will just relax for a moment we might get out of here alive, mmm."

Vimes reached up and carefully pushed the end of Detritus's crossbow toward a less threatening direction.

Inigo talked very fast in what seemed to Vimes to be a torrent of perfect Dwarfish, although he was sure he heard the occasional "mmm." He opened his leather case and produced a couple of documents affixed with big waxy seals. These were inspected with considerable suspicion. The dwarf pointed at Cheery and Detritus. Inigo flapped a hand impatiently, the universal symbol for dismissing that which was not important. More papers were examined.

Eventually, with more universal body language meaning "I *could* do something bad to you but right now it's just too much bother," the dwarf waved Inigo away, gave Vimes a look that suggested that, against all physical evidence, Vimes was beneath him and strode back to his troops.

An order was barked. The dwarfs set off again, leaving the road and heading off toward the forest.

"Well, that all seems sorted out," said Inigo, getting back into the coach. "Miss Littlebottom was a bit of a sticking point, but a dwarf does respect very complicated documents. Something's up. He wouldn't say what it was. He wanted to search the coach."

"The hell with that. What for?"

"Who knows? I persuaded him that we have diplomatic immunity."

"And what did you tell him about me?"

"I tried to convince him that you were a bloody idiot, Your Grace. Mph, mhm."

"Oh really?" Vimes heard Lady Sybil repress a laugh.

"It was necessary, believe me. Street Dwarfish wasn't a good idea, Your Grace. But when I pointed out that you were an aristocrat, he—"

"I am *not* an—well, I'm not *really* a—"

"Yes, Your Grace. But if you'll be advised by me, a lot of diplomacy lies in appearing to be a lot more stupid than you are. You've made a good start, Your Grace. And now, I think we'd better be moving, mhm."

"I'm glad to see you're being less deferential, Inigo," said Vimes, as they got under way again.

"Oh well, Your Grace, I've gotten to know you better now."

Gaspode had confused recollections of the rest of that night. The pack moved fast, and he realized that most of them were running ahead of Carrot, to flatten down the snow.

It wasn't flat enough for Gaspode. Eventually a wolf picked him up by the scruff of the neck and carried him bodily, while making muffled comments about the foul taste.

The snow stopped after a while and there was a slip of moonlight behind the clouds.

And all around, near and far, was the howl. Occasionally the pack would stop, in a clearing or on the crisp white brow of a hill, and join in.

Gaspode limped to Angua while the cries went up around them. "What's this for?" he said.

"Politics," said Angua. "Negotiation. We're crossing territories."

Gaspode glanced at Gavin. He hadn't joined in the howl but sat a little way off, regally dividing his attention between Carrot and the pack.

"*He* has to ask permission?" he said.

"He has to make sure they'll let me through."

"Oh. That's giving him problems?"

"None that he can't bite through."

"Oh. Er . . . is the howl saying anything about *me*?"

" 'Small, horrible, smelly dog.' "

"Ah, right."

They set off again a few minutes later, down a long snow-crusted slope in the moonlight toward the forest again, and Gaspode saw shadows angling fast across the snowfield toward them. For a moment he was flanked by two packs, the old and the new, and then their original escort dropped away.

So we've got a new honor guard, he thought, as he ran in the center of a wall of blurred gray legs. Wolves we haven't met before. I just hope the howl added "doesn't taste nice."

Then Carrot fell over in the snow. It was a moment before he pushed himself up again.

The wolves circled uncertainly, occasionally glancing at Gavin. Gaspode caught up with Carrot, jumping awkwardly through the snow.

"You all right?"

"Hard . . . to . . . run . . ."

"I don't want to, you know, worry you or anything," whined Gaspode, "but we're not exactly among friends here, know what I mean? Our Gavin isn't going to win the prize of the wolf with the waggiest tail *anywhere*."

"When did he last sleep?" Angua demanded, pushing her way through the wolves.

"Dunno, really," said Gaspode. "We've been moving pretty fast the last few days . . ."

"No sleep, no food and no proper clothing," snarled Angua. "Idiot!"

There was growling and whining from some of the wolves around Gavin. Gaspode sat down by Carrot's head and watched as Angua . . . argued.

He couldn't speak pure wolf and, besides, gesture and body language played a far greater part than it did in canine. But you didn't have to be bright to see that things weren't going well. There was def'nitly a lot of Atmosphere in the atmosphere. And Gaspode had a feeling that, if things went all pear-shaped in a hurry, one small dog had all the survival chances of a chocolate kettle on a very hot stove.

There was a lot of whining and growling. One wolf—Gaspode mentally named him Awkward—was not happy. It looked as though a number of wolves were agreeing with him. One of them bared its teeth at Angua.

Then Gavin stood up. He shook some snowflakes off his coat, looked around in an offhand fashion and padded toward Awkward.

Gaspode felt every hair on his body stand on end.

The other wolves crouched back. Gavin ignored them. When he was a few feet away from Awkward, he put his head on one side and said, "Hrurrrm?"

It was almost a pleasant noise. But right down inside Gaspode's bones it bounced a harmonic which said: At this point, we could go two ways. There is the easy way, and that is very easy.

You'll never *know* about the hard way.

Awkward held eye contact for a while, and then looked down.

Gavin snarled something. Half a dozen of the wolves, led by Angua, loped off toward the forest.

They returned twenty minutes later. Angua was human again—at least, Gaspode corrected himself, human *shaped*—and the wolves were harnessed to a big dog sled.

"Borrowed it from a man in the village over the hill," she said, as it slid to a halt by Carrot.

"Nice of him," said Gaspode, and decided not to pursue the subject. "I'm surprised to see wolves in harness, though."

"Well, this *was* the easy way," said Angua.

It's odd, Gaspode mused, as he lay in the sled alongside the slumbering Carrot. He was so int'rested when Bum talked about the howl and how it could send messages right up into the mountains. If I was a suspicious dog, I'd wonder if he *knew* that she'd come back for him if he was really in trouble, if he decided to gamble everything on it . . .

He poked his head out from under the blanket. Snow stung his eyes. Running alongside the sled, only a few feet away from Carrot, and glowing silver in the moonlight, was Gavin.

This is me, thought Gaspode, stuck between the humans and the wolves. It's a dog's life.

This is the life, thought Acting Captain Colon. Hardly any paperwork was coming up here now, and by dint of much effort he'd entirely cleared the backlog. It was a lot quieter, too.

When Vimes was here—and Fred Colon suddenly found himself thinking the word "Vimes" without prefixing it with the word

"Mister"—the main office was full of so much noise and bustle you could hardly hear yourself speak. Completely inefficient, that was. How could anyone hope to get anything done?

He counted the sugar again. Twenty-nine. But he'd had two in his tea, so that was all right. Toughness was paying off.

Colon went and opened his door a fraction so that he could just see down into the office. It was amazing how you could catch them out that way.

Quiet. And neat, too. Every desk was clear. Much better than the mess you used to get.

He went back to the desk and counted the sugar lumps.

There were twenty-seven.

Ah-ha! Someone was trying to drive him mad. Well, two could play at that game.

He counted the lumps again.

There were twenty-six, and there was a knock at the door.

This caused it to swing inward, and Colon to jump up in evil triumph.

"Ah-ha! Burst in on me, eh? . . . oh . . ."

The "oh" was because the knocker was Constable Dorfl, the golem. He was taller than the doorway and strong enough to tear a troll in half; he'd never done this, since he was an intensely moral being, but not even Colon was going to pick an argument with someone who had glowing red holes where his eyes should be. Ordinary golems would not harm a human because they had magic words in their head that ordered them not to. Dorfl had no magic words, but he didn't harm people because he'd decided that it wasn't moral. This left the worrying possibility that, given enough provocation, he might think again.

Beside the golem was Constable Shoe, saluting smartly.

"We've come to pick up the wages chitty, sir," he said.

"The what?"

"The wages chitty, sir. The monthly chitty, sir. And then we take it to the palace and bring back the wages, sir."

"I don't know anything about that!"

"I put it on your desk yesterday, sir. Signed by Lord Vetinari, sir."

Colon couldn't hide the flicker in his eyes. The black ash in the fireplace was, by now, overflowing.

Shoe followed his gaze.

"I haven't seen any such thing," said Colon, while the color drained from his face like a sucked popsicle.

"I'm sure I did, sir," said Constable Shoe. "I wouldn't forget a thing like that, sir. In fact, I distinctly remember saying to Constable Visit, 'Washpot, I'm just going to take this—'"

"Look, you can see I'm a busy man!" snapped Colon. "Get one of the sergeants to sort it out!"

"There's no sergeants left except Sergeant Flint, sir, and he spends all his time going around asking people what he should be doing," said Constable Shoe. "Anyway, *sir*, it's the senior officer who must sign the chitty—"

Colon stood up, leaning on his knuckles, and shouted, "Oh, I 'must,' must I? That's a nerve and no mistake! 'Must,' eh? Most of you lot are lucky anyone even gives you a job! Bunch of zombies and loonies and lawn ornaments and rocks! I've had it up to here with you!"

Shoe leaned back out of range of the spittle.

"Then I am afraid I must take this up with the Guild of Watchmen, sir," he said.

"Guild of Watchmen? Hah! And since when has there been a Guild of Watchmen?"

"Dunno. What's the time now?" said Corporal Nobbs, ambling into the room. "Got to be a couple of hours, at least. Morning, Captain."

"What are you doing here, Nobby?"

"That's Mister Nobbs to you, Captain. And I'm president of the Guild of Watchmen, since you ask."

"There's no such bloody thing!"

"All legit, Captain. Registered at the Palace and everything. Amazin' how people rushed to join, too." He pulled his grubby notebook. "Got a few matters to take up with you, if you have a moment. Well, I *say* a few—"

"I'm not putting up with this!" bellowed Colon, his face crimson. "This is high treason! You're all sacked! You're all—"

"We're all on strike," said Nobby, calm in the face.

"You can't go on strike while I'm sacking you!"

"Our strike headquarters are in the back room of the Bucket, on Gleam Street," said Nobby.

"Here, that's my boozer! I forbid you to go on strike in my own pub!"

"We shall be there when you wish to talk terms. Come, brothers. We are now officially in a dispute situation."

They marched out.

"Don't bother to come back!" Colon shouted after them.

Bonk wasn't what Vimes had expected. In fact he'd find it hard to say what he *had* expected, except that this wasn't it.

It occupied a narrow valley with a white-water river winding through it. There were city walls. They were not like those of Ankh-Morpork, which had become at first a barrier to expansion and then a source of masonry for it. These had an inside and an outside.

There were castles on the hills. There were castles on most hills in these parts. And there were high gates across the road.

Detritus thumped on the side of the coach. Vimes stuck his head out.

"Dere's guys in der road," said the troll. "Dey got halibuts."

Vimes looked out of the windows. There were half a dozen guards, and they did indeed have halberds.

"What are *they* after?" he said.

"I expect they'll also want to see our papers and make a search of the coaches," said Inigo.

"Papers are one thing," said Vimes, getting out of the coach, "but no one is rummaging in our stuff. I know that trick. They're not looking *for* anything, they just want to show us who's boss. You come along and do the translating." He added, "Don't worry, I'll be diplomatic."

The two men barring the way did have helmets and they were holding weapons, but their uniforms did not conform to normal uniformity. No guards, Vimes thought, should be dressed in red, blue and yellow. People would be able to see them coming. Vimes liked a uniform you could lurk in.

He pulled out his badge and held it up, advancing with an ingratiating smile.

"Just repeat this, Mister Skimmer," Vimes raised his voice. "Hello, fellow officer, as you can see I am Commander V—"

A blade swung around. If Vimes hadn't stopped, he'd have walked into it.

Inigo stepped forward, leather case already open, one hand holding several impressive pieces of paper, mouth already framing some suitable sentences. A guard took one of the pieces of paper and stared at it.

"This is a studied insult," said Inigo, contriving to speak out of the corner of his mouth while maintaining a smile. "Someone wishes to see how you react, mmm, mhm."

"Them?"

"No. We are being watched."

The paper was handed back. There was a terse conversation.

"The captain of the guard says there are special circumstances and he will search the coaches," said Inigo.

"No," said Vimes, taking in the expression on the captain's white face. "I know when people are playing silly buggers, 'cos I've done it myself."

He pointed to the door of his coach.

"See this?" he said. "Tell him this is an *Ankh-Morpork* crest. And *this* is an Ankh-Morpork coach, property of Ankh-Morpork. If they lay hands on it, that will constitute an act of *war* against Ankh-Morpork. Tell him that."

He saw the man lick his lips nervously as Inigo translated. Poor sod, he thought. He didn't ask for this. He was probably expecting a quiet day on the gate. But someone gave him some orders.

Inigo said, "He says he's very sorry, but those are his instructions, and he quite understands if His Grace wishes to make a complaint at the highest level, mmm, mhm."

A guard turned the handle of the coach door. Vimes slammed it shut.

"Tell him the war will start right now," he said. "And then it'll work its way up."

"Your Grace!"

The guards looked at Detritus. It was quite hard to hold the Piecemaker nonchalantly, and he wasn't even making the attempt.

Vimes maintained eye contact with the captain of the guard. If the man had any sense, he'd realize that if Detritus fired the thing it'd kill them all, besides sending the coach backward at high speed.

Please just let him have the sense to know when to fold, he prayed.

Out of the corner of his ear, he could hear the guards whispering to one another. He caught the word "Wilinus."

The captain stepped back and saluted.

"He apologizes for any inconvenience and hopes you will enjoy your stay in his beautiful city," said Inigo. "He particularly hopes you will visit the Chocolate Museum in Prince Vodorny Square, where his sister works."

Vimes saluted.

"Tell him I think he is an officer with a great future," said Vimes. "A future which, I trust, is going to very soon include opening the damn gates."

The captain had nodded to the men before Inigo was halfway through the translation. *Aha* . . .

"And ask him his name," he said. The man was bright enough not to respond until this had been translated.

"Captain Tantony," Inigo said.

"I shall remember it," said Vimes. "Oh . . . and tell him he has a fly on his nose."

Tantony won a prize. His eyes barely flickered. Vimes grinned.

As for the town itself . . . it was just a town. Roofs were steeper than in Ankh-Morpork, some maniac with a fretsaw had been allowed to amuse himself on the wooden architecture, and there was more paint than you saw back home. Not that this told you anything; many a rich man had become rich by, metaphorically, not painting his house.

The coaches bowled over the cobbles. Not the right sort of cobbles, of course. Vimes knew that.

The coach stopped again. Vimes stuck his head out of the window. Two rather scruffier guards had barred the road this time.

"Ah, I *recognize* this one," said Vimes grimly. "I reckon that this time we've just met Colonesque and Nobbski."

He stepped out and walked up to them.

"Well?"

The fatter of the two hesitated, and then held out his hand.

"Pisspot," he said.

"Inigo?" said Vimes quietly, without turning his head.

"Ah," said Inigo, after some muttered exchanges. "Now the problem seems to be Sergeant Detritus. No trolls are allowed in this part of town during the hours of daylight, apparently, without a passport signed by their . . . owner. Uh . . . in Bonk the only trolls allowed are prisoners of war. They have to carry identification."

"Detritus is a citizen of Ankh-Morpork and my sergeant," said Vimes.

"However, he *is* a troll. Perhaps in the interests of diplomacy you could write a short—"

"Do *I* need a pisspot?"

"A passport . . . no, Your Grace."

"Then he doesn't, either."

"Nevertheless, Your Grace—"

"There is *no* nevertheless."

"But it may be advisable to—"

"There's no advisable, either."

A few other guards had drifted over. Vimes was aware of watching eyes.

"He could be ejected by force," said Inigo.

"Now *there's* an experiment I wouldn't want to miss," said Vimes.
Detritus made a rumbling noise. "I don't mind goin' back if—"

"Shut up, Sergeant. You're a free troll. That's an order."

Vimes permitted himself another brief scan of the growing, silent crowd. And he saw the fear in the eyes of the men with the halberds. They did not want to be doing this, any more than the captain had.

"I'll tell you what, Inigo," he said, "tell the . . . guards that the Ambassador from Ankh-Morpork commends them for their diligence, congratulates them on their dress sense and will see that their instruction is obeyed forthwith. That should do it, shouldn't it?"

"Certainly, Your Grace."

"And now turn the coach around, Detritus. Coming, Inigo?"

Inigo's expression changed rapidly.

"We passed an inn about ten miles back," Vimes went on. "Ought to make it by dark, do you think?"

"But *you* can't go, Your Grace!"

Vimes turned, very slowly.

"Would you repeat that, Mister Skimmer?"

"I mean—"

"We are *leaving*, Mister Skimmer. What you do, of course, is up to you."

He sat down inside the coach. Opposite him, Sybil made a fist and said, "Well done!"

"Sorry, dear," said Vimes, as the coach turned. "It didn't look like a very good inn."

"Serves them right, the little bullies," said Sybil. "You showed them."

Vimes glanced out and saw, at the edge of the crowd, a black coach with dark windows. He could make out a figure in the gloom within. The luckless guards were looking at it, as if for instructions. It waved a gloved hand languidly.

He started counting under his breath.

After eleven seconds Inigo trotted alongside the coach and jumped onto the running board.

"Your Grace, apparently the guards acted quite without authority and will be punished—"

"No they didn't. I was looking at 'em. They'd been given an *order*," said Vimes.

"Nevertheless, diplomatically it would be a good idea to accept the explan—"

"So that the poor buggers can be hung up by their thumbs?" said Vimes. "No. Just you go back and tell whoever's giving the orders that all our people can go anywhere they like in this city, d'you see, whatever shape they are."

"I don't think you can actually demand *that*, sir—"

"Those lads had old Burleigh and Stronginthearm weapons, Mister Skimmer. Made in Ankh-Morpork. So did the men on the gate. Trade, Mister Skimmer. Isn't that part of what diplomacy is all about? You go back and talk to whoever's in the black carriage, and then you'd better get them to lend you a horse, because I reckon we'll have gone a little way by then."

"You could perhaps wait—"

"Wouldn't dream of it."

In fact the coach was outside the gates of the town before Skimmer caught it up again.

"There will not be a problem with either of your requests," he panted, and for a moment there appeared to be a touch of admiration in his expression.

"Good man. Tell Detritus to turn around again, will you?"

"You're grinning, Sam," said Sybil, as Vimes sat back.

"I was just thinking that I could take to the diplomatic life," said Vimes.

"There is something else," said Inigo, getting into the coach. "There's some . . . historical artifact owned by the dwarfs, and there's a rumor—"

"How long ago was the Scone of Stone stolen?"

Inigo's mouth stayed open. Then he shut his mouth and his eyes narrowed.

"How in the *world* did you know that, Your Grace? Mmm?"

"By the pricking of my thumbs," said Vimes, his face carefully blank. "I've got very odd thumbs, when it comes to pricking."

"Really?"

"Oh yes."

Dogs had a much easier sex life than humans, Gaspode decided. That was something to look forward to, if he ever managed to have one.

It wasn't going to start here, that was definite. The female wolves snapped at him if he came too close, and they weren't just warnings, either. He was having to be very careful where he trod.

The really *odd* thing about human sex, though, was the way it went on even when people were fully clothed and sitting on opposite sides of a fire. It was in the things they said and did not say, the way they looked at one another and looked away.

The packs had changed again, overnight. The mountains were higher, the snow was crisper. Most of the wolves were sitting at some distance from the fire that Carrot had made—just enough distance, in fact, to establish that they were proud wild creatures that didn't have to rely on this sort of thing but close enough to get the benefit.

And then there was Gavin, sitting a little way off, turning to look from one to the other.

"Gavin's people *hate* my family," Angua was saying. "I told you, it's always wolves who suffer when werewolves get too powerful. Werewolves are smarter at escaping hunters. That's why wolves much prefer vampires. Vampires leave them alone. Werewolves sometimes *hunt* wolves."

"I'm surprised," said Carrot.

Angua shrugged. "Why? They hunt humans, don't they? We're not nice people, Carrot. We're all pretty dreadful. But my brother Wolfgang is something *special*. Father's frightened of him and so's Mother if she'd only admit it, but she thinks he'll make the clan powerful, so she indulges him. He drove my other brother away and he killed my sister."

"How—?"

"He *said* it was an accident. Poor little Elsa. She was a yennork, just like Andrei. That's a werewolf that doesn't Change, you know? I'm sure I've mentioned it. Our family throws them up from time to time. Wolfgang and I were the only classic bi-morphs in the litter. Elsa looked human all the time, even at full moon. Andrei was always a wolf."

"You mean you had a human sister and a wolf brother?"

"*No*, Carrot. They were both *werewolves*. But the, well, the little . . . switch . . . inside them didn't work. Do you understand? They always stayed the same shape. In the old days, the clan would kill off a yennork quickly, and Wolfgang is a traditionalist when it comes to nastiness. He says they made the blood impure. You see, a yennork would go off and be a human or be a wolf but they'd still be *carrying* the werewolf . . . blood, and then they'd marry and have children . . . or pups . . . and, well, that's where the fairy-tale monsters come from. People with a *bit* of wolf and wolves with that extra capacity for violence that is so very human." She sighed, and glanced momentarily at Gavin. "But Elsa was harmless. After that, Andrei didn't wait for it to happen to him. He's a sheepdog over in Borogravia now. Doing well, I hear. Wins championships," she added sourly.

She poked the fire aimlessly.

"Wolfgang's got to be stopped. He's plotting something with some of the dwarfs. They meet in the forest, Gavin says."

"He sounds very well informed for a wolf," said Carrot. Angua almost snarled at him.

"He's not stupid, you know. He can understand more than eight hundred words. A lot of humans get by on less! *And* he's got a sense of smell that's almost as good as mine! The wolves see *everything*. The werewolves are out all the time now. They're chasing people down . . . the Game, we call it. The wolves get the blame. It looks like they're breaking the Arrangement. And there's been these meetings, right out in the forest where they think no one will see them. Some dwarfs have got some sort of nasty scheme, by the sound of it. They asked Wolfgang for help! That's like asking a vulture to pick your teeth."

"What can you do?" said Carrot. "If even your parents can't control him—"

"We used to fight when we were younger. 'Rough and tumble,' he'd call it. But I could send him off howling. Wolfgang hates to think there's anyone who can beat him, so I don't think he'll relish the thought of me turning up. He's got plans. This part of Uberwald has always, well, worked because no one was too powerful, but if the dwarfs start squabbling among themselves then Wolfgang's the lad to take advantage, with his stupid uniforms and his stupid flag."

"I don't think I want to see you fighting, though."

"Then you can look the other way! I didn't ask you to follow me! Do you think I'm proud of this? I've got a brother who's a sheepdog!"

"A *champion* sheepdog," said Carrot earnestly.

Gaspode watched Angua's expression. It was one you'd never get on a dog.

"You mean that," she said at last. "You actually mean that, don't you . . . you really do. And if you'd met him it wouldn't worry you, would it? To you everyone's a person. I have to sleep in a dog basket seven nights a month and that doesn't worry you, either, does it?"

"No. You know it doesn't."

"It should! Don't ask me why, but it should! You're so . . . unthinkingly *nice* about it! And sooner or later a girl can have too much nice!"

"I don't *try* to be nice . . ."

"I know. I know. I just wish you'd . . . oh, I don't know . . . *complain* a bit. Well, not exactly *complain*. Just sigh, or something."

"Why?"

"Because . . . oh, because it'd make me feel better! Oh, it's too hard to explain. It's probably a werewolf thing."

"I'm sorry—"

"And don't be sorry all the time, either!"

Gaspode curled up so close to the fire that he steamed. Dogs had it down a lot better, he decided.

The building that was to be the embassy was set back from the road on a quiet side street. They rattled under an arch into a small rear courtyard containing some stables. It reminded Vimes of a large coaching inn.

"It's really only a consulate at the moment," said Inigo, leafing through his papers. "We should be met by . . . ah, yes, Wando Sleeps. Been here for several years, mhm."

Behind the coaches a pair of gates were swung shut. There was the sound of heavy bolts shooting home. Vimes stared at the apparition that came limping back toward the coach door.

"He looks it," he said.

"Oh, I don't think *this* is—"

"Good evening, marthterth, mithtreth . . ." said the figure. "Welcome to Ankh-Morpork. I'm Igor."

"Igor who?" said Inigo.

"Jutht Igor, thir. *Alwayth* . . . jutht Igor," said Igor calmly, unfolding the step. "I'm the odd-job man."

"You don't say?" said Vimes, mesmerized.

"Have you had a terrible accident?" said Lady Sybil.

"I did thpill tea down my thirt thith morning," said Igor. "Kind of you to notice."

"Where's Mister Sleeps?" said Inigo.

"I'm afraid Marthter Thleeps ith nowhere to be found. I wath rather hoping you would know what'd happened to him."

"Us?" said Inigo. "Mhm, mmm! We assumed he was here!"

"He left rather urgently two weeks ago," said Igor. "He did not vouchthafe to me where he wath going. Do go inthide, and I will thee to the baggage."

Vimes glanced up. A little bit of snow was falling now, but there was enough light to see that, across the whole courtyard, was an iron mesh. With the bolted doors and the walls of the building all around, they were in a cage.

"Jutht a little leftover from the old dayth," said Igor cheerfully. "Nothing to worry about, thir."

"What a fine figure of a man," said Sybil weakly, as they stepped inside.

"More than one man, by the look of him."

"Sam!"

"Sorry. I'm sure his heart's in the right place."

"Good."

"Or someone's heart, anyway."

"Sam, really!"

"All right, all right, but you must admit he does look a bit . . . odd."

"None of us can help the way we're made, Sam."

"He looks as if he tried—good grief . . ."

"Oh dear," said Lady Sybil.

Vimes was not against hunting, if only because Ankh-Morpork seldom offered any better game than the large rats you got along the waterfront. But the sight of the walls of the new embassy might have been enough to make the keenest hunter take a step back and cry, "Oh, I say, hold on . . ."

The previous occupant had been keen on hunting, shooting and fishing and, to have covered every single wall with the resultant trophies, he must have been doing all three at the same time.

Hundreds of glass eyes, obscenely alive in the light of the fire in the huge hearth, stared down at Vimes.

"It's just like my grandfather's study," said Lady Sybil. "There was a stag's head in there that used to frighten the life out of me."

"There's just about *everything* here . . . oh no . . ."

"My gods . . ." whispered Lady Sybil.

Vimes looked around desperately. Detritus was just entering, carrying some of the trunks.

"Stand in front of it," Vimes hissed.

"I'm not that tall, Sam! Or that wide!"

The troll looked up at them, then at the trophies, and then grinned. It's colder up here, Vimes thought. He's quicker on the uptake.* Even Nobby won't play poker with him in the winter. Damn!

"Something wrong?" said Detritus.

Vimes sighed. What was the point? He'd spot it sooner or later.

"I'm sorry about this, Detritus," he said, standing aside.

Detritus looked at the horrible trophy and nodded.

"Yeah, dere used to be a lot of dat sort of fing in der old days," he said calmly, putting down the luggage. "Dey wouldn't be de real diamond teef, o'course. Dey'd take dem out and put bigger glass ones in."

"You don't *mind*?" said Lady Sybil. "It's a troll's head! Someone actually mounted a troll's head and put it on the wall!"

"Ain't mine," said Detritus.

"But it's so *horrible!*"

Detritus stood in thought for a moment, and then opened the stained wooden box that contained all he had felt it necessary to bring.

"Dis is de old country, after all," he said. "So if it'd made you feel better . . ."

He pulled out a smaller box and rummaged among what appeared to be bits of rock and cloth until he found something yellowy-brown and round, like a shallow cup.

"Should've bunged it away," he said, "but it's all I got to remember my old granny by. She kept fings in it."

"It's a bit of human skull, isn't it," said Vimes, at last.

"Yep."

"Whose?"

---

* Detritus's silicon-based brain was, as with most trolls, highly sensitive to changes in temperature. When the thermometer was very low he could be dangerously intellectual.

"Anyone ask dat troll dere *his* name?" said Detritus, and the glint in his eye had a brittle edge to it for a moment. Then he carefully put the bowl away. "Tings were diff'rent in dem days. Now you don't chop our heads off an' we don't make drums outa your skin. Everyt'ing is hunky-dory. Dat's all we have to know."

He picked up the boxes again and followed Lady Sybil toward the staircase. Vimes took another look at the trophy head. The teeth *were* longer, far longer than they'd be on a real troll. A hunter'd have to be very brave and very lucky to go up against a fighting troll and survive. It'd be so much easier to go after an old one and later replace the ground-down stumps with sparkly fangs.

My gods, the things we do . . .

"Igor?" he said, as the odd-job man lurched past under the weight of two more bags.

"Yeth, Your Exthelenthy?"

"I'm an Excellency?" said Vimes to Inigo.

"Yes, Your Grace."

"And still My Grace as well?"

"Yes, Your Grace. You are His Grace His Excellency the Duke of Ankh-Morpork, Commander Sir Samuel Vimes, Your Grace."

"Hang on, hang on . . . His Grace cancels out the Sir, I know that. It's like having an ace in poker."

"Strictly speaking this is true, Your Grace, but great score is set by titles here and it is best to play with a full deck, mmm."

"I was once blackboard monitor at school," said Vimes sharply. "For a whole term. Would that help? Dame Venting said no one could clean a blackboard like me."

"A useful fact, Your Grace, which may possibly be helpful in the event of a tie-breaker, mmm, mhm," said Inigo, his face carefully blank.

"We Igorth have alwayth preferred 'marthter,'" said Igor. "What wath it you were requiring?"

Vimes gestured toward the heads that covered every wall.

"I want them taken down as soon as possible. I can do this, can't I, Mister Skimmer?"

"You are the ambassador, sir. Mmm, mmm."

"Well, they're coming down. All of them."

Igor gave the camphor-smelling multitude a worried look.

"Even the thwordfith?"

"Even the swordfish," said Vimes firmly.

"And the thnow leopardth?"

"Both of them, yes."

"What about the troll?"

"*Especially* the troll. See to it."

Igor could have been said to have looked as if his world had fallen down around his ears were it not for the fact that he *already* looked as if this had happened.

"What do you want to do with them, mathter?"

"That's up to you. Throw them in the river, maybe. Ask Detritus about the troll . . . maybe it should be buried, or something. Is there any supper?"

"There'th walago,* noggi,** sclot,*** swinefletht and thauthageth," said Igor, still clearly upset about the trophies. "I'll thop tomorrow, if Her Ladythip giveth me inshtructionth."

"Is swineflesh the same as pork?" said Vimes. People in drought-

---

* A kind of pastry made from curtains.

** Buckwheat dumplings stuffed with stuff.

*** Bread made from parsnips, and widely considered to be much tastier than the dull wheat kind.

stricken areas would have paid good money to have Igor pronounce "sausages."

"Yes," said Inigo.

"And what's in the sausages?"

"Er . . . meat?" said Igor, looking as though he was ready to run.

"Good. We'll give them a try."

Vimes went upstairs and followed the sound of conversation until he reached a bedroom, where Sybil was laying clothes on a bed the size of a small country. Cheery was assisting her.

The walls were carved panels of wood. The bed was carved panels of wood. The Mad Fretworker of Bonk had been hard at work here, too. Only the floors weren't wood; they were stone, and radiated cold.

"It's a bit like the inside of a cuckoo clock, isn't it," said Sybil. "Cheery has volunteered to be my lady's maid for now."

Cheery saluted.

"Why not?" said Vimes. After a day like this, a lady's maid with a long flowing beard now seemed perfectly normal.

"The floors are a bit chilly, though. Tomorrow I shall measure up for some carpets," said Sybil firmly. "I know we won't be here long, but we ought to leave something for the next people."

"Yes, dear. That would be a good idea."

"There's a bathroom through there," said Sybil, nodding. "There's hot springs near here, apparently. They pipe them in. You'll feel better for a hot bath."

Ten minutes later Vimes was happy to agree. The water was a funny color and smelled a little of what he would politely call bad eggs, but it was good and hot and he could feel it drawing the tension out of his muscles.

A distressing scent of secondhand baked beans sloshed around him as he lay back. At the other end of the huge bath, the lump of pumice stone that he'd been using to rasp the dead skin off his feet banged against the side. Vimes watched it, unseeing, while he filed the thoughts of the day.

Things *were* starting to smell, just like the bathwater. The Scone of Stone had been stolen, had it? Now *there* was a coincidence.

It had been a complete shot in the dark. But lately he was on the lucky side when it came to nocturnal targets. Someone had pinched the replica Scone, and now the *real* one had gone missing, and someone in Ankh-Morpork who was good at making rubber molds had been found dead. You didn't need the brains of Detritus in a snowdrift to suspect a connection.

A recollection nagged at him. Someone had said something and he'd thought it odd at the time but then something else had happened and it had gone out of his mind. Something about . . . a welcome to Bonk. Only . . .

Well, he was here. No doubt about that.

Absolute confirmation of the fact was brought forth half an hour later, at supper.

Vimes cut into a sausage, and stared.

"What is *in* these? All this . . . pink stuff?" he demanded.

"Er . . . that's the meat, Your Grace," said Inigo, on the other side of the table.

"Well, where's the texture? Where's the white bits and the yellow bits and those green bits you always hope are herbs?"

"To a connoisseur here, Your Grace, an Ankh-Morpork sausage would not be considered a sausage, mph, mhm."

"Oh really? So what would he call it?"

"A loaf, Your Grace. Or possibly a log. Here, a butcher can be hanged if his sausages are not all meat, and at that it must be from a named domesticated animal, and I perhaps should add that by name I mean that it should not have been called 'Spot' or 'Ginger,' mmm, mmm. I'm sure that if Your Grace would prefer the more genuine Ankh-Morpork taste, Igor could make up some side dishes of stale bread and sawdust."

"Thank you for that patriotic comment," said Vimes. "However, these are . . . okay, I suppose. They just came as a bit of a shock, that's all. No!"

He put his hand over his mug to prevent Igor from filling it with beer.

"Ith there thomething wrong, marthter?"

"Just water, please," said Vimes. "No beer."

"The marthster doth not drink . . . beer?"

"No. And perhaps in a mug without a face on it?" He took another look at the stein. "Why's it got a lid, by the way? Are you afraid of the rain getting in?"

"I've never been quite certain of that one," said Inigo, as Igor shuffled off. "From observation, though, I believe the purpose of the stein is to stop the beer being spilled while using the mug to conduct the singing, mmm, mmm."

"Ah, the old quaffing problem," said Vimes. "What a clever idea." Sybil patted him on the knee.

"You're not in Ankh-Morpork anymore, dear," she said.

"Now we're alone, Your Grace," said Inigo, leaning closer, "I'm very worried about Mister Sleeps. The acting consul, you remember? He seems to have vanished, mmm, mmm. Some of his personal items have gone, too."

"Holiday?"

"Not at a time like this, sir! And—"

There was a thud of wood against wood as Igor re-entered, pointedly carrying a stepladder. Inigo sat back.

Vimes found that he was yawning.

"We'd better talk about that in the morning," he said, as the ladder was dragged toward the horrible hunting trophies. "It's been a long day, what with one thing and another."

"Of course, Your Grace."

The bed's mattress was so soft that Vimes sank into it nervously, afraid it might close over the top of his head. That was just as well, because the pillow was . . . well, everyone *knew* a pillow was a sack full of feathers, didn't they? Not an apprentice eiderdown like this thing.

"Just fold it up, Sam," said Sybil, from the depths of the mattress. "G'night."

"G'night."

"Sam . . . ?"

There was a snore from Sam Vimes. Sybil sighed, and turned over.

Vimes awoke a few times, when there were two thuds from downstairs.

"Snow leopards," he muttered, and drifted away again.

There was a louder crash.

"Moose," murmured Lady Sybil.

"Elk?" mumbled Vimes.

"Def'nitly moose."

Some time later there was a muffled scream, a thud, and a sound very much like the sound made when a huge wooden ruler is held against a desk and twanged.

"Swordfish," said Sam and Sybil together, and went back to sleep.

* * *

"You should present your credentials to the rulers of Bonk," said Inigo in the morning.

Vimes was looking out of the window. Two guards in the rainbow-colored uniforms were standing stiffly to attention outside the embassy.

"What're *they* doing here?" he said.

"Guarding," said Inigo.

"Guarding who from what?"

"Just generally guarding, mmm. I suppose it's thought that guards give such a *finished* look to an important building."

"What was that you said about credentials?"

"They're just formal letters from Lord Vetinari, confirming your appointment. Mph, mmm . . . the lore is a little complex, but at the moment the order of precedence is the future Low King, the Lady Margolotta and the Baron von Uberwald. Each, of course, will pretend that you are not calling on the other two. It's called the Arrangement. It's an awkward system but it keeps the peace."

"If I understood your briefing," said Vimes, still watching the guards, "in the days of Imperial Uberwald the whole bloody show was run by the werewolves and the vampires and everyone else was lunch."

"Somewhat simplistic but broadly true, mmm," said Inigo, brushing some dust off Vimes's shoulder.

"And then it all broke up and the dwarfs became powerful because there's dwarfs from one end of Uberwald to the other and they all keep in touch . . ."

"Their system certainly survives political upheaval, yes."

"And then . . . what was it? A diet of beetles?"

"The Diet of Bugs, mmm. Diet being an Uberwaldean word for meeting, and Bugs being an important town further up river, famous for its pastries made from flax. Everyone came to an . . . arrangement. No one would wage war on any of the others, and everyone could live in peace. No garlic to be grown, no silver to be mined. And the werewolves and vampires promised that those things wouldn't be needed. Mmm, mmm."

"Seems a bit trusting," said Vimes.

"It appears to have worked, mhm."

"What did the humans think about it all?"

"Well, humans have always been a bit of background noise in the history of Uberwald, Your Grace."

"It must be a bit dull for the undead, though."

"Oh, the bright ones know the old days can't come back."

"Ah, well . . . that's always the trick, isn't it? Finding the bright ones?" Vimes put on his helmet. "And what're the dwarfs like?"

"The future Low King is considered pretty clever, Your Grace. Mhm."

"How does he stand on Ankh-Morpork?"

"He can take Ankh-Morpork or leave it alone, Your Grace. On balance, I believe he doesn't much like us."

"I thought it was Albrecht that didn't like us?"

"No, Your Grace. Albrecht is the one who would be happy to see Ankh-Morpork burned to the ground. Rhys merely wishes we didn't exist."

"I thought he was one of the good guys!"

"Your Grace, I did hear you express some negative sentiments about Ankh-Morpork on the way here, mhm, mhm."

"Yes, but I *live* there! I'm *allowed* to! That's *patriotic*!"

"Across the whole of the world, Your Grace, there inexplicably appear to be definitions of, mmm, mhm, 'good guy' which do not automatically mean 'likes Ankh-Morpork.' You will find out, I daresay. The other two are a lot easier to deal with. It may have been the Lady Margolotta who tried the little trick with the guards last night. She was the one who got me to bring you back, anyway. She has invited you for drinks."

"Oh."

"She's a vampire, mmm, mmm."

"*What?*"

Inigo sighed.

"Your Grace, I thought you understood. Vampires are simply part of Uberwald. This is where they belong. I'm afraid this is something you will have to come to terms with. I understand that now they . . . obtain blood by arrangement. Some people are . . . impressed by a title, Your Grace."

"Good grief . . ."

"Quite so. In any case, you will be safe. Remember your diplomatic immunity, mmm, mhm."

"I didn't quite see that working in the Wilinus Pass the other day."

"Oh, they were common bandits."

"Really? Has your man Sleeps turned up? Haven't you taken this to the Watch here?"

"There's no Watch here, as you understand the term. You saw them. They're . . . gate guards, enforcers for the city rulers, mhm, mmm, not officers of the law. But . . . inquiries are being made."

"Does Sybil come with me for this bit?" said Vimes, and thought: *We* were guards like that, not so long ago . . .

"It is usually done by the new ambassador and his guards."

"Well, Detritus is staying here to keep an eye on her, all right? She said this morning she really thinks this place would be better for some decent carpet, and there's no stopping her when she's in a tape-measure mood. I'll take Cheery and one of the lads from out-side, for the look of the thing. I assume you're coming?"

"I won't be required, sir. Mmm. The new coachman knows the way, Morporkian is the diplomatic language, after all, and . . . I shall be making inquiries."

"Delicate ones?"

"Indeed, Your Grace."

"If he's been killed, won't that be an act of war?"

"Yes and no, Your Grace."

"What? Sleeps was—*is* our man!"

Inigo looked awkward. "It would depend on . . . exactly where he was and what he was doing . . ."

Vimes gave him a blank look, and then the penny dropped and operated his brain.

"Spying?"

"Acquiring information. Everyone does it, mm, mmm."

"Yes, but if you find a diplomat going too far you just send him home with a sharp note, don't you?"

"Around the Circle Sea, Your Grace, that is the case. Here . . . they may have a different approach . . ."

"Something rather sharper than a note?"

"Exactly. Mmm."

Captain Tantony was one of the guards. There was some minor difficulty, but the argument that, since he was guarding Vimes, he might as well be where Vimes *was*, eventually carried some weight. Tantony had the look of an agonizingly logical man.

He kept giving Vimes curious looks as the coach rattled out of the town. Beside him, Cheery sat with her legs dangling. Vimes noticed, although it was not the kind of thing he generally made a habit of noticing, that the shape of her breastplate had been subtly altered, probably by the same armorer that Angua went to, to indicate that the chest underneath it was not quite the same shape of chest that you got under the armor of, say, Corporal Nobbs, although of course probably no one had a chest the same shape as that of Corporal Nobbs.

She was wearing her high-heeled iron boots, too.

"Look, you don't have to come," he said out loud.

"Yes, I do."

"I mean I could go and get Detritus instead. Although I suppose there'd be even more upshot if I took a troll into a dwarf mine . . . I mean, rather than a . . . a . . ."

". . . girl," said Cheery helpfully.

"Er . . . yes." Vimes felt the coach slow to a halt, even though they hadn't left the town yet, and he looked out.

In front of them, across a small square, was a fort of sorts, but with much larger gates than you'd expect for its size. As Vimes stared at them, they were swung open from within.

Inside, there was a slope. All the fort consisted of was four walls around a large, sloping tunnel.

"The dwarfs live *underneath* the town?" he said, as the light from outside was gradually replaced by the infrequent glow of torches. But they clearly showed the coach was rattling past a long, long line of stationary carts. The pools of light revealed horses, and drivers talking in groups.

"Under quite a lot of Uberwald," said Cheery. "This is just the nearest entrance, sir. We'll probably have to stop in a minute, because the horses don't like—ah."

The coach stopped again, and the coachman banged on the side to indicate that this was the end of the line. The queue of carts wound off down another tunnel, but the coach had stopped in a small cave with a big door. A couple of dwarfs were waiting there. They had axes slung across their backs, although by dwarf standards this counted merely as "politely dressed" rather than "heavily armed." Their attitude, however, was in the international language of people guarding gates everywhere.

"Commander Sam Vimes, Ankh-Morpork Ci— ambassador from Ankh-Morpork," said Vimes, handing one of them his papers. At least it was not hard to assume a lofty air with dwarfs.

To his surprise, the document was read thoroughly, one dwarf looking over the other one's shoulder and pointing out interesting subclauses. The official seal was carefully examined.

One guard pointed to Cheery.

"*Kra'k?*"

"My official guard," said Vimes. "Included in 'associated members of staff' on page two," he added helpfully.

"Mhust searhch thy coash," said the guard.

"No. Diplomatic immunity," said Vimes. "Tell 'em, Cheery."

They listened to Cheery's urgent Dwarfish. Then the other guard, whose face had indicated that there was something on his mind and it was jumping up and down, nudged his companion and pulled him aside.

There was a torrent of whispers. Vimes couldn't understand, but he caught the word "Wilinus." And, shortly afterward, the word "*hr'grag,*" Dwarfish for "thirty."

"Oh gods," he said. "And a dog?"

"Good guess, sir," said Cheery.

The document was handed back, hurriedly. Vimes could read the body language, even written smaller than usual—there was probably an expensive problem here, so the guards were inclined to leave it to someone who earned more money than they did.

One of them pulled a bellpull by the door. After some time, the door slid open, revealing a small room.

"We have to go in, sir," said Cheery.

"But there's no other doors!"

"It's all right, sir."

Vimes stepped inside. The dwarfs slid the door back, leaving them in the room lit only by one candle.

"Some kind of waiting room?" said Vimes.

Somewhere far off, something went *clonk*. The floor trembled for a moment, and then Vimes had an uneasy sensation of movement.

"The room *moves*?" he said.

"Yes, sir. Several hundred feet down, probably. I think it's all done by counterweights."

They stood silently, unsure of what to say, as walls around them creaked and groaned. Then there was a rattle, a passing sensation of weight, and the room stopped moving.

"Wherever we're headed, keep your ears open," said Vimes. "Something's going on, I can feel it . . ."

The door slid back.

Vimes looked out onto the night sky, underground. The stars were all around him . . . below him . . .

"I think we went down . . . too far," he said. And then his brain made sense of what his eyes had seen. The moving room had brought them out somewhere on the side of a huge cave. He was looking at a thousand points of candlelight, spread out on the cavern floor and in other galleries. Now that he could grasp the scale of things, he realized that many of them were moving.

The air was full of one huge sound made up of thousands of voices, echoed and re-echoing. Occasionally a shout or a laugh would stand out, but mostly it was just an endless sea of sound, beating on the shores of the eardrum.

"I thought you people lived in little mines," said Vimes.

"Well, *I* thought humans lived in little cottages, sir," said Cheery, taking a candle from a large rack beside the door and lighting it. "And then I saw Ankh-Morpork."

There was something recognizable about the way the lights were moving. A whole constellation of them was heading in toward one invisible wall, where reflected light now indicated, very faintly, the mouth of a large tunnel. In front of it was a row of lights.

Think of it as a lot of people heading for something which one row of people was . . . guarding.

"People down there aren't happy," said Vimes. "That looks like a mob to me. Look, you can tell by the way they move . . ."

"Commander Vimes?"

He turned. In the gloom he could make out several dwarfs, each with a candle fixed to his helmet. In front of them was, presumably, another dwarf.

He'd seen clothes like this in Ankh-Morpork, but always scurrying away. This was . . . a *deep-down* dwarf.

It was wearing some sort of robe made of overlapping leather plates. Instead of the small round iron helmet which Vimes had always thought dwarfs were born with, it had a pointed leather hat with more leather flaps all around it. The one at the front had been tied up, to allow the wearer to look out at the world, or at least that part of it that was underground. The general effect was of a mobile cone.

"Er . . . yes, that's me," said Vimes.

"Welcome to Shmaltzberg, Your Excellency. I am the king's *jar'ahk'haga*, which in your language you would call—"

But Vimes's lips had been moving fast as he tried to translate. "Ideas . . . taster?" he said.

"Hah! That would be a way of putting it, yes. My name . . . is Dee. Would you care to follow me? This should not take long."

The figure swept away. One of the other dwarfs prodded Vimes very gently, indicating that he should follow.

The sound from far below redoubled. Someone was yelling.

"Is there some problem?" said Vimes, catching up with the fast-moving Dee.

"We have no problems."

Ah, he's already lied to me, thought Vimes. We're being diplomatic.

Vimes trailed after the dwarf through more caves. Or tunnels . . . it was hard to tell, because in the darkness Vimes could only rely on a sense of the space around him. Occasionally they passed the lighted entrance to another cave or tunnel. Several guards, with candles on their helmets, stood at each one.

The well-honed copper's radar was beeping at him continuously. Something bad was going on. He could smell the tension, the sense of quiet panic. The air was thick with it. Occasionally other dwarfs scuttled past, distracted, on some mission. Something *very* bad. People didn't know what to do next, so they were trying to do *everything*. And, in the middle of this, important officials had to stop what they were doing because some idiot from some distant city had to hand over a piece of paper.

Eventually a door opened in the darkness. It led into a large, roughly oblong cave that, with its book-lined walls and paper strewn tables, had the look of an office about it.

"Do be seated, Commander."

A match burst into life. One candle was lit, all lost and alone in the dark.

"We try to make guests feel welcome," said Dee, scuttling behind his desk. He pulled off his pointed hat and, to Vimes's amazement, put on a pair of thick smoked glasses.

"You had papers?" he said. Vimes handed them over.

"It says here 'His Grace,'" the dwarf said, after reading them for a while.

"Yes, that's me."

"And there's a sir."

"That's me, too."

"And an Excellency."

"'Fraid so." Vimes narrowed his eyes. "I was blackboard monitor for a while, too."

There was the sound of angry voices from behind a door at the far end of the room.

"What does a blackboard monitor do?" said Dee, raising his voice.

"What? Er . . . I had to clean the blackboard after lessons."

The dwarf nodded. The voices grew louder, more intense. Dwarfish was such a good language to be annoyed in.

"Erasing the teachings when they were learned!" said Dee, shouting to be heard.

"Er . . . yes!"

"A task only given to the trustworthy!"

"Could be, yes!"

Dee folded up the letter and handed it back, glancing briefly at Cheery.

"Well, these seem to be in order," he said. "Would you care for a drink before you go?"

"Sorry? I thought I had to present myself to your king." The swearing from the other side of the door was threatening to burn through the woodwork.

"Oh, that won't be necessary," said Dee. "At the moment he should not be bothered with—"

"—trivial matters?" said Vimes. "I thought it was how the thing ought to be done. I thought dwarfs always did the thing that ought to be done."

"At the moment it . . . would not be advisable," said Dee, talking very loudly again in an effort to drown out the noise. "I'm sure you understand."

"Let's assume I'm very stupid," said Vimes.

"I assure you, Your Excellency, that what I see the king sees, and what I hear the king hears."

"That's certainly true at the moment, isn't it?"

Dee drummed his fingers on his desk.

"Your Excellency, I have spent only long enough in your . . . city to gain a general insight into your ways, but I might feel you are making fun of me."

"May I speak freely?"

"From what I have heard of you, Your Monitorship, you usually do."

"Have you found the Scone of Stone yet?"

The expression on Dee's face told Vimes that he had scored. And that, almost certainly, the next thing the dwarf said would be another lie.

"What a strange and untruthful thing to say! There is no possibility that the Scone could have been stolen! This has been firmly declared! This is not a lie we wish to hear repeated!"

"You told me I—" Vimes tried. By the sound of it, there was a fight going on behind the door now.

"The Scone will be seen by all at the coronation! This is not a matter for Ankh-Morpork or anyone else! I protest this intrusion into our private affairs!"

"I merely—"

"Nor do we have to show the Scone to any prying trouble-maker! It is a sacred trust and well-guarded!"

Vimes kept quiet. Dee was better than Done It Duncan.

"Every person leaving the Scone Cave is carefully watched! The Scone cannot be removed! It is perfectly safe!"

Dee was shouting now.

"Ah, I understand," said Vimes quietly.

"Good!"

"So . . . you *haven't* found it yet, then."

Dee opened his mouth, shut it again and then slumped back in his seat.

"I think, Your Grace, that you had better—"

The door at the other end of the room rolled back. Another dwarf, cone-shaped in his robes, stamped out, stopped, glared around him, went back to the doorway again to shout some after-thoughts to whomever was beyond and then made to head out of the room. He was brought up short when he almost walked into Vimes.

The dwarf tilted its head to look up at him. There was no real face there, just the suggestion of the glint of angry eyes between the leather flaps.

"Arnak-Morporak?"

"Yes."

Vimes didn't understand the words that followed, but the nasty tone was unmistakable. The important thing was to keep smiling. That was the diplomatic way.

"Why, thank you," he said. "And may I say it—"

There was a grunt from the dwarf. He'd seen Cheery.

"*Ha'ak!*" he shouted.

Vimes heard a gasp. There were other dwarfs clustered around the doorway. Then he glanced down at Cheery. Her eyes were shut. She was trembling.

"Who is this dwarf?" he said to Dee.

"This is Albrecht Albrechtson," said the Ideas-taster.

"The runner-up?"

"Yes," said Dee hoarsely.

"Then can you tell the creature that if he uses that word again in the presence of myself or any of my staff there will be, as we diplomats say, repercussions. Wrap that up in diplomacy and give it to him, will you?"

The corners of Vimes's ears picked up a suggestion that not every dwarf listening was ignorant of the language. A couple of dwarfs were already heading purposefully toward them.

Dee babbled a stream of hysterical Dwarfish just as the other dwarfs caught up with the gaping Albrecht and led him quietly but firmly away, but not before one of them had whispered something to the Ideas-taster.

"The . . . er . . . the king wishes to see you," he mumbled.

Vimes looked toward the doorway.

More dwarfs were hurrying through it now. Some of them were dressed in what Vimes thought of as "normal" dwarf clothing, others in the heavy black leathers of the deep-down clans. All of them glared at him as they went past.

Then there was just empty floor, all the way to the door.

"Do you come, too?" he said.

"Not unless he asks for me," said Dee. "I wish you luck, Your Monitorship."

Beyond the door . . . was a room of bookshelves, stretching up, stretching away. Here and there a candle merely changed the density of the darkness. There were lots of them, though, punctuating the distance. Vimes wondered how *big* this room must be—

"In here is a record of every marriage, every birth, every death, every movement of a dwarf from one mine to another, the succession of the king of each mine, every dwarf's progress through *k'zakra*, mining claims, the history of famous axes . . . and other matters of note," said a voice behind him. "And perhaps most importantly, every decision made under dwarf law for fifteen hundred years is written down in this room, look you."

Vimes turned. A dwarf, short even by dwarf standards, was standing behind him.

He seemed to be expecting a reply.

"Er . . . every decision?"

"Oh yes."

"Er . . . were they all good?" said Vimes.

"The important thing is that they were all made," said the king. "Thank you, young . . . dwarf, you may straighten up."

Cheery was bowing.

"Sorry, should I be doing that?" said Vimes. "You're . . . not the king, are you?"

"Not yet."

"I . . . I'm . . . I'm sorry, I was expecting someone more . . . er . . ."

"Do go on."

". . . someone more . . . kingly."

The Low King sighed.

"I meant . . . I mean, you look just like an ordinary dwarf," said Vimes weakly.

This time the king smiled. He was slightly shorter than average for dwarfs, and dressed in the usual almost-uniform of leather and home-forged chain mail. He looked old, but dwarfs started looking old around the age of five years and were still looking old three hundred years later, and he had that musical cadence to his speech that Vimes associated with Llamedos. If he'd asked Vimes to pass the ketchup in Gimlet's Whole Food Delicatessen, Vimes wouldn't have given him a second look.

"This diplomacy business," said the king, "are you getting the hang of it, do you think?"

"It doesn't come easy, I must admit . . . er, Your Majesty."

"I believe you have been, up until now, a watchman in Ankh-Morpork?"

"Er, yes."

"And you had a famous ancestor, I believe, who was a regicide? Took an ax, he did, and cut the head off?"

Here it comes, thought Vimes.

"Yes, Stoneface Vimes," he said, as levelly as possible. "I've always thought that word was a bit unfair, though. It was only one king. It wasn't as if it was a *hobby*."

"You don't like kings," said the dwarf.

"I don't meet many, sir. Not in Ankh-Morpork," said Vimes, hoping that this would pass for a diplomatic answer. It seemed to satisfy the king.

"I went to Ankh-Morpork once, when I was a young dwarf," he said, walking toward a long table piled high with scrolls.

"Er . . . really?"

"Lawn ornament, they called me. And . . . what was it . . . ah, yes . . . shortass. Some children threw stones at me."

"I'm sorry."

"I expect you will tell me that sort of thing doesn't happen anymore?"

"It doesn't happen as much. But you always get idiots who don't move with the times."

The king gave Vimes a piercing glance.

"Indeed. The times . . . But now they are always Ankh-Morpork's times, see?"

"I'm sorry?"

"When people say 'we must move with the times' they really mean 'you must do it my way.' That is what I'm tellin' you. And there are *some* who would say that Ankh-Morpork is . . . a kind of vampire. It bites, and what it bites it turns into copies of itself. It sucks, too. It seems all our best go to Ankh-Morpork, where they live in squalor. You leave us dry."

Vimes was at a loss. It was clear that the little figure now sitting at the long table was a lot brighter than he was, although right now he felt as dim as a penny candle in any case. It was also clear that the king hadn't slept for quite some time. He decided to go for honesty.

"Can't really answer that, sir," he said, adopting a variant on his talking-to-Vetinari approach. "But . . ."

"Yes?"

"I'd wonder . . . you know, if I were a king . . . I'd wonder why people were happier living in squalor in Ankh-Morpork than staying back home . . . sir."

"Ah. You're telling me how I should think, now?"

"No, sir. Just how I think. But . . . there's dwarf bars all over Ankh-Morpork, and they've got mining tools wired to the wall, and there's dwarfs in 'em every night quaffing beer and singing sad songs about how they wish they were back in the mountains digging for gold. But if you said to them, fine, the gate's open, off you go and send us a postcard, they'd say, 'Oh, well, yeah, I'd love to, but we've just got the new workshop finished . . . maybe *next* year we'll go to Uberwald.'"

"They come back to the mountains to die," said the king.

"They *live* in Ankh-Morpork."

"Why is this, do you think?"

"I couldn't say, sir. Because no one tells them how to, I suppose."

"And now you want our gold and iron," said the king. "Is there *nothing* we can keep?"

"Don't know about that, either, sir. I wasn't trained for this job."

The king muttered something under his breath. Then, much louder, he said: "I can offer you no favors, Your Excellency. These are difficult times, see."

"But my real job is finding things out," said Vimes, a little louder. "If there is anything that I could do to—"

The king thrust the papers at Vimes.

"Your letters of accreditation, Your Excellency. Their contents have been noted!"

And that shuts *me* up, Vimes thought.

"I would ask you one thing, though," the king went on.

"Yes, sir?"

"*Really* thirty men and a dog?"

"No. There were only seven men. I killed one of them because I had to."

"How did the others die?"

"Er . . . victims of circumstances, sir."

"Well, then . . . your secret is safe with me. Good morning, Miss Littlebottom."

Cheery looked stunned.

The king gave her a brief smile.

"Ah, the rights of the individual, a famous Ankh-Morpork invention, or so they say. But what rights are they, really, and whence do they come? Thank you, Dee, His Excellency was just leaving. You may send in the Copperhead delegation."

As Vimes was ushered out he saw another party of dwarfs assembled in the anteroom. One or two of them nodded at him as they were herded in.

Dee turned back to Vimes.

"I hope you didn't tire his majesty."

"Someone else has already been doing that, by the look of it."

"These are sleepless times," said the Ideas-taster.

"Scone turned up yet?" said Vimes, innocently.

"Your Excellency, if you persist in this attitude a complaint will go to your Lord Vetinari!"

"He does so look forward to them. Was it this way out?"

It was the last word said until Vimes and his guards were back in the coach and the doors to daylight were opening ahead of them.

Out of the corner of his eye Vimes saw that Cheery was shaking.

"Certainly hits you, doesn't it, the cold air after the warmth underground . . ." he ventured.

Cheery grinned in relief.

"Yes, it does," she said.

"Seemed quite a decent sort," said Vimes. "What was that he muttered when I said I hadn't been trained?"

"He said 'Who has?,' sir."

"It sounded like it. All that arguing . . . it's not a case of sitting on the throne and saying 'do this, do that,' then."

"Dwarfs are very argumentative, sir. Of course, many wouldn't agree. But none of the big dwarf clans are happy about this. You know how it is—the Copperheads didn't want Albrecht, and the Shmaltzburgers wouldn't support anyone called Glodson, the Ankh-Morpork dwarfs were split both ways, and Rhys comes from a little coal-mining clan near Llamedos that isn't important enough to be on anyone's side . . ."

"You mean he didn't get to be king because everyone liked him but because no one disliked him enough?"

"That's right, sir."

Vimes glanced at the crumpled letter that the king had thrust into his hand.

By daylight he could see the faint scribble on one corner. There were just two words.

MIDNIGHT, SEE?

Humming to himself, he tore the piece of paper off and rolled it into a ball.

"And now for the damn vampire," he said.

"Don't worry, sir," said Cheery. "What's the worst she can do? Bite your head off?"

Vimes grunted. "Thank you for that, Corporal. Tell me . . . those robes some of the dwarfs were wearing . . . I know they wear them on the surface so they're not polluted by the nasty sunlight, but why wear them down there?"

"It's traditional, sir. Er . . . they were worn by the . . . well, it's what you'd call the knockermen, sir."

"What did they do?"

"Well, you know about firedamp? It's a gas you get in mines sometimes. It explodes."

Vimes saw the images in his mind as Cheery explained . . .

The miners would clear the area, if they were lucky. And the knockerman would go in, wearing layer after layer of chain mail and leather, carrying his sack of wicker globes stuffed with rags and oil. And his long pole. And his slingshot.

Down in the mines, all alone, he'd hear the knockers . . . Agi Hammerthief and all the other things that made noises, deep under the earth. There could be no light, because light would mean sudden, roaring death. The knockerman would feel his way through the utter dark, far below the surface.

There was a type of cricket that lived in the mines. It chirruped loudly in the presence of firedamp. The knockerman would have one in a box, tied to his hat.

When it sang, a knockerman who was either very confident or extremely suicidal would step back, light the torch on the end of his pole, and thrust it ahead of him. The more careful knockerman would step back rather more, and slingshot a ball of burning rags into the unseen death. Either way, he'd trust in his thick leather clothes to protect him from the worst of the blast.

It was an honorable trade but, at least to start with, it didn't run in families. They didn't *have* families. Who'd marry a knockerman? They were dead dwarfs walking. But sometimes a young dwarf would ask to become one; his family would be proud, wave him goodbye, and then speak of him as if he were dead, because that made it easier.

Sometimes, though, knockermen came back. And the ones that survived went on to survive again, because surviving is a matter of practice. And sometimes they would talk a little of what they heard, all alone in the deep mines . . . the tap-tapping of dead dwarfs trying to get back into the world, the distant laughter of Agi Hammerthief, the heartbeat of the turtle that carried the world.

Knockermen became kings.

Vimes, listening with his mouth open, wondered why the hell it was that dwarfs believed that they had no religion and no priests. Being a dwarf *was* a religion. People went into the dark for the good of the clan, and heard things, and were changed, and came back to tell . . .

And then, fifty years ago, a dwarf tinkering in Ankh-Morpork had found that if you put a simple fine mesh over your lantern flame it'd burn blue in the presence of the gas but wouldn't explode. It was a discovery of immense value to the good of dwarfkind and, as so often happens with such discoveries, almost immediately led to a war.

"And afterward there were two kinds of dwarfs," said Cheery sadly. "There's the Copperheads, who all use the lamp and the patent gas exploder, and the Shmaltzburgers, who stick to the old ways. Of course we're all *dwarfs*," she said, "but relations are rather . . . restrained."

"I bet they are."

"Oh, no, all dwarfs recognize the need for the Low King, it's just that . . ."

". . . they don't quite see why knockermen are still so powerful?"

"It's all very sad," said Cheery. "Did I tell you my brother Snorey went off to be a knockerman?"

"I don't think so."

"He died in an explosion somewhere under Borogravia. But he was doing what he wanted to do." After a moment she added, conscientiously, "Well, up to the moment when the blast hit him. After that, I don't think so."

Now the coach was rumbling up the mountain on one side of the town. Vimes looked down at the little round helmet beside him. Funny how you think you know about people, he thought.

The wheels clattered over the wood of a drawbridge.

As castles went, this one looked as though it could be taken by a small squad of not very efficient soldiers. Its builder had not been thinking about fortifications. He'd been influenced by fairy tales and possibly by some of the more ornamental sorts of cake. It was a castle for looking at. For defense, putting a blanket over your head might be marginally safer.

The coach stopped in the courtyard. To Vimes's amazement, a familiar figure in a shabby black coat came shuffling up to open the door.

"Igor?"

"Yeth, marthter?"

"What the hell are you doing here?"

"Er . . . I'm opening thif here door, marthter," said Igor.

"But why aren't you—"

Then it stole over Vimes that Igor was different. *This* Igor had both eyes the same color, and some of his scars were in different places.

"Sorry," he mumbled. "I thought you were Igor."

"Oh, you mean my *couthin* Igor," said Igor. "He workth down at the embathy. How'th he getting on?"

"Er . . . he's looking . . . well," said Vimes. "Pretty . . . well. Yes."

"Did he mention how Igor'th getting on, thir?" said Igor, shambling away so fast that Vimes had to run to keep up. "Only none of uth have heard from him, not even Igor, who'th alwayth been very clothe."

"I'm sorry? Is your whole family called Igor?"

"Oh yeth, thir. It avoidth confuthion."

"It does?"

"Yeth, thir. Anyone who ith anyone in Uberwald wouldn't dream of employing any other thervant but an Igor. Ah, here we are, thir. The mithtreth ith expecting you."

They'd walked under an arch and Igor was opening a door with far more studs in it than was respectable. This led to a hallway.

"Are you sure you want to come?" said Vimes to Cheery. "She is a vampire."

"Vampires don't worry me, sir."

"Lucky for you," said Vimes. He glanced at the silent Tantony. The man was looking as strained as Vimes felt.

"Tell our friend here he won't be needed and he's to wait for us in the coach, the lucky devil," he said. "But don't translate that last bit."

Igor opened an inner door as Tantony almost ran out of the hall.

"Hith Grathe Hith Exthelenthy—"

"Ah, Sir Samuel," said Lady Margolotta. "Do come in. I know you don't like being Your Grace. Isn't this tiresome? But it has to be done, doesn't it."

It wasn't what he'd expected. Vampires weren't supposed to wear pearls, or sweaters in pink. In Vimes's world they didn't wear sensible flat shoes, either. Or have a sitting room in which every conceivable piece of furniture was upholstered in chintz.

Lady Margolotta looked like someone's mother, although possibly someone who'd had an expensive education and a pony called Fidget. She moved like someone who had grown used to her body and, in general, looked like what Vimes had heard described as "a woman of a certain age." He'd never been quite certain what age that was.

But . . . things weren't quite right. There were *bats* embroidered on the pink sweater, and the chintzy pattern on the furniture had a sort of . . . *bat* look. The little dog with a bow round its neck, lying curled on a cushion, looked more like a rat than a dog. Vimes was less certain about that one, though; dogs of that nature tended to look a bit ratlike in any case. The effect was as if someone had read the music but had never heard it played.

He realized she was politely waiting for him, and bowed, stiffly.

"Oh, don't bother with that, please," said Lady Margolotta. "Do take a seat." She walked over to the cabinet and opened it. "Do you fancy a Bull's Blood?"

"Is that the drink with the vodka? Because—"

"No," said Lady Margolotta quietly. "This, I am afraid, is the other kind. Still, ve have that in common, don't ve? Neither of us drinks . . . alcohol. I believe you vere an alcoholic, Sir Samuel."

"No," said Vimes, completely taken aback, "I was a drunk. You have to be richer than I was to be an alcoholic."

"Ah, vell said. I have lemonade, if you vish. And Miss Littlebottom? Ve don't have beer, you'll be pleased to hear."

Cheery looked at Vimes in amazement.

"Er . . . perhaps a sherry?" she said.

"Certainly. You may leave us, Igor. Isn't he a treasure?" she added, as Igor retired.

"He certainly looks as though he's just been dug up," said Vimes. This was not going according to his mental script.

"Oh, all Igors look like that. He's been in the family for almost two hundred years. Most of him, anyvay."

"Really . . . ?"

"Extremely popular with the young ladies, for some reason. All Igors are. I've found it best not to speculate vhy." Lady Margolotta gave Vimes a bright smile. "Vell, here's to your stay, Sir Samuel."

"You know a lot about me," said Vimes weakly.

"Most of it good, I assure you," she said. "Although you're inclined to forget your papervork, you get exasperated easily, you are far too sentimental, you regret your own lack of education and distrust erudition in others, you are immensely proud of your city and you vonder if you may be a class traitor. My . . . friends in Ankh-Morpork were unable to find out anything very bad and, believe me, they are pretty good at that sort of thing. And you loathe vampires."

"I—"

"Quite understandable. Ve're dreadful people, by and large."

"But *you*—"

"I try to look on the bright side," said Lady Margolotta. "But, anyvay—how did you like the king?"

"He's very . . . quiet," said Vimes the diplomat.

"Try cunning. He vill have found out a lot more about you than you did about him, I'm sure. Vould you like a biscuit? I don't eat them myself, of course, but there's a little man down in the town that does vonderful chocolate . . . Igor?"

"Yes, mithtreth," said Igor. Vimes nearly sprayed his lemonade across the room.

"He was out of the room!" he said. "I saw him go! I heard the door shut!"

"Igor has strange vays. Do give Sir Samuel a napkin, Igor."

"You said the king was cunning," said Vimes, mopping lemonade off his breeches. Igor put down a plate of biscuits and shuffled out of the room.

"Did I? No, I don't think I could possibly have said that. It's not the diplomatic thing to say," said Lady Margolotta smoothly. "I'm sure ve all support the new Low King, the choice of dvarfdom in general, even if they thought they vere getting a traditionalist and got an unknown quantity."

"Did you just say that last bit?" said Vimes, awash on a sea of diplomacy and damp trousers.

"Absolutely not. You know their Scone of Stone has been stolen?"

"They say it hasn't," said Vimes.

"Do you believe them?"

"No."

"The coronation cannot go ahead without it, did you know that?"

"We'll have to wait until they bake another one?" said Vimes.

"No. There will be no more Low Kings," said Lady Margolotta. "Legitimacy, you see. The Scone represents continuity all the vay to B'hrian Bloodaxe. They say he sat on it vhile it vas still soft and left his impression, as it vere."

"You mean kingship has passed from bu—backside to backside?"

"Humans believe in crowns, don't they?"

"Yes, but at least they're at the other end!"

"Thrones, then." Lady Margolotta sighed. "People set such store by strange things. Crowns. Relics. Garlic . . . Anyvay . . . there will be a civil var over the leadership which Albrecht vill surely vin, and he'll cease all trading with Ankh-Morpork. Did you know that? He thinks the place is evil."

"I *know* it is," said Vimes. "And I *live* there."

"I've heard that he plans to declare all dvarfs there *d'hrarak*," the vampire went on.

Vimes heard Cheery gasp. "It means 'not dwarfs.'"

"That's very big of him," said Vimes. "I shouldn't think our lads'll worry about that."

"Um," said Cheery.

"Quite so. The young lady looks vorried, and you'd do vell to listen to her, Sir Samuel."

"Excuse me," said Vimes. "But what is all this to you?"

"You really don't drink at all, Sir Samuel?"

"No."

"Not even vun?"

"No," said Vimes, more sharply. "You'd know that, if you knew anything about—"

"Yet you keep half a bottle in your bottom drawer as a sort of permanent test," said Lady Margolotta. "Now that, Sir Samuel, suggests a man who vears his hair shirts on the inside."

"I want to know who's been saying all this!"

Lady Margolotta sighed. Vimes got the impression that he'd failed another test. "I am rich, Sir Samuel. Vampires tend to be. Didn't you know? Lord Vetinari, I know, believes that information is currency. But *everyone* knows that currency has *always* been information. Money doesn't need to talk, it merely has to listen."

She stopped and sat watching Vimes, as if she'd suddenly decided to listen. Vimes moved uncomfortably under the steady gaze.

"How is Havelock Vetinari?" she said.

"The Patrician? Oh . . . fine."

"He must be quite old now."

"I've never really been certain how old he is," said Vimes. "About my age, I suppose."

Then she stood up suddenly. "This *has* been an interesting meeting, Sir Samuel. I trust Lady Sybil is vell?"

"Er . . . yes."

"Good. I am so glad. Ve vill meet again, I am sure. Igor vill see you out. My regards to the baron, vhen you see him. Pat him on the head for me."

"What the hell was that all about, Cheery?" said Vimes, as the coach set off down the hill again.

"Which bit, sir?"

"Practically all of it, really. Why should Ankh-Morpork dwarfs object if someone says they're not dwarfs? They *know* they're dwarfs."

"They won't be subject to dwarf law, sir."

"I didn't know they were."

"I mean . . . it's like . . . how you live your life, sir. Marriages, burials . . . that sort of thing. Marriages won't be legal. Old dwarfs won't be allowed to be buried back home. And that'd be terrible. Every dwarf dreams of going back home when he's old and starting up a little mine."

"Every dwarf? Even the ones who were *born* in Ankh-Morpork?"

"Home can mean all sorts of things, sir," said Cheery. "There's other things, too. Contracts won't be valid. Dwarfs like good solid rules, sir."

"We've got laws in Ankh-Morpork, too. More or less."

"Between themselves dwarfs prefer to use their own, sir."

"I bet the Copperhead dwarfs won't like it if that happens."

"Yes, sir. There'll be a split. And another war." She sighed.

"But why was she going on about drink?"

"I don't know, sir."

"I don't like 'em. Never have, never will."

"Yes, sir."

"Did you see that rat?"

"Yes, sir."

"I think she was laughing at me."

The coach rolled through the streets of Bonk once more.

"How big a war?"

"Probably a worse one than the one fifty years ago, I expect," said Cheery.

"I don't recall people talking about that one," said Vimes.

"Most humans didn't know about it," said Cheery. "It mostly took place underground. Under mining passages and digging invasion tunnels and so on. Perhaps a few houses fell into mysterious holes and people didn't get their coal, but that was about it."

"You mean dwarfs just try to collapse mines on other dwarfs?"

"Oh yes."

"I thought you were all law-abiding?"

"Oh yes, sir. Very law-abiding. Just not very merciful."

Ye gods, thought Vimes, as the coach rolled over the bridge on the center of the town, I haven't been sent to a coronation. I've been sent to a war that hasn't started yet.

He glanced up. Tantony was watching him intently, but looked away quickly.

Lady Margolotta watched the coach until it reached the gates of the town. She stood back a little from the window. There was a slight overcast, but habits of preservation died hard.

"What a very *angry* man, Igor."

"Yeth, mithtreth."

"You can see it piling up behind his patience. I vonder how far he can be pushed?"

"I've brought the hearthe around, mithreth."

"Oh, is it that late? Ve had better be going, then. Everyone feels despondent if I miss a meeting, you know."

The castle on the other side of the valley was much more rugged than Lady Margolotta's confectionery item. Even so, the gates were wide open and didn't look as though they were often closed.

The main door was tall and heavy-looking. The only thing that suggested it hadn't been ordered from the standard castle catalog was the smaller, narrow door, a few feet high, set into it.

"What's that for?" said Vimes. "Even a dwarf would bump their head."

"I suppose it depends on what shape you are when you go in," said Cheery darkly.

The main door opened as soon as Vimes had laid his hand on the wolf's-head knocker. But he was ready this time.

"Good morning, Igor," he said.

"Good day, Your Exthelency," said Igor, bowing.

"Igor and Igor send their regards, Igor."

"Thank you, Your Exthelency. Thince you mention it, could I put a parthel on your coach for Igor?"

"You mean the Igor at the embassy?"

"That's who I thaid, thir," said Igor, patiently. "He athked me if I could lend him a hand."

"Yes, no problem there."

"Good. It'th well wrapped up and the ithe will keep it nithe and frethh. Would you thtep thith way? The marthter ith changing at the moment."

Igor shambled into a wide hall, one side of which was mostly fireplace, and bowed out.

"Did he say what I thought he said?" said Vimes. "About the hand and ice?"

"It's not what it sounds like, sir," said Cheery.

"I hope so. My gods, look at that damned thing!"

A huge red flag hung from the rafters. In the middle of it was a black wolf's head, its mouth full of stylized flashes of lightning.

"Their new flag, I think," said Cheery.

"I thought it was just a crest with the doubled-headed bat?"

"Perhaps they thought it was time for a change, sir—"

"Ah, Your Excellency! Isn't Sybil with you?"

The woman who had entered was Angua, but padded some-what with years. She was wearing a long, loose green gown, very old-fashioned by Ankh-Morpork standards, although there were some styles that never go out of style on the right figure. She was brushing her hair as she walked across the floor.

"Er . . . she's staying at the embassy today. We had rather a difficult journey. You would be the Baroness Serafine von Uberwald?"

"And you're Sam Vimes. Sybil's letters are all about you. The baron won't be long. We were out hunting and lost track of time."

"I expect it's a lot of work, seeing to the horses," said Vimes politely. Serafine's smile went strange for a moment.

"Hah. Yes," she said. "Can I get Igor to fetch you a drink?"

"No, thank you."

She sat down on one of the overstuffed chairs and beamed at him.

"You've met the new king, Your Excellency?"

"This morning."

"I believe he's having trouble."

"What makes you think that?" said Vimes. Serafine looked startled.

"I thought everyone knew?"

"Well, I've hardly been here five minutes," said Vimes. "I probably don't count as everyone."

Now, he was pleased to note, she looked puzzled.

"We . . . just heard there was some problem," she said.

"Oh, well . . . a new king, a coronation to organize . . . a few problems are bound to occur," he said. Well, he thought, so *this* is diplomacy. It's lying, only for a better class of people.

"Yes. Of course."

"Angua is well," said Vimes.

"Are you sure you won't have a drink?" said Serafine quickly, standing up. "Ah, here is my husband—"

The baron entered the room like a whirlwind which had swept up several dogs. They bounded ahead of him and danced around him.

"Hello! Hello!" he boomed.

Vimes looked at an enormous man—not fat, not tall, just built to perhaps one-tenth over scale. He didn't so much have a face with a beard as a beard with, peeking over the top in that narrow gap between the mustache and the eyebrows, small remnants of face. He bore down on Vimes in a cloud of leaping bodies, hair and a smell of old carpets.

Vimes was ready for the handshake when it came but even so had to grimace as his bones were ground together.

"Good of you to come, hey? Heard so much about you!"

But not enough, Vimes thought. He wondered if he'd ever have the use of his hand again. It was still being gripped. The dogs had transferred their attention to him. He was being sniffed.

"Greatest respect for Ankh-Morpork, hey?" said the baron.

"Er . . . good," said Vimes. Blood was getting no farther than his wrist.

"Have seat!" the baron barked. Vimes had been trying to avoid the word, but that was exactly how the man spoke—in short, sharp, sentences, every one an exclamation.

He was herded toward a chair. Then the baron let go of his hand and flung himself onto the huge carpet, the excited dogs piling on top of him.

Serafine made a noise somewhere between a growl and the "tch!" of wifely disapproval. Obediently the baron pushed the dogs aside and flung himself into a chair.

"You'll have to take us as you find us," said Serafine, smiling with her mouth alone. "This has always been a very *informal* household."

"It is a very nice place," said Vimes weakly, staring around the enormous room. Trophy heads lined the walls, but at least there were no trolls. No weapons, either. There were no spears, no rusty old swords, not even a broken bow had been hung up anywhere, which was practically against the law of castle furnishing. He stared at the wall again, and then at the carving over the fireplace. And then his gaze traveled down.

One of the dogs, and Vimes had to be clear about this, he was using the term *dogs* merely because they were indoors and that was a place where the word *wolf* was not usually encountered, was watching him. He'd never seen such an appraising look on a creature's face. It was weighing him up.

There was something familiar about the pale gold hair that was a sort of mane. In fact, the dog looked quite like Angua, but heavier set. And there was another difference, which was small yet horribly significant. As with Angua, he had this sensation of movement stilled; but, whereas Angua always looked as if she was poised to flee, this one looked poised to leap.

"The embassy is to your liking? We owned it, you know, before we sold it to Lord V . . . Ve . . ."

"Vetinari," said Vimes, reluctantly taking his eyes off the wolf.

"Of course, your people made a lot of changes," she went on.

"We've made a few more," said Vimes, recalling all those patches of shiny woodwork where the hunting trophies had been removed. "I must say I was really impressed with the bathroo— I'm sorry?"

There had been almost a yelp from the baron. Serafine was glaring at her husband.

"Yes," she said sharply, "I gather interesting things have been done."

"You're so lucky to have the thermal springs," said Vimes. And *this* was diplomacy, too, he thought, when you let your mouth chatter away while you watched people's eyes. It's just like being a copper. "Sybil wants to go to take the waters at Bad Heisses Bad—"

Behind him he heard a faint growl from the baron and saw the look of annoyance flash across Serafine's face.

"I'm saying the wrong thing?" he said innocently.

"My husband is a little unwell at the moment," said Serafine, in the special wife voice which Vimes recognized as meaning "he thinks he's fine right now but just you wait until I get him alone."

"I suppose I'd better present my credentials," said Vimes, pulling out the letter.

Serafine reached across quickly and took it from his hand.

"I shall read it," she said, smiling sweetly. "Of course, it's a mere formality. Everyone's heard of Commander Vimes. I mean no offense, of course, but we were a little surprised when the Patrician—"

"Lord Vetinari," said Vimes helpfully, putting a slight stress on the first syllable and hearing the growl on cue.

"Yes, indeed . . . said that you would be coming. We were expecting one of the more . . . experienced . . . diplomats . . ."

"Oh, I can hand around the thin cucumber sandwiches like anything," said Vimes. "And if you want little golden balls of chocolate piled up in a heap, I'm your man."

She gave him a slow, blank stare.

"Your pardon, Your Excellency," she said. "Morporkian is not my first language, and I fear we may have inadvertently misled one another. I gather that you are, in real life, a pol*ice*man?"

"In real life, yes," said Vimes.

"We've always been against a police force in Bonk," said the baroness. "We feel it interferes with the liberties of the individual."

"Well, I have certainly heard that argument advanced," said Vimes. "Of course, it depends on whether the individual you are thinking of is yourself or the one climbing out of the bathroom"—he noted the grimace—"window with the family silver in a sack."

"Happily, security has never been a problem for us," said Serafine.

"I'm not surprised," said Vimes. "I mean . . . because of all the walls and gates and things."

"I do hope you will bring Sybil to the reception this evening. But I see that we are keeping you, and I know you must have much to do. Igor will show you out."

"Yeth, mithtreth," said Igor, behind Vimes.

Vimes could feel the river of fury building up behind the levees of his mind.

"I shall tell Sergeant Angua you asked after her," he said, standing up.

"Indeed," said Serafine.

"But right now I'm looking forward to a really relaxing *bath*," said Vimes, and watched with satisfaction as both the baron and his wife flinched. "Good day to you."

Cheery marched along beside him across the hallway.

"Don't say a word until we're out of here," hissed Vimes.

"Sir?"

"Because I want to *get* out of here," said Vimes.

Several of the dogs had followed him out. They weren't growling, they hadn't bared their teeth, but they were carrying themselves with rather more purpose than Vimes had come to associate with groin-sniffers in general.

"I've put the parthel in the coach, Your Exthelenthy," said Igor, opening the coach door and knuckling his forehead.

"I'll be *sure* to give it to Igor," said Vimes.

"Oh, not to Igor, thir. Thif ith for *Igor*."

"Oh, right."

Vimes looked out of the windows as the horses trotted away. The golden-haired wolf had come to the steps and was watching him leave.

He sat back as the coach rumbled out of the castle, and closed his eyes. Cheery was wise enough to remain silent.

"No weapons on the walls, did you notice?" he said, after a while. His eyes were still shut, as if he were looking at a picture on the back of them. "Most castles like that have the things hanging all over the place."

"Well, they *are* werewolves, sir."

"Does Angua ever talk about her parents?"

"No, sir."

"They didn't want to talk about her, that's certain."

Vimes opened his eyes. "Dwarfs?" he said. "I've always got on with dwarfs. And werewolves . . . well, never had a problem with werewolves. So why is the only person who hasn't tried to blow me out this morning the blood-sucking vampire?"

"I don't know, sir."

"Big fireplace they had."

"Werewolves like to sleep in front of the fire at night, sir," said Cheery.

"The baron certainly didn't seem comfortable in a chair, I spotted that. And what was that motto carved into that great big mantelpiece? 'Homini . . .'"

"'Homo Homini Lupus,' sir," said Cheery. "It means 'Every man is a wolf to another man.'"

"Hah! Why haven't I promoted you, Cheery?"

"Because I get embarrassed about shouting at other people, sir. Sir, did you notice the strange thing about the trophies they had on the wall?"

Vimes shut his eyes again. "Stag, bears, some kind of mountain lion . . . What're you asking me, Corporal?"

"And did you notice something just below them?"

"Let's see . . . I think there was just space below them."

"Yes, sir. With three hooks in it. You could just make them out." Vimes hesitated.

"Do you mean," he said carefully, "three hooks that might have had trophies hanging from them until they were removed?"

"Very much that sort of hook, sir, yes. Only perhaps the heads haven't been hung up yet?"

"Trolls' heads?"

"Who knows, sir?"

The coach entered the town.

"Cheery, have you still got that silver chain-mail vest you used to have?"

"Er . . . no, sir. I stopped because it seemed a bit disloyal to Angua, sir. Why?"

"Just a passing thought. Oh, ye gods . . . is that Igor's parcel under the seat?"

"I think so, sir. But look, I know about Igors. If that's a real hand, the original owner hasn't got a use for it, believe me."

"What? He cuts bits off dead people?"

"Better than live people, sir."

"You know what I mean!"

"Sir, it's considered good manners, if one of the Igors has helped you, to put it in your will that they can help themselves to any . . .

bits of you that might help someone else. They never ask for any money. They're very respected in Uberwald. Very good men with a scalpel and a needle. It's a kind of vocation, really."

"But they're covered in scars and stitches!"

"They won't do to anyone else what they are not prepared to try on themselves."

Vimes decided to explore the full horror of this. It took his mind off the missing trophies.

"Are there any . . . Igorinas? Igorettes?"

"Well, any Igor is considered a good catch for a young lady . . ."

"He is?"

"And their daughters tend to be very attractive."

"Eyes at the same height, that sort of thing?"

"Oh yes."

But the door, when it was finally opened in response to impatient knocking, revealed not the switchback features of Igor but the business end of Detritus's crossbow, which was marginally worse.

"It's us, Sergeant," said Vimes.

The crossbow was removed, and the door opened farther.

"Sorry, sir, but you said I was to be on guard," said Detritus.

"There's no need to—"

"Igor's been hurt, sir."

Igor was sitting in the huge kitchen, a bandage around his head. Lady Sybil was fussing over him.

"I went to look for him a couple of hours ago and there he was, flat on the snow," she said. She leaned closer to Sam Vimes. "He doesn't remember very much."

"Can you recall what you were doing, old chap?" said Vimes, sitting down.

Igor gave him a bleary look.

"Well, thir, I went out to unpack the foodthtuffth from the other coach, and I'd just got hold of thomething and then all the lighth went out, thir. I reckon I mutht've thlipped."

"Or someone hit you?"

Igor shrugged. For a moment, both of his shoulders were at the same level.

"There's nothing on the coach worth stealing!" said Lady Sybil.

"Not unless someone was dying for a knuckle sandwich," said Vimes. "Was anything taken?"

"I checked everything against der list Her Ladyship gave me, sir," said Detritus, meeting Vimes's gaze. "There wasn't anything missing, sir."

"I'll just go and take a look for myself," said Vimes.

When they were outside he walked over to the coach and looked at the snow around it. The cobbles were visible here and there. Then he looked up at the grating.

"All right, Detritus," he said. "Talk to me."

"Just a feelin', sir," rumbled the troll. "I know 'fick' is my middle name . . ."

"I didn't know you had a *first* name, Sergeant."

"I don't fink this was one of dem accidents dat happens by accident."

"He *might* have fallen off the coach when he was unloading it," said Vimes.

"An' I might be the Fairy Clinkerbell, sir."

Vimes was impressed. This was low-temperature thinking from Detritus.

"Der street doors is open," said Detritus. "I reckon Igor disturbed someone who was pinchin' stuff."

"But you said nothing was missing."

"Maybe der thief took fright, sir."

"What, at seeing Igor? Could be . . ."

Vimes looked at the bags and boxes. Then he looked again. Things had been thrown down any old how. That wasn't how you unpacked a coach, unless you were looking for something in a real hurry. No one would go to these lengths to steal food.

"Nothing was missing . . ." He rubbed his chin. "Who *packed* the coach, Detritus?"

"Dunno, sir. I fink Her Ladyship just ordered a lot of stuff."

"And we left in a bit of a rush, too . . ." Vimes stopped. Best to leave it there. He had an idea but . . . well, where was the evidence? You could say: Nothing that should have been there was missing, so what must have been taken was something that *shouldn't* have been there. No. For now, it was just something to remember.

They walked into the hall, and Vimes's eye fell on a pile of cards on a table by the door.

"Dere's been a lot of visitors," said Detritus.

Vimes took a handful of cards. Some of them had gold edging.

"Dem diplomatics all want you to come for drinky-poos an' stories about chickens," the troll added helpfully.

"Cocktails, I think you'll find," said Vimes, reading through the pasteboards. "Hmm . . . Klatch . . . Muntab . . . Genua . . . Lancre . . . *Lancre?* It's a kingdom you could spit across! They've got an embassy here?"

"No, sir, mostly dey've got a letterbox."

"Will we all fit in?"

"Dey've rented a house for der coronation, sir."

Vimes dropped the invitations back onto the table.

223

"I don't think I can face any of this stuff," he said. "A man can only drink so much fruit juice and listen to so many bad jokes. Where is the nearest clacks tower, Detritus?"

"About fifteen miles hubward, sir."

"I'd like to find out what's going on back home. I think that this afternoon Lady Sybil and I will have a nice quiet ride in the country. It'll take her mind off this."

And then, he thought, I'll wait until midnight, see?

And it's still only lunchtime.

In the end, Vimes took Igor as driver and guide, and the guards Tantony and the one he would forever think of as Colonesque. Skimmer still hadn't returned from whatever nefarious expedition was occupying his time, and Vimes was damned if he'd leave the embassy unguarded.

Yet another word for diplomat, Vimes mused, was "spy." The only difference was that the host government knew who you were. The game was to outwit them, presumably.

The sun was warm, the breeze was cold, the mountain air made every peak look as if Vimes could reach out and touch it. Outside the town snow-covered vineyards and farms clung to slopes that in Ankh-Morpork would be called walls, but after a while the pine forests closed in. Here and there, at a curve in the road, the river was visible far below.

Up on the box, Igor was crooning a lament.

"He told me Igors heal very fast," said Lady Sybil.

"They'd have to."

"Mister Skimmer said they are very gifted surgeons, Sam."

"Except cosmetically, perhaps."

The coach slowed.

"Do you come up here a lot, Igor?" said Vimes.

"Mister Thleep used to have me drive over onthe a week to collect methages, marthter."

"I'd have thought it'd be easier to have a pickup tower in Bonk."

"The counthil are dead againtht it, thir."

"And you?"

"I am very modern in my outlook, thir."

The tower was quite close now, and loomed. The first twenty feet or so were of stone with narrow, barred windows. Then there was a broad platform from which the main tower grew. It was a sensible arrangement. An enemy would find it hard to break in or set fire to it, there was enough storage room inside to see out a siege, and the enemy would be aware that the lads inside would have signaled for help thirty seconds after the attack began. The company had money. They were like the coaching agents in that respect. If a tower went out of action, someone would be along to ask expensive questions. There was no law here; the kind of people who'd turn up would be inclined to leave a message to the world that towers were not to be touched.

Everyone should know this, and therefore it was odd to see that the big signal arms were stationary.

The hairs rose on Vimes's neck.

"Stay in the carriage, Sybil," he said.

"Is there something wrong?"

"I'm not . . . sure," said Vimes, who was sure. He stepped down and nodded to Igor.

"I'm going to have a look inside," he said. "If there is any . . . trouble, you're to get Lady Sybil back to the embassy, all right?"

Vimes leaned back into the coach and, trying not to look at Sybil, lifted up one of the seats and pulled out the sword he had hidden there.

"Sam!" she said, accusingly.

"Sorry, dear. I thought I ought to carry a spare . . ."

There was a bellpull by the door of the tower. Vimes tugged at it, and heard a clang somewhere above.

When nothing else happened, he tried the door. It swung open.

"Hello?"

There was silence.

"This is the Wa—" Vimes stopped. It wasn't the Watch, was it. Not out here. The badge didn't work. He was just an inquisitive trespassing bastard.

"Anyone there?"

The room was piled high with sacks, boxes and barrels. A wooden stairway led up to the next floor. Vimes climbed up into a combined bedroom and mess room; there were only two bunks, their covers pulled back.

A chair was on the floor. A meal was on the table, knife and fork laid down carefully. On the stove something had boiled dry in an iron pot. Vimes opened the firebox door, and there was a *whoomph* as the inrushing air rekindled the charred wood.

And, from above, the *chink* of metal.

He looked at the ladder and trapdoor to the next floor. Anyone climbing it would be presenting their head at a convenient height for a blade or a boot—

"Tricky, isn't it, Your Grace," said someone above him. "You'd better come up. Mmm, mhm."

"*Inigo?*"

"It's safe enough, Your Grace. There's only me here. Mmm."

"That counts as safe, does it?"

Vimes climbed the ladder. Inigo was sitting at a table, leafing through a stack of papers.

226

"Where's the crew?"

"That, Your Grace," said Inigo, "is one of the mysteries, mmm, mmm."

"And the others are—?"

Inigo nodded toward the steps leading upward. "See for yourself."

The controls for the arms had been comprehensively smashed. Laths and bits of wire dangled forlornly from their complex framework.

"Several hours of repair work for skilled men, I'd say," said Inigo, as Vimes returned.

"What happened here, Inigo?"

"I would say the men who lived here were forced to leave, mmm, mhm. In some disorder."

"But it's a fortified tower!"

"So? They have to cut firewood. Oh, the company has rules, and then they put three young men in some lonely tower for weeks at a time and they expect them to act like clockwork people. See the trapdoor up to the controls? That should be locked at all times. Now you, Your Grace, and myself as well, because we are . . . are—"

"—bastards?" Vimes supplied.

"Well, yes . . . mmm . . . we'd have devised a system that meant the clacks couldn't even be operated unless the trapdoor was shut, wouldn't we?"

"Something like that, yes."

"And we'd have written into the rules that the presence of *any* visitor in the tower would, mhm, be automatically transmitted to the neighboring towers, too."

"Probably. That'd be a start."

"As it is, I suspect that any harmless-looking visitor with a nice fresh apple pie for the lads would be warmly welcomed," sighed

Inigo. "They do two-month shifts at a time. Nothing to look at but trees, mmm."

"No blood, not much sign of a struggle," said Vimes. "Have you checked outside?"

"There should be a horse in the stable. It's gone. We're more or less on rock here. There's wolf tracks, but there's wolf tracks everywhere around here. And the wind's blown the snow. They've . . . gone, Your Grace."

"Are you *sure* the men let someone in through the door?" Vimes said. "Anyone who could land on the platform could be in one of these windows in an instant."

"A vampire, mmm?"

"It's a thought, isn't it."

"There's no blood around . . ."

"It's a shame to waste good food," said Vimes. "Think of those poor starving children in Muntab. What are *these*?"

He pulled a box from under the lower bunk. Inside it were two long tubes, about a foot long, open at one end.

"'Badger and Normal, Ankh-Morpork,'" he read aloud. "'Mortar Flare (Red). Light Fuse. Do Not Place In Mouth.' It's a firework, Mister Skimmer. I've seen them on ships."

"Ah, there was something . . ." Inigo leafed through the book on the table. "They could send up an emergency flare if there's a big problem. Yes . . . the tower nearest Ankh-Morpork will send out a couple of men and a bigger squad comes up from the depot down on the plains. They take a downed tower very seriously."

"Yes, well, it could cost them money," said Vimes, peering into the mouth of the mortar. "We need this tower working, Inigo. I don't like being stuck out here."

"The roads aren't too bad yet. They could be here by tomorrow evening— I'm sure you shouldn't do that, sir!"

Vimes had pulled the mortar out of its tube. He looked at Inigo quizzically.

"They won't go off until you light the charge in the base," he said. "They're safe. And they'd make a stupid weapon, 'cos you can't aim them worth a damn and they're only made of cardboard in any case. Come on, let's get it onto the roof."

"Not until dark, Your Grace, mmm. That way two or three towers on each side will see it, not just the closest."

"But the closest towers are watching they'll certainly see—"

"We don't know that there is anyone there to watch, sir. Perhaps what happened here has happened there, too? Mmm?"

"Good grief! You don't think—"

"No, I don't think, sir, I'm a civil servant. I advise other people, mmm, mmm. Then *they* think. My advice is that an hour or two won't hurt, sir. My advice is that you return with Lady Sybil *now*, sir. I will send up a flare as soon as it is dark and make my way back to the embassy."

"Hold on, I *am* Commander in—"

"Not here, Your Grace. Remember? Here you are a civilian in the way, mhm, mmm. I'll be safe enough—"

"The crew weren't."

"They weren't me, mhm, mhm. For the sake of Lady Sybil, Your Grace, I *advise* you to leave *now*."

Vimes hesitated, hating the fact that Inigo was not only right but was, despite his claim to mindlessness, doing the thinking that he should be doing. He was supposed to be out for an afternoon's drive with his wife, for heaven's sake.

"Well . . . all right. Just one thing, though. Why are *you* here?"

"The last time Sleeps was seen he was on his way up here with a message."

"Ah. And am I right in thinking that your Mister Sleeps was not exactly the kind of diplomat that hands around the cucumber sandwiches?"

Inigo smiled thinly.

"That's right, sir. He was . . . the other sort. Mmm."

"Your sort."

"Mmm. And now *go*, Your Grace. The sun will be setting soon. Mmm, mmm."

Corporal Nobbs, President and Convenor of the Guild of Watchmen, surveyed his troops.

"All right, one more time," he said. "Whadda we want?"

The strike meeting had been going on for some time, and it had been going on in a bar. The watchmen were already a little forgetful.

Constable Ping raised his hand.

"Er . . . a proper grievance procedure, a complaints committee, an overhaul of the promotion procedures . . . er . . ."

"—better crockery in the canteen," someone supplied.

"—freedom from unwarranted accusations of sucrose theft," said someone else.

"—no more than seven days straight on nights—"

"—an increase in the boots allowance—"

"—at least three afternoons off for grandmother's funerals per year—"

"—not having to pay for our own pigeon feed—"

"—another drink." This last demand met with general approval.

Constable Shoe got to his feet. He was still, in his spare time, organizer of the Campaign for Dead Rights, and he knew how this sort of thing went.

"No, no, no, no, *no*," he said. "You've got to get it a lot simpler than that. It's got to have *bounce*. And rhythm. Like 'Whadda we want? *Dum*-dee-*dum*-dee. When do we want it? Now!' See? You need one simple demand. Let's try it again. Whadda we want?"

The watchmen looked at one another, no one quite wanting to be the first.

"Another drink?" someone volunteered.

"Yeah!" said someone at the back. "When do we want it? NOW!"

"Well, that one seems to have worked," said Nobby, as the policemen crowded round the bar. "What else are we going to need, Reg?"

"Signs for the picket," said Constable Shoe.

"We've got to picket?"

"Oh yes."

"In that case," said Nobby firmly, "we've got to have a big metal drum to burn old scrap wood in, while we're pickin' at it."

"Why?" said Reg.

"You *got* to stand around warmin' your hands over a big drum," said Nobby. "That's how people know you're an official picket and not a bunch of bums."

"But we *are* a bunch of bums, Nobby. People think we are, anyway."

"All right, but let's be warm ones."

The sun was a finger's width above the rim when Vimes's coach set off from the tower. Igor whipped the horses up. Vimes looked out of the window at the road's edge, a few feet away and several hundred feet above the river.

"Why so fast?" he shouted.

"Got to be home by thunthet!" Igor shouted. "It'th *tradithional*."

The big red sun was moving through bars of cloud.

"Oh, let him, dear, if it gives the poor soul any pleasure," said Lady Sybil, shutting the window. "Now, Sam, what happened at the tower?"

"I don't really want to worry you, Sybil . . ."

"Well, now that you've got me *really* worried, you may as well tell me. All right?"

Vimes gave in and explained the little that he knew.

"Someone's killed them?"

"Possibly."

"The same people that ambushed us back in that gorge?"

"I don't think so."

"This isn't turning out to be much of a holiday, Sam."

"It's not being able to *do* anything that makes me sick," said Vimes. "Back in Ankh-Morpork . . . well, I'd have leads, contacts, some kind of a map. Everyone here is . . . well, hiding something, I think. The new king thinks I'm a fool, the werewolves treated me as if I was something the cat dragged in . . . the only person who's been halfway civil was a vampire!"

"Not the cat," said Sybil.

"What?" said Vimes, mystified.

"Werewolves hate cats," said Sybil. "I distinctly remember that. Definitely not cat people."

"Hah. No. Dog people. They don't like words like *bath* or *vet*, either. I reckon if you threw a stick at the baron he'd leap out of his chair to catch it—"

"I suppose I ought to tell you about the carpets," said Sybil, as the coach rocked around a corner.

"What, isn't he house-trained?"

"I meant the carpets in the embassy. You know I said I'd measure up for them? But the measurements aren't right, on the first floor . . ."

"I don't want to sound impatient, dear, but is this a carpet moment?"

"Sam?"

"Yes, dear?"

"Just stop thinking like a husband and start listening like a . . . a copper, will you?"

Vimes marched into the embassy and summoned Detritus and Cheery.

"You two are coming with us to the ball tonight," he said. "It'll be posh. Have you got anything to wear apart from your uniform, Sergeant?"

"No, sir."

"Well, go and see Igor. There's a good man with a needle if I ever saw one. How about you, Cheery?"

"I do, er, have a gown," said Cheery, looking down shyly.

"You do?"

"Yes, sir."

"Oh. Well. Good. I'm putting the two of you on the embassy staff, too. Cheery, you're . . . you're Military Attaché."

"Oh," said Detritus, disappointed.

"And, Detritus, you're Cultural Attaché."

The troll brightened up considerably. "You will not regret dis, sir!"

"I'm sure I won't," said Vimes. "Right now, I'd like you to come with me."

"Is dis a cultural matter, sir?"

"Broadly. Perhaps."

Vimes led the troll and Sybil up the stairs and into the office, where he stopped in front of a wall.

"This one?" he said.

"Yes," said his wife. "It's hard to notice until you measure the rooms, but that wall really is rather thick—"

Vimes ran his hands along the paneling, looking for anything that might go *click*. Then he stood back.

"Give me your crossbow, Sergeant."

"Here we are, sir."

Vimes staggered under its weight, but managed to get it pointed at the wall.

"Is this wise, Sam?" said Sybil.

Vimes stood back to take aim, and the floorboard moved under his heel. A panel in the wall swung gently.

"You scared der hell out of it, sir," said Detritus loyally.

Vimes carefully handed the crossbow back, and tried to look as though he'd meant things to happen this way.

He'd expected a secret passage. But this was a tiny workroom. There were jars on shelves, with labels . . . NEW SUET STRATA, AREA 21, GRADE A FAT, THE BIG HOLE. There were lumps of crumbling rock, with neat cardboard tags attached to them saying things like LEVEL #3, SHAFT 9, DOUBLE-PICK MINE.

There was a set of drawers. One of them was full of makeup, including a selection of mustaches.

Wordlessly, Vimes opened one of a stack of notebooks. The first pages had a pencil-drawn street map of Bonk, with red lines threading through it.

"Good grief, look at this," he breathed, flicking onward. "Maps. Drawings. There's pages of stuff about the assaying of fat deposits.

Huh, says here '. . . the new suets, while initially promising, are now suspected of having high levels of BCBs and are likely to be soon exhausted.' And *here* it says 'A werewolf putsch is clearly planned in the chaos following the loss of the Scone' . . . 'K. reports that many of the younger werewolves now follow W., who has changed the nature of the Game'. . . This stuff . . . this stuff is *spying*. I wondered how Vetinari always seems to know so much!"

"Did you think it came to him in dreams, dear?"

"But there's loads of details here . . . notes about people, lots of figures about dwarf mining production, political rumors . . . I didn't know we did this sort of thing!"

"You use spies all the time, dear," said Sybil.

"I do not!"

"Well, what about people like Foul Ole Ron and No Way José and Cumbling Michael?"

"That is *not* spying, that is *not* spying! That's just 'information received.' We couldn't do the job if we didn't know what's happening on the street!"

"Well . . . perhaps Havelock just thinks in terms of . . . a bigger street, dear."

"There's loads more of this muck, look. Sketches, more bits of ore . . . what the hell's this?"

It was oblong, and about the size of a cigarette packet. There was a round glass disk on one face, and a couple of levers on one side.

Vimes pushed one of them. A tiny hatch opened on one side, and the smallest head that he'd ever seen that could speak said " 's?"

"I know dat!" said Detritus. "Dat's a nano-imp! Dey cost over a hundred dollars! Dey're really *small*!"

"No one's bloody fed me for a fortnight!" the imp squeaked.

"It's an iconograph small enough to fit in a *pocket*," said Vimes. "Something for a spy . . . it's as bad as Inigo's damn one-shot crossbow. And look . . ."

Steps led downward. He took them carefully, and swung open the little door at the end.

Wet heat slapped into him.

"Pass me down a candle, will you, dear?" he said. And by its light he looked out into a long dank tunnel. Crusted pipes, leaking steam at every joint, lined the far wall.

"A way in and out where no one will see him, too," he said. "What a dirty world we live in . . ."

The clouds had covered the sky and the wind was whipping thick snowflakes around the tower when Inigo finished setting up the red mortar on the platform below the big square shutters.

He lit a couple of matches but the wind streamed them out before he could even cup his hands around them.

"Damn. Mmm, mmm."

He slid down the ladder and into the warmth of the tower. It'd be better to spend the night here, he thought, as he rummaged in drawers. The night didn't hold many terrors for him, but this storm had the feel of another big snow and the mountain roads would soon be treacherous.

Finally an idea struck him, and he opened the door of the stove and pulled out a smoldering log on the tongs.

It burst into flame when he carried it out at the top of the tower, and he directed them into the touch hole at the base of the tube.

The mortar fired with a *phut* that was lost in the wind. The flare itself tumbled invisibly up into the snow and then, a few seconds later, exploded a hundred feet overhead, casting a brief red glare over the forests.

Inigo had just gotten back into the room when there was a knock at the door, down at ground level.

He paused. There was a window and hatch at this level; the designers of the tower had at least realized that it would be a good idea to be able to look down and see who was a-knocking.

There was no one there.

When he'd climbed back into the room, the knock came again.

He hadn't locked the door after Vimes went. A bit late to regret that now, he realized. But Inigo Skimmer had trained in an academy that made the School of Hard Knocks look like a sandpit.

He lit a candle and crept down the ladder in the darkness, shadows fleeing and dancing among the stacks of provisions.

With the candle set down on a box, he pulled the one-shot crossbow from inside his coat and, with an effort, cocked it against the wall. Then he flexed his left arm and felt the palm dagger ease itself into position.

He clicked his heels in a certain way and sensed the tiny blades slide out from the toes.

And Inigo settled down to wait.

Behind him, something blew the candle out.

As he turned, and the crossbow's one bolt whirred into darkness, and the palm dagger scythed at nothing, it occurred to Inigo Skimmer that you could knock on *either* side of a door.

They really *were* very clever . . .

"Mhm, m—"

Cheery twirled, or at least attempted to. It was not a movement that came naturally to dwarfs.

"You look very . . . nice," said Lady Sybil. "It goes all the way to the ground, too. I don't think anyone could possibly complain."

Unless they were remotely fashion conscious, she had to admit.

The problem was that the . . . well, she had to think of them as the *new* dwarf women—hadn't quite settled on a look.

Lady Sybil herself usually wore ball gowns of a light blue, a color often chosen by ladies of a certain age and girth to combine the maximum of quiet style with the minimum of visibility. But dwarf girls had heard about sequins. They seemed to have decided in their bones that, if they were going to overturn thousands of years of subterranean tradition, they weren't going to go all through that for no damn twinset and pearls.

"And red is *good*," said Lady Sybil sincerely. "Red is a very nice color. It's a nice red dress. Er. And the feathers. Er. The bag to carry your ax, er—"

"Not glittery enough?" said Cheery.

"No! No . . . if I was going to carry a large ax on my back to a diplomatic function, I think I'd want it glittery, too. Er. It is such a very *large* ax, of course," she finished lamely.

"You think perhaps a smaller one might be better? For evening wear?"

"That would be a start, yes."

"Perhaps with a few rubies set in the handle?"

"Yes," said Lady Sybil weakly. "Why not, after all?"

"What about me, Ladyship?" Detritus rumbled.

Igor had certainly risen to the occasion, applying to a number of suits found in the embassy wardrobes the same pioneering surgical skills that he used on unfortunate loggers and other people who may have strayed too close to a band saw. It had taken him just ninety minutes to construct something around Detritus. It was definitely evening dress. You couldn't get away with it in daylight. The troll looked like a wall with a bow tie.

"How does it all feel?" said Lady Sybil, playing for safety.

"It are rather tight around der—what's this bit called?"

"I really have no idea," said Lady Sybil.

"It makes me lurch a bit," said Detritus. "But I feel very diplomatic."

"Not the crossbow, however," said Lady Sybil.

"*She* got her ax," said Detritus accusingly.

"Dwarf axes are accepted as a cultural weapon," said Lady Sybil. "I don't know the etiquette here, but I suppose you could get away with a club." After all, she added to herself, it's not as though anyone would try to take it off you.

"Der crossbow ain't cultural?"

"I'm afraid not."

"I could put, like, glitter on it."

"Not enough, I'm afraid— Oh, Sam . . ."

"Yes, dear?" said Vimes, coming down the stairs.

"That's just your Watch dress uniform! What about your ducal regalia?"

"Can't find it anywhere," said Vimes innocently. "I think the bag must have fallen off the coach in the pass, dear. But I've got a helmet with feathers in it and Igor's buffed up the breastplate until he could see his face in it, although I'm not sure why." He quailed at her expression. "Duke is a military term, dear. No soldier would ever go to war in tights. Not if he thought he might be taken prisoner."

"I find this *highly* suspicious, Sam."

"Detritus will back me up on this," said Vimes.

"Dat's right, sir," the troll rumbled. "You distinctly said to say dat—"

"Anyway, we'd better be goi— Good grief, is that Cheery?"

"Yes, sir," said Cheery nervously.

Well, thought Vimes, she comes from a family where people go off in strange clothes to face explosions far away from the sun.

"Very nice," he said.

Lamps were lit all along the tunnel to what Vimes had come to think of as Downtown Bonk. Dwarf guards waved the coach through after mere glances at the Ankh-Morpork crest. The ones around the giant elevator were more uncertain. But Sam Vimes had learned a lot from watching Lady Sybil. She didn't mean to act like that, but she'd been born to it, into a class which had always behaved this way: You went through the world as if there was *no possibility* that anyone would stop you or question you, and most of the time that's exactly what didn't happen.

There were others in the elevator as it rumbled downward. Mostly they were diplomats that Vimes didn't recognize, but there was also, now, in a roped-off corner, a quartet of dwarf musicians playing pleasant yet slightly annoying music that ate its way into Vimes's head as the interminable descent went on.

When the doors opened he heard Sybil gasp.

"I thought you said it was like a starry night down here, Sam!"

"Er . . . they've certainly turned the wick up . . ."

Candles by the thousand burned in brackets all around the walls of the huge cavern, but it was the chandeliers that caught the eye.

There were scores of them, each at least four stories high. Vimes, always ready to look for the wires behind the smoke and mirrors, made out the dwarfs working inside the gantries and the baskets of fresh candles being lowered through holes in the ceiling. If the Fifth Elephant wasn't a myth, at least one whole toe must be being burned tonight.

"Your Grace!"

Dee was advancing through the crowds.

"Ah, Ideas-taster," said Vimes, as the dwarf approached, "do allow me to introduce the Duchess of Ankh-Morpork . . . Lady Sybil."

"Uh . . . er . . . yes . . . indeed . . . so delighted to make your acquaintance . . ." Dee murmured, caught off-guard by the charm offensive. "But, er . . ."

Sybil had picked up the code. Vimes loathed the word "duchess," so if he was using it then he wanted her to out-dutch everyone. She enveloped Dee's pointy head in delighted Duchessness.

"Mister Dee, Sam has told me *so* much about you!" she trilled. "I understand you're *quite* the right-hand man—"

"—dwarf—" hissed Vimes.

"—dwarf to his majesty! Please, you *must* tell me how you have achieved such a *delightful* lighting effect here!"

"Er . . . lots of candles . . ." Dee muttered, glaring at Vimes.

"I think Dee wishes to discuss some political matters with me, dear," said Vimes smoothly, putting his hand on the dwarf's shoulder. "If you'll just take the others down, I'll join you shortly, I'm sure." And he knew that no power in the world was going to prevent Sybil sweeping on down to the reception. That woman could *sweep*. Things stayed swept after she'd gone past.

"You brought a troll, you brought a *troll*!" muttered Dee.

"And he's an Ankh-Morpork citizen, remember," said Vimes. "Covered by diplomatic immunity and a rather bad suit."

"Even so—"

"There is no 'even so,'" said Vimes.

"We are at *war* with the trolls!"

"Well, that's what diplomacy is all about, isn't it?" said Vimes. "A way to *stop* being at war? Anyway, I understand it's been going on for five hundred years, so obviously no one is trying very hard."

"There will be complaints at the very highest level!"

Vimes sighed. "More?" he said.

"Some are saying Ankh-Morpork is deliberately flaunting its wickedness at the king!"

"The king?" said Vimes pleasantly. "He's not *exactly* king yet, is he? Not until the coronation, which involves a certain . . . object . . ."

"Yes, but of course that is a mere formality . . ."

Vimes moved closer.

"But it isn't, is it?" he said quietly. "It is the thing and the whole of the thing. Without the magic, there is no king. Just someone like you, unaccountably giving orders."

"Someone called Vimes teaches me about royalty?" said Dee, miserably.

"And without the thing, all the bets are off," said Vimes. "There will be a war. Explosions underground."

There was a tinny little sound as he took out his watch and opened it.

"My word, it's midnight," he said.

"Follow me," Dee muttered.

"Am I being taken to see something?" said Vimes.

"No, Your Excellency. You are being taken to see where something is not."

"Ah. Then I want to bring Corporal Littlebottom."

"*That?* Absolutely not! That would be a desecration of—"

"No, it wouldn't," said Vimes. "And the reason is, she *won't* come with us because we're *not* going, are we? You're certainly not taking the representative of a potentially hostile power into your confidence and revealing that your house of cards is missing a card on the bottom layer, are you? Of course not. We are not having this conversation. For the next hour or so we'll be nibbling tidbits in this room. I haven't even just said this, and you didn't hear me. But Corporal Littlebottom is the best scene-of-crime officer I've got, and so I want her to come along with us."

"You've made your point, Your Excellency. Graphically, as always. Fetch her, then."

Vimes found Cheery standing back to back, or at least back to knees, with Detritus. They were surrounded by a ring of the curious. Whenever Detritus raised his hand to sip his drink, the nearby dwarfs jumped back hurriedly.

"Where are we going, sir?"

"Nowhere."

"Ah. That sort of place."

"But things are looking up," said Vimes. "Dee has discovered a new pronoun, even if he does spit it."

"Sam!" said Lady Sybil, advancing through the throng. "They're going to perform 'Bloodaxe and Ironhammer'! Isn't that wonderful?"

"Er . . ."

"It's an opera, sir," Cheery whispered. "Part of the Koboldean Cycle. It's *history*. Every dwarf knows it by heart. It's about how we got laws, and kings . . . and the Scone, sir."

"I sang the part of Ironhammer when we did it at finishing school," said Lady Sybil. "Not the full five-week version, of course. It'd be marvelous to see it done here. It's really one of the great romances of history."

"Romances?" said Vimes. "Like . . . a love story?"

"Yes. Of course."

"Bloodaxe and Ironhammer were both . . . er . . . weren't both . . ." Vimes began.

"They were both *dwarfs*, sir," said Cheery.

"Ah. Of course." Vimes gave up. All dwarfs were dwarfs. If you tried to understand their world from a human point of view, it all went wrong. "Do, er, enjoy it, dear. I've got to . . . the king wants me to . . . I'll just be somewhere else for a while . . . politics . . ."

He hurried away, with Cheery trailing behind him.

Dee led the way through dark tunnels. When the opera began it was a whisper far away, like the sea in an ancient shell.

Eventually they stopped at the edge of a canal, its waters lapping at the darkness. A small boat was tethered there, with a waiting guard. Dee urged them into it.

"It is important that you understand what you are seeing, Your Grace," said Dee.

"Practically nothing," said Vimes. "And I thought *I* had good night vision."

There was a clink in the gloom, and then a lamp was lit. The guard was punting the boat under an arch and into a small lake. Apart from the tunnel entrance, the walls rose up sheer.

"Are we at the bottom of a well?" said Vimes.

"That is quite a good way of describing it." Dee fished under his seat. He produced a curved metal horn and blew one note, which echoed up the rock walls.

After a few seconds another note floated down from the top. There was a clanking, as of heavy, ancient chains.

"This is quite a short lift compared to some up in the mountains," said Dee, as an iron plate ground across the entrance, sealing it. "There's one half a mile high that will take a string of barges . . ."

Water boiled beside the boat. Vimes saw the walls begin to sink.

"This is the *only* way to the Scone," said Dee behind him.

Now the boat was rocking in the bubbling water and the walls were blurred.

"Water is diverted into reservoirs up near the peaks. Then it is simply a matter of opening and closing sluices, you see?"

"Yes," mumbled Vimes, experiencing vertigo and seasickness in one tight green package.

The walls slowed. The boat stopped shaking. Smoothly, the water lifted them over the lip of the well and into a little channel, where there was a dock.

"Any guards below?" Vimes managed, stepping out onto the blessedly solid stone.

"There are usually four," said Dee. "For tonight I . . . arranged matters. The guards understand. No one is proud of this. I must tell you, I disapprove *most strongly* of this enterprise."

Vimes looked around the new cave. A couple of dwarfs were standing on a lip of stone which overlooked what was now a placid pool. By the look of it, they were the ones who operated the machinery.

"Shall we proceed?" said the dwarf.

There was a passage leading off the cave, which rapidly narrowed. Vimes had to bend almost double along one length. At one point metal plates clanked under his feet, and he felt them shift slightly. Then he was standing almost upright again, passing under another arch, and there . . .

Either the dwarfs had cut into a huge geode, or they had with great care lined this small cave with quartz crystals until every surface reflected the light of the two small candles that stood on pillars in the middle of the sandy floor. The effect dazzled even Vimes, after the darkness of the tunnels.

"Behold," said Dee gloomily, "where the Scone should be . . ."

A round flat stone, midway between the candles and only a few inches high, clearly contained nothing.

Behind it, water bubbled up in a natural basin and split into two streams that flowed around the stone and disappeared again into another stone funnel.

"All right," said Vimes. "Tell me everything."

"It was found missing three days ago," said Dee. "Dozy Longfinger found it gone when he unlocked the door to replace the candles."

"And his job is . . . ?"

"Captain of the Candles."

"Ah."

"It's a very responsible position."

"I've seen the chandeliers. And how often does he go in there?"

"He went in there every day."

"Went?"

"He no longer holds the position."

"Because he's a prime suspect?" said Vimes.

"Because he's dead."

"And how did that happen?" said Vimes, slowly and deliberately.

"He . . . took his own life. We are certain of this, because we had to break down the door of his cave. He'd had been Captain of the Candles for sixty years. I do not think he could bear the thought of suspicion falling on him."

"To me he *does* sound a likely suspect."

"He did not steal the Scone. We know that much."

"But the robes you people wear could hide practically anything. Was he searched?"

"Certainly not! But . . . I shall demonstrate," said Dee. He walked off along the narrow, metal-floored corridor.

"Can you see me, Your Excellency?"

"Yes, of course."

The floor rattled as Dee came back. "Now this time I will carry something . . . your helmet, if you please? Just for the demonstration . . ."

Vimes handed it to him. The Ideas-taster walked back down the corridor. When he was halfway, a gong boomed and two metal grids dropped down out of the ceiling. A few seconds after that guards appeared at the far grille, peering in suspiciously.

Dee said a few words to them. The faces vanished. After a while, the grilles rose slowly.

"The mechanism is complex and quite old but we keep it in good working order," he said, handing Vimes his helmet. "If you weigh more going out than going in, the guards will want to know why. It is unavoidable, it is still accurate to within a few ounces, and does not violate privacy. The only way to beat it would be to fly. Can thieves fly, Your Excellency?"

"Depends on which sort," said Vimes absently. "Who else goes in there?"

"Once every six days the chamber is inspected by myself and two guards. The last inspection was five days ago."

"Does anyone else go in there?" said Vimes. He noticed that Cheery had picked up a handful of the off-white sand that formed the floor of the Scone cave and was letting it run between her fingers.

"Not lately. When the new king is crowned, of course, the Scone will often be brought forth for various ceremonial purposes."

"Do you only get that white sand in here?"

"Yes. Is that important?"

Vimes saw Cheery nod.

"I'm not . . . sure," he said. "Tell me, what intrinsic value has the Scone?"

"Intrinsic? It's priceless!"

"I know it's valuable as a symbol, but what is its value in *itself*?"

"Priceless!"

"I'm trying to work out why a thief might want to steal it," said Vimes, as patiently as he could.

Cheery had lifted up the flat round stone and was looking underneath it. Vimes pursed his lips.

"What is . . . *she* doing?" said Dee. The pronoun dripped with distaste.

"Constable Littlebottom is looking for clues," said Vimes. "They are what we call . . . signs, which may help us. It's a skill."

"Would this letter speed your search?" said Dee. "It has writing on it. That is what we call . . . signs, which may help you."

Vimes looked at the proffered paper. It was brown, and quite stiff, and covered in runes.

"I, er, can't read those," he said.

"It's a skill," said Dee, solemnly.

"I can, sir," said Cheery. "Allow me?"

She took the paper and read it.

"Er . . . it appears to be a ransom note, sir. From . . . the Sons of Agi Hammerthief. They say they have the Scone and will . . . they say they'll destroy it, sir."

"Where's the money?" said Vimes.

"No money, sir. They say Rhys must renounce all claim to be Low King."

"There are no other conditions," said Dee. "The note turned up on my desk. But *everyone* puts paperwork on my desk these days."

"Who are the Sons of Agi Hammerthief?" said Vimes, looking at Dee. "And why didn't you tell me about this before?"

"We don't know. It is just a made-up name. Some . . . malcontents, we assume. And I was told *you* would ask *me* questions."

"But this isn't a real crime anymore, is it?" said Vimes. "This is politics. Why can't the king just renounce all claim, get the Scone back, and then say he had his fingers crossed? If it's done under duress—"

"We take our ceremonies seriously, Your Excellency. If Rhys renounces the throne, he cannot change his mind the next day. If he allows the Scone to be destroyed, then the kingship has no legitimacy and there will—"

"—be trouble," said Vimes. And it'll spread to Ankh-Morpork, he added to himself. At the moment it's only riots.

"Who'll become king if he abdicates?"

"Albrecht Albrechtson, as everyone knows."

"And that will be trouble, too," said Vimes. "Civil war, from what I hear."

"The king says," said Dee quietly, "that he intends to step down nevertheless. Better any king than chaos. Dwarfs do not like chaos."

"It's going to be chaos either way, though," said Vimes.

"There have been rebellions against kings before. Dwarfdom survives. The crown continues. The lore abides. The Stone remains. There is . . . a sanity to come back to."

Oh, my gods, thought Vimes. Thousands of dwarfs die but that's all right if a lump of rock survives. "I'm not a policeman here. What can I do?"

"This hasn't happened!" shrieked Dee, his nerve cracking. "But everyone knows foreigners from Ankh-Morpork do not mind their own business!"

"Ah . . . you mean . . . given that you don't want people to know about this . . . it would look bad if you appeared to be too excited . . . but you can't be blamed if a stupid flatfoot pokes his nose into things . . . ?"

Dee waved his hands in the air. "This wasn't my idea!"

"Look, the security you have got here would disgrace a child's piggy bank. I can think of two or three ways of getting the Scone out of here. What about the secret passage into this room?"

"I know of no secret passage into this room!"

"Oh, *good*. At least we've ruled out *something*. Go and wait by the boat. Corporal Littlebottom and I have to talk about some things."

Dee left reluctantly. Vimes waited until the dwarf was visible in the glow of the candles beyond the weighing bridge.

"What a mess," he said. "Locked-room mysteries are even worse when they leave the room unlocked."

"You're thinking that Dozy might have worn bags of sand under his robes, aren't you, sir," said Cheery.

No, thought Vimes. I wasn't. But now I know how a dwarf would solve this.

"Possibly," he said aloud. "Grubby white sand can't be uncommon. You'd add a bit of sand every day, yes? Just enough not to trigger the scales. Finally you've got . . . how much does the Scone weigh?"

"About sixteen pounds, sir."

"All right. Dump the sand on the floor, shove the Scone under your robes and . . . it might just work."

"Risky, sir."

"But no one thinks anyone is really going to *try* to steal the Scone. Would you try to tell me that four guards sitting in that little guardhouse on a twelve-hour shift will be alert *all* the time? That's enough for a hand of poker!"

"I suppose they rely on the fact that they'd know when a boat came up, sir."

"Right. Big mistake. And you know what? I *bet* that when a boat's just gone down, that's the time they're least alert. Cheery, if a human could get in here, they could get into the Scone room. They'd have to be nimble and a good swimmer, but they could do it."

"The guards on the gates were pretty keen, sir."

"Well, *yes*. Guards always are, just after a theft. Smart as foxes and sharp as knives, just in case anyone wonders if it was *them* who dropped off to sleep at the wrong time. I'm a *copper*, Cheery. I know how dull guarding can be. Especially when you know that no one is ever going to steal what you're guarding."

He scuffed the sand with his boot.

"They were looking hard at every cart that went in or out this morning. But that was because the Scone had *been* stolen. It's at times like this you get very official, very efficient and very pointless activity. Don't try to tell me that last week they opened every barrel and prodded every load of hay. Even the stuff coming *in*? Can you see Dee? Is he looking at me?"

Cheery peered around Vimes.

"No, sir."

"Good."

Vimes walked over to the tunnel, pressed his back against a wall, took a deep breath and walked his legs up the opposite wall. Then he eased his way out over the plates of the weigh-bridge, inched along with feet and shoulder blades and, wincing at every protest from his knees, eventually dropped down. He strolled over to Dee, who was talking to the guards.

"How did—"

"Never mind," said Vimes. "Let's just say I'm longer than a dwarf, shall we?"

"Have you solved it?"

"No. But I have an idea."

"Really? Already?" said Dee. "And what is that?"

"I'm still working it out," said Vimes. "But it's lucky the king told you to ask me, Dee. One thing I *have* found out is that no dwarf will give you the right answer."

The opera was just ending as Vimes slipped into the seat beside Sybil.

"Have I missed anything?" he said.

"It's very good. Where *have* you been?"

"You wouldn't believe me."

He stared, unseeing, at the stage. A couple of dwarfs were engaged in a very careful mock battle.

All right, then. If it was politics it was . . . well, politics. There was nothing he could do about politics. So . . . think about it as a crime . . .

What was the *simple* solution? Best to start with the first rule of policing: Suspect the victim. Vimes wasn't quite sure who the victim was here, though. So . . . suspect the witness. That was *another* good rule. That meant the late Dozy. He *could* have walked out with the Scone days before he "discovered" the loss. He could have done just about anything. The way the thing was guarded was a joke. Nobby and Colon could have done it better. *Much* better, he corrected himself, because they had devious little minds and that was what made them coppers . . . the guards on the Scone were honorable dwarfs, the *last* people you wanted to entrust with anything. You wanted sneaky people for a job like this.

But . . . it made no *sense*. He'd be the prime suspect. Vimes wasn't well up on dwarf law, but he suspected that there was not a huge friendly future in store for a prime suspect, especially if no other solution was forthcoming.

Maybe he'd snapped after sixty years of changing candles? That didn't sound right. Anyone who could put up with a job like that for ten years would probably run in their groove for the rest of eternity. Anyway, Dozy had now gone to the great big gold mine in the sky or deep underground or whatever it was dwarfs believed in. He wasn't going to be answering any questions.

He *could* solve this, Vimes told himself. Everything he needed was there, if only he asked the right questions and thought the right way.

But his Vimesish instincts were trying to tell him something else.

This was *a* crime—if holding a piece of property to ransom *was* technically a crime—but it wasn't *the* crime.

There was another crime here. He knew it in the same way that a fisherman spots the shoal by the ripple on the water.

The fight on stage continued. It was slowed by the need to stop after every gingerly exchanged ax blow for a song, probably about gold.

"Er . . . what's this all about?" he said.

"It's nearly over," whispered Sybil. "They've only performed the bit concerning the baking of the Scone, really, but at least they've included the Ransom Aria. Ironhammer escapes from prison with the help of Skalt, steals the Truth that Agi has hidden, conceals it by baking it into the Scone and persuades the guards around Bloodaxe's camp to let him pass. The dwarfs believe that Truth was once a, a *thing* . . . a sort of ultimate rare metal, really . . . and the last bit of it is inside the Scone. And the guards can't resist, because of the sheer power of it. The song is about how love, like truth, will always reveal itself, just as the grain of Truth inside the Scone makes the whole thing true. It is actually one of the finest pieces of music in the world. Gold is hardly mentioned at all."

Vimes stared. He got lost in any song more complex than the sort with titles like "Where Has All the Custard Gone (Jelly's Just Not the Same)."

"Bloodaxe and Ironhammer," he muttered, aware that dwarfs around them were giving him annoyed looks, "which one was—"

"Cheery told you. They were both dwarfs," said Sybil, sharply.

"Ah," said Vimes glumly.

He was always a little out of his depth in these matters. There were men, and there were women. He was clear on that. Sam Vimes was an uncomplicated man when it came to what poets called "the lists of love."* In some parts of the Shades, he knew, people adopted a more pick-and-mix approach. Vimes looked upon this as he looked upon a distant country; he'd never been there, and it wasn't his problem. It just amazed him what people got up to when they had time on their hands.

He just found it hard to imagine a world without a map. It wasn't that the dwarfs ignored sex, it really didn't seem *important* to them. If humans thought the same way, his job would be a lot simpler.

There seemed to be a deathbed scene now. It was a little hard for Vimes, with his shaky command of Ankh-Morpork street Dwarf-

---

* He'd noticed that sex bore some resemblance to cookery: It fascinated people, they sometimes bought books full of complicated recipes and interesting pictures, and sometimes when they were really hungry they created vast banquets in their imagination—but at the end of the day they'd settle quite happily for egg and chips, if it was well done and maybe had a slice of tomato.

ish, to follow what was going on. Someone was dying, and someone else was very sorry about it. Both the main singers had beards you could hide a chicken in. They weren't bothering to act, apart from infrequently waving an arm in the direction of the other singer.

But there were sobs all around him, and occasionally the trumpeting of a blown nose. Even Sybil's lower lip was trembling.

It's just a song, he wanted to say. It's not *real*. Crime and streets and chases . . . *they're* real. A song won't get you out of a tight corner. Try waving a large bun at an armed guard in Ankh-Morpork and see how far it gets you . . .

He shouldered his way through the throng after the performance, which from the humans present had received the usual warm reception that such things always got from people who hadn't really understood what was going on but rather felt that they should have.

Dee was talking to a black-clad, heavily built young man who looked vaguely familiar to Vimes. Vimes must have looked familiar to him as well, because he gave him a nod just short of offensiveness.

"Ah, Your Grace Vimes," he said. "And did you enjoy the opera?"

"Especially the bit about the gold," said Vimes. "And you are—?"

The man clicked his heels. "Wolf von Uberwald!"

Something went *bing* in Vimes's head. And his eyes picked up details—the slight lengthening of the incisors, the way the blond hair was so thick around the collar—

"Angua's brother?" he said.

"Yes, Your Grace."

"Wolf the wolf, eh?"

"Thank you, Your Grace," said Wolf solemnly. "That is very funny. Indeed, yes! It is quite some time since I heard that one! Your Ankh-Morpork sense of humor!"

"But you're wearing silver on your . . . uniform. Those . . . insignias. Wolf heads biting the lightning . . ."

Wolf shrugged. "Ah, the kind of thing a policeman would notice. But they are nickel!"

"I don't recognize the regiment."

"We are more of a . . . movement," said Wolf.

The stance was Angua's, too. It was the poised, fight-or-flight look, as if the whole body was a spring eager to unwind and "flight" wasn't an option. People in the presence of Angua when she was in a bad mood tended to turn up their collars without quite knowing why. But the eyes were different. They weren't like Angua's. They weren't even like the eyes of a wolf.

No animal had eyes like that, but Vimes saw them occasionally in some of Ankh-Morpork's less salubrious drinking establishments, where if you were lucky you'd get out the door before the drink turned you blind.

Colon called that sort of person a "bottle covey," Nobby preferred "soddin' nutter" but whatever the name Vimes recognized a head-butting, eye-gouging, down-and-dirty bastard when he saw one. In a fight you'd have no alternative but to lay him out or cut him down, because otherwise he'd do his very best to kill you. Most bar fighters wouldn't usually go that far, because killing a copper was known to be bad news for the murderer and anyone else who knew him, but your true nutter wouldn't worry about that because, while he was fighting, his brain was somewhere else.

Wolf smiled.

"There is a problem, Your Grace?"

"What? No. Just . . . thinking. I feel I've met you before . . . ?"

"You called on my father this morning."

"Ah, yes."

"We don't always Change for . . . visitors, Your Grace," said Wolf. There was an orange light in his eyes now. Up until then, Vimes had thought that "glowing eyes" was just a figure of speech.

"If you'll excuse me, I do need to talk to the Ideas-taster for a moment," said Vimes. "Politics."

Dee followed him into a quiet spot.

"Yes?"

"Did Dozy go to the Scone Cave at the same time every day?"

"I believe so. It depended on his other duties."

"So he *didn't* go in at the same time every day. Right. When does the guard change?"

"At each three o'clock."

"Did he go in before the guard change or afterward?"

"That would depend on—"

"Oh dear. Don't the guards write anything down?"

Dee stared at Vimes.

"Are you saying he could have gone in twice in one day?"

"Very *good*. But I'm saying *someone* might have. A dwarf comes up in a boat alone, carrying a couple of candles . . . would the guards take that much interest? And if *another* dwarf carrying a couple of candles came up an hour or so later, when the new guards were there . . . well, is there any real risk? Even if our faker was noticed, he'd just have to mutter something about . . . oh, bad candles or something. Damp wicks. Anything."

Dee looked distant.

"It is still a great risk," he said at last.

"If our thief was keeping an eye on the guard changes, and knew where the real Dozy was, it'd be worth it, wouldn't it? For the Scone?"

Dee shuddered, and then nodded. "In the morning the guards will be closely questioned," he said.

"By me."

"Why?"

"Because I know what kind of questions get answers. We'll set up an office here. We'll find out the movements of everyone and talk to all the guards, okay? Even the ones on the gates. We'll find out who went in and out."

"You already think you know something . . ."

"Let's say some ideas are forming, shall we?"

"I will . . . see to matters."

Vimes straightened up and walked back to Lady Sybil, who stood like an island in a sea of dwarfs. She was talking animatedly to several of them who Vimes vaguely recognized as performers in the opera.

"What have you been up to, Sam?" she said.

"Politics, I'm afraid," said Vimes. "And . . . trusting my instincts. Can you tell me who's watching us?"

"Oh, it's *that* game, is it?" said Sybil. She smiled happily, and in the tones of someone chatting about inconsequential things, said, "Practically everyone. But if I was handing out prizes, I'd choose the rather sad lady in the little group just off to your left. She's got fangs, Sam. And pearls, too. They don't exactly accessorize."

"Can you see Wolfgang?"

"Er . . . no, not now you come to mention it. That's odd. He was around a moment ago. Have you been upsetting people?"

"I think I may let people upset themselves," said Vimes.

"Good for you. You do that so well."

Vimes half turned, like someone just taking in the view. In among the human guests, the dwarfs moved and clustered. Five or six would come together, and talk animatedly. Then one would drift away and join another group. He might be replaced. And sometimes an entire group would spread out like the debris of an explosion, each member heading toward another group.

Vimes got the impression that there was some kind of structure behind all this, some slow, purposeful dance of information. Mineshaft meetings, he thought. Small groups, because there wouldn't be room for more. And you don't talk too loudly. And then when the group decides, every member is an ambassador for that decision. The word spreads out in circles. It's like running a society on formal gossip.

It occurred to him that it was also a way in which two plus two could be debated and weighed and considered and discussed until it became four-and-a-bit, or possibly an egg*

Occasionally a dwarf would stop and stare at him before hurrying away.

"We're supposed to go in for supper, dear," said Sybil, indicating the general drift toward a brightly lit cave.

"Oh dear. Quaffing, do you think? Rats on sticks? Where's Detritus?"

"Over there, talking to the cultural attaché from Genua. That's the man with the glazed expression."

As they got closer Vimes heard Detritus's voice in full expansive explanation: "—and den dere's dis big room wid all seats in it, wid red walls and dem big gold babies climbin' up der pillar only,

---

* Vimes had once discussed the Ephebian idea of "democracy" with Carrot, and had been rather interested in the idea that everyone** had a vote until he found out that while he, Vimes, would have a vote, there was no way in the rules that anyone could prevent Nobby Nobbs from having one as well. Vimes could see the flaw there straightaway.

** Apart from women, children, slaves, idiots and people who weren't really our kind of people.

don't worry, 'cos dey're not *real* gold babies, dey're only made of plaster or somethin' . . ." There was a pause as Detritus considered matters. "An' also I don't reckon it's real gold, neither, 'cos some bugger'd have pinched it if it was . . . And in front of der stage dere's dis big pit where all der musicians sits. And dat's about it for dat room. In der *next* room der's all dese marble pillars, an' on der floor dey got red carpeting—"

"Detritus?" said Lady Sybil. "I do hope you're not monopolizing this gentleman."

"No, I bin tellin' him all about der culture we got in Ankh-Morpork," said Detritus airily. "I know just about every inch of der op'ra house."

"Yes," said the cultural attaché, in a stunned voice. "And I must say I'm particularly interested in visiting the art gallery and seeing"—he shuddered—"'. . . der picture of dis woman, I don't reckon der artist knew how to do a smile prop'ly, but the frame's got to be worth a bob or two.' It sounds like the experience of a lifetime. Good evening to you."

"You know, I don't fink he knows a lot of culture," said Detritus, as the man strode away.

"Do you think people will miss us if we slip away?" said Vimes, looking around. "It's been a long day and I want to think about things—"

"Sam, you are the *ambassador*, and Ankh-Morpork is a world power," said Sybil. "We can't just sneak off! People will *comment*."

Vimes groaned. So Inigo was right: When Vimes sneezes, Ankh-Morpork blows its nose.

"Your Excellency?"

He looked down at two dwarfs.

"The Low King will see you now," said one of them.

"Er . . ."

"We will have to be officially presented," Lady Sybil hissed.

"What, even Detritus?"

"Yes!"

"But he's a troll!" It had seemed amusing at the time.

Vimes was aware of a drift in the crowds across the floor of the huge cave. There was a certain movement to them, a flow in the current of people toward one end of the cave. There was really no option but to join it.

The Low King was on a small throne under one of the chandeliers. There was a metal canopy over it, already encrusted with marvelous stalactites of wax.

Around him, watching the crowd, were four dwarfs, tall for dwarfs, and looking rather menacing in their dark glasses. Each one was holding an ax. They spent all their time staring very hard at people.

The king was talking to the Genuan ambassador. Vimes looked sideways at Cheery and Detritus. Suddenly, bringing them here wasn't such a good idea. In his official robes, the king looked a lot more . . . distant, and a lot harder to please.

Hang on, he told himself. They *are* Ankh-Morpork citizens. They're not doing anything *wrong*.

And then he argued: They're not doing anything wrong *in Ankh-Morpork*.

The line moved along. Their party was almost in the presence. The armed dwarfs were all watching Detritus now, and holding their axes in a slightly less relaxed way.

Detritus appeared not to notice.

"Dis place is even more cult'ral than the op'ra house," he said, gazing around respectfully. "Dem chandeliers must weigh a ton."

He reached up and rubbed his head, and then inspected his fingers.

Vimes glanced up. Something warm, like a buttered raindrop, hit his cheek.

As he brushed it away, he saw the shadows move . . .

Things happened with treacle slowness. He saw it as if he were watching himself from a little way away.

He saw himself push Cheery and Sybil roughly, heard himself shout something, and watched himself dive toward the king, snatching the dwarf up as an ax clanged into his backplate.

Then he was rolling, with the angry dwarf in his arms, and the chandelier was halfway through its fall, candle flames streaming, and there was Detritus, raising his hands with a calculating look on his face . . .

There was a moment of stillness and silence as the troll caught the descending mountain of light. And then physics returned, in an exploding cloud of dwarfs, debris, molten wax and tumbling, flaring candles.

Vimes woke up in utter darkness. He blinked and touched his eyes to make sure that they were open.

Then he sat up and his head thumped against stone, and *then* there was light, vicious yellow and purple *lights*, filling his life very suddenly. He lay back until they went away.

He took a personal itinerary. His cloak, helmet, sword and armor had all gone. He was left in his shirt and breeches, and while this place was not freezing, it had a clamminess that was already working its way through to his bones.

Right . . .

He wasn't sure how long it took him to get a feel for the cell, but a feel it was. He moved by inches, waving his arms ahead of him like a man practicing a very slow martial art against the darkness.

Even then, the senses became unreliable in the total black. He followed the wall carefully, followed another wall, followed a wall which yielded, under his fingertips, the outline of a small door with a handle, and found the wall which had the stone slab against it on which he'd awoken.

What made this all the harder was having to do this with his head sunk against his chest. Vimes wasn't a very tall man. If he had been, he'd probably have cracked his skull when he woke up.

Without any other aids to rely on, he walked the length of the walls using his copper's pace. He knew exactly how long it took him, swinging his legs easily, to walk across the Brass Bridge back home. A little bit of muzzy mental arithmetic was needed, but eventually he decided that the room was ten feet square.

One thing that Vimes did not do was shout "Help! Help!" He was in a cell. Someone had *put* him in a cell. It was reasonable to assume, therefore, that whoever had done this wasn't interested in his opinions.

He groped his way to the stone slab again and lay down. As he did so, something rattled.

He patted his pockets and brought out what felt and sounded very much like a box of matches. There were only three left.

So . . . resources = the clothes he stood up in, and a few matches.

Now to work out what the hell was going on.

He remembered seeing the chandelier. He *thought* he remembered seeing Detritus actually catch the thing. And there had been a lot of screaming and shouting and running around, while in his arms the king swore at Vimes as only a dwarf could swear. Then someone had hit him.

There was also an ache across his back where an ax had been turned aside by his armor. He felt a twitch of national pride at that thought. Ankh-Morpork armor had stood up to the blow! Admittedly, it *was* probably made in Ankh-Morpork by dwarfs from Uberwald, using steel smelted from Uberwald iron, but it damn well was Ankh-Morpork armor, just the same.

There was a pillow on the slab, made in Uberwald.

As Vimes turned his head, the pillow went, very faintly, *clink*. This was a sound he didn't associate with feathers.

In the darkness, he picked up the sack and, after resorting to his teeth, managed to rip a hole in the heavy material.

If what he drew up had ever been part of a bird, it wasn't one Vimes would ever like to meet. It *felt* very much like Inigo's One-Shot. A finger inserted very gingerly into the end told Vimes that it was loaded, too.

Just one shot, he remembered. But it was one people didn't know you had . . .

On the other hand, the Tooth Fairy probably wasn't responsible for putting it in the pillow, unless she'd been having to face some particularly difficult children lately.

He slipped it back into the bag when he became aware of a light. It was the faintest glow, showing that the door contained a barred window and that there were shadowy figures on the other side of it.

"Are you awake, Your Grace? This is very unfortunate."

"Dee?"

"Yes."

"And you've come to tell me this has all been some terrible mistake?"

"Alas, no. I am convinced of your innocence, of course."

"Really? Me, too," growled Vimes. "In fact I'm *so* convinced of my innocence I don't even know what it is I'm innocent of! Let me out or—"

"—or you will stay in, I am afraid," said Dee. "It is a very strong door. You are not in Ankh-Morpork, Your Grace. I will of course communicate your predicament to your Lord Vetinari as soon as possible, but I understand that the message tower has been badly damaged—"

"My *predicament* is that you've locked me up! Why? I saved your king, didn't I?"

"There is . . . conflict . . ."

"Someone let that chandelier down!"

"Yes, indeed. A member of your staff, it appears."

"You know that can't be true! Detritus and Littlebottom were with me when—"

"Mister Skimmer was on your staff?"

"He . . . Yes, but . . . I . . . he wouldn't—"

"I believe you have such a thing in Ankh-Morpork called the Guild of Assassins?" said Dee, calmly. "Correct me if I am wrong."

"He was up at the tower!"

"The *damaged* tower?"

"It was damaged before he—" Vimes stopped. "Why would he smash up one of the towers?"

"I did not say he would," said Dee. The flat calm was still there. "And then, Your Grace, it has been *suggested* that you gave a signal just before the thing came down . . ."

"What?"

"A hand to the cheek, or something. It has been suggested that you anticipated the event."

"The thing was swaying! Look, let me talk to Skimmer!"

"Do you have supernatural powers, Your Grace?"

Vimes hesitated.

"He's dead?"

"We believe he became entangled in the winch mechanism in the process of releasing the chandelier. Three dwarfs were dead around him."

"He wouldn't—"

Vimes stopped again. Of course he wouldn't. It's just that he's a member of this Guild we have, and you certainly know that, don't you—

Dee must have seen his expression.

"Quite so, quite so. Everything will be investigated thoroughly. The innocent have nothing to fear."

The news that they have nothing to fear is guaranteed to strike fear into the hearts of innocents everywhere.

"What have you done with Sybil?"

"Done, Your Grace? Why . . . nothing. We are not barbarians. We have heard nothing but good reports of your wife. She is upset, of course."

Vimes groaned. "And Detritus and Littlebottom?"

"Well, of course they were under your command, Your Grace. And one is a troll and the other is . . . dangerously different. And that is why, and precisely for that reason, that they are under house arrest in your own embassy. We do respect the traditions of diplomacy, and we will not have it said that we have acted out of malice." Dee sighed. "And then, of course, there is the *other* matter—"

"Are you going to accuse me of stealing the Scone, too?"

"You laid hands on the king."

Vimes stared. "Huh? A ton of candlestick was about to fall on him!"

"This has been pointed out—"

"And I'm imprisoned for saving him from an assassination attempt I planned?"

"Are you?"

"No! Look, the thing was coming down, what else should I have done? Tugged at the carpet and try to drag him away?"

"Yes, yes, I understand. But precedent in this area is very clear. In 1345, when the king at the time fell into a lake, not one member of his staff dared touch him because of the ruling, and the subsequent finding was that they had acted correctly. It is forbidden to touch the king. I have of course explained to the conclave that this is not the Ankh-Morpork way, but . . . this is not Ankh-Morpork."

"I don't need everyone reminding me about that!"

"You will remain . . . our guest while investigations continue. Food and drink will be brought to you."

"And light?"

"Of course. Excuse our lack of consideration. Stand back from the door, please. The guards with me are armed and they are . . . uncomplicated people."

The grille on the door was swung back. A glowing wire cage was put on the ledge.

"What's this? A sick glow-worm?"

"It is a kind of beetle, yes. You will find that it will very soon seem quite bright. We are very accustomed to darkness."

"Look," said Vimes, as the grille was shut again, "you *know* this is ridiculous! I . . . don't know what the position is with Mister Skimmer, but I damn well intend to find out! And there's the Scone theft, I'm pretty certain I'm close to working that out, too. If you let me return to the embassy, where else could I go?"

"We would not wish to find out. You may just feel that life would be more pleasant in Ankh-Morpork."

"Really? And how would we get there?"

"You may have friends in unexpected places."

Vimes thought of the evil little weapon in the pillow.

"You will not be badly treated. This is our way," said Dee. "I will return when I have news."

"Hey—"

But Dee was a retreating shape in the crepid, almost-not-there light.

In Vimes's cell, the glow beetle was doing its best. All it managed to achieve, though, was to turn the darkness into a variety of green shadows. You could find your way with it without walking into walls, but that was about the extent of it.

One shot, that they didn't know you had.

That'd *probably* get him out of the door. Into a corridor. Underground. Full of dwarfs.

On the other hand . . . it was amazing how the evidence could stack up against you when people wanted it to.

Anyway, Vimes was an ambassador! What happened to diplomatic immunity? But that was hard to argue when you were faced by uncomplicated people with weaponry; there was a risk that they'd experiment to see if it was true.

One shot they didn't expect . . .

Sometime later there was a rattling of keys and the door was pulled open. Vimes could make out the shape of two dwarfs. One was holding an ax, the other was bearing a tray.

The dwarf with the ax motioned Vimes to step back.

An ax wasn't a good idea, Vimes considered. It was always the weapon of choice among dwarfs, but it wasn't sensible in a confined space.

He raised his hands and, as the other dwarf walked cautiously over to the stone slab, let them move toward the back of his neck.

These dwarfs were nervous of him. Perhaps they didn't see humans very often.

They'd remember this one.

"Want to see a trick?" said Vimes.

"*Grz'dak?*"

"Watch *this*," said Vimes, and brought his hands around and shut his eyes just before the match flared.

He heard the ax drop as its owner tried to cover his face. That was an unexpected bonus, but there wasn't time to thank the god of desperate men. Vimes plunged forward, kicked as hard as he could and heard an "oof" of expelled breath. Then he leapt into the patch of darkness that contained the other dwarf, found a head, spun around and rammed it into an unseen wall.

The other dwarf was trying to get to his feet. Vimes fumbled for him in the gloom, pulled him up by his jerkin and rasped: "*Someone* left me a weapon. They wanted me to kill you. Remember that. *I could have killed you.*"

He punched the dwarf in the stomach. This was no time to play by the Marquis of Fantailler rules.*

Then he turned, snatched the little cage containing the light beetle and headed for the door.

---

* The Marquis of Fantailler got into many fights in his youth, most of them as a result of being known as the Marquis of Fantailler, and wrote a set of rules for which he termed "the noble art of fisticuffs" which mostly consisted of a list of places where people weren't allowed to hit him. Many people were impressed with his work and later stood with noble chest outthrust and fists balled in a spirit of manly aggression against people who hadn't read the Marquis's book but *did* know how to knock people senseless with a chair. The last words of a surprisingly large number of people were "Stuff the bloody Marquis of Fantailler—"

There was a feeling of passageway, stretching off in both directions. Vimes paused for just long enough to sense the draft on his face, and headed that way.

Another glow beetle was hanging in a cage a little distance off. It illuminated, if such a bright word could be used for a light that merely made the darkness less black, a huge circular opening in which a fan turned lazily.

The blades were so slow that Vimes was able to step between them, into the velvet cavern beyond.

Someone really wants me dead, he thought, as he inched his way along the nearest invisible wall with his face to the draft. One shot they weren't expecting . . . but *someone* was expecting it, weren't they?

If you want to get a prisoner out of the clink, then you gave him a key, or a file. You didn't give him a weapon. A key might get him out; a weapon would get him killed.

He stopped, one foot over emptiness. The glow beetle revealed a hole in the floor. It had the huge suckingness of depth.

Then he gripped the beetle's basket between his teeth, took a few steps back and completely misjudged the distance. He hit the other side of the hole with every rib, both arms flat on the floor beyond.

A bit of Ankh-Morpork sense of humor hissed between his teeth.

He scrabbled his way onto the cave floor and got his breath back. Then he took the one-shot out of his pocket, fired it into the floor, tossed it into the hole—it clattered and echoed for some time—and moved on, keeping his face toward the cold air.

This wasn't a tunnel anymore. It was the bottom of a shaft. But the green glow lit up something heaped in the middle.

Vimes picked up a handful of snow and, when he looked up, a flake melted on his face.

He grinned in the dark. The beetle light just caught the edge of the spiral stairs fixed to the rock.

"Stairs" turned out to be a generous description. When the shaft had been cut, the dwarfs had made holes in the stone and hammered thick balks of timber into them. He tried one or two. They seemed sturdy enough. With care, he'd be able to scramble . . .

He was a long way up before one snapped. He flung out his hands and caught the next one, his grip slipping on the wet wood. The glow beetle disappeared downward and Vimes, swinging back and forth from his precarious handhold, watched the circle of dim green light dwindle to a dot, and vanish.

Then the realization crept over him that there was no *way* he would be able to pull himself up. His fingers were numb, but the rest of his entire *life* consisted of the amount of time they could maintain a grip on the clammy step above him.

Call it a minute, perhaps.

There were a lot of things that could profitably be done in a minute, but most of them couldn't be done with no hands while hanging in darkness over a long drop.

He lost his grip. A moment later he smacked into the spiral of logs one turn below, which parted company with the wall.

Man and timber fell one more turn. Vimes landed with a rib-bending thump across one step, while those around it gave way. Rocking gently on the one tough log, he listened to the thuds and booms as the fallen timber continued to the bottom of the shaft.

"——!" Vimes had intended to swear, but the fall had knocked the breath out of him.

He hung like a folded pair of old trousers.

It had been a long time since he'd slept. Whatever he'd been doing on the slab, it hadn't been sleep. Normal sleep didn't leave your mouth feeling as though glue had been poured into it.

And only this morning the new ambassador for Ankh-Morpork had strolled out to present his credentials. Only this evening Ankh-Morpork's commander of police had set out to solve a simple little theft. And now he was dangling halfway up a freezing shaft, with a few inches of old and unreliable wood between him and a brief trip to the next world.

All he could hope for was that his whole life wasn't going to pass before his eyes. There were some bits of it he didn't want to remember.

"Ah . . . Sir Samuel. Bad luck. You were doing so well."

He opened his eyes.

A faint purple light just above him illuminated the form of the Lady Margolotta. She was sitting on empty space.

"Can I give you a lift?" she said.

Vimes shook his head, muzzily.

"If it makes you feel any better, I really *don't* like doing this," said the vampire. "It's so . . . *expected* of one. Oh dear. That rotten old log doesn't look very—"

The log snapped. Vimes landed spread-eagled on the turn below, but only for a moment. Several stairs broke and dropped him a further flight. This time, he caught hold of one and was, once again, dangling.

Lady Margolotta descended regally.

Far below, the broken wood boomed.

"Now, in theory this might be an almost survivable way of getting back down," said the vampire. "Unfortunately, I fear that the descending logs have smashed many of the ones below."

Vimes shifted. His handhold seemed secure. It might just be possible to pull himself up . . .

"I knew you were behind this," he muttered, trying to will some life into his shoulder muscles.

"No, you didn't. You knew that the Scone wasn't stolen, though."

Vimes stared at the serenely floating shape.

"The dwarfs wouldn't think that—" he began. The log under him gave the little nasty movement that announces to any luckless passengers that it is about to land.

Lady Margolotta drifted closer.

"I know you hate vampires," she said. "It's quite usual, for your personality type. It's the . . . penetrative aspect. But if I vas you, right now, I'd ask myself . . . do I hate them with all my life?"

She held out a hand.

"Just one bite'll end all my troubles, eh?" Vimes snarled.

"One bite would be one too many, Sam Vimes."

The wood cracked. She grabbed his wrist.

If he'd thought about it at all, Vimes would have expected to be dangling from a vampire now. Instead, he was simply floating.

"Don't *think* of letting go," said Margolotta, as they rose gently up the shaft.

"*One bite would be too many?*" said Vimes. He recognized the mangled mantra. "You're a . . . a *teetotaler?*"

"Almost four years now."

"No blood at all?"

"Oh yes. Animal. It's rather kinder to them than slaughter, don't you think? Of course, it makes them docile, but frankly a cow is unlikely ever to vin the Thinker of the Year award. I'm on a vagon, Mister Vimes."

"*The* wagon. We call it *the* wagon," said Vimes weakly. "And . . . that replaces human blood?"

"Like lemonade replaces vhisky. Believe me. However, the intelligent mind can find a . . . substitute." The sides of the shaft dropped away and they were in clear, freezing air, which knifed through Vimes's shirt. They drifted sideways a little, and then Vimes was dropped into knee-deep snow.

"One of the better things about our dwarfs is that they don't often try something new and they never let go of anything old," said the vampire, hovering over the snow. "You weren't hard to find."

"Where am I?" Vimes looked around at rocks and trees mounded in snow.

"In the mountains, quite a long way viddershins of the town, Mister Vimes. Goodbye."

"You're going to leave me *here*?"

"I'm sorry? *You* vere the one who escaped. I am certainly not here. Me, a vampire, interfering in the affairs of the dwarfs? Unthinkable! But let us just say . . . I like people to have an even chance."

"It's freezing! I haven't even got a coat! What is it you *want*?"

"You have freedom, Mister Vimes. Isn't that vhat everyone vants? Isn't it supposed to give you a lovely varm glow?"

Lady Margolotta disappeared into the snow.

Vimes shivered. He hadn't realized how warm it had been underground. Or what time it was. There was a dim, a very dim light. Was this just after sunset? Was it almost dawn?

The flakes were piling up on his damp clothes, driven by the wind.

Freedom could get you killed.

Shelter . . . that was *essential*. The time of day and a precise location were no use to the dead. They always knew what time it was and where they were.

He moved away from the open shaft and staggered into the trees, where the snow wasn't so deep. It gave off a light, fainter than a sick beetle, as if snow somehow absorbed it from the air as it fell.

Vimes wasn't good at forests. They were things you saw on the horizon. If he'd thought about them at all, he'd imagined a lot of trees, standing like poles, brown at the bottom, bushy and green at the top.

Here there were humps, and bumps, and dark branches weighted and creaking under the snow. It fell around him with a hiss. Occasionally lumps of the stuff would slide from somewhere above, and there would be another shower of frigid crystals as a branch sprang back.

There *was* a track of sorts, or at least a wider, smoother expanse of snow. Vimes followed it, on the basis that there was no more sensible choice. The warm glow of freedom only lasted so long.

Vimes had city eyes. He'd watched coppers develop them. A trainee copper who glanced once at a street was just learning, and if he didn't learn quicker he'd become highly experienced at dying. One who'd been on the streets for a while paid attention, took in details, noted shadows, saw background and foreground and the people who were trying not to be in either. Angua looked at streets like that. She worked at it.

The long-term coppers, like even Nobby when he was on a good day, glanced once at a street and that was enough, because they'd seen everything.

Maybe there were . . . country eyes. Forest eyes. Vimes saw trees, mounds, snow and not much else.

The wind was getting up, and began to howl among the trees. Now the snow *stung*.

Trees. Branches. Snow.

Vimes kicked a mound beside the track. Snow slid off dark pine needles.

He dropped to his hands and knees and pushed forward . . .

Ah . . .

It was still cold, and there was some snow on the dead needles, but the weighted branches had spread around the trunk like a tent. He pulled himself in, congratulating himself. It was windless here and, contrary to all common sense, the blanket of snow above him seemed to make it *warmer*. It even smelled warm . . . sort of . . . animal . . .

Three wolves, lying lazily around the trunk of the tree, were watching him with interest.

Vimes added metaphorical freezing to the other sort. The animals didn't seem frightened.

Wolves!

And that was about it. It made as much sense to say: Snow! Or: Wind! Right now, those were more certain killers.

He heard somewhere that wolves wouldn't attack you if you faced them down.

The trouble was that he *was* going to sleep soon. He could feel it creeping over him. He wasn't thinking right, and every muscle ached.

Outside, the wind moaned. And His Grace the Duke of Ankh-Morpork fell asleep.

He awoke with a snort and, to his surprise, all his arms and legs as well. A drop of chilled water, melted from the roof just above by the heat of his body, ran down his neck. His muscles didn't hurt anymore. He couldn't *feel* most of them.

And the wolves had gone. There was trampled snow at the far end of the makeshift lair, and light so bright that he groaned.

It turned out to be daylight, from a bright sky bluer than any Vimes had seen, so blue that it seemed to shade into purple at the zenith. He stepped out into a sugar-frosted world, crunchy and glittering.

Wolf tracks led away between the trees. It occurred to Vimes that following them would not be a life-enhancing move; perhaps last night had been understood as time out, but today was a new day and probably the search was on for breakfast.

The sun felt warm, the air was cold, his breath hung in front of him.

There should be people around, shouldn't there? Vimes was hazy on rural issues, but weren't there supposed to be charcoal burners, woodcutters and . . . he tried to think . . . little girls taking goodies to granny? The stories Vimes had learned as a kid suggested that all forests were full of bustle, activity and the occasional scream. But this place was silent.

He set off in a direction that appeared to head downward, on general principles. Food was the important thing. He'd still got a couple of matches, and he could probably make a fire if he had to be out here another night, but it was a long time since the canapés at the reception.

This is Ankh-Morpork, trudging over and through the snow . . .

After half an hour he reached the bottom of a shallow valley, where a stream splashed between encroaching banks of ice. It steamed.

The water was warm to the touch.

He followed the banks for some way. They were crisscrossed with animal tracks. Here and there the water pooled in deep hollows that smelled of rotten eggs. Around them the leafless bushes were heavy with ice, where the steam had frozen.

Food could wait. Vimes stripped off his clothes and stepped into one of the deeper pools, yelping at the heat, and then lay back.

Didn't they do something like this up in Nothingfjord? He'd heard stories. They had hot steamy baths and then ran around in the snow hitting one another with birch logs, didn't they? Or something. There was nothing really daft that some foreigner wouldn't do, somewhere.

Gods, it felt *good*. Hot water *was* civilization. Vimes could feel the stiffness in his muscles melting away in the warmth.

After a moment or two he splashed over to the bank and rummaged through his clothes until he found a flattened packet of cigars, containing a couple of things that, after the events of the past twenty-four hours, looked like fossilized twigs.

He had two matches.

Well, the hell with it. Anyone could light a fire with one match.

He lay back in the water. That had been a good decision. He could feel himself coming back together again, pulled into shape by the heat within and without—

"Ah. Your Grace . . ."

Wolf von Uberwald was sitting on the other bank. He was stark naked. A little vapor rose off him, as if he'd just been exerting himself. Muscles gleamed as though they'd been oiled. They probably had been.

"A run in the snow is such a thing, is it not?" said Wolf pleasantly. "You are certainly learning the ways of Uberwald, Your Grace. Lady Sybil is alive and well and free to go back to your city when the passes are cleared. I know you would wish to hear that."

Other figures were approaching through the trees, men and women, all of them as unselfconsciously naked as Wolf.

Vimes realized he was a dead man bathing. He could see it in Wolf's eyes.

"Nothing like a hot dip before breakfast," he said.

"Ah, yes. We also have not, as yet, breakfasted," said Wolf. He stood up, stretched, and cleared the pool from a standing start. Vimes's breeches were picked up and examined.

"I threw Inigo's damn thing away," said Vimes. "I don't think a friend put it there."

"It is all a great game, Your Grace," said Wolf. "Do not reproach yourself! The strongest survive, which is as it should be!"

"Dee planned this, did he?"

Wolf laughed. "The dear little Dee? Oh, he had a plan. It was a good little plan, although a touch insane. Happily, it will no longer be required!"

"You want the dwarfs to go to war?"

"Strength is *good*," said Wolf, folding Vimes's clothes neatly. "But like some other good things, it only remains good if it is not possessed by too many people." He tossed the clothes as far as he could.

"What *is* it you want me to say, Your Grace?" said Wolf. "Something like 'you are going to die anyway so I might as well tell you,' perhaps?"

"Well, it'd be a help," said Vimes.

"You *are* going to die anyway." Wolf smiled. "Why don't *you* tell *me*?"

Talking gained time. Maybe those woodcutters and charcoal burners would be along at any minute.

If they hadn't brought their axes everyone was going to be in *big* trouble.

"I'm . . . pretty sure why the replica Scone was stolen in Ankh-Morpork," said Vimes. "I've just got the inkling of an idea that a copy was made of it, which was smuggled here on one of our coaches. Diplomats don't get searched."

"Well done!"

"Shame Igor came to unload when one of your boys was there, wasn't it?"

"Oh, it's hard to hurt an Igor!"

"You don't care, do you?" said Vimes. "A bunch of dwarfs want Albrecht on the thro—the Scone because they want to hang onto that old-time certainty, and *you* just want dwarfs fighting. And old Albrecht wouldn't even get the right Scone back!"

"Let us say that just now we find our interests converge, shall we?" said Wolf.

Out of the corner of his eye, Vimes saw the other werewolves spreading out around the pool.

"And now you've set me up," he said. "Pretty amateurishly, I'd say. But impressive, because Dee couldn't have had much time after he thought I was getting close. It would have worked, too. People aren't good eyewitnesses. I *know*. They believe what they want to see and what people told them they saw. It was a nice touch giving me that damn one-shot. He really must have hoped I'd kill to escape—"

"Is it not time you got out of that . . . pool?" said Wolfgang.

"You mean *bath*?" said Vimes. Yes, there was a wince. Vimes registered it. Oh, you're walking upright and talking, my lad, and you look strong as an ox—but something between a human and a wolf has a bit of dog in them, doesn't it?"

"We have an ancient custom here," said Wolf, looking away. "And it is a good one. Anyone can challenge us. It's a little . . . chase. The great Game! A competition, if you like. If they outrun us, they win four hundred crowns. That is a very good sum! A man may start a small business with it. Of course, as I can see you realize, if they *don't* outrun us . . . the question of money does not arise!"

"Does anyone ever win?" said Vimes. Come *on*, woodcutters, the people need wood!

"Sometimes. If they train well and know the country! Many a successful man in Bonk owes his start in life to our little custom. In your case, we will give you, oh, an hour's lead. For the sport of it!" He pointed. "Bonk is five miles in that direction. The lore says that you must not enter a dwelling until you get there."

"And if I don't run?"

"Then it will be a really short event! We do not like Ankh-Morpork. We do not want you here!"

"That's odd," said Vimes.

Wolf's broad brow wrinkled.

"Your meaning?"

"Oh, it's just that everywhere I go in Ankh-Morpork I seem to bump into people who came from Uberwald, you see. Dwarfs, trolls, humans. All beavering away quite happily and writing letters home saying, come on, it's great here—they don't eat you alive for a dollar."

Wolf's lip curled, revealed a glint of incisor. Vimes had seen that look on Angua's face. It meant she was having a bad hair day. And a werewolf can have a bad hair day all over.

He pushed his luck. It was clearly too weak to move by itself.

"Angua's getting on well—"

"Vimes! Mister Civilized! Ankh-Morpork! You will *run*!"

Hoping that his legs would support him, Vimes climbed out on the snow of the bank, as slowly as he dared. There was laughter from the werewolves.

"You go into the water wearing *clothes*?"

Vimes looked down at his streaming legs.

"You've never seen drawers before?" he said.

Wolf's lip curled again. He glanced triumphantly at the others. "Behold . . . civilization!" he said.

Vimes puffed life into his cigar, and looked around the frozen woodland with as much hauteur as he could muster.

"Four hundred crowns, did you say?" he said.

"Yes!"

Vimes sneered at the forest again.

"What is that in Ankh-Morpork dollars, do you know? About a dollar fifty?"

"The question will not arise!" Wolf bellowed.

"Well, I don't want to have to spend it all here—"

"*Run!*"

"Under the circumstances, then, I won't ask if you have the money on you."

Vimes walked away from the werewolves, glad that they couldn't see his face and very much aware that the skin on his back wanted to crawl around to his front.

He kept moving calmly, his wet drawers beginning to crackle in the frosty air, until he was certain he was out of sight of the pack.

So, let's see . . . they've got better strength than you, they know the country, and if they're as good as Angua they could track a fart through a skunk's breakfast, and your legs hurt already.

So what are the plusses here? Well . . . you've made Wolf really angry.

Vimes broke into a run.

Not much of a plus there then, all things considered.

Vimes broke into a *faster* run.

Off in the distance, wolves began to howl.

There is a saying: It won't get better if you picket.

Corporal Nobbs or, rather, Guild President C. W. St. J. Nobbs, reflected on this. A little early snow was fizzling in the air over the metal drum which, in approved strike fashion, was glowing red-hot in front of the Watch House.

A main problem, as he saw it, was that there was something philosophically wrong with picketing a building that no one except a watchman wanted to enter in any case. It is impossible to keep people out of something that they don't want to go into. It can't be done.

The chant hadn't worked. An old lady had given him a penny.

"Colon, Colon, Colon! Out! Out! Out!" shouted Reg Shoe happily, waving his placard.

"That doesn't sound right, Reg," said Nobby. "Sounds like surgery."

He looked at the other placards. Dorfl was holding a large, closely worded text, detailing their grievances in full, with references to Watch procedures and citing a number of philosophical texts. Constable Visit's sandwich board, on the other hand, proclaimed: WHAT PROFITETH IT A KINGDOM IF THE OXEN BE DE-FLATED? RIDDLES II, V3

Somehow, these cogent arguments did not seem to be bringing the city to its knees.

He turned at the sound of a coach pulling up and looked up at a door which had a crest consisting mainly of a black shield. And above that, looking out of the window, was the face of Lord Vetinari.

"Ah, none other than Corporal Nobbs," said Lord Vetinari.

At this point Nobby would have given quite a lot to be *anyone* other than Corporal Nobbs.

He wasn't sure whether, as a striker, he should salute. He saluted anyway, on the basis that a salute was seldom out of place.

"I gather you have withdrawn your labor," Lord Vetinari went on. "In your case, I am sure this presented a good deal of difficulty."

Nobby wasn't certain about that sentence, but the Patrician seemed quite amiable.

"Can't stand by when the security of the city's concerned, sir," he said, oozing affronted loyalty from every unblocked pore.

Lord Vetinari paused long enough for the peaceful, everyday sounds of a city apparently on the brink of catastrophe to filter into Nobby's consciousness.

"Well, of course I wouldn't dream of interfering," he said at last. "This is Guild business. I'm sure His Grace will understand fully when he returns." He banged on the side of the coach. "Drive on."

And the coach was gone.

A thought that had been nudging Nobby for some time chose this moment to besiege him once again.

Mr. Vimes is going to go spare. *He's going to go mental.*

Lord Vetinari sat back in his seat, smiling to himself.

"Er . . . did you *mean* that, sir?" said the clerk Drumknott, who was sitting opposite.

"Certainly. Make a note to have the kitchen send them down cocoa and buns around three o'clock. Anonymously, of course. It's been a crime-free day, Drumknott. Very unusual. Even the Thieves' Guild is lying low."

"Yes, my lord. I can't imagine why. When the cat's away . . ."

"Yes, Drumknott, but mice are happily unencumbered by apprehensions of the future. Humans, on the other hand, are. And they know that Vimes is going to be back in a week or so, Drumknott. And Vimes will not be happy. Indeed, he will not. And when a commander of the Watch is unhappy, he tends to spread it around with a big shovel."

He smiled again. "This is the time for sensible men to be honest, Drumknott. I only hope Colon is stupid enough to let it continue."

The snow fell faster.

"How beautiful the snow is, sisters . . ."

Three women sat at the window of their lonely house, looking out at the white Uberwald winter.

"And how cold the vind is," said the second sister.

The third sister, who was the youngest, sighed. "Why do we always talk about the weather?"

"Vhat else is there?"

"Well, it's either freezing cold or baking. I mean, that's it, really."

"That is how things are in Mother Uberwald," said the oldest sister, slowly and sternly. "The vind and the snow and the boiling heat of summer . . ."

"You know, I bet if we cut down the cherry orchard, I'm sure we could put in a roller skating rink—"

"No."

"How about a conservatory? We could grow pineapples."

"No."

"If we moved to Bonk we could get a big apartment for the cost of this place—"

"This is our home, Irina," said the eldest sister. "Ah, a home of lost illusions and thwarted hopes . . ."

"We could go out dancing and everything."

"I remember vhen ve lived in Bonk," said the middle sister dreamily. "Things vere better then."

"Things vere *alvays* better then," said the oldest sister.

The youngest sister sighed, and looked out of the window. She gasped.

"There's a man running through the cherry orchard!"

"A *man*? Vot could he possibly vant?"

The youngest sister strained to see.

"It's looks like he wants . . . a pair a trousers . . ."

"Ah," said the middle sister dreamily. "Trousers vere better then."

The hurrying pack stopped in a chilly blue valley when the howling filled the air.

Angua loped back to the sledge, lifted out her bag of clothes with her jaws, glanced at Carrot and disappeared among the drifts. A few moments later she walked back again, doing up her shirt.

"Wolfgang's got some poor devil playing the Game," she said. "I'm going to put a stop to it. It was bad enough that Father kept the tradition going, but at least he played fair. Wolfgang cheats. They *never* win."

"Is this the Game you told me about?"

"That's right. But Father played by the rules. If the runner was bright and nimble he got four hundred crowns and Father had him to dinner at the castle."

"If he *lost*, then your father had him for dinner out in the woods."

"Thank you for reminding me."

"I was trying not to be nice."

"You may have an undiscovered natural talent," said Angua. "But no one *had* to run, is my point. I won't apologize. I've been a copper in Ankh-Morpork, remember. City motto: You May Not Get Killed."

"Actually, it's—"

"Carrot! I *know*. And *our* family motto is Homo Homini Lupus. 'A man is a wolf to other men'! How *stupid*. Do you think they
mean that men are shy and retiring and loyal and kill only to eat?
Of course not! They *mean* that men act like *men* toward other men,
and the worse they are, the more they think they're really being like
wolves! Humans hate werewolves because they see the wolf in us,
but wolves hate us because they see the human inside—and I don't
blame them!"

Vimes veered away from the farmhouse and sprinted toward the
nearby barn. There had to be something in there. Even a couple of
sacks would do. The chafing qualities of frozen underwear can be
seriously underestimated.

He'd been running for half an hour. Well, for twenty-five
minutes, really. The other five had been spent limping, wheezing,
clutching at his chest and wondering how you knew if you were
having a heart attack.

The inside of the barn was . . . barnlike. There were stacks of
hay, dusty farm implements . . . and a couple of threadbare sacks,
hanging on a nail. He snatched one, gratefully.

Behind him, the door creaked open. He spun around, clutching the sack to him, and saw three very somberly dressed women
watching him carefully. One of them was holding a kitchen knife
in a trembling hand.

"Have you come here to ravish us?" she said.

"Madam! I'm being pursued by werewolves!"

The three looked at one another. To Vimes, the sack suddenly
seemed far too small.

"Vill that take you all day?" said one of the women.

Vimes held the sack more tightly.

"Ladies! Please! I need trousers!"

"Ve can see that."

"And a weapon, and boots if you've got them! Please?"

They went into another huddle.

"We have the gloomy and purposeless trousers of Uncle Vanya," said one, doubtfully.

"He seldom vore them," said another.

"And I have an ax in my linen cupboard," said the youngest. She looked guiltily at the other two. "Look, just in case I ever needed it, all right? I wasn't going to chop anything *down*."

"I would be so grateful," said Vimes. He took in the good but old clothes, the faded gentility, and played the only card in his hand. "I am His Grace the Duke of Ankh-Morpork, although I appreciate this fact is not evident at the—"

There was a three-fold sigh.

"Ankh-Morpork!"

"You haf a magnificent opera house and many fine galleries."

"Such vonderful avenues!"

"A veritable heaven of culture and sophistication and unattached men of quality!"

"Er . . . I said *Ankh-Morpork*," said Vimes. "With an *A* and an *M*."

"Ve have always dreamed of going there."

"I'll have three coach tickets sent along immediately after I get home," said Vimes, his mind's ear hearing the crunch of speeding paws over snow. "But, dear ladies, if you could fetch me those things—"

They hurried away, but the youngest lingered by the door.

"Do you have long, cold winters in Ankh-Morpork?" she said.

"Just muck and slush, usually."

"Any cherry orchards?"

"I don't think we have any, I'm afraid."

She punched the air.

"Yesss!"

A few minutes later Vimes was alone in the barn, wearing a pair of ancient black trousers that he'd tied at the waist with rope, and holding an ax which was surprisingly sharp.

He had five minutes, perhaps. Wolves probably didn't stop to worry about heart attacks.

There was no point in simply running. They could run faster. He needed to stay near civilization and its hallmarks, like trousers.

Maybe *time* was on Vimes's side. Angua was never very talkative about her world, but she *had* said that, in either shape, a werewolf slowly lost some of the skills of the *other* shape. After several hours on two legs her sense of smell dropped from uncanny to merely good. And after too long as a wolf . . . it was like being drunk, as far as Vimes understood it; a little inner part of you was still trying to give instructions, but the rest of you was acting stupid. The human part started to lose control . . .

He looked around the barn again. There was a ladder to an upper gallery. He climbed it, and looked out of a glassless window across a snowy meadow. There was a river in the distance, and what looked very much like a boathouse.

Now . . . how would a werewolf think?

The werewolves slowed as they reached the building. Their leader glanced at a lieutenant, and nodded. He loped off in the direction of the boathouse. The others followed Wolf inside. The last became human for a moment to pull the doors shut and drop the bar across.

Wolf stopped near the center of the barn. Hay had been scattered over the floor in great fluffy piles.

He scraped gently with a paw, and wisps fell away from a rope that was stretched taut.

Wolf took a deep breath. The other werewolves, sensing what was going to happen, looked away. There was a moment of struggling shapelessness, and then he was rising slowly on two feet, blinking in the dawn of humanity.

That's interesting, thought Vimes, up on the gallery. For a second or two after Changing, they're not entirely up on current events . . .

"Oh, Your Grace," said Wolf, looking around. "A *trap*? How very . . . civilized."

He caught site of Vimes, who was standing on the higher floor, by the window.

"What was it supposed to do, Your Grace?"

Vimes reached down to the oil lamp.

"It was supposed to be a decoy," he said.

He hurled the lamp down onto the dry hay, and flicked his cigar after it. Then he grabbed the ax and climbed through the window just as the spilled fat oil *whump*ed.

Vimes dropped into the deep snow and ran toward the boathouse.

There were other tracks leading to it, not human. When he reached the door he swung wildly at the darkness just inside, and his reward was a cut-off yelp.

The skiff that was housed in the tumbledown shed was a quarter full of dark water, but he didn't dare think about bailing yet. He grabbed the dusty oars and rowed with considered effort and not much speed out onto the river.

He groaned. Wolf was trotting across the snow, with the rest of the pack behind him. They all seemed to be there.

Wolf cupped his hands.

"Very civilized, Your Grace! But, you see, when you set fire to a barn full of wolves, they panic, Your Grace! But when they're werewolves, one of them just opens the door! You cannot *kill* werewolves, Mister Vimes!"

"Tell that to the one in the boathouse!" Vimes shouted, as the current took the boat.

Wolf looked into the shadows for a moment, and then cupped his hands again.

"He *will* recover, Mister Vimes!"

Vimes swore under his breath, because despite all his hopes a couple of werewolves had plunged into the water upstream and were swimming strongly toward the opposite bank. But that was *another* doggy thing, wasn't it? Leap joyfully into any water outdoors, but fight like hell against a tub.

Wolfgang had started to trot along the bank. The ones in the water emerged on the *far* bank. Now they were keeping pace with the boat on both sides.

The current was carrying him faster now. Vimes started to bail with both hands.

"You can't outrun the river, Wolf!" he shouted.

"We don't have to, Mister Vimes! That is not the question! The question is, can you outswim the waterfall? See you later, Civilized!"

Vimes looked around. In the distance, the river ahead had a foreshortened look. When he concentrated, the inner ear of terror could hear a distant roaring.

He snatched the oars again and tried to row upstream and, yes, it was possible to make headway against the current. But he couldn't keep rowing faster than wolves could run, and taking on two at once on the shore, when they were ready and waiting for him, was not an option.

If he went over the falls now, he might get to the bottom before they did.

That wasn't a good sentence, however he tried it.

He took his hands off the oars and pulled in the mooring rope. If I make a couple of loops, he thought, I can strap the ax onto my back—

He had a mental picture of what could happen to a man who plunged into the cauldron below a waterfall with a sharp piece of metal attached to his body—

GOOD MORNING.

Vimes blinked. A tall dark-robed figure was now sitting in the boat.

"Are you Death?"

IT'S THE SCYTHE, ISN'T IT. PEOPLE ALWAYS NOTICE THE SCYTHE.

"I'm going to die?"

POSSIBLY.

"*Possibly?* You turn up when people are *possibly* going to die?"

OH YES. IT'S QUITE THE NEW THING. IT'S BECAUSE OF THE UNCERTAINTY PRINCIPLE.

"What's that?"

I'M NOT SURE.

"That's very helpful."

I THINK IT MEANS PEOPLE MAY OR MAY NOT DIE. I HAVE TO SAY IT'S PLAYING HOB WITH MY SCHEDULE, BUT I TRY TO KEEP UP WITH MODERN THOUGHT.

The roar was a lot louder now. Vimes lay back in the boat and gripped the sides.

I'm talking to Death, he thought, to take my mind off things.

"Didn't I see you last month? I was chasing Bigger-than-Small-Dave Dave along Peach Pie Street and I fell off that ledge?"

THAT IS CORRECT.

"But I landed on that cart. I didn't die!"

BUT YOU *MIGHT* HAVE.

"But I thought we all had some kind of hourglass thing that said *when* we were going to die?"

Now the roar was almost physical. Vimes redoubled his grip on the boat.

OH YES. YOU DO, said Death.

"But we might not?"

NO. YOU WILL. THERE IS NO DOUBT ABOUT THAT.

"But you said—"

YES, IT IS A BIT HARD TO UNDERSTAND, ISN'T IT? APPARENTLY THERE'S THIS THING CALLED THE TROUSERS OF TIME, WHICH IS QUITE ODD, BECAUSE TIME CERTAINLY DOESN'T—

The boat went over the waterfall.

Vimes had a thunderous sensation of pounding, thudding water, followed by the echoing ringing in his ears as he hit the pool below. He fought his way to what passed for the surface and felt the current take him, slam him into a rock and then roll him away in the white water.

He flailed blindly and caught another rock, his body swinging around into a pool of comparative calm. As he fought for breath he saw a gray shape leaping from stone to stone and then another dose of hell was unleashed as it landed, snarling, beside him.

He grabbed it desperately and hung on as it struggled to bite him. Then a paw flailed to gain purchase on the slippery stone and then, in sudden difficulties, responding automatically . . . it *Changed* . . .

It was as if the wolf shape became small and a man shape became bigger, in the same space, at the same time, with a moment of horrible distortion as the two forms passed through one another.

And then there was that moment he'd noticed before, a second of confusion—

It was just long enough to ram the man's head against the rock with every ounce of strength he could scrape together. Vimes thought he heard a crack.

He pushed himself back out into the current and let it carry him on, while he simply struggled to stay near the surface. There was blood in the water.

He'd never killed someone with his bare hands before. Truth to tell, he'd never deliberately killed at all. There had been deaths, because when people are rolling down a roof and trying to strangle one another, it's sheer luck who is on top when they hit the ground. But that was *different*. He went to bed every night believing that.

His teeth were chattering and the bright sun made his eyes ache, but he felt . . . good.

He wanted to beat his chest and scream, in fact.

They'd been trying to *kill* him!

Make them stay wolves, said a little inner voice. The more time they spent on four legs, the less bright they'd become.

A deeper voice, red and raw, from much, much further inside, said: Kill 'em all!

The rage was boiling up now, fighting against the chill.

His feet touched bottom.

The river was broadening here, into something wide enough to be called a lake. A wide ledge of ice had crept out from the bank, covered here and there with blown snow. Fog drifted across it, fog with a sulfurous smell.

There were still cliffs on the far side of the river. One solitary werewolf, companion to the one now drifting on the current, was watching him from the nearest bank.

Clouds were sliding across the sun and snow was falling again, in large, raggedy flakes.

Vimes waded to the rim of ice and tried to pull himself up out of the water, but it creaked ominously under his weight and cracks zigzagged across its surface.

The wolf came closer, moving with caution. Vimes made another desperate attempt; a slab of ice came free and tipped up, and he disappeared under the water.

The creature waited a few moments and then inched farther out over the ice, growling as fine cracks spread out like stars under its paws.

A shadow moved in the shallow water below it. There was an explosion of water and breath as Vimes broke through the ice under the werewolf, grabbed it around the waist, and fell back.

A claw ripped along Vimes's side, but he gripped as hard as he could with arms and legs as they rolled under the ice. It was a desperate test of lung capacity, he knew. But *he* wasn't the one who'd just had the air squeezed out of him. He held on, while the water clanged in his ears and the thing scrabbled and scratched at him and then, when there was nothing else left but to let go or drown, he punched his way up to the air.

Nothing lashed at him. He cracked his way through the ice to the bank, dropped on his hands and knees, and threw up.

Howling started, all around the mountains.

Vimes looked up. Blood was coursing down his arms. The air stank of rotten eggs.

And there, high on a hill a mile or so off, was the clacks tower.

. . . with its stone walls and door that could be bolted . . .

He stumbled forward.

The snow underfoot was already giving way to coarse grass and moss. The air was hotter now, but it was the clammy heat of a fever. And then he looked around, and realized where he was.

There was bare dirt and rock in front of him, but here and there parts of it were moving and going *blup*.

Everywhere he looked, there were fat geysers. Rings of ancient, congealed, yellow fat, so old and rancid that even Sam Vimes wouldn't dip his toast in it unless he was really hungry, encircled sizzling little pools. There were even black floating bits, which on a second glance turned out to be insects that were slow learners in a hot fat situation.

Vimes recalled something Igor had said. Sometimes, dwarfs working the high strata, where the fat had congealed into a kind of tallow millennia ago, occasionally found strange ancient animals, perfectly preserved but fried to a crisp.

Probably . . . Vimes found himself laughing, out of sheer exhaustion . . . probably battered to death.

Mwahahaa.

The snow was heavy now, making the fat pools spit.

He sagged to his knees. He ached all over. It wasn't just that his brain was writing checks that his body couldn't cash. It had gone beyond that. Now his feet were borrowing money that his legs hadn't got, and his back muscles were looking for loose change under the sofa cushions.

And still nothing was coming up behind him. Surely they must've crossed the river by now?

Then he saw one. He could have sworn it hadn't been there a moment ago. Another one trotted out from behind a nearby snowdrift.

They sat watching him.

"Come on, then!" Vimes yelled. "What are you waiting for?"

The pools of fat hissed and bubbled around Vimes. It was warm here, though. If they weren't going to move, then neither was he.

He focused on a tree on the edge of the fat geysers. It looked barely alive, with greasy splashes on the end of the longer branches, but it also looked climbable. He concentrated on it, tried to estimate the distance and whatever speed he might be capable of.

The werewolves turned to look at it, too.

Another one had entered the clearing at a different point. There were three watching him now.

They weren't going to run until he ran, he realized. Otherwise it wouldn't be *fun*.

He shrugged, turned away from the tree . . . and then turned back and ran. By the time he was halfway there he was afraid his heart was going to climb up his throat, but he ran on, jumped awkwardly, caught a low branch, slipped, struggled gasping to his feet, grabbed the branch again and managed to pull himself up, expecting at every second the first tiny puncture as teeth broke his skin . . .

He rocked on the greasy wood. The werewolves hadn't moved, but they were watching him with interest.

"You *bastards*," Vimes growled.

They got up and picked their way carefully toward the tree, without hurrying. Vimes climbed a little farther up the tree.

"Ankh-Morpork! Mister Civilized! Where are your weapons now, Ankh-Morpork?"

It was Wolfgang's voice. Vimes peered around the snowdrifts, which were already filling up with violet shadows as the afternoon died.

"I got two of you!" he shouted.

"Yes, they will have big headaches later on! We are *werewolves*, Ankh-Morpork! Quite hard to stop!"

"You said that you—"

"Your Mister Sleeps could run much faster than you, Ankh-Morpork!"

"Fast enough?"

"No! And the man with the little black hat could *fight* better than you, too!"

"Well enough?"

"No!" shouted Wolfgang cheerfully.

Vimes growled. Even Assassins didn't deserve that kind of death.

"It'll be sunset soon!" he shouted.

"Yes! I lied about the sunset!"

"Well, wake me up at dawn, then. I could do with the sleep!"

"You will freeze to death, Civilized Man!"

"Good!" Vimes looked around at the other trees. Even if he could jump to one, they were all conifers, painful to land in and easy to fall out of.

"Ah, this must be the famous Ankh-Morpork sense of humor, yes?"

"No, that was just irony," Vimes shouted, still looking for an arboreal escape route. "You'll know when we've got onto the famous Ankh-Morpork sense of humor when I start talking about breasts and farting!"

So what were his options? Well, he could stay in the tree, and die, or run for it, and die. Of the two, dying in one piece seemed better.

You're doing very well for a man of your age.

Death was sitting on a higher branch of the tree.

"Are you following me, or what?"

Are you familiar with the phrase 'Death was his constant companion'?

"But I don't usually *see* you!"

Possibly you are in a state of heightened awareness caused by lack of food, sleep and blood?

"Are you going to help me?"

Well . . . yes.

"When?"

Er . . . when the pain is too much to bear. Death hesitated, and then went on, Even as I say it I realize that this isn't the answer you were looking for, however.

The sun was near the horizon now, getting big and red.

Racing the sun . . . that was another Uberwald sport, wasn't it? Be home safe before the sun sets.

Half a mile or more, through deep snow in rising ground . . .

Someone was climbing up the tree. He felt it shake. He looked down. In the cold blue gloom, a naked man was quietly pulling himself from branch to branch.

Vimes was enraged. They weren't supposed to do this!

There was a grunt from below as the climber slipped and recovered on the greasy wood.

How are you feeling, in yourself?

"Shut *up*! Even if you *are* a hallucination!"

There must be *something* about werewolves he could use . . .

You have a second's grace when they were changing shape, but they knew he knew that . . .

No weapons. That's what he'd noticed in the castle. You *always* got weapons in castles. Spears, battleaxes, ridiculous suits of armor, huge old swords . . . Even the vampire had a few rapiers on the walls. That was because, sometimes, even vampires had to use a weapon.

Werewolves didn't. Even Angua hesitated before reaching for a sword. To a werewolf, a physical weapon would always be the *second* choice.

Vimes locked his legs together and swung around the branch as the werewolf came up. He caught it a blow on the ear and, as it looked up, managed another blow right on the nose.

It gave him a ringing slap and that would have ended it, except that it also pulled itself a little farther up the tree and brought itself in the range of the Vimes Elbow.

It justified the capital letter. It had triumphed in a number of street fights. Vimes had learned early on in his career that the graveyards were full of people who'd read the Marquis of Fantailler. The whole *idea* of fighting was to stop the other bloke hitting you as soon as possible. It wasn't to earn *marks*. Vimes had often fought in circumstances where being able to use the hands freely was a luxury, but it was amazing how a well-placed elbow could make a point, possibly assisted by a knee.

He drove it into the werewolf's throat, and was rewarded with a horrible noise. Then he grabbed a handful of hair and pulled, let go and slammed the palm of his hand into its face in a mad attempt to prevent it having a second to think. He couldn't allow that—he could see the size of the man's muscles.

The werewolf reacted, instead.

There was that sudden moment of morphological inexactitude. A nose turned into a muzzle while Vimes's fist was en route, but when the wolf opened its mouth to lunge at him two things occurred to it.

One was that it was high in a tree, not a tenable position for a shape designed for fast-paced living on the ground. The other was gravity.

"Down there it's the lore," Vimes panted, as its paws scrabbled for purchase on the greasy branch. "But up here it's *me*."

He reached up, grabbed the branch above him and kicked down with his feet.

There was a yelp, and another yelp as the wolf slid and hit the next branch down.

About halfway toward the ground it tried to change back again, combining in one falling shape all the qualities of something not good at staying in trees with something not good at landing on the ground.

"Gotcha!" screamed Vimes.

In the forest all around, a howling went up.

The branch he was clinging to . . . snapped. For a moment he hung by the gloomy trousers of Uncle Vanya, caught on a snag, and then their ancient fabric ripped off him and he dropped.

His progress was a little faster, since the falling werewolf had removed a lot of branches on the way down, but the landing was softer because the werewolf was just getting to its feet.

Vimes's flailing hand grabbed a broken branch.

A *weapon*.

Thought more or less stopped when his fingers closed. Whatever replaced it in the pathways of his brain was gushing up from somewhere else, thousands of years old.

The werewolf struggled up and turned on him. The branch caught it across the side of the head.

Steam rose off Sir Samuel Vimes as he lurched forward, snarling incoherently. He smacked the club down again. He roared. There were no words there. It was a sound from before words. If there was any meaning in it at all, it was a lament that he couldn't cause enough pain . . .

The wolf whined, stumbled, rolled over . . . and Changed.

The human extended a bleeding hand toward him in supplication.

"Ple-ease . . ."

Vimes hesitated, club raised.

The red rage drained away.

In one movement, changing from man to wolf as it moved, the werewolf sprang.

Vimes went backward into the snow. He could feel the breath and the blood, but not the pain—

No talons ripped, no teeth tore.

And the weight was lifted. Hands pulled the body off him.

"Bit of a close one there, sir," said a voice cheerfully. "Best not to give them any quarter, really." There was a spear right through the werewolf.

"Carrot?"

"We'll get a fire going. It's easy if you dip the wood in the fat springs first."

"Carrot?"

"I shouldn't think you've eaten. There's not much game this close to the town, but we've still got some—"

"Carrot?"

"Er . . . yes, sir?"

"What the hell are you doing here?"

"It's all a bit complicated, sir. Here, let me help you up—"

Vimes shook him off as he tried to help him to his feet.

"I got this far, thank you, I think I'm capable of standing up," he said, and forced his legs to support him.

"You seem to have lost your trousers, sir."

"Yes, it's the famous Ankh-Morpork sense of humor once again," growled Vimes.

"Only . . . Angua will be back soon, and . . . and . . ."

"Sergeant Angua's family, Captain, are in the habit of running around the woods in the snow stark bol—stark naked!"

"Yes, sir, but . . . I mean . . . you know . . . it's not really . . ."

"I'll give you five minutes to find a clothes shop, shall I? Otherwise— Look, where the hell are all the werewolves, eh? I was expecting to drop into a heap of snarling jaws, and now you're here, thank you very much, and there's no werewolves!"

"Gavin's people chased them away, sir. You must've heard the howl go up."

"Gavin's people, eh? Well, that's good! That's very good! I'm pleased about that! Well done, Gavin! Now . . . *who the hell is Gavin!*"

A howl went up from a distant hill.

"That's Gavin," said Carrot.

"A wolf? Gavin's a wolf? I've been saved from werewolves by *wolves?*"

"It's all right, sir. When you think about it, it's not really any different from being saved from werewolves by people."

"When I think about it, I think perhaps I was better off lying down," said Vimes weakly.

"Let's get to the sleigh, sir. I was trying to say we have *got* your clothes. That's how Angua tracked you."

Ten minutes later Vimes was sitting in front of a fire with a blanket around him, and the world seemed to make a little more sense. A slice of venison was going down well, and Vimes was far too hungry to bother much that the butcher appeared to have used his teeth.

"The wolves spy on the werewolves?" he said.

"Sort of, sir. Gavin keeps an eye on things for Angua. They're . . . old friends."

The moment of silence went on just slightly too long.

"He sounds like a very bright wolf," said Vimes, in the absence of anything more diplomatic to say.

"More than that. Angua thinks he might be part werewolf, from way back."

"Er . . . can that happen?"

"She says so. Did I tell you that he came all the way into Ankh-Morpork? A big city? Can you imagine what that must have been like?"

Vimes turned at a faint sound behind him.

A large wolf was standing at the edge of the firelight. It was looking at him intently. It wasn't just the look of an animal, sizing him up on the level of food/threat/thing. Behind that stare, wheels were turning. And there was a small but rather proud mongrel at his side, scratching furiously.

"Is that . . . Gaspode?" said Vimes. "The dog that's always hanging around the Watch House?"

"Yes, he . . . helped me get here," said Carrot.

"I just don't want to ask," said Vimes. "Any minute now a door's going to open in a tree and Fred and Nobby are going to step out, am I right?"

"I hope not, sir."

Gavin lay down a short distance from the fire, and started watching Carrot.

"Captain?" said Vimes.

"Yes, sir?"

"You'll notice I haven't pressed you on why you're here as well as Angua?"

"Yes, sir."

"Well?" said Vimes. And now he thought he recognized the look on Gavin's face, even though it was on a face of an unusual shape. It was the look you got on the face of a gentleman lounging on a corner by a bank, watching the comings and goings, seeing how the place worked . . .

"I was admiring your diplomacy, sir."

"Hmm? What?" said Vimes, still staring at the wolf.

"I appreciated the way you were avoiding asking questions, sir."

Angua walked into the firelight. Vimes saw her glance around the circle, and squat down on the snow *exactly* halfway between Carrot and Gavin.

"They're miles away now. Oh . . . hello, Mister Vimes."

There was some more silence.

"Is anyone going to tell me something?" said Vimes.

"My family are trying to upset the coronation," said Angua. "They're working with some dwarfs that don't want—that want to keep Uberwald separate."

"I think I've worked that one out. Running for your life through a freezing cold forest gives you a bit of an insight."

"I have to tell you, sir . . . my brother killed the clacky signalers. His scent's all over the place up there."

Gavin made a noise in his throat.

"And another man that Gavin didn't recognize, except that he spent a lot of time hiding in the forest and watching our castle."

"I think that might have been a man called Sleeps. One of our . . . agents," said Vimes.

"He did well. He managed to get to a boat a few miles downriver. Unfortunately, there was a werewolf waiting in it."

"It was a waterfall that did it for me," said Vimes.

"Permission to speak honestly, sir?" said Angua.

"Don't you always?"

"They could have got you any time they liked, sir. Really they could. They wanted you to get as far as the tower before they *really* attacked. I expect Wolfgang thought that'd be nicely symbolic, or something."

"I got three of them!"

"Yes, sir. But you wouldn't have been able to get three of them all at once. Wolfgang was having some . . . fun. That's how he's always played the Game. He's good at thinking ahead. He likes ambushes. He likes some poor soul to get within a few yards of the finish before he leaps out on them." Angua sighed. "Look, sir, I don't want there to be trouble—"

"He's been killing people!"

"Yes, sir. But my mother's just a rather ignorant snob and my father's half-gone now, he spends so much time as a wolf he hardly knows how to act human anymore. They don't live in the real world. They really think Uberwald can stay the same. There isn't a lot up here, really . . . but it's ours. Wolfgang's a murderous idiot who thinks that werewolves were born to rule. The trouble is, sir . . . he hasn't broken the lore."

"Oh, ye gods!"

"I bet he could find plenty of witnesses to say that he gave everyone the start the lore requires. That's the rules of the Game."

"And meddling with the dwarfs' affairs? He's stolen the Scone or swapped it or . . . something, I haven't worked it all out yet, but one poor dwarf's already dead because of it! Cheery and Detritus are under arrest! Inigo is dead! Sybil's locked up somewhere! And you're saying it's all okay?"

"Things are different here, sir," said Carrot. "It wasn't until ten years ago they replaced trial by ordeal here with trial by lawyer, and that was only because they found that lawyers were nastier."

"I've got to get back to Bonk. If they've harmed Sybil I don't care *what* the damn lore is."

"Mister Vimes! You look done in as it is!" said Carrot.

"I'll keep going. Come on. Get some of the wolves to pull the sleigh—"

"You don't *get* them to, sir. You ask Gavin if they will," said Carrot.

"Oh. Er . . . can you explain the situation to him?"

I'm standing in the cold in the middle of a forest, thought Vimes a moment later, watching a quite handsome young woman growling a conversation with a wolf who is watching her. This does not often happen. Not in Ankh-Morpork, anyway. It's probably a daily occurrence up here.

Eventually six wolves allowed themselves to be harnessed, and Vimes was carried up the hill to the road.

"Stop!"

"Sir?" said Carrot.

"I want a weapon! There's got to be something I can use in the tower!"

"Sir, you can use my sword! And there's the . . . hunting spears . . ."

"You know what you can do with the hunting spears!"

Vimes kicked the door at the base of the tower. Fresh snow had blown in, smoothing the edges of wolf and human tracks.

He felt drunk. Bits of his brain were going on and off. His eyeballs felt as though they were lined with toweling. His legs seemed only vaguely under his control.

Surely the signalers must've had *something*?

Even the sacks and barrels had gone. Well, there were plenty of peasants in the hills, and winter was coming on, and the men who'd been here certainly didn't have any use for the food anymore. Even Vimes wouldn't call *that* theft.

He climbed up to the next floor. The thrifty people of the forest had been up here, too. But they hadn't taken the bloodstains off the floor, or Inigo's little round hat which inexplicably was wedged into the wooden wall.

He pulled it out, and saw where the thin felt on the brim had been pushed back to reveal the razor-shape edge.

An assassin's hat, he thought. And then . . . no, *not* an assassin's hat. He remembered the street fights he'd seen when he was a kid, among the hard-drinking men who thought that even bare-knuckle fighting was posh. Some of them would sew a razor blade into the brim of their cap, for a bit of help in a melee. This was the hat of a man who was always looking for that extra edge.

It hadn't worked here.

He dropped it on the floor, and his eye caught, in the gloom, the box of mortars. Even that had been ransacked, but the tubes had simply been scattered across the floor. The gods alone knew what the scavengers thought they were.

He put them back in their box. Inigo was right about them, at least. A weapon so inaccurate that it probably couldn't hit a barn wall from inside the barn was no good as a weapon. But other things had been scattered around, too. The men who'd been living rough here had left a few personal items. Pictures had been thumbtacked to the wall. There was a diary, a pipe, someone's shaving gear . . . Boxes had been tipped out on the floor . . .

"We'd better get on, sir," said Carrot, from the ladder.

They'd been killed. They'd been sent racing off into the dark with monsters at their heels, and then some blank-faced peasants who'd done nothing to help had come in here and picked over the little things they'd left behind . . .

Damn it! Vimes growled and swept everything into the box and dragged it over to the ladder.

"We'll drop this lot off at the embassy," he said. "I'm not leaving any here for scavengers. Don't think about arguing with me."

"Wouldn't dream of it, sir. Wouldn't *dream* of it."

Vimes paused.

"Carrot? That wolf and Angua . . ." He stopped. How the hell did you continue a sentence like that?

"They're old friends, sir."

"They are?"

There was nothing but the usual completely open honesty anywhere in Carrot's expression.

"Oh . . . we . . . that's good, then . . ." Vimes finished.

A minute later, they were on their way again. Angua was running as a wolf far ahead of the sleigh, alongside Gavin. Gaspode had curled up under the blankets.

And here I am again, thought Vimes, racing the sunset. Heaven knows why . . . I'm in the company of a werewolf and a wolf that looks worse, and sitting in a sleigh drawn by wolves which I can't steer. Try looking *that* one up in the manual.

He dozed among the blankets, half-open eyes watching the disk of the sun flickering between pine trees.

How could you steal the Scone from its cave?

He'd said there were dozens of ways and there were, but they were all risky. They all depended too much on luck and sleepy guards. And this didn't feel like a crime that was going to rely on luck. It had to work.

The Scone wasn't important. It *was* important that the dwarfs ended in disarray—no king, violent arguments and fighting in the dark. And it would stay dark in Uberwald, too. And it seemed to be important that the king was blamed . . . after all, he was the one who'd lost the Scone . . .

Whatever the plan was, it had to be done quickly. Well, the clacks would have been useful. What had Wolfgang said? "Those clever men in Ankh-Morpork"? Not dwarfs, but *men*.

Rubber Sonky, floating in his vat . . .

You dipped in a wooden hand, and out of the vat you got a glove . . . hand in glove . . .

It wasn't where you've got it, it's where people think it is. That's what matters. That's the magic.

He remembered the very first thought he'd had, when he saw Cheery staring at the floor of the Scone's cave, and the little policemen in Vimes's head started to clamor.

"What, sir?" said Carrot.

"Hmm?" Vimes forced his eyes open.

"You just shouted, sir."

"What did I shout?"

"You shouted 'The bloody thing was never bloody stolen!,' sir."

"The bastards! I *knew* I nearly had it! It all fits together if you don't think like a dwarf! Let's make sure Sybil is all right and then, Captain, we're going to—"

"Prod buttock, sir?"

"Right!"

"Only one thing, sir . . ."

"What?"

"You are an escaped criminal, aren't you?"

For a moment there was only the sound of the runners skimming over the snow.

"We-ell," said Vimes, "this isn't Ankh-Morpork, I know. Everyone keeps telling me. But, Captain, wherever you are, wherever you go, watchmen are always watchmen."

A solitary light burned in the window. Captain Colon sat by the candle, staring at nothing.

Regulations called for the Watch House to be manned at all hours, and that's what he was doing.

The floorboards in the room below creaked into a new position. For many months now they'd been walked on around the clock, because the main office never had fewer than half a dozen people in it. Chairs, too, accustomed to being warmed continuously by a relay of bottoms, groaned gently as they cooled.

There was only one thought buzzing around Fred Colon's head now.

Mr. Vimes is going to go completely bursar. He's going to go totally Librarian-poo.

His hand went down to the desk and came back automatically, while he looked straight ahead.

There was the *crunch* of a sugar lump being eaten.

Snow was falling again. The watchman that Vimes had named Colonesque was leaning in his box by the hubward gate of Bonk. He'd perfected the art, and it *was* an art form, of going to sleep upright with his eyes open. It was one of the things you learned, on endless nights.

A female voice by his ear said, "Now, there are two ways this could go."

His position didn't change. He continued to stare straight ahead.

"You haven't seen anything. That's the truth, isn't it? Just nod."

He nodded, once.

"Good man. You didn't hear me arrive, did you? Just nod."

Nod.

"So you won't know when I've gone, am I right? Just nod."

Nod.

"You don't want any trouble. Just nod."

Nod.

"They don't pay you enough for this. Just nod."

This time the nod was quite emphatic.

"You get more than your fair share of night watches as it is, anyway."

Colonesque's jaw dropped. Whoever was standing in the shadows was clearly reading his mind.

"Good man. You just stand here, then, and make sure no one steals the gate . . ."

Colonesque took care to continue to stare straight ahead. He heard the thud and creak of the gate being opened and closed.

It occurred to him that the speaker had not in fact mentioned what the *other* way was, and he was quite relieved about that.

"What was the other way?" said Vimes, as they hurried through the snow.

"We'd go and look for another way in," said Angua.

There were few people on the streets, which were whitening with the new snow again except where wisps of steam escaped from the occasional grating. In Uberwald, it seemed, sunset made its own curfew. This was just as well, because Gavin was growling continuously under his breath.

Carrot came back from the next corner.

"There's dwarfs on guard all around the embassy," he said. "They don't look open to negotiation, sir."

Vimes looked down. They were standing on a grating.

Captain Tantony of the Bonk Watch was not happy with this duty.

He'd been at the opera last night, and later on he'd thought he saw things happening in a way which, the burger-master had instructed him, hadn't happened. Of course, the thing to do was obey orders. You were safe if you obeyed orders. Everyone in the Watch knew that. But these didn't feel like safe orders.

He'd heard they did things differently in Ankh-Morpork. Milord Vimes would arrest anyone, they said.

Tantony had set up a desk in the embassy's hall, so that he could keep an eye on the main doors. He'd taken some pains to position his men around the inside of the building; he didn't trust the dwarfs on guard outside. They'd said they'd gotten orders to kill Vimes on sight, and that didn't make any sense. There had to be *some* sort of a trial, didn't there?

There was a faint noise from upstairs. He stood up carefully and reached for his crossbow.

"Corporal Svetlz?"

There was another little sound.

Tantony went to the bottom of the stairs.

Vimes appeared at the top of them. There was blood on his shirt, and crusted on the side of his face. To the captain's horror, he began to walk down the steps.

"I *will* shoot you!"

"That's the order, is it?" said Vimes.

"Yes! Stop there!"

"But I'm going to be shot *anyway*, there's no point *in* stopping, is there?" said Vimes. "I don't think you're the kind to do that, Captain. You've got a brain." Vimes steadied himself on the banister rail. "Shouldn't you have called for the rest of the guards by now, by the way?"

"I tell you to *stop!*"

"You know who I am. If you're going to fire that damn thing, do it now. But first, I suggest it would be a really *good* career move to tug the bellpull over there. What's the worst that would happen? You've still got the bow pointed at me. There's something you really ought to know."

Tantony gave him a suspicious look, but took a few steps sideways and tugged the rope.

Igor stepped out from behind a pillar.

"Yeth, marthter?"

"Tell this young man where he is, will you?"

"He'th in Ankh-Morpork, marthter," said Igor calmly.

"See?" said Vimes. "And don't glare at Igor like that. I missed it when he welcomed me here, but it's true. This is an *embassy*, my son," he went on, walking forward again, "and that means it's officially on the soil of the home counti y. Welcome to Ankh-Morpork. There's thousands of Uberwald people living in our city. You don't want to go starting a *war*, do you?"

"But . . . but . . . they said . . . my orders . . . you are a criminal!"

"The word is *accused*, Captain. We don't kill people in Ankh-Morpork just because they're *accused*. Well, not on purpose. And not because someone tells us to."

Vimes took the crossbow out of his unresisting hands, and fired it into the ceiling.

"Now send your men away," he said.

"I'm in *Ankh-Morpork*?" said the captain.

Even in his current state, Vimes thought he recognized the harmonics.

"That's *right*," he said, putting an arm around him. "A city which, incidentally, always has a job in the Watch for a young man of ability—"

Tantony's body stiffened. He pushed Vimes's arm away.

"You insult me, milord. This is my country!"

"Ah." Vimes was aware of Carrot and Angua watching from the landing.

"But . . . I will not see *it* dishonored, either," said the captain. "This isn't right. I *saw* what happened last night. You swept up the king and your troll *caught* the chandelier! And then they said you'd tried to kill the king and you'd killed dwarfs when you escaped . . ."

"Are you in charge of the Watch here?"

"No. That's the job of the burgermaster."

"And who gives him *his* orders?"

"Everyone," said Tantony bitterly. Vimes nodded. Been there, he thought. Been there, done that, bought the doublet . . .

"Are you going to stop me taking my people out of here?"

"How can you do that? The dwarfs surround us!"

"We're going to use . . . diplomatic channels. Just show me where everyone is, and we'll be off. If it's any help, I can hit you over the head and tie you up . . ."

"That will not be required. The dwarf and the troll are in the cellar. Her Ladyship is . . . I assume she's wherever the baron took her . . ."

Vimes felt the little trickle of superheated ice down his spine.

"Took her?" he said hoarsely.

"Well . . . yes." Tantony stepped back from Vimes's expression. "She knew the baroness, sir! She said they were old friends! She said they could sort it all out! And then . . ." Tantony's voice became a mumble, seared into silence by the look on Vimes's face.

When Vimes spoke, it was in a monotone as threatening as a spear.

"You are standing there in your shiny breastplate and your silly helmet and your sword without a single notch in the blade and your stupid trousers and *you* are telling *me* that you let my *wife* be taken away by *werewolves*?"

Tantony took a step backward.

"It was the baron—"

"And you don't argue with barons. Right. You don't argue with anyone. Do you know what? I'm ashamed, *ashamed* to think that something like you is called a watchman. Now give me those keys."

The man had gone red.

"You've obeyed many orders," said Vimes. "Don't . . . even . . . think . . . about . . . disobeying . . . that . . . one."

Carrot reached the bottom of the stairs and put a hand on his shoulder.

"Steady, Mister Vimes."

Tantony looked from one to the other and made a life decision.

"I hope you . . . find your lady, milord." He produced a bunch of keys and handed them over. "I really do."

Vimes, still fighting for breath, wordlessly passed the keys to Carrot.

"Let them out," he said.

"Are you going to the werewolves' castle?" Tantony panted.

"Yes."

"You won't stand a chance, milord. They do as they please."

"Then they've got to be stopped."

"You can't. The old one understood the rules, but Wolfgang . . . he doesn't obey anything!"

"All the more reason to stop him, then. Ah, Detritus." The troll saluted. "You've got your bow, I see. Treated you well, did they?"

"Dey called me a ficko troll," said Detritus, darkly. "One of dem kicked me inna rocks."

"Was it this one?"

"No."

"But he is their captain," said Vimes, stepping away from Tantony. "Sergeant, I order you: Shoot him down."

In one movement the troll had the crossbow balanced on his shoulder and was sighting along the massive package of arrows. Tantony went pale.

"Well, go on," said Vimes. "It was an order, Sergeant."

Detritus lowered the bow.

"I ain't dat fick, sir."

"I gave you an *order!*"

"Den you can do wid that order what Boulder der Lintel did wid his bag of gravel, sir! Wid respect, o'course."

Vimes walked across and patted the shaking Tantony on his shoulder.

"Just making a point," he said.

"However," said Detritus, "if you can find der man dat kicked me inna rocks, I should be happy to get him a flick around der earhole. I know which one it was. He's der one walkin' wid der limp."

Lady Sybil drank her wine carefully. It didn't taste very nice. In fact, quite a lot of things weren't very nice.

She wasn't a good cook. She'd never been taught proper cookery;

at her school it had always been assumed that other people would be doing the cookery and that in any case it would be for fifty people using at least four types of fork. Such dishes as she had mastered were dainty things on doilies.

But she cooked for Sam because she vaguely felt that a wife ought to and, besides, he was an eater who entirely matched her kitchen skills. He *liked* burnt sausages and fried eggs that went *boing* when you tried to stick a fork in them. If you gave him caviar, he'd want it in batter. He was an easy man to feed, if you always kept some lard in the house.

But the food here tasted as though it had been cooked by someone who had never even *tried* before. She'd seen the kitchens, when Serafine had given her the little tour, and they'd just about do for a cottage. The game larders, on the other hand, were the size of barns. She'd never seen so many dead things hanging up.

It was just that she was certain that venison shouldn't be served boiled, with potatoes that were crunchy. If they were potatoes, of course. Potatoes weren't usually gray. Even Sam, who *liked* the black lumpy bits you got in some mashed potatoes, would have commented. But Sybil had been brought up properly; if you can't find something nice to say about the food, find *something* to be nice about.

"These are . . . really *very* interesting plates," she said, dutifully. "Er . . . are you *sure* there's been no more news?" She tried to avoid watching the baron. He was ignoring Sybil and his wife and was prodding the meat around on his plate as if he'd forgotten what a knife and fork were for.

"Wolfgang and his friends are still out searching," said Serafine. "But this is terrible weather for a man to be on the run."

"He is *not* on the run!" snapped Sybil. "Sam is *not* guilty of *anything!*"

"Of course, of course. All the evidence is circumstantial. Of course," said the baroness soothingly. "Now, I suggest that as soon as they have the passes clear, you and the, er, the staff get back to the safety of Ankh-Morpork before the real winter hits. We know the country, my dear. If your husband is alive, we can soon do something about it."

"I will not have him shamed like this! You *saw* him save the king!"

"I'm sure he did, Sybil. I'm afraid I was talking to my husband at the time, but I don't disbelieve you for a *minute*. Er . . . is it true that he killed all those men in the Wilinus Pass?"

"What? But . . . they were bandits!" At the other end of the table the baron had picked up a lump of meat and was trying to tear it apart with his teeth.

"Well, of course. Yes. Of course."

Sybil pinched the bridge of her nose. Most of her would not have considered Sam Vimes guilty of murder, actual *murder*, even on the evidence of three gods and a message written on the sky. But . . . stories did get back to her, in a roundabout way. Sam got wound up about things. Sometimes he unwound all at once. There'd been that . . . bad business with that little girl and those men over at Dolly Sisters, and when Sam had broken in to the men's lodging he found one of them had stolen one of her shoes, and she'd heard Detritus say that if he hadn't been there only Sam would have walked out of the room alive . . .

She shook her head.

"I really would like a bath," she said. There was a clatter from the other end of the table.

"Dear, you will have to eat your dinner in the Changing room," said the baroness, without looking around. She flashed Lady Sybil

319

a brief, brittle smile. "We do not, in fact, have a . . . have such a, a device in the castle." A thought occurred to her. "We use the hot springs. So much more hygienic."

"Out in the forest?"

"Oh, it's quite close. And a quick run around in the snow really tones up the body."

"I think perhaps I shall have a lie-down instead," said Lady Sybil, firmly. "But thank you all the same."

She made her way to the musty bedroom, fuming in a ladylike way.

She couldn't bring herself to like Serafine, and this was shocking, because Lady Sybil even liked Nobby Nobbs, and that took breeding. But the werewolf scraped across her nerves like a file. She remembered that she'd never liked her at school, either.

Among the other unwanted baggage that had been heaped on the young Sybil to hamper her progress through life was the injunction to be pleasant to people and say helpful things. People took this to mean that she didn't think.

She'd hated the way Serafine had talked about dwarfs. She'd called them "subhuman." Well, obviously most of them lived *underground*, but Sybil rather liked dwarfs. And Serafine spoke of trolls as if they were *things*. Sybil hadn't met many trolls, but the ones she knew seemed to spend their lives raising their children and looking for the next dollar just like everyone else.

Worst of all, Serafine simply assumed that Sybil would naturally agree with her stupid opinions because she was a lady. Sybil Ramkin had not had an education in these things, moral philosophy not having featured much in a curriculum that was heavy on flower-arranging, but she had a shrewd idea that in any possible debate the right side was where Serafine wasn't.

She'd only ever written all those letters to her because it was what you did. You always wrote letters to old friends, even if you weren't very friendly with them.

She sat on the bed and stared at the wall until the shouting started, and when the shouting started she knew Sam was alive and well, because only Sam made people that angry.

She heard the key click in the lock.

Sybil rebelled.

She was large, and she was kind. She hadn't enjoyed school much. A society of girls is not a good one in which to be large and kind, because people are inclined to interpret that as "stupid" and, worse, "deaf."

Lady Sybil looked out of the window. She was two floors up.

There were bars across the window, but they'd been designed to keep something out; from the inside, they could be lifted out of their slots. And there were musty but heavy sheets and blankets on the bed. None of this might have suggested very much to the average person, but life in a rather strict school for well brought-up young ladies can give someone a real insight into the tricks of escapology.

Five minutes after the key had turned, there was only one bar in the window and it jerked and creaked in the stonework, suggesting that quite a heavy weight was on the sheets that had been neatly knotted around it.

Torches streamed all along the castle walls. The ghastly red and black flag snapped in the wind. Vimes looked over the side of the bridge. The water was a long way down, and pure white even before it reached the waterfall. Forward and back were the only possible directions here.

He reviewed his troops. Unfortunately, this did not take long. Even a policeman could count up to five. Then there was Gavin and his wolves, who were lurking in the trees. And finally, very definitely finally, there was Gaspode, the Corporal Nobbs of the canine world, who'd attached himself to the group uninvited.

What else was on his side? Well, the enemy preferred not to use weapons. This bonus evaporated somewhat when you remembered that they had, at will, some very nasty teeth and claws.

He sighed, and turned to Angua.

"I know this is your family," he said. "I won't blame you if you hang back."

"We'll see, sir, shall we?"

"How are we going to get in, sir?" said Carrot.

"How would *you* go about it, Carrot?"

"Well, I'd start by knocking, sir."

"Really? Sergeant Detritus, forward please."

"Sir!"

"Blow the bloody doors off!"

"Yessir!"

Vimes turned back to Carrot as the troll gazed thoughtfully at the door and began making extra turns on his crossbow's winch, grunting as the springs fought back. Their fight was unsuccessful.

"This isn't Ankh-Morpork, see?" said Vimes.

Detritus hoisted the bow onto his shoulders and took a step forward.

There was a *thunk*. Vimes didn't see the bundle of arrows leave the bow. They were probably already fragments by the time they'd gone about a few feet. Halfway toward the doors the expanding cloud of splinters exploded into flame from the air friction.

What hit the doors was a fireball as angry and unstoppable as the Fifth Elephant and traveling at an appreciable fraction of local light speed.

"My gods, Detritus," muttered Vimes, as the thunder died away. "That's not a crossbow, that's a national emergency . . ."

A few bits of charred door crashed onto the cobbles.

"The wolves won't come in, Mister Vimes," said Angua. "Gavin will follow me, but they won't come, not even for him."

"Why not?"

"Because they're wolves, sir. They don't feel at home in houses."

The only sound was the squeak-squeak of Detritus winding up his bow again.

"The hell with it," said Vimes, drawing his sword and stepping forward.

Lady Sybil untucked her dress from her underwear and stepped carefully across the little courtyard. She was somewhere around the rear of the castle, as far as she could make out.

She flattened herself as best she could against the wall when she heard a sound, and tightened her grip on one of the iron bars that had formerly graced the window.

A large wolf came around the corner, holding a bone in its mouth. It did not look as if it was expecting her, and certainly wasn't expecting the iron bar.

"Oh, I'm terribly sorry," said Sybil automatically, as it folded up onto the cobbles.

There was an explosion on the other side of the castle. That sounded like Sam.

* * *

"Do you think they heard us, sir?" said Carrot.

"Captain, people in *Ankh-Morpork* probably heard us. So where are all the werewolves?"

Angua pushed forward. "This way," she said.

She led them up a flight of low steps to the door of the keep, and tried one of the doors. It swung back slowly.

There were torches in the hall, too.

"They'll leave us somewhere to run," she said. "We *always* leave people somewhere to run . . ."

A pair of smaller doors at the far end of the hall were pushed open. No handles, Vimes noted. Paws can't use handles.

Wolfgang stepped in. A couple dozen werewolves escorted him, fanning out around the room and sitting down . . . *sprawling* down and then watching the intruders with keen interest.

"Ah, Civilized!" said Wolfgang cheerfully. "You won the Game! Would you like another go? When people have a second Game we give them a handicap! We bite one of their legs off! Good joke, hey?"

"I think I prefer the Ankh-Morpork sense of humor," said Vimes. "Where's my wife, you bastard?" He could still hear the sound of Detritus winding. That was the trouble with the big bow. It was only a quick-fire weapon by geological standards.

"And Delphine! *Look* at what the dog dragged in!" said Wolfgang, ignoring Vimes. He stepped forward. Vimes heard a growl begin in Angua's throat, a sound which could cause instant obedience in many of Ankh-Morpork's criminal population when they encountered it in a dark alley. There was a deeper rumble from Gavin.

Wolfgang stopped.

"You haven't got the brains for this, Wolfie," said Angua. "And you couldn't plot your way out of a wet paper bag. Where's Mother?"

She looked around at the lolling werewolves. "Hello, Uncle Ulf . . . Aunt Hilda . . . Magwen . . . Nancy . . . Unity . . . The pack's all here, then? Except for Father, who I expect is off rolling in something. What a family—"

"I want these disgusting people out of here *right* away," said the baroness, stepping into the hall. She glared at Detritus. "How dare you bring a troll into this house!"

"O-kay, it's all wound up," said Detritus cheerfully, hoisting the humming bow onto his shoulder. "Where should I fire it, Mister Vimes?"

"Good grief, not in *here*! This is an enclosed building!"

"Only up until I pull dis trigger, sir."

"How very *civilized*," said the baroness. "How very Ankh-Morpork. You think you merely have to threaten and the lesser races back down, eh?"

"Have you seen your gates lately?" said Vimes.

"We're *werewolves*," snapped the baroness—and it *was* a snap, the words sharp and clipped as though they were barked. "Stupid toys like that don't frighten us."

"But it'll slow you down for a while. Now bring out Lady Sybil!"

"Lady Sybil is resting. You are in no position to make demands, Mister Vimes. We are not the criminals here."

As Vimes's mouth dropped open, she went on: "The Game is not against the lore. It has been played for a thousand years. And what else is it that you think we have done? Stolen the dwarfs' pet rock? We—"

"You *know* it wasn't stolen," said Vimes. "And I know—"

"You *know* nothing! You suspect everything. You have that kind of mind."

"Your son said—"

"My son unfortunately has honed to perfection every muscle in his body except the ones for thinking with," said the baroness. "In civilized Ankh-Morpork I daresay you can barge into people's houses and stamp around, but here in our barbaric backwater the lore requires something beyond mere assertion."

"I can smell the fear," said Angua. "It's pouring off you, Mother."

"Sam?"

They looked up. Lady Sybil was standing at the top of some stone stairs leading to a lower floor, looking bewildered and angry. She was holding an iron bar with a bend in it.

"Sybil!"

"*She* told me you were on the run and they were all trying to save you . . . but that wasn't right, was it . . ."

It's a terrible thing to admit to yourself, but when the shoulder blades are pressed firmly against the brickwork then any weapon will do, and right now Vimes saw Sybil loaded and ready to fire.

She got on with people. Practically from the moment she'd been able to talk she'd been taught how to listen. And when Sybil listened to people she made them feel good about themselves. It was probably something to do with being a . . . a big girl. She tried to make herself seem small, and by default that made those around her feel bigger. She got on with people almost as well as Carrot. No wonder even the dwarfs liked her.

She had pages to herself in *Twurp's Peerage*, huge ancestral anchors biting into the past, and dwarfs also respected someone who knew their great-great-great-grandfather's full name. And Sybil couldn't lie, you could see her redden when she tried it. Sybil was a rock. She made Detritus look like a sponge.

"We've been having a lovely run in the woods, dear," he said. "Now please come here, because I think we're going to see the king. And I'm going to tell him everything. I've worked it out at last . . ."

"The dwarfs will *kill* you," said the baroness.

"I can probably outrun a dwarf," said Vimes. "And now we're leaving. Angua?"

Angua hadn't moved. Her eyes were still fixed on her mother, and she was still growling.

Vimes recognized the signs. You spotted them in the bars of Ankh-Morpork every Saturday night. Hackles rose, and people climbed up them, and then all that was needed was for someone to break a bottle. Or blink.

"We are *leaving*, Angua," he repeated. The other werewolves were standing up and stretching.

Carrot reached out and took her arm. She turned, snarling. It was over in a fraction of a second, and in reality her head had hardly moved before she got a grip on herself.

"Sor thiz iz therr boy?" said the baroness, her voice slurring. "You betrrray yourrr people for *thizz*?"

Her ears were lengthening, Vimes was sure. The muscles in her face were moving strangely, too.

"And what else hass Anrk-Morrporrk taught you?"

Angua shuddered.

"Self-control," she muttered. "Let's go, Mister Vimes."

The werewolves closed in as they backed toward the steps.

"Don't turn your back," said Angua levelly. "Don't run."

"Don't need telling," said Vimes. He was watching Wolfgang, who was moving obliquely across the floor, his eyes fixed on the retreating party.

They'll have to bunch up to follow us through the doorway, he thought. He glanced at Detritus. The giant crossbow was weaving back and forth as the troll tried to keep all the wolves in the field of fire.

"Fire it," said Angua.

"But they're your family!" said Sybil.

"They'll heal soon enough, believe me!"

"Detritus, don't shoot unless you have to," Vimes ordered, as they headed toward the drawbridge.

"He has to *now*," said Angua. "Sooner or later Wolfgang will leap, and the others will take—"

"There's something you ought to know, sir," said Cheery. "You really ought to know it, sir. It's really *important*."

Vimes looked across the drawbridge. Figures massed in the dark. Torchlight glinted off armor and weaponry, blocking the way.

"Well, things couldn't get any worse," he said.

"Oh, they could if there were snakes in here with us," said Lady Sybil.

Carrot turned at the sound of Vimes's snort of laughter.

"Sir?"

"Oh, nothing, Captain. Keep your eyes on the bastards, will you? We can deal with the soldiers later."

"Just say the word, sir," said Detritus.

"You arrre trrapped now," snarled the baroness. "Watchman! Do yourr duty!"

A figure was walking across the bridge, carrying a torch.

Captain Tantony reached Vimes, and glared at him.

"Stand aside, sir," he said. "Stand aside, or by gods, ambassador or not, I'll arrest you!"

Their eyes met.

Then Vimes looked away.

"Let's let him through," he said. "The man's decided he's got a duty to do."

Tantony nodded slightly, and then marched on across to the bridge until he was a few feet from the baroness. He saluted.

"Take these people away!" she said.

"Lady Serafine von Uberwald?" said Tantony woodenly.

"You *know* who I am, man!"

"I wish to talk to you concerning certain charges made in my presence."

Vimes closed his eyes. Oh, you poor dumb idiot . . . I didn't mean you to actually—

"You *what*?" said the baroness.

"It has been alleged, my lady, that a member or members of your family have been involved in a conspiracy to—"

"How *darrre* you!" screamed Serafine.

And Wolfgang leapt, and the future became a series of flickering images.

In midair he changed into the wolf.

Vimes grabbed the bottom of Detritus's bow and forced it upward at the same time as the troll pulled the trigger.

Carrot was running before Wolfgang landed on Captain Tantony's chest.

The *sound* of the bow echoed around the castle, above the noise of a thousand whirring fragments scything through the sky.

Carrot reached Wolfgang in a flat dive. He hit the wolf with his shoulder, and the two of them were bowled over.

Then, like some moving magic lantern show coming back up to speed, the scene exploded.

Carrot got to his feet and—

It must be because we're abroad, thought Vimes. He's trying to do things *properly*.

He'd squared up to the werewolf, fists balled, a stance taken straight from Fig. 1 of *The Noble Art of Fisticuffs*, which looked impressive right up to the point when your opponent broke your nose with a quart mug.

Carrot had a punch like an iron bar, and landed a couple of heavy blows on Wolfgang as he got up. The werewolf seemed more puzzled than hurt.

Then he changed shape, caught a fist in both hands and gripped it hard. To Vimes's horror he stepped forward, without apparent effort, forcing Carrot back.

"Do not try anything, Angua," said Wolf, grinning happily. "Or else I will break his arm. Oh, perhaps I will break his arm anyway! Yes!"

Vimes even heard the crack. Carrot went white. Someone holding a broken arm has all the control they need. Another idiot, thought Vimes. When they're down you don't let them get back up! Damn the Marquis of Fantailler! Policing by consent was a good theory, but you had to get your opponent to lie still first.

"Ah! And he has other bones!" said Wolfgang, pushing Carrot away. He glanced toward Angua. "Get back, get back. Or I'll hurt him some more! No, I shall hurt him some more *anyway*!"

Then Carrot kicked him in the stomach.

Wolfgang went over backward, but turned this into a backflip and a midair spin. He landed lightly, leapt back at the astonished Carrot and punched him twice in the chest.

The blows sounded like shovels hitting wet concrete.

He grabbed the falling man, lifted him over his head with one hand and hurled him down onto the bridge in front of Angua.

"Civilized man!" he shouted. "Here he is, sister!"

Vimes heard a sound down beside him. Gavin was watching intently, making urgent little noises in his throat. A tiny part of Vimes, the little rock hard core of cynicism, thought: All right for you, then.

Steam was rising off Wolfgang. He shone in the torchlight. The blond hair across his shoulders gleamed like a slipped halo.

Angua knelt down by the body, face impassive. Vimes had been expecting a scream of rage.

He heard her crying.

Beside Vimes, Gavin whined. Vimes stared down at the wolf. He looked at Angua, trying to lift Carrot, and then he looked at Wolfgang. And then back again.

"Anyone else?" said Wolfgang, dancing back and forth on the boards. "How about you, Civilized?"

"Sam!" hissed Sybil. "You can't—"

Vimes drew his sword. It wouldn't make any difference, now. Wolfgang wasn't playing now, he wasn't punching and running away. Those arms could push a fist through Vimes's rib cage and out the other side—

A blur went past at shoulder height. Gavin struck Wolfgang in the throat, knocking him over. They rolled across the bridge, Wolfgang changing back to wolf shape to lock jaw against jaw. They broke, circled, and went for one another again.

Dreamlike, Vimes heard a small voice say: "He wouldn't last five minutes back home fightin' like that. The silly bugger's gonna get *creamed*, fightin' like that! Stuff the Marquis of flamin' Fantailler!"

Gaspode was sitting bolt upright, stubby tail vibrating.

"The daftie! *This* is how you win a dogfight!"

As the wolves rolled over and over, Wolfgang tearing at Gavin's belly, Gaspode arrived growling and yapping and launched himself in the general direction of the werewolf's hindquarters.

There was a yip. Gaspode's growling was suddenly muffled. Wolfgang leapt vertically. Gavin sprang. The three hit the parapet of the bridge together, knocked the crumbling stones aside, hung for a moment in a snarling ball and then dropped down into the roaring whiteness of the river.

The whole of it, from the moment Tantony had crossed the bridge, had taken much less than a minute.

The baroness was staring down into the gorge. Keeping his eye on her, Vimes spoke to Detritus.

"Are you sure you're werewolf-proof, Sergeant?"

"Pretty much, sir. Anyway, I got the bow wound up again."

"Go into the castle and fetch the resident Igor, then," said Vimes calmly. "If anyone even tries to stop you, shoot them. And shoot anyone standing near them."

"No problem about dat, sir."

"We're not at home to Mister Reasonable, Sergeant."

"I do not hear him knockin', sir."

"Go to it, then. Sergeant Angua?"

She did not look up.

"Sergeant Angua!"

Now she looked up.

"How can you be so . . . so *cool*?" she snarled. "He's *hurt* . . ."

"I know. Go and talk to those watchmen hanging around on the other end of the bridge. They look scared. I don't want any accidents. We're going to need them. Cheery, cover Carrot and Tantony with something. Keep them warm."

I wish there was something to keep *me* warm, he thought. The thoughts came slowly, like drips of freezing water. He felt that ice would crackle off him if he moved, that frost would sparkle in his footsteps, that his mind was full of crisp snow.

"And now, madam," he said, turning back to the baroness, "you will give me the Scone of Stone."

"He'll be back!" hissed the baroness. "That fall was *nothing*! And he'll *find* you."

"For the last time . . . the stone of the dwarfs. The wolves are waiting out there. The dwarfs are waiting down in the city. Give me the stone, and we all might survive. This is diplomacy. Don't let me try anything else."

"I have only to say the word—"

Angua began to growl. Sybil strode toward and grabbed the baroness.

"You never answered a single letter! All those years I wrote to you!"

The baroness stared at her in amazement, as people so often did when struck with Sybil's sharp non sequiturs.

"If you know we've got the Scone," she said to Vimes, "then you know it's not the real one. And much good may it do the dwarfs!"

"Yes, you had it made in Ankh-Morpork. Made in Ankh-Morpork! They should have stamped it on the bottom. But some-one killed the man who did it. That's murder. It's against the law." Vimes nodded at the baroness. "It's a thing we have."

Gaspode dragged himself out of the water and stood, shivering, on the shingle. Every single part of him felt bruised. There was a nasty ringing noise in his ears. Blood dripped down one leg.

The last few minutes had been a little hazy, but he *did* recall they'd involved a lot of water that had hit him like hammers.

He shook himself. His coat jangled where the water was already freezing.

Out of habit, he walked over to the nearest tree and, wincing, raised a leg.

Excuse me.

A busy, reflective silence followed.

"That was not a good thing you just did," said Gaspode.

I'm sorry. Perhaps this is not the right moment.

"Not for me, no. You may have caused some physical damage here."

It's hard to know what to say.

"Trees don't normally talk back, is my point." Gaspode sighed. "So . . . what happens now?"

I beg your pardon?

"I'm dead, right?"

No. No one is more surprised than me, I may say, but your time does not appear to be now.

Death pulled out an hourglass, held it up against the cold stars for a moment and stalked away along the riverbank.

"'Scuse me, there's no chance of a lift, is there?" said Gaspode, struggling after him.

None whatsoever.

"Only, being a short dog in deep snow is not good for the ol' wossnames, if you get my—"

Death had stopped at a little bay. An indistinct shape lay in a few inches of water.

"Oh," said Gaspode.

Death leaned down. There was a flash of blue, and then he vanished.

Gaspode shivered. He paddled into the water, and nudged Gavin's sodden fur with his nose.

"Shouldn't be like this," he whined. "If you was a human, they'd put you in a big boat on the tide and set fire to it, an' everyone'd see. Shouldn't just be you an' me down here in the cold."

There was something that had to be done, too. He knew it in his bones. He crawled back to the bank and pulled himself up onto the trunk of a fallen willow.

He cleared his throat.

Then he howled.

It started badly, hesitantly, but it picked up and got stronger, richer . . . and when he paused for breath the howl went on and on, passing from throat to throat across the forest.

The sound wrapped him as he slid off the log and struggled on toward higher ground. It lifted him over the deeper snow. It wound around the trees, a plaiting of many voices becoming something with a life of its own. He remembered thinking: Maybe it'll even get as far as Ankh-Morpork.

Maybe it'll get much farther than that.

Vimes was impressed by the baroness. She fought back in a corner.

"I know nothing about any deaths—"

A howl came up from the forest. How many wolves were there? You never saw them . . . and then, when they cried out, it sounded as though there was one behind every tree. This one went on and on—it sounded like a cry thrown into a lake of air, the ripples spreading out across the mountains.

Angua threw her head back and screamed. Then, breath hissing between her teeth, she advanced on the baroness, fingers flexing.

"Give him . . . the damn stone," she hissed. "Will any . . . of . . . you . . . face me? *Now?* Then . . . give him the stone!"

"What theems to be the throuble?"

Igor lurched through the stricken gates, trailed by Detritus. He caught sight of the two bodies and hurried over like a very large spider.

"Fetch the stone," growled Angua. "And then . . . we . . . will leave. I can *smell* it. Or do you . . . want me to *take* it?"

Serafine glared at her, then turned on her heel and ran back into the ruins of the castle. The other werewolves shrank back from Angua as if her stare were a whip.

"If you can't help these men," said Vimes to the kneeling Igor, "your future does not look good."

Igor nodded. "Thith one," he said, indicating Tantony, "fleth woundth, I can thitch him up a treat, no problem. *Thith* one"—he tapped Carrot—". . . nasty break on the arm." He glanced up. "Marthter Wolfgang been playing again?"

"Can you make him well?" snapped Vimes.

"No, it'th hith lucky day," said Igor. "I can make him *better.* I've got some kidneyth jutht in, a lovely little pair, belonged to young Mr. Crapanthy, hardly touched a drop of thtrong licker, shame about the avalanchthe . . ."

"Does he *need* them?" said Angua.

"No, but you thould never mith an opportunity to improve yourthelf, I alwayth thay."

Igor grinned. It was a strange sight. The scars crawled around his face like caterpillars.

"Just see to the arm," said Vimes, firmly.

The baroness reappeared, flanked by several werewolves. They also backed away as Angua spun around.

"Take it," said Serafine. "Take the wretched thing. It is a fake. No crime has been committed!"

"I'm a policeman," said Vimes. "I can always find a crime."

The sleigh slid under its own weight down the track toward Bonk, the town's watchmen running alongside it and giving it the occasional push. With their captain down they were lost and bewildered and in no mood to take orders from Vimes, but they did what Angua commanded because Angua was of the class that traditionally gave them orders . . .

The two casualties were bedded down on blankets.

"Angua?" said Vimes.

"Yes, sir?"

"There's wolves keeping pace with us. I can see them running between the trees."

"I know."

"Are they on our side?"

"Let's just say . . . they're not on anyone else's side yet, shall we? They don't like me much but they know . . . Gavin did, and right now that is what's important. Some of them are out looking for my brother."

"Would he have survived that? It was a long way down."

"Well, it wasn't fire or silver. There's nothing but white water for miles. It probably hurt a lot, but we heal amazingly well, sir."

"Look, I'm sorry that—"

"No, Mister Vimes, you're not. You shouldn't be. Carrot just didn't understand what Wolfgang is like. You can't beat something like him in a fair fight. Look, I know he's family, but . . . personal is not the same as important. Carrot always said that."

"*Says* that," said Lady Sybil sharply.

"Yes."

Carrot opened his eyes.

"What . . . happened back there?" he said.

"Wolfgang hit you," said Angua. She wiped his brow.

"What with?" Carrot tried to push himself upward, winced and fell back.

"What have I always told you about the Marquis of Fantailler?" said Vimes.

"Sorry, sir."

Something bright rose from the distant forests. It vanished, and then a green light expanded into existence. A moment later came the *pop* of the flare.

"The signalers have got to the tower," said Vimes.

"Can't this damn thing go any faster?" said Angua.

"I mean, we can contact Ankh-Morpork," said Vimes. After everything, he felt curiously cheered by this. It was as if a special human howl had gone up. He wasn't floundering around loose now. He was floundering on the end of a very long line. That made all the difference.

It was a small public room over a shop in Bonk and, since it belonged to everybody, it looked as though it didn't belong to anyone. There was dust in the corners, and the chairs that were currently arranged in a ragged circle had been chosen for their ability to be stacked neatly rather than sat on comfortably.

Lady Margolotta smiled at the assembled vampires. She liked these meetings.

The rest of the group were a pretty mixed bunch, and she wondered what their motives were. But perhaps they at least shared one conviction—that what you were made as, wasn't what you had to be or what you might become . . .

And the trick was to start small. Suck, but don't impale. Little steps. And then you found that what you really wanted was power, and there were much politer ways of getting it. And then you realized that power was a bauble. Any thug had power. The true prize was *control*. Lord Vetinari knew that. When heavy weights were balanced on the scales, the trick was to know where to place your thumb.

And all control started with the self.

She stood up. They watched her with slightly worried yet friendly faces.

"My name, in the short form, is Lady Margolotta Amaya Katerina Assumpta Crassina von Uberwald, and I am a vampire . . ."

They chorused: "Hello, Lady Margolotta Amaya Katerina Assumpta Crassina von Uberwald!"

"It has been five years now," said Lady Margolotta. "And I am still taking one night at a time. One neck would always be one too many. But . . . there are compensations . . ."

There were no guards on the gate of Bonk, but there was a cluster of dwarfs outside the embassy as the cart slid to a halt. The wolves in the traces jerked nervously and whined at Angua.

"I'll have to let them go," she said, getting out. "They've only come this far because they're frightened of me . . ."

Vimes wasn't surprised. At the moment, anything would be frightened of Angua.

Even so, a squad of dwarfs was hurrying to the sledge.

It'd take them a few seconds to get a grip on things, Vimes realized. There were uptown guards here, and an Igor, and a werewolf.

They'd be puzzled as well as suspicious. That should give him a tiny crack to lever open. And, ashamed as he was to say it, an arrogant bastard always had the edge.

He glared at the lead dwarf. "What is your name?" he demanded.

"You are under—"

"You know the Scone of Stone was stolen?"

"You . . . what?"

Vimes reached around and pulled a sack out of the sleigh.

"Bring those torches closer!" he shouted, and because he delivered the command in a tone that said there was no *doubt* that it'd be obeyed, it *was* obeyed. I've got twenty seconds, he thought, and then the magic goes away.

"Now look at this," he said, lifting the thing out of the sack.

Several dwarfs fell to their knees. The murmuring spread out. Another howl, another rumor . . . in his current state he could see, in his mind's bloodshot eye, the towers in the night, clicking and clacking, delivering to Genua *exactly* the message that had been sent from Ankh-Morpork.

"I want to take this to the king," he said, in the hushed silence.

"*We* will take it—" the dwarf began, moving forward.

Vimes stepped aside.

"Good evenin', boys," said Detritus, standing up in the sleigh.

The tortured noises the bow's springs were making under their preternatural stress sounded like some metal animal in extreme pain. The dwarf was a couple of feet away from several dozen arrow points.

"On the *other* hand," said Vimes, "we could continue talking. You look like a dwarf who likes to talk."

The dwarf nodded.

"First of all, is there any reason why the two wounded men I have here couldn't be taken inside before they die of their wounds?"

The bow twitched in Detritus's hands.

The dwarf nodded.

"They can go inside and be treated?" said Vimes.

The dwarf nodded again, still looking into a bundle of arrows bigger than his head.

"Capital. See how we get on when we simply talk? And *now* I suggest that you arrest me."

"You *want* me to arrest you?"

"Yes. And Lady Sybil. We place ourselves under your personal jurisdiction."

"That's right," said Sybil. "I demand to be arrested." She drew herself up and out, righteous indignation radiating like a bonfire, causing the dwarfs to back away from what was clearly an unexploded bosom.

"And since the arrest of its ambassador will certainly cause . . . difficulties with Ankh-Morpork," Vimes went on, "I strongly suggest you take us directly to the king."

By blessed chance, the distant tower sent up another flare. Green light illuminated the snows for a moment.

"What's that mean?" said the dwarf captain.

"It means that Ankh-Morpork knows what's going on," said Vimes, praying that it did. "And I don't reckon you want to be the dwarf who started the war."

The dwarf spoke to the dwarf beside him. A third dwarf joined them. Vimes couldn't follow the hurried conversation, but right behind him Cheery whispered: "It's a bit beyond him. He doesn't want anything to happen to the Stone."

"Good."

The dwarf turned back to Vimes.

"What about the troll?"

"Oh, Detritus will stay in the embassy," said Vimes.

This seemed to lighten the tone of the debate somewhat, but it still appeared to be heavy going.

"What's happening now?" whispered Vimes.

"There's no precedent for anything like this," muttered Cheery. "You're supposed to be an assassin, but you've come back to see the king and you've got the Scone—"

"No precedent?" said Sybil. "Yes there bloody well is, pardon my Klatchian . . ."

She took a deep breath, and began to sing.

"Oh," said Cheery, shocked.

"What?" said Vimes.

The dwarfs were staring at Lady Sybil as she changed up through the gears into full, operatic voice. For an amateur soprano she had an impressive delivery and range, a touch too wobbly for the professional stage but exactly the kind of high coloratura to impress the dwarfs.

Snow slid off roofs. Icicles vibrated. Good grief, thought Vimes, impressed, with a spiky corset and a hat with wings on it she could be ferrying dead warriors off a battlefield . . .

"It's Ironhammer's 'Ransom' song," said Cheery. "Every dwarf knows it! Er, it doesn't translate well, but . . . 'I come now to ransom my love, I bring a gift of great wealth, none but the king can have power over me now, standing in my way is against all the laws of the world, the value of truth is greater than gold' . . . er, there's always been some debate about that last line, sir, but generally considered acceptable if it's a really big truth—"

Vimes looked at the dwarfs. They were fascinated, and one or two of them were mouthing along to the words.

"Is it going to work?" he whispered.

"It's hard to think of a bigger precedent than this, sir. I mean . . . it's the song of songs! The ultimate appeal! It's built into dwarf law, almost! They *can't* refuse. It'd be . . . not being a dwarf, sir!"

As Vimes watched, one dwarf pulled a fine chain-mail handkerchief out of his pocket and blew his nose with a wet, jingling noise. Several others were in tears.

When the last note died away there was silence, and then the sudden thunder of axes banging on shields.

"It's all right!" said Cheery. "They're clapping!"

Sybil, panting with the effort, turned to her husband. She gleamed in the torchlight.

"Do you think that was all right?" she said.

"By the sound of it, you're an honorary dwarf," said Vimes. He held out his arm. "Shall we go?"

News was going on ahead. Dwarfs were pouring out of the entrance to Downtown when the duke and duchess arrived.

There were dwarfs behind them now. They were being swept along. And all the time, hands would reach out to touch the Scone as it passed.

Dwarfs crowded into the elevator with them. Down below the roar of conversation stopped abruptly as Vimes stepped out and raised the Scone above his head. Then the rock echoed and re-echoed to one enormous cheer.

They can't even see it, said Vimes. To most of them, it's a tiny white dot. And that was what the plotters had known, wasn't it? You don't have to steal something to hold it hostage . . .

"They are to be arrested!"

Dee was hurrying forward, with more guards behind him.

"Again?" said Vimes. He kept the stone aloft.

"You attempted to kill the king! You escaped from your cell!"

"That's something about which we could hear more evidence," said Vimes, as calmly as he could. The Scone was getting heavier. "You can't keep people in the dark all the time, Dee."

"You shall certainly not see the king!"

"Then I will drop the Scone!"

"Do so! It won't—"

Vimes heard the gasp of the dwarfs behind him.

"It won't what?" he said, quietly. "It won't matter? But this is the *Scone!*"

One of the dwarfs that had accompanied them from the embassy shouted something, and several others took it up.

"Precedent is on your side," Cheery translated. "They say they can always kill you *after* you've seen the king."

"Well, not exactly what I was hoping but it'll have to do." Vimes looked at Dee again. "You *said* you wanted me to find the thing, didn't you? And now, how fitting that I return it to its rightful owner . . ."

"You . . . the king is . . . you may give it to me," said Dee, pulling himself up to the height of Vimes's chest.

"Absolutely not!" snapped Lady Sybil. "When Ironhammer returned the Scone to Bloodaxe, would he have given it to Slogram?"

There was a general chorus of dissent.

"Of course not," said Dee, "Slogram was a trait—"

He stopped.

"I think," said Vimes, "that we had better see the king, don't you think?"

"You can't demand that!"

Vimes indicated the press of dwarfs behind them.

"You're going to be *amazed* at how difficult it's going to be for you, explaining that to them," he said.

It took half an hour to see the king. He had to be roused. He had to dress. Kings don't hurry.

In the meantime, Vimes and Sybil sat in an anteroom on chairs too small for them, surrounded by dwarfs who weren't themselves sure if they were a prisoner escort or an honor guard. Other dwarfs were peering around the doorway; Vimes could hear the buzz of excited conversation.

They weren't wasting much time looking at him. Their gaze always fell on the Scone that he held in his lap. It was clear that most of them hadn't even seen it before.

You poor little sods, he thought. This is what you all believe in, and before the day's out you're going to be told it's just a bad fake. You'll *see* it's a forgery. And that about wraps it up for your little world, doesn't it? I set out to solve a crime and I'm going to end up committing a bigger one.

I'm going to be lucky to get out of here alive, aren't I?

A door was rolled open. A couple of what Vimes thought of as the *heavy* dwarfs stepped through and gave everyone the official, professional look which said that for your comfort and convenience we have decided not to kill you right at this very moment.

The king entered, rubbing his hands.

"Ah, Your Excellency," he said, pronouncing the word as a statement of fact rather than a welcome. "I see you have something that belongs to us."

Dee detached himself from the crowd at the door.

"I must make a serious accusation, sire!" he said.

"Really? Bring these people into the law room. Under guard, of course."

He swept away. Vimes looked at Sybil, and shrugged. They followed the king, leaving the hubbub of the main cavern behind.

Once again, Vimes was in the room with too many shelves and too few candles. The king sat down.

"Is the Scone heavy, Your Excellency?"

"Yes!"

"It is weighted with history, see? Put it down on the table with *extreme* care, please. And . . . Dee?"

"That . . . thing," said Dee, pointing a finger, "that *thing* is . . . a fake, a copy. A forgery! Made in *Ankh-Morpork*! Part of a plot which, I am sure can be proven, involves milord Vimes! It is *not* the Scone!"

The king lifted a candle a little closer to the Scone and gave it a critical look from several angles.

"I have seen the Scone many times before," he said at last, "and I would say that this appears to be the true thing and the whole of the thing."

"Sire, I demand—that is, I advise you to demand a closer inspection, sire."

"Really?" said the king mildly. "Well, I am not an expert, see? But we are fortunate, are we not, that Albrecht Albrechtson is here for the coronation? All of dwarfdom knows, I think, that he is *the* authority on the Scone and its history. Have him summoned. I daresay he is close at hand. I should say just about everyone is on the other side of that door now."

"Indeed, sire." The look of triumph on Dee's face as he swept past Vimes was almost obscene.

"I think we're going to need another song to get us out of this one, dear," murmured Vimes.

"I'm afraid I can only remember that one, Sam. The others were mainly about gold."

Dee returned, with Albrecht and a following of other senior and somewhat magisterial dwarfs.

"Ah, Albrecht," said the king. "Do you see this on the table? It is claimed that this is not the true thing and the whole of the thing. Your opinion is sought, please." The king nodded at Vimes. "My friend understands Morporkian, Your Excellency. He just chooses not to pollute the air by speaking it. Just his way, see?"

Albrecht glared at Vimes and then stepped up to the table.

He looked at the Scone from several angles. He moved the candles, and leaned down so that he could inspect the crust closely.

He took a knife from his belt, tapped the Scone with it, and listened with ferocious care to the note produced. He turned the Scone over. He sniffed at it.

He stood back, his face screwed up in a scowl, and then said, *"H'gradz?"*

The dwarfs muttered among themselves, and then, one by one, nodded.

To Vimes's horror, Albrecht chipped a tiny piece from the Scone and put it in his mouth.

Plaster, thought Vimes. Fresh plaster from Ankh-Morpork. And Dee will talk his way out of it—

Albrecht spat the piece out into his hand, and looked up at the ceiling for a moment, while he chewed.

Then he and the king exchanged a long, thoughtful stare.

"P'akga," said Albrecht, at last, *"a p'akaga-ad . . ."*

Behind the outbreak of murmuring, Vimes heard Cheery translate: "'It is the thing, and the whole of—'"

"Yes, yes," said Vimes. And he thought: By gods, we're good. Ankh-Morpork, I'm proud of you. When we make a forgery, it's better than the real damn thing.

Unless . . . unless I've missed something . . .

"Thank you, gentlemen," said the king. He waved a hand. The dwarfs filed out, reluctantly, with many backward glances at Vimes.

"Dee? Please fetch my ax from my chamber, will you?" the king said. "Yourself, please. I don't want anyone else to handle it. Your Excellency, you and your lady will remain here. Your . . . dwarf must leave, however. The guards are to be posted on the door. Dee?"

The Ideas-taster hadn't moved.

"*Dee?*"

"Wh' . . . yes, sire?"

"You do what I tell you!"

"Sire, this man's ancestor once killed a king!"

"I daresay the family have got it out of their system! Now do as I say!"

The dwarf hurried away, turning to stare at Vimes for a moment as he left the cave.

The king sat back.

"Sit down, Your Monitorship. And your lady, too." He put one elbow on the arm of the chair and cupped his chin on his hand. "And now, Mister Vimes, tell me the truth. Tell me everything. Tell me the truth that is more valuable than small amounts of gold."

"I'm not sure I know it anymore," said Vimes.

"Ah. A good start," said the king. "Tell me what you suspect, then."

"Sire, I'd swear that thing is as fake as a tin shilling."

"Oh. Really?"

"The *real* Scone wasn't stolen, it was destroyed. I reckon it was smashed and ground up and mixed with the sand in its cave. You see, sire, if people see that something's gone, and then you turn up with something that looks like it, they'll think 'this must be it, it *must* be, because it isn't where we thought it was.' People are like that. Something disappears and something very much like it turns up somewhere else and they think it must somehow have got from one place to the other . . ." Vimes pinched his nose. "I'm sorry, I haven't had much sleep . . ."

"You are doing very well for a sleepwalking man."

"The . . . thief was working with the werewolves, I think. They were behind the 'Sons of Agi Hammerthief' business. They were going to blackmail you off the throne . . . well, you *know* that. To keep Uberwald in the dark. If you didn't step down there'd be a war, and if you did Albrecht would get the fake Scone."

"What else do you think you know?"

"Well, the fake was made in Ankh-Morpork. We're good at making things. I *think* someone had the maker killed, but I can't find out more until I get back. I *will* find out."

"You make things very well in your city, then, to fool Albrecht. How do you think that was done?"

"You want the truth, sire?"

"By all means."

"Is it possible that Albrecht was involved? Find out where the money is, my old sergeant used to say."

"Hah. Who was it said 'Where there are policemen, you find crimes'?"

"Er . . . *me*, sir, but—"

"Let *us* find out. Dee should have had time to think. Ah . . ."

The door opened. The Ideas-taster stepped through, carrying a dwarfish ax. It was a mining ax, with a pick point on one side, in order to go prospecting, and a real ax blade on the other, in case anyone tried to stop you.

"Call the guards in, Dee," said the king. "And His Excellency's young dwarf. These things should be seen, see."

Oh, good grief, thought Vimes, watching Dee's face as the others shuffled in, there must be a manual. Every copper knows how this goes. You let 'em know you know they've done something wrong, but you don't tell 'em what it is and you certainly don't tell 'em how *much* you know, and you keep 'em off balance, and you just talk quietly and—

"Place your hands upon the Scone, Dee."

Dee spun around. "Sire?"

"Place your hands upon the Scone. Do as I say. Do it now."

—you keep the threat in view but you never refer to it, oh no. Because there's nothing you can do to them that their imagination isn't already doing to themselves. And you keep it up until they break, or in the case of my old dame school, until they feel their boots get damp.

And it doesn't even leave a mark.

"Tell me about the death of Longfinger, the candle captain," said the king, after Dee, with a look of hollow apprehension, had touched the Scone.

The words rushed out. "Oh, as I told you, sire, he—"

"If you do not keep your hands pressed upon the Scone, Dee, I will see to it that they are fixed there. Tell me *again*."

"I . . . he . . . took his own life, sire. Out of shame."

The king picked up his ax and turned it so that the long point faced outward.

"Tell me again."

Now Vimes could hear Dee's breathing, short and fast.

"He took his own life, sire!"

The king smiled at Vimes. "There's an old superstition, Your Excellency, that since the Scone contains a grain of Truth it will glow red-hot if a lie is told by anyone touching it. Of course, in these more modern times, I shouldn't think anyone believes it." He turned to Dee.

"Tell me again," he whispered.

As the ax moved slightly, the reflected light of the candles flashed along the blade.

"He took his own life! He did!"

"Oh yes. You said. Thank you," said the king. "And do you recall, Dee, when Slogram sent false word of Bloodaxe's death in battle to Ironhammer, causing Ironhammer to take his own life in grief, where was the guilt?"

"It was Slogram's, sir," said Dee promptly. Vimes suspected the answer had come straight from some rote-remembered teaching.

"Yes."

The king let the word hang in the air for a while, and then went on: "And who gave the order to kill the craftsman in Ankh-Morpork?"

"Sire?" said Dee.

"Who gave the order to kill the craftsman in Ankh-Morpork?" The king's tone did not change. It was the same comfortable, sing-song voice. He sounded as though he would carry on asking the question forever.

"I know nothing about—"

"Guards, press his hands firmly against the Scone."

They stepped forward. Each one took an arm.

"Again, Dee. Who gave the order?"

Dee writhed as if his hands were burning.

"I . . . I . . ."

Vimes could see the skin whiten on the dwarf's hands as he strained to lift them from the stone.

But it's a *fake*. I'd swear he destroyed the real one, so he *knows* it's a fake, surely? It's just a lump of plaster, probably still damp in the middle! Vimes tried to think. The original Scone had been in the cave, hadn't it? Was it? If it wasn't, where had it been? The *werewolves* thought they had a fake, and it certainly hadn't left his sight since. He tried to think through the fog of fatigue.

He'd half-wondered, once, whether the original Scone had been the one in the Dwarf Bread Museum. That would have been the way to keep it safe. No one would try to steal something that everyone knew was a fake . . . The whole *thing* was the Fifth Elephant, nothing was what it seemed, it was all a fog . . .

Which one *was* real?

"Who gave the order, Dee?" said the king.

"Not me! I said they must take all necessary steps to preserve secrecy!"

"To whom did you say this?"

"I can give you names!"

"Later, you will. I promise you, boyo," said the king. "And the werewolves?"

"The baroness suggested it! That is true!"

"Uberwald for the werewolves. Ah, yes . . . 'joy through strength.' I expect they promised you all sorts of things . . . You may take your hands off the Scone. I do not wish to distress you further. But . . . why? My predecessors spoke highly of you, you are a dwarf of power and influence . . . and then you let yourself become a pawn of the werewolves. Why?"

"Why should they be allowed to get away with it?" Dee snapped, his voice breaking with the strain.

The king looked across at Vimes.

"Oh, I suspect the werewolves will regret that they—" he began.

"Not *them*! The . . . ones in Ankh-Morpork! Wearing . . . makeup and dresses and . . . and abominable things!" Dee pointed a finger at Cheery. "*Ha'ak!* How can you even *look* at it! You let *her*"—and Vimes had seldom heard a word sprayed with so much venom—"*her* flaunt herself, *here*! And it's happening everywhere because people have not been firm, not obeyed, have let the old ways slide! Everywhere there are reports . . . they're eating away at everything dwarfish with their . . . their soft clothes and paint and beastly ways. How can you be king and allow this? Everywhere they are doing it and you do nothing! Why should *they* be allowed to do this?" Now Dee was sobbing. "*I* can't! And I work so hard . . . so hard . . ."

Vimes saw that Cheery, to his amazement, was blinking back tears.

"I see," said the king. "Well, I suppose that is an explanation."

He nodded to the guards. "Take . . . *her* away. Some things must wait a day or two."

Cheery saluted, suddenly.

"Permission to go with her, sire?"

"What on earth for, young . . . young dwarf?"

"I expect she'd like someone to talk to, sir. I know I would."

"Indeed? Well, if your commander has no objection . . . Off you go, then."

The king leaned back when the guards had left with their prisoner and the prisoner's new counselor.

"Well, Your Excellency?"

"This *is* the real Scone?"

"You are not certain?"

"Dee was!"

"Dee . . . is in a difficult state of mind." The king looked at the ceiling. "I think I will tell you this because, Your Excellency, I really do not want you going through the rest of your time here asking silly questions. Yes, this is the true Scone."

"But how could—"

"Wait! So was the one that is, yes, ground to dust in the cave by Dee in her . . . madness," the king went on. "So were the . . . let me see . . . five before that. Still untouched by time after fifteen hundred years? What romantics we dwarfs are! Even the very best dwarf bread crumbles after a few hundred."

"Fakes?" said Vimes. "They were *all* fakes?"

Suddenly the king was holding his mining ax again. "This, milord, is my family's ax. We have owned it for almost nine hundred years, see. Of course, sometimes it needed a new blade. And sometimes it has required a new handle, new designs on the metalwork, a little refreshing of the ornamentation . . . but is this not the nine-hundred-year-old ax of my family? And *because* it has changed gently over time, it is still a pretty good ax, y'know. *Pretty* good. Will you tell me if *this* is a fake, too?"

He sat back again.

Vimes remembered the look on Albrecht's face.

"He *knew*."

"Oh yes. A number of . . . more senior dwarfs know. The knowledge runs in families. The first Scone crumbled after three hundred years when the king of the time touched it. My ancestor was a guard who witnessed it, see. He . . . got accelerated promotion, you could say. I'm sure you understand me. After that, we were a little more prepared. We should have been looking for a new one in fifty years or so in any case. I'm *glad* this one was made in the large dwarf city of Ankh-Morpork, and I wouldn't be at all surprised if it turns out to be an excellent keeper. Look, they've even got the currants right, see?"

"But Albrecht could have exposed you!"

"Expose *what*? He is not king, but I will be very surprised if one of his family is not king again, in the fullness of time. What goes around comes around, as the Igors say." The king leaned forward.

"You have been laboring under a misapprehension, I reckon. You think that because Albrecht dislikes Ankh-Morpork and has . . . old-fashioned ideas, he is a bad dwarf. But I have known him for two hundred years. He is honest and honorable . . . more so than me, that I'm sure of. Five hundred years ago he would have made a fine king. Today, perhaps not. Perhaps . . . hah . . . the ax of my ancestors needs a different handle. But now I am king and he accepts that with all his heart because if he did not, he'd think he wasn't a dwarf, see? Of course he will now oppose me at every turn. Being Low King was never an easy job. But, to use one of *your* metaphors, we are all floating in the same boat. We may certainly try to push one another over the side, but only a maniac like Dee would make a hole in the bottom."

"Corporal Littlebottom thought there'd be a war—" said Vimes, weakly.

"Well, there are always hotheads. But while we argue who steers the boat, we don't deny that it's an important voyage . . . I see you are tired. Let your good lady take you home. But . . . as a nightcap . . . what is it, Your Excellency, that Ankh-Morpork wants?"

"Ankh-Morpork wants the names of the murderers," mumbled Vimes.

"No, that is what Commander Vimes wants. What is it that *Ankh-Morpork* wants? Gold? So often it is gold. Or iron, perhaps? You use a lot of iron."

Vimes blinked. His brain had finally given up. There was nothing left anymore. He wasn't certain he could even stand up.

He remembered a word.

"Fat," he said blankly.

"Aha. The Fifth Elephant. Are you sure? There's some good iron now. Iron makes you strong. Fat only makes you slippery."

"Fat," parroted Vimes, feeling the darkness closing in. "Lots of fat."

"Well, certainly. The price is ten Ankh-Morpork cents a barrel but, Your Excellency, since I have come to know you, I feel that perhaps—"

"Five cents a barrel for grade one high-rendered, three cents for grade two, ten cents per barrel for heavy tallow, safe and delivered to Ankh-Morpork," said Sybil. "And all from the Shmaltzberg Bend levels and measured on the Ironcrust scale. I have some doubt about the long-term quality of the Big Tusk wells."

Vimes tried to focus on his wife. She seemed, inexplicably, a long way away.

"Wha'?"

"Er . . . I caught up with some reading when I was in the embassy, Sam. The, er, notebooks. Sorry."

"Would you beggar us, madam?" said the king, throwing up his hands.

"We may be flexible on delivery," said Lady Sybil.

"Klatch would pay at least nine for grade one," said the king.

"But the Klatchian ambassador isn't sitting here," said Sybil.

The king smiled. "Or married to you, my lady, much to his loss. Six, five and fifteen."

"Six dropping to five after twenty thousand, three and half across the board for grade two, I can give you thirteen on tallow."

"Acceptable, but give me fourteen on white tallow and I'll allow seven on the new pale suets we are finding. They are making an acceptable candle, look you."

"Six, I'm afraid. You haven't plumbed the full extent of those deposits, and I think it may be reasonable to expect high levels of scrattle and BCBs in the lower layers. Besides, I think your forecasts about the amount of those deposits are erring on the optimistic side."

"Wha' BCBs?" murmured Vimes.

"Burnt Crunchy Bits," said Sybil. "Mostly unbelievably huge and ancient animals, deep fried."

"You astonish me, Lady Sybil," said the king. "I did not know you were trained in fat extraction?"

"Cooking Sam's breakfasts is an education in itself, Your Majesty."

"Oh well, far be it for a mere king to argue. Six, then. Price to remain stable for two years—" The king saw Sybil's mouth open. "All right, all right, three years. I'm not an unreasonable king."

"Prices on the dock?"

"How can I refuse?"

"Agreed, then."

"The paperwork will be with you in the morning. And now we really must go our separate ways," said the king. "I can see His Excellency has had a long day. Ankh-Morpork will be swimming in fat. I can't imagine what you'll use it all for . . ."

"Make light," said Vimes, and, as darkness fell at last, fell forward gently into the welcoming arms of sleep.

Sam Vimes woke up to the smell of hot fat.

Softness enveloped him. It practically imprisoned him.

For a moment he thought it was snow, except that snow wasn't usually this warm. Finally, he identified it as the cloudlike softness of the mattress on the ambassadorial bed.

He let his attention drift back to the fat smell. It had . . . overtones. There was a definite burnt component. Since Sam Vimes's range of gastronomic delight mainly ranged from "well fried" to "caramelized," it was definitely promising.

He shifted position and regretted it immediately. Every muscle in his body squealed in protest. He lay still and waited for the fire in his back to die down.

Bits and pieces of the last two days assembled themselves in his head. Once or twice he winced. Had he *really* gone through the ice like that? Was it Sam Vimes who'd stepped up to fight the werewolf, despite the fact that the thing was strong enough to bend a sword in a circle? And had Sybil won a lot of fat off the king? And . . .

Well, here he was in a nice warm bed and by the smell of it there was breakfast on the way.

Another piece of recollection floated into place.

Vimes groaned, and forced his legs out of the bed. No, Wolfgang couldn't have survived that, surely . . .

Naked, he staggered into the bathroom and spun the huge taps. Hot pungent water gushed out.

A minute later, he was lying full length again. It was rather too hot, but he could remember the snows, and maybe from now on he could never be hot enough.

Some of the pain washed away.

Someone rapped on the door.

"It's me, Sam."

"Sybil?"

She came in, carrying a couple of very large towels and some fresh clothes.

"Good to see you up again. Igor's frying sausages. He doesn't like doing it. He thinks they should be boiled. And he's doing slumpie and fikkun haddock and distressed pudding. I didn't want the food to go to waste, you see. I don't think I want to stay for the rest of the celebrations."

"I know what you mean. How's Carrot?"

"Well, he says he doesn't want sausages."

"What? He's al— he's up?"

"Sitting up, at least. Igor's a marvel. Angua said it was a bad break, but he's just got some sort of device that . . . well, Carrot's not even got a sling on now!"

"Sounds a useful man to have around," said Vimes, pulling on his civilized trousers.

"Angua says Igor's got an icehouse in the cellars and there's frozen jars of, of . . . well, let's just say he suggested that you might like liver and onions for breakfast and I said no."

"I like liver and onions," said Vimes. He thought about it. "Up until now, anyway."

"I think the king wants us to go, as well. In a polite way. A lot of very respectful dwarfs came round here with paperwork first thing this morning."

Vimes nodded grimly. It made sense. If *he* were king he'd want Vimes out of here, too. Here's some grateful thanks, a nice trading agreement, terribly sorry to see you go, do call again, only not too soon . . .

Breakfast was everything he'd dreamed of. Then he went to see the invalid.

Carrot was pale, gray under the eyes, but smiling. He was sitting up in bed, drinking fatsup.

"Hello, Mister Vimes! We won, then?"

"Didn't Angua tell you?"

"She went off with the wolves when I was asleep, Lady Sybil said."

Vimes recounted the events of the night as best he could.

Afterward, Carrot said: "Gavin was a very noble creature. I am sorry he is dead. I'm sure we would have got on well."

You mean every word of it, Vimes thought. I know you do. But it works out all right for you, doesn't it? It always does. If it had been the other way about, if it had been Gavin that attacked Wolf first, then I *know* it would have been you that went over the falls with the bastard. But it wasn't you, was it. If you were dice, you'd always roll sixes.

And the dice don't roll themselves. If it wasn't against everything he wanted to be true about the world, Vimes might just then have believed in some huge destiny controlling people. And gods help the other people who were around when a big destiny was alive in the world, bending every poor bugger around itself . . .

He wondered, not for the first time, but perhaps for the first time so articulately that his lips almost moved, if he might ever, one day, have to stand in its way . . .

Out loud, he said: "Poor old Gaspode went over, too."

"How? What was he doing?"

"Er . . . you could say he had our lad's full attention," said Vimes, coming back to the present. "A real streetfighter."

"Poor little soul. He was a good dog at heart."

And once again words that would have sounded trite and wrong on anyone else's lips were redeemed by the way Carrot said them.

"And what about Tantony?" said Vimes.

"Left this morning, Lady Sybil said."

"Good grief! And Wolfgang played tic-tac-toe on his chest!"

"Igor's a dab hand with a needle, sir."

Afterward, a thoughtful Sam Vimes stepped out into the coach yard. An Igor was already loading the luggage.

"Er . . . which one are you?" said Vimes.

"I'm *Igor*, marthter."

"Ah. Right. And, er . . . are you happy here, Igor? We could do with a . . . man of your talents in the Watch, and no mistake."

Igor looked down from the top of the coach.

"In Ankh-Morpork, marthter? My word. *Everyone* wanth to go to Ankh-Morpork, marthter. It'th a very tempting offer. But I know where my duty lieth, Your Exthelenthy. I must get the plathe ready for the *next* exthelenthy."

"Oh, surely—"

"However, fortuitouthly my nephew Igor ith looking for a pothition, marthter. He thould do well in Ankh-Morpork. He'th rather too modern for Uberwald, to tell you the truth."

"Good lad, is he?"

"Hith heart'th in the right place. I know that for *thertain*, thir."

"Er . . . good. Well, get a message to him, then. We're leaving as soon as we can."

"He will be tho exthited, thir! I've heard that in Ankh-Morpork bodieth just lie around in the thtreeth for anyone to take away!"

"It's not *quite* as bad as that, Igor."

"Ithn't it? Oh well, you can't have everything. I'll tell him directly."

Igor lurched off in a sort of high-speed totter.

I wonder why they all walk like that, thought Vimes. They must have one leg shorter than the other. Either that or they're not good at choosing boots.

He sat down on the steps to the house, and fished out a cigar.

So that was it, then. Bloody politics again. It was always bloody politics, or bloody diplomatics. Bloody lies in smart clothing. Once you got off the streets criminals just flowed through your fingers. The king and Lady Margolotta and Vetinari . . . they always looked at some sort of *big picture*. Vimes knew he was, and always would be, a little picture man. Big picture people ran the world, and they said what was a crime and what wasn't. And Dee was useful, so she'd probably get, oh, a few days breaking bread or whatever it was they gave you here for being naughty. After all, all she'd destroyed was a fake, wasn't it?

Was it?

But she'd *thought* she was committing a much bigger crime. That ought to mean something, in Sam Vimes's personal gallery of little pictures.

And the baroness was as guilty as hell. People had *died*. As for Wolfgang . . . well, some people were just built guilty. It was as simple as that. Anything they did became a crime, simply because it was them doing it.

He blew out a stream of smoke.

People like that shouldn't be allowed to simply *die* their way out of things.

But . . . he hadn't, had he.

The wolves had gone a long way down the river, Sybil had said, on both banks. There wasn't a sniff of him. Farther down was a mass of rapids and falls, miles of them . . .

If he'd gone downstream . . .

But upstream there was nothing but wild water, too, right up to the town . . .

No, he couldn't . . . surely no one could swim up a waterfall . . .

A chilly little feeling began at the back of Vimes's neck. Ice formed in his muscles.

Any sensible person would get right out of the country, wouldn't they? He tried *hard* to believe this. The wolves were out hunting, Tantony wouldn't remember Wolfgang fondly and if Vimes judged the king correctly then the dwarfs would have some dark little revenge in store, too.

The trouble was that, if you formed a picture in your mind of a sensible person, and tried to superimpose it on a picture of Wolfgang, you couldn't get them to meet *anywhere*.

There was an old saying, wasn't there? As a dog returneth to his vomit, so a fool returneth to his folly. Well, that got Wolfgang coming *and* going.

Vimes stood up, and turned around carefully. There was no one there. Sounds came in from the street gateway—people laughing, the sound of harness, the clank of a shovel clearing up last night's snow.

He sidled into the embassy, keeping his back to the wall. He groped his way toward the stairs, peering into every doorway. He ran across the expanse of the hallway, did a tumbling roll and ended up against the far wall.

"Is there anything wrong, sir?" said Cheery. She was watching him from the top of the stairs.

"Er . . . have you seen anything odd?" said Vimes, dusting himself off self-consciously, "And I do realize that we're talking about a house with Igor in it."

"Could you give me a hint, sir?"

"Wolfgang, godsdammit!"

"But he's dead, sir. Isn't he?"

"Not dead enough!"

"Er . . . what do you want me to do?"

"Where's Detritus?"

"Polishing his helmet, sir!" said Cheery, on the point of panic.

"What the hell is he wasting time with that for?"

"Er . . . er . . . because we're supposed to leave for the coronation in ten minutes, sir?"

"Oh . . . yes . . ."

"Lady Sybil told me to come and find you. In a very *distinct* tone of voice, sir."

At that point Lady Sybil's voice boomed along the corridor.

"Sam Vimes! You come here!"

"That one, sir," Cheery added helpfully.

Vimes trailed into the bedroom. Sybil was wearing another blue dress, a tiara and a firm expression.

"Is it a posh do?" said Vimes. "I thought if I put on a clean shirt—"

"Your official dress uniform is in the dressing room," said Sybil.

"It was rather a long day yesterday—"

"This is a *coronation*, Samuel Vimes. It is not a come-as-you-are! Go and get dressed, quickly. Including, and I don't want to have to say this twice, the helmet with the feathers."

"But not the red tights," said Vimes, hoping against hope. "Please?"

"The red tights, Sam, go without saying."

"They go at the knees," said Vimes, but it was the grumble of the defeated.

"I'll ring for Igor to come and help you."

"Things will have come to a pretty pass when I can't put my own tights on, dear, thank you."

Vimes dressed hurriedly, listening for . . . anything. Some creak in the wrong place, perhaps.

At least this was a Watch uniform, even if it did have buckled shoes. It included a sword. The duking outfit didn't allow for one, which had always struck Vimes as amazingly stupid. You got made a duke for being a fighter, and then they gave you nothing to fight with.

There was a tinkle of glass, back in the bedroom, and Lady Sybil was astonished to see her husband enter at a run with his sword raised.

"I dropped the top of a scent bottle, Sam!" she said. "What's up with you? Even Angua says he's probably miles away and in no shape to cause trouble! Why're you so nervy?"

Vimes sheathed the sword, and tried to relax.

"Because our Wolfgang's a damn bottle covey, dear. Any normal person, they crawl off if they get a beating. Or they have the sense to stay down, at least. But sometimes you get one who just won't let go. Eight-stone weaklings who'll try to head-butt Detritus. Evil little bantamweight bastards who'll bust a bottle on the bar and try to attack five watchmen all at once. You know what I mean? Idiots who'll go on fighting long after they should stop. The only way to put 'em down is to put 'em out."

"I think I recognize the type, yes," said Lady Sybil, with an irony that failed to register with Sam Vimes until some days later. She picked some lint off his cloak.

"He's going to be back. I can feel it in my water," mumbled Vimes.

"Sam?"

"Yes?"

"Can I have your attention for a couple of minutes? Wolfgang is not your problem now. And I really need to talk to you very quietly for a little while without you running off after werewolves." She said it as if this was a minor character flaw, like a tendency to leave his boots where people could trip over them.

"Er . . . they run after *me*," he pointed out.

"But there's always people being found dead or trying to kill you—"

"I don't *ask* them to, dear."

"Sam, I'm going to have a baby."

Vimes's head was full of werewolves and his automatic husbandry circuitry cut in to respond with "yes, dear," or "choose any color you like" or "I'll get someone to sort it out." Fortunately his brain itself had its own sense of self-preservation and, not wishing to be inside a skull that was stoved in by a bedside lamp, rewrote Sybil's words in white-hot fire across his inner eyeball and then went and hid.

That's why the response came out as a weak "What? How?"

"The normal way, I hope."

Vimes sat down on the bed. "And . . . not right now?"

"I very much doubt it. But Mrs. Content says it's definite, and she's been a midwife for fifty years."

"Oh." Some more brain functions crept back. "Good. That's . . . good."

"It'll probably take a while to sink in."

"Yes." Another neuron lit up. "Er . . . everything will be all right, will it?"

"What do you mean?"

"Er, you're rather, you're not as . . . you . . ."

"Sam, my family have *bred* for breeding. It's an aristocratic tradition. It's practically what being an aristocrat *means*. Of course everything will be all right."

"Oh. Good."

Vimes sat and stared. His head felt like some vast sea that had just been parted by a prophet. Where there should have been activity, there was just bare sand and the occasional floundering fish. But huge steep waves were tottering on either side, and in a minute they would crash down and cause cities to flood, a hundred miles away.

More glass tinkled, somewhere downstairs.

"Sam, Igor's probably just dropped something," said Sybil, seeing his expression. "That's all. Probably just knocked a glass over."

There was a snarl, and a scream, abruptly cut off.

Vimes leapt off the bed. "Lock the door after me and push the bed against it!" He paused for a moment in the doorway. "Without straining yourself!" he added, and ran for the stairs.

Wolfgang was trotting across the hall.

He was different this time. Wolf ears sprouted from a head that was still human. His hair had grown around him like a mane. Patches of fur were tufted on his skin, and were mostly streaked with blood.

The rest of him . . . was having trouble deciding what it was. One arm was trying to be a paw.

Vimes reached for his sword, and remembered that it was back on the bed. He rummaged in his pockets.

He knew the other thing was here, he remembered picking it up off the dressing table . . .

His fingers closed on his badge. He held it out.

"Stop! In the name of the law!"

Wolfgang looked up at him, one eye glowing yellow. The other was a mess.

"Hello, Civilized," he growled. "You wait for me, hey?"

He ducked into the corridor that led to the room where Carrot lay. Vimes tried to catch him up, saw claw-tipped fingers curl around the door and haul it out of its frame.

367

Carrot was reaching for his sword—

And then Wolfgang was flying backward under the full weight of Angua. They landed back in the hall, a rolling ball of fur, claws and teeth.

When werewolf fights werewolf, there are advantages to either shape. It's an eternal struggle to get a position where hands beat claws. And body shapes have lives of their own, a dangerous attribute if it is allowed to act unchecked. A cat's instinct is to jump on something that moves, but this is not a correct action if what is moving has a fizzing fuse. The mind has to fight its own body for control and the other body for survival. Mix this together, and the noise suggests that there are four creatures in the whirling ball of rage. And each one of them has brought several friends. And none of them like any of the others.

A shadow made Vimes spin around. Detritus, in shining armor, was aiming the Piecemaker over the banisters.

"Sergeant! No! You'll hit Angua, too!"

"Not a problem, sir," said Detritus, "'cos it won't kill 'em, so all we have to do, see, is sort out der bits that are Wolfgang an' belt him over der head when he gets himself back together—"

"If you fire that in here his bits will be mixed up with our bits and they won't be *big* bits! Put the damn thing *down*!"

Wolfgang couldn't control his shape well, Vimes saw. He couldn't quite manage to be full wolf or full human, and Angua was making the most of that. She was ducking, weaving . . . biting.

But even if you put him down you couldn't put him out.

"Mister Vimes!" Now it was Cheery, beckoning urgently from the passage that led to the kitchen. "You ought to come here right now!"

She was white-faced. Vimes nudged Detritus. "If they separate, just grab him, right? Just try to hold him still!"

Igor was lying in the kitchen, surrounded by broken glass. Wolfgang must have landed on him, and then took out his perpetual anger on a soft target. The patchwork man was bleeding heavily and lay like a doll that had been flung hard against a wall.

"Marthter," he groaned.

"Can you do anything for him, Cheery?"

"I wouldn't know where to *start*, sir!"

"Marthter, you got to remember thith, right?" Igor groaned.

"Er . . . yes . . . what?"

"You got to get me into the icehouthe downthtairth and let Igor know, underthtand?"

"Which Igor?" said Vimes desperately.

"Any Igor!" Igor clutched at Vimes's sleeve. "Me heart'th had it, but me liver'th right ath ninepence, tell him! Nothing wrong with my brain that a good bolt of lightnin' won't sort out. Then Igor can have me right hand, he'th got a cuthtomer waiting. There's yearth of good thervice left in my lower intethtine. Left eye not up to much, but I darethay thome poor thoul can find a uthe for it. The right knee ith nearly new. Old M'th Prodzky down the road would value my hip jointh, tell him. Got all that?"

"Yes . . . yes, I think so."

"Right. Remember . . . what goeth around, cometh around . . ."

Igor sank down.

"He's gone, sir," said Cheery.

But he'll soon be up and on someone else's feet, Vimes thought. He didn't say it aloud. Cheery was softhearted. Instead he said: "Can you get him into his icehouse? By the sound of it Angua's winning—"

He ran back into the hall. It was a wreck. As he arrived Angua managed to get a headlock on Wolfgang and ran him into a wooden pillar. He staggered, and she spun and scythed his legs from under him with a kick.

I taught her that, Vimes thought, as her brother landed heavily. Some of that dirty fighting—that's *Ankh-Morpork* fighting, that is.

But Wolfgang was up again like a rubber ball and somersaulting over her head. That brought him to the front door. He smashed it open with a blow and leapt out into the street.

And . . . that was it. A room full of debris, snowflakes blowing in and Angua sobbing on the floor.

He picked her up. She was bleeding in a dozen places. That was as much of a diagnosis as Sam Vimes, not used these days to surveying naked young women at close quarters, thought he could decently attempt.

"It's all right, he's gone," he said, because he had to say something.

"It's *not* all right! He'll lie low for a while and then he'll be back! I *know* him! It won't matter where we go! You've *seen* him! He'll just track us down and follow us and then he'll kill Carrot!"

"Why?"

"Because Carrot's mine!"

Sybil advanced down the stairs, carrying Vimes's crossbow.

"Oh, you poor thing . . ." she said. "Come here, let's find something to cover you up. Sam, isn't there something you can do?"

Vimes stared at her. Built into Sybil's expression was the unquestioning assumption that he *could* do something.

An hour ago he'd been having breakfast. Ten minutes ago he'd been putting on this stupid uniform. In a real room, with his wife. And it had been a real world, with a real future. And suddenly the dark was back, spattered with red rage.

And if he gave in to it, he'd lose. That was the beast screaming, inside, and Wolfgang was a better beast. Vimes knew he didn't have the knack, the mindless, driving nastiness; sooner or later his brain would start operating, and kill him.

Perhaps, said his brain, you *start* by using me . . .

"Ye-es," he said. "Yes . . . I think there is *something* I can do . . ."

Fire and silver, thought Vimes. Well, silver's in pretty short supply in Uberwald.

"You want I should come?" said Detritus, who could pick up signals.

"No, I think . . . I think I want to make an arrest. I don't want to start a war. Anyway, you need to wait here in case he doubles back. But you could lend me your penknife . . ."

Vimes found a sheet in one of the broken boxes, and tore off a long strip. Then he took his crossbow from his wife.

"You see, *now* he's committed a crime in Ankh-Morpork," he said. "That makes him *mine*."

"Sam, we're not—"

"You know, everyone kept telling me I wasn't in Ankh-Morpork so often that I believed it. But this embassy *is* Ankh-Morpork and, right now"—he hefted the bow—"I *am* the law."

"Sam?"

"Yes, dear?"

"I know that look. Don't hurt anyone else, will you?"

"Don't worry, dear. I'm going to be *civilized* about it."

There was a cluster of dwarfs in the street outside, surrounding one lying on the snow and in a pool of blood.

"Which way?" said Vimes, and if they didn't understand his words they understood the question. Several of them pointed along the street.

As he walked Vimes cradled the crossbow and lit a thin cigar.

Now *this* he understood. It wasn't damn politics, where good and bad were just, apparently, two ways of looking at the same thing or, at least, were described like that by the people who were on the side Vimes thought of as "bad."

It was all too complicated and, where it was complicated, it meant that someone was trying to fool you. But on the street, in hot pursuit, it was all so clear. Someone was going to be still standing at the end of the chase, and all you had to concentrate on was making sure it was you.

On a street corner a cart had overturned and its driver was kneeling by a horse that had been ripped open.

"Which way?"

The man pointed.

The new street was wider, busier, and there were a number of elegant coaches, moving slowly through the crowds. Of course . . . the coronation.

But that belonged to the world of the Duke of Ankh-Morpork and, right now, he wasn't here. There was only Sam Vimes, who didn't much like coronations.

There were screams up ahead, and the flow of people suddenly turned against Vimes, so that he appeared to be heading upstream, like a salmon.

The street opened into a large square. People were running now, which suggested to Vimes that he was still going in the right direction. It was pretty clear that you'd find Wolfgang somewhere no one else wanted to be.

A flurry of movement on one side of him became a squad of the town guard, at the trot. They halted. One of them walked back. It was Tantony.

He looked Vimes up and down.

"I have you to thank for last night?" he said. There were fresh scars on his face, but they were already healing. We've *got* to get an Igor, Vimes told himself.

"Yes," said Vimes. "The good bits and the bad bits."

"And you see what happens when you stand up to a werewolf?"

Vimes opened his mouth to say "Is that a uniform you're wearing, Captain, or is it just fancy dress?" but stopped himself in time.

"No, it's what happens when you're fool enough to stand up to a werewolf with no backup and no firepower," he said. "I'm sorry, but we all have to learn that lesson. Integrity makes very poor armor."

The man reddened.

"What is your business here?" he said.

"Our hairy friend just murdered someone in the embassy, which is—"

"Yes, yes, Ankh-Morpork territory. But *this* isn't! I am the watchman here!"

"I'm in hot pursuit, Captain. You know the term?"

"I . . . I . . . that doesn't apply!" Tantony snapped.

"Really?" Vimes raised an eyebrow. "Surely *every* copper knows about the rule of hot pursuit. You can chase the suspect over your legal boundary if you're in hot pursuit. Of course, there may be a bit of legal argy-bargy once he's *caught*, but we can save that for later."

"I intend to arrest him myself for crimes committed today!"

"You're too young to die. Besides, I saw him first. Tell you what . . . after he's killed me, you can have a go. Fair enough?" He looked Tantony in the eye. "Now get out of the way."

"You know I could have you arrested."

"Probably, but up until now I'd got you down as an intelligent man."

Tantony nodded, and proved Vimes right.

"And is there *nothing* you would have us do?"

"Well, yes. You could scrape up my remains if this doesn't work."

Vimes felt the man's stare on the back of his neck as he set off again.

There was a statue in the middle of the square. It was of the Fifth Elephant. Some ancient craftsman had tried to achieve in bronze and stone the moment when the allegorical animal had thundered down out of the sky and gifted the country its incredible mineral wealth. Around it were idealized and rather heavyset figures of dwarfs and men, holding hammers and swords, and striking noble attitudes; they probably represented Truth, Industry, Justice and Mother's Home-Made Fat Pancakes, for all Vimes knew, but he felt truly far from home in a country where, apparently, no one wrote graffiti on public statues.

A man was sprawled on the cobbles, with a woman kneeling beside him. She looked tearfully at Vimes and said something in Uberwaldean. All he could do was nod.

Wolfgang jumped down from a perch on top of the statue to Bad Sculpting and landed a few yards away, grinning.

"Mister Civilized! You want another Game?"

"You see this badge I am holding up?" said Vimes.

"It is a very small one!"

"But you see it?"

"Yes, I see your little badge!" Wolfgang started to move sideways, arms hanging loosely by his sides.

"And I'm armed. Did you hear me tell you I'm armed?"

"With that silly bow?"

"But you just heard me say I'm armed, yes?" said Vimes, loudly, turning to face the moving werewolf. He puffed on his cigar, letting a glow build up.

"Yes! Is this what you call civilized?"

Vimes grinned. "Yes, this is how we do it."

"My way is better!"

"And now you're under arrest," said Vimes. "Come along and make no fuss and we'll tie you securely and hand you over to whatever passes for justice around here. I realize this may be difficult."

"Hah! Your Ankh-Morpork sense of humor!"

"Yes, any minute now I'll drop my trousers. So . . . you're resisting arrest?"

"Why these stupid questions?" Now Wolfgang was almost dancing.

"Are you resisting arrest?"

"Yes indeed! Oh yes! Good joke!"

"Look at me laughing."

Vimes tossed the crossbow aside and swung a tube out from under his cloak. It was made of cardboard, and a red cone protruded from one end.

"A stupid silly firework!" shouted Wolfgang, and charged.

"Could be," said Vimes.

He didn't bother to aim. These things were never designed for accuracy. He simply removed his cigar from his mouth and, as Wolfgang ran toward him, pressed it into the fuse hole.

The mortar jerked as the charge went off and its payload came out tumbling slowly and trailing smoke in a lazy spiral. It looked like the stupidest weapon since the toffee spear.

Wolfgang danced back and forth under it, grinning, and as it passed several feet over his head he leapt up gracefully and caught it in his mouth.

And then it exploded.

The flares were made to be seen twenty miles away. Even with his eyes tightly shut, Vimes saw the glare through the lids.

When the body had stopped rolling, Vimes looked around the square. People were watching from the coaches. The crowds were silent.

There were a lot of things he could say. "Son of a bitch!" would have been a good one. Or he could say "Welcome to civilization!" He could have said "Laugh this one off!" He might have said "Fetch!"

But he didn't, because if he had said any of those things, then he'd know that what he had just done was murder.

He turned away, tossed the empty mortar over his shoulder and muttered: "The hell with it."

At times like this, teetotalism bit down hard.

Tantony was watching.

"Don't say a word out of place," said Vimes, without altering his stride. "Just don't."

"I thought . . . those things shot very fast . . ."

"I cut the charge down," said Vimes, tossing Detritus's penknife in the air and catching it again. "I didn't want to *hurt* anyone."

"I heard you warn him that you were armed. I heard him twice resist arrest. I heard everything. I heard everything you wanted me to hear."

"Yes."

"Of course, he might not have known that law."

"Oh, really? Well, *I* didn't know it was legal in these parts to chase some poor sod across the country and maul him to death and, do you know, that didn't stop anyone."

The crowds parted ahead of Vimes. He could hear whispers around him.

"On the *other* hand," said Tantony, "you did only fire that thing to warn him . . ."

"Huh?"

"*Clearly* you were not to know that he would automatically try to catch the . . . explosive," said Tantony, and it seemed to Vimes that he was rehearsing the line. "The . . . doglike qualities of a were-wolf would hardly have occurred to a man from the big city."

Vimes held his gaze for a moment, and then patted him on the shoulder.

"Hold on to that thought," he said.

A coach pulled to a halt beside him as he continued on his way. It slid to a stop so silently, not a jingle of harness, not a clop of horseshoe, that Vimes jumped sideways out of shock.

The horses were black, with black plumes on their heads. The coach was a hearse, the traditional long glass windows now filled with smoked black glass. There was no driver; the reins were simply loosely knotted on a brass railing.

A door swung open. A veiled figure leaned out.

"Your Excellency? *Do* let me give you a lift back to the embassy. You look so tired."

"No, thank you," said Vimes grimly.

"I apologize for the emphasis on black," said Lady Margolotta. "It is rather expected of one on these occasions, I'm afraid—"

Vimes swung himself up and into the carriage with furious speed.

"You tell *me*," he growled, waving a finger under her nose, "how *anyone* can swim up a vertical waterfall? I was prepared to believe *anything* about that bastard, but even he couldn't have managed that . . ."

"Certainly that is a puzzle," said the vampire calmly, as the driverless coach moved on. "Superhuman strength, possibly?"

"And now he's gone and that's one up for the vampires, eh?"

"I would like to think that it's going to be a blessing for the whole country." Lady Margolotta leaned back. Her rat with the bow around its neck watched Vimes suspiciously from its pink cushion. "Wolfgang was a sadistic murderer, a throwback who frightened even his own family. Delphine . . . sorry, Angua . . . will have some peace of mind. An intelligent young lady, I've always thought. Leaving here was the best thing she ever did. The darkness will be a little less frightening. The world will be a better place."

"And I've handed you Uberwald?"

"Don't be stupid. Uberwald is huge. This is one small part of it. And now it's going to change. You have been a breath of fresh air."

Lady Margolotta drew a long holder from her bag and inserted a black cigarette. It lit itself.

"Like you, I have found consolation in a . . . different vice," she said. "Black Scopani. They grow the tobacco in total darkness. Do try some. You could waterproof roofs with it. I believe Igor makes cigars by rolling the leaves between his thighs." She blew out a stream of smoke. "Or someone's thighs, anyway. Of course, I am sorry for the baroness. It must be so hard for a werewolf, realizing that she's raised a monster. As for the baron, give him a bone and he's happy for hours." Another stream of smoke. "Do look after Angua. Happy Families is not a popular game among the undead."

"You helped him come back! Just like you did for me!"

"Oh, he'd have come back anyway, in time. Some time when you weren't expecting him. He'd track Angua like a wolverine. Best that things ended today." She gave him an appraising look through the smoke. "You're good at anger, Your Grace. You save it up for when you need it."

"You couldn't have known I'd beat him. You left me in the snow. I wasn't even armed!"

"Havelock Vetinari would not have sent a fool to Uberwald." More smoke, which writhed in the air. "At least, not a *stupid* fool."

Vimes's eyes narrowed. "You've *met* him, haven't you."

"Yes."

"And taught him all he knows, right?"

She blew smoke down her nostrils, and gave him a radiant smile.

"I'm sorry? You think *I* taught him? My dear sir . . . As for what I've got out of all this . . . well, a little breathing space. A little influence. Politics is more interesting than blood, Your Grace. And much more fun. Beware the reformed vampire, sir—the craving for blood is only a craving, and with care it can be diverted along different channels. Ah, I believe we are here," she added, although Vimes could have sworn that she hadn't so much as glanced out of the window.

The door opened.

"If my Igor's still there, do tell him I will see him Downtown. So nice to have met you. I'm sure we shall meet again. And do please present my fondest regards to Lord Vetinari."

The door shut behind Vimes. The coach moved off.

He swore, under his breath.

The hall was full of Igors. Several of them touched their forelocks, or at least the approximate line of stitch marks, when they saw him. All of them were carrying heavy metal containers of varying sizes, on which frost crystals were forming.

"What's this?" he said. "Igor's funeral?" Then it sunk in. "Oh, my gods . . . with party loot bags? Everyone gets something to take home?"

"You could say that, thir, you could put it that way," said an Igor, as the rest filed past. "It may theem odd to you, but *we* think that putting bodieth in the ground ith rather gruethome. All thothe wormth and thingth." He tapped the tin box under his arm. "Thith way, he'll be mothtly up and about again in no time," he added brightly.

"Reincarnation on the installment plan, eh?" said Vimes weakly.

"Motht amuthing, thir," said the Igor gravely. "But it'th amathing what people need. Heartth, liverth, handth . . . we keep a litht, thir, of detherving catheth. By tonight there will be thome very lucky people in thethe parth—"

"And these parts in some very lucky people?"

"Well done, thur. I can thee you are a wit. And I'm sure one day thome poor thoul will have a really nathty brain injury, and"—he tapped the chilly box again—"what goeth around, cometh around."

He nodded at Cheery, and at Vimes.

He limped off, but suddenly a very similar voice was *behind* Vimes. Another Igor came out of the kitchens, carrying a dusty black suit on a hanger and, in his other hand, a pair of boots.

"A bit worn, but I darethay some poor thoul will be grateful," he said. "Thorry we're all ruthing off, thir. Tho much to do, you know how it ith."

"I can imagine," said Vimes, and unfortunately he could. But, then, he thought: The ax of my grandfather, the king called it. You change things around, you replace every bit, but the ax survives. There will always be an Igor.

"They're really rather selfless people, sir," said Cheery, when the last Igor had lurched off. "They do a lot of good work for people."

"I know, I know. But—"

"Yes, sir. I know what you mean, sir. Everyone's in the drawing room. Lady Sybil said you'd be back. She said anyone with that look in their eye comes back."

"We're all going to the coronation. Might as well see this through. Is that what you'll be wearing, Cheery?"

"Yes, sir."

"But it's just . . . ordinary dwarf clothes. Trousers and everything."

"Yes, sir."

"But Sybil said you'd got a fetching little green number and a helmet with a feather in it."

"Yes, sir."

"You're free to wear whatever you want, you know that."

"Yes, sir. And then I thought about Dee. And I watched the king when he was talking to you, and . . . well, I *can* wear what I like, sir. That's the point. I don't *have* to wear that dress. I can wear what I like. I don't *have* to wear something just because other people *don't* want me to. Anyway, it made me look a rather stupid lettuce."

"That's all a bit complicated for me, Cheery."

"It's probably a dwarf thing, sir."

"And a female thing," said Vimes.

"Well, sir . . . yes. A dwarf thing and a female thing," said Cheery. "And they don't come much more complicated than that."

Vimes pushed open the doors to the drawing room.

"It's over," he said, as they turned to look at him.

"Did you hurt anyone else?" said Sybil.

"Only Wolfgang."

"He'll be back," said Angua, flatly.

"No."

"You killed him?"

"No. I put him down. I see you're up, Captain."

Carrot got to his feet, awkwardly, and saluted.

"Sorry I haven't been much use, sir."

"You just chose the wrong time to fight fair. Are you well enough to come?"

"Er . . . Angua and I want to stay here, if it's all right with you, sir. We've got things to talk about." Carrot looked down. "And . . . er . . . do," he added.

It was the first coronation Vimes had attended. He'd expected it to be . . . stranger, touched somehow by glory.

Instead it was dull, but at least it was *big* dull, dullness distilled and honed and cultivated over thousands of years until it had developed an impressive shine, as even grime will if you polish it long enough. It was dullness hammered into the shape and form of ceremony.

It had also been timed to test the capacity of the average bladder.

A number of dwarfs read passages from ancient scrolls. There were what sounded like excerpts from the Koboldean Saga, and Vimes wondered desperately if they were in for another opera, but these were over after a mere hour. There were more readings by different dwarfs. At one point the king, who had been standing alone in the center of a circle of candlelight, was presented with a leather bag, a small mining ax and a ruby. Vimes didn't catch the meaning of any of this, but by the sounds behind him it was clear that each item was of huge and satisfying significance to the thousands who were standing behind him. Thousands? No, there must be tens of thousands, he thought. The bowl of the cavern was full of tier upon tier of dwarfs. Maybe a hundred thousand . . .

. . . and he was in the front row. No one had said anything. The four of them had simply been led there and left, although the murmurings suggested that the presence of Detritus was causing considerable comment. Senior, long-bearded and richly clothed dwarfs were all around them, and the troll stood out like a tower.

Someone was being taught something. Vimes wondered who the lesson was directed at.

Finally, the Scone was brought in, small and dull and yet carried by twenty-four dwarfs on a large bier. It was laid, reverentially, on a stool.

He could sense the change in the air of the huge cavern, and once again he thought: There's no magic, you poor devils, there's no history. I'll bet my wages the damn thing was molded with rubber from a vat that had last been used in the preparation of Sonky's Eversure Dependables, and there's your holy relic for you . . .

There were still more readings, much shorter this time.

Then the dwarfs who had been participating in the endless and baffling hours withdrew from the center of the cavern, leaving the king looking as small and alone as the Scone itself.

He stared around him and, although it was surely impossible for him to have seen Vimes among the thousands in the gloom, it did seem that his gaze rested on the Ankh-Morpork party for a fraction of a second.

The king sat down.

A sigh began. It grew louder and louder, a hurricane made up of the breath of a nation. It echoed back and forth among the rocks until it drowned out all other sounds.

Vimes had half expected the Scone to explode, or crumble, or flash red-hot. Which was stupid, said a dwindling part of himself—it was a fake, a nonsense, something made in Ankh-Morpork for money, something that had already cost lives. It was not, it *could* not be real.

But in the roaring air he knew that it was, in the minds of all who needed to believe, and in a belief so strong that fact was not the same as truth . . . he knew that for now, and yesterday, and to-morrow, it was both the thing, and the whole of the thing.

Angua noticed that Carrot was walking better even as they reached the forest below the falls, and the shovel over his shoulder hardly burdened him at all.

There were wolf prints all over the snow.

"They won't have stayed," she said, as they walked between the trees. "They felt things keenly when he died but . . . wolves look to the future. They don't try to remember things."

"They're lucky," said Carrot.

"They're realistic, it's just that the future contains the next meal and the next danger. Is your arm all right?"

"It feels as good as new."

They found the freezing mass of fur lying at the water's edge. Carrot pulled it out of the water, scraped off the snow higher up the shingle and started to dig.

After a while he took off his shirt. The bruises were already fading.

Angua sat and looked over the water, listening to the thud of the spade and the occasional grunt when Carrot hit a tree root. Then she heard the soft slither of something being pulled over snow, a pause, and then the sound of sand and stones being shoveled into a hole.

"Do you want to say a few words?" said Carrot.

"You heard the howl last night. That's how wolves do it," said Angua, still looking out across the water. "There aren't any other words."

"Perhaps just a moment's silence, then—"

She spun round. "Carrot! Don't you *remember* last night? Didn't you wonder what I might become? Didn't you worry about the future?"

"No."

"Why the hell not?"

"It hasn't happened yet. Shall we get back? It'll be dark soon."

"And tomorrow?"

"I'd like you to come back to Ankh-Morpork."

"Why? There's nothing for me there."

Carrot patted the soil over the grave.

"Is there anything left for you here?" he said. "Besides, I—"

Don't you dare say the words, Angua thought. Not at a time like this.

And then they both became aware of the wolves. They were creeping through the trees, darker shadows in the evening light.

"They're hunting," said Angua, grabbing Carrot's arm.

"Oh, don't worry. They don't attack human beings for no reason."

"Carrot?"

"Yes?" The wolves were closing in.

"I'm not human!"

"But last night—"

"That was different. They remembered Gavin. *Now* I'm just a werewolf to them . . ."

She watched him turn to look at the advancing wolves. The hairs were up on their backs. They were growling. They moved with the strange sidle of those whose hatred could just manage to overcome their fear. And at any moment that balance in one of them was going to tip all the way, and then it would be all over.

There was a leap, and it was Carrot who made it. He grabbed the lead wolf by its neck and tail and held on as it struggled and snapped. Its frantic efforts to escape resulted only in it running in a circle with Carrot in the middle, the other wolves back away from the whirl of gray. Then, as it stumbled, he bit it on the back of the neck. It screamed.

Carrot let go, and stood up. He looked at the circle of wolves. They shied away from his gaze.

"Hmmm?" he said.

The wolf on the ground whined, and got to its feet awkwardly.

"Hmmm?"

It tucked its tail between its legs and backed off, but it still seemed to be attached to Carrot by an invisible lead.

"Angua?" said Carrot, still watching it carefully.

"Yes?"

"Can you speak wolf? I mean, in this shape?"

"A bit. Look, how did you know what to do?"

"Oh, I've watched animals," said Carrot, as if that was an explanation. "Please tell them . . . tell them if they go away now, I won't harm them."

She managed to bark out the words. It had all changed, in such a tiny handful of seconds. Now Carrot wrote the script.

"And now tell them that although I'm going away, I may be back. What's the name of this one?" He nodded at the cowering wolf.

"That's Eats Wrong Meat," Angua whispered. "He was . . . he's the leader now that Gavin's gone."

"Then tell them that I'm quite happy that he should go on leading. Tell them all that."

They watched her intently. She knew what they were thinking. He'd beaten the leader. It was all Sorted Out. Wolves did not have a lot of mental space for uncertainty. Doubt was a luxury for species that did not live one meal away from starvation. They still had a Gavin-shaped hole in their minds and Carrot had stepped into it. Of course, it wouldn't last long. But it didn't need to.

He always, always finds a way in, she thought. He doesn't think about it, he doesn't plot, he simply slides in. I saved him because he couldn't save himself, and Gavin saved him because . . . because . . . because he had some reason . . . and I'm almost, almost certain that Carrot doesn't know how he manages to wrap the world around him. Almost certain. He's good and kind and born to be a king of the ancient sort that wore oak leaves and ruled from a seat under a tree, and though he tries hard he never has a cynical thought.

I'm almost certain.

"Let's go now," said Carrot. "The coronation will be over soon, and I don't want Mister Vimes to worry."

"Carrot! I've got to know something . . ."

"Yes?"

"*That* might happen to me. Have you ever thought about that? He was my brother, after all. Being two things at the same time, and never quite being one . . . we're not the most stable of creatures . . ."

"Gold and muck come out of the same shaft," said Carrot.

"That's just a dwarf saying!"

"It's true, though. You're not him."

"Well . . . if it happened . . . if it did . . . would you do what Vimes did? Carrot? Would it be you who picked up a weapon and came after me? I know you won't lie. I've got to know. Would it be *you*?"

A little snow slid down from the trees. The wolves watched. Carrot looked up for a moment, at the gray sky, and then nodded.

"Yes."

She sighed.

"Promise?" she said.

Vimes was surprised at how quickly the coronation became a working day. There was a flourish of echoing horns, a general flow of the crowd and, gradually, a queue in front of the king.

"They haven't even given him time to get comfy!" said Lady Sybil, as they headed toward the exit.

"Our kings are . . . working kings," said Cheery, and Vimes detected a dash of pride in her voice. "But now is the time when the king awards favors."

A dwarf caught up with Vimes and tugged his cloak respectfully.

"The king wishes to see you now, Your Excellency," he said.

"There's an almighty queue!"

"Nevertheless"—the dwarf gave a polite cough—"the king wishes to see *you* now. All of you."

They were led to the front of the queue. Vimes felt many eyes boring into the small of his back.

The king dismissed the previous supplicant with a regal nod as the Ankh-Morpork party was deftly inserted at the top of the line, supplanting a dwarf whose beard went down to his knees.

He looked at them for a moment, and then the internal filing system threw up a card.

"Ah, it's yourselves, good as new," he said. "Now, what was it I was going to do? Oh, I remember . . . Lady Sybil?"

She curtsied.

"Classically, we give rings at this time," said the king. "Between ourselves, many dwarfs consider this a bit . . . well, bath salts, see. But I believe they are still welcome and so this, Lady Sybil, is, perhaps, a token of things to come."

It was a thin silver ring. Vimes was taken aback at this parsimony, but Sybil could graciously accept a bunch of rats.

"Oh, how wond—"

"We normally give gold," the king went on. "Very popular, and of course you can sing about it. But this has . . . rarity value, see. It is the first silver that had been mined in Uberwald in hundreds of years."

"I thought there was a rule that—" Vimes began.

"I ordered the mines reopened last night," said the king, pleasantly. "It seemed . . . an auspicious time. We shall soon have silver for sale, Your Excellency, but if Lady Sybil doesn't get involved in the negotiations and bankrupt us, I for one shall be very grateful," the king added. "Miss Littlebottom, I see, has not graced us with a sartorial extravaganza today?"

Cheery stared.

"You're not wearing a dress," prompted the king.

"No, sire."

"Although I do notice a few unobtrusive touches of mascara and lipstick."

"Yes, sire," squeaked Cheery, on the point of death through shock.

"That's nice. Do be sure to let me know the name of your dressmaker," the king went on pleasantly. "I may have some custom for her in the fullness of time. I've thought long and hard—"

Vimes blinked. Cheery had gone pale. Had anyone else heard that? Had *he*?

Sybil nudged him in the ribs.

"Your mouth's open, Sam," she whispered.

So he *had* heard it . . .

He heard the king's voice again.

"—and a bag of gold is always acceptable."

Cheery was still staring.

Vimes shook her gently by the shoulder.

"Th—thank you, sire."

The king held out his hand. Vimes wobbled Cheery again. Completely hypnotized, she extended her hand. The king took it and shook it.

Shocked whispers were spreading, behind Vimes. The king had shaken the hand of a self-declared *female* . . .

"And that leaves . . . Detritus," said the king. "What a dwarf should give a troll is of course a bit of a puzzle, but it occurs to me that what I should give you is what I would *give* a dwarf. A bag of gold, then, for whatever purpose you choose to put it, and—"

He stood up. He held out his hand.

Dwarfs and trolls were still fighting in the farther regions of Uberwald, Vimes knew. Elsewhere, there was at best the sort of peace you got when both sides were busy rearming.

The whispering stopped. Silence spread out in a widening circle, all across the floor of the cave.

Detritus blinked. Then he took the hand very carefully, trying not to crush it.

The whispering started again. And this time, Vimes knew, it'd go for miles.

It occurred to him that in two handshakes the white-bearded, elderly dwarf had done more than a dozen devious plots could have achieved. By the time those ripples reached the edge of Uberwald, they would be tidal waves. Thirty men and a dog would be nothing by comparison.

"Hmm?"

"I said, what can a king give a Vimes?" said the king.

"Er . . . nothing, I think," said Vimes absently. Two handshakes! And very quietly, smiling, the king had turned the customs of the dwarfs upside down. And so gently, too, that they'd spend years arguing about it.

"Sam!" snapped Sybil.

"Well, then, I shall give something to your descendants," said the king, apparently unperturbed. A long flat box was brought to him. He opened it to reveal a dwarf ax, the new metal glinting on its nest of black cloth.

"This will become, in time, the ax of someone's grandfather," said the king, lifting it out. "And no doubt over the years it will need a new handle or a new blade and over the centuries the shape will change in line with fashion, but it will always be, in every detail and respect, the ax I give you today. And because it'll change with the times, it'll always be sharp. There's a grain of Truth in that, see. So nice to have met you. Do enjoy your journey home, Your Excellency."

The four were silent in the coach back to the embassy. Then Cheery said: "The king said—"

"I heard," said Vimes.

"That was as good as saying that *he* is a sh—"

"Things are going to change," said Lady Sybil. "That's what the king was saying."

"I never shook hands with no king before," said Detritus. "No dwarf, either, come to that."

"You shook hands with me once," said Cheery.

"Watchmen don't count," said Detritus firmly. "Watchmen is *watchmen*."

"I wonder if it'll change anything?" said Lady Sybil.

Vimes stared out of the window. It'd probably make people feel good, he thought. But trolls and dwarfs had been fighting for centuries. Ending that sort of thing took more than a handshake. It was just a symbol.

On the other hand . . . the world wasn't moved by heroes or villains or even by policemen. It might as well be moved by symbols. All he knew was that you couldn't hope to try for the big stuff, like world peace and happiness, but you might just about be able to achieve some tiny deed that'd make the world, in a small way, a better place.

Like shooting someone.

"I forgot to say that I thought it was very kind of you, Cheery," said Lady Sybil, "yesterday, when you comforted Dee."

"She would have had me killed by the werewolves," said Vimes. He felt this was a point worth making.

"Yes, of course. But . . . it was kind, anyway," said Sybil.

Cheery looked at her feet, avoiding Lady Sybil's gaze. Then she coughed nervously and pulled a small piece of paper out of her sleeve, which she handed wordlessly to Vimes.

He unfolded it, and read it. It was a list of names and addresses.

"She gave you these?" he said. "Some of these are *very* senior dwarfs in Ankh-Morpork . . ."

"Yes, sir," said Cheery. She coughed again. "I *knew* she wanted someone to talk to, and . . . er . . . I suggested a few things she might like to talk about. Sorry, Lady Sybil. It's very hard to stop being a copper."

"I worked that one out a long time ago," said Sybil.

"You know," said Vimes, to break the silence, "if we leave at first light tomorrow, we could be through the pass before sundown . . ."

And it was a comfortable night, somewhere in the depths of the feather mattress. Vimes awoke a couple of times, and thought he could hear voices. Then he'd sink back into the softness, and dream of warm snow.

He was shaken awake by Detritus.

"It's gettin' light, sir."

"Mm?"

"And dere's a Igor an' a . . . a young man out in der hall," said Detritus. "He got a big jar full of noses and a rabbit covered in ears."

Vimes tried to get back to sleep. Then he sat bolt upright.

"What?"

"It's all covered in ears, sir."

"You mean one of those rabbits with big floppy ears?"

"You better come and see dis rabbit," sniffed the troll.

Vimes left Sybil wallowing in sleep, pulled on his dressing gown and pattered barefoot down to the freezing hall.

An Igor was waiting anxiously in the middle of the floor. Vimes was getting the hang of Igor-recognition,* and this was a new one. He was with a much younger . . . er . . . man, probably barely out of his teens, at least in places, but already the scars and stitching indicated that relentless urge toward self-improvement that was the hallmark of a good Igor. They just never seemed to be able to get the eyes level.

"Your Exthelenthy?"

"You're . . . Igor, right?"

"Amathing gueththth, thir. We haven't met before, but I work for Dr. Thaumic on the other thide of the mountain, and thith is my thon, Igor." He smacked the young man around the back of his head. "Thay hello to Hith Grathe, Igor!"

"I don't believe in the peerage," said young Igor, sulkily. "Nor shall I call any man marthter."

"Thee?" said his father. "Thorry about this, Your Grathe, but thith is the younger generation for you. I hope you can find a job for him in the big thity, 'coth he'th totally unemployable in Uberwald. But he'th a very good thurgeon, even if he *doeth* have funny ideaths. He'th got his grandfather's handth, you know."

"I can see the scars," said Vimes.

"Lucky little devil, they thould have been mine by rightth, but he wath old enough to go into the lottery."

---

* The key was in the pattern of scars.

"You *want* to join the Watch, Igor?" said Vimes.

"Yes, sir. I believe Ankh-Morpork is where the future lies, thir."

His father leaned closer to Vimes. "We don't menthion hith thlight thpeech impedient, marthter," he whispered. "Of courthe, it counth againtht him here, you know, in the Igor buthinethth, but I'm thure people will be kind to him in Ankh-Morpork."

"Yes, indeed," said Vimes, removing his handkerchief and absentmindedly dabbing his ear. "And . . . er . . . this rabbit?"

"He's Eerie, thir," said young Igor.

"Good name. Good name. Er . . . is that why he's got human ears all over his back?"

"Early experiment, thir."

"And . . . er . . . the noses?"

There were about a dozen of them, in a large screw-top pickle jar. And they were . . . just noses. Not cut off of anyone, as far as Vimes could see. They had little legs, and were jumping hopefully up and down against the glass, like puppies in a pet shop window. He thought he would hear faint "whee!" noises.

"The wave of the future, thir," said young Igor. "I grow them in special vats. I can do eyes and fingers, too!"

"But they've got little legs!"

"Oh, they wither off in a few hours after they're attached, thir. And they *want* to be useful, my little noses. Bio-artificing for the nexth century, thir. None of that outmoded cutting-up of old bodies—"

His father smacked his head again. "You thee? You thee? Where'th the point in that? Wathtrel! I hope you can do thomething with him, marthter, becauthe I've justht about given up! Not worth breaking down for thpareth, ath we thay!"

Vimes sighed. Still, losing small extremities was a daily hazard in the Watch and the lad was, after all, an Igor. It wasn't as if there *were* any normal people in the Watch. He could afford to put up with a nose breeder in exchange for surgery that didn't involve screaming and buckets of boiling pitch.

He indicated a box beside the young man. It was growling, and rocking from side to side.

"You haven't got a dog, too, have you?" he said, trying to make it sound like a joke.

"That's my tomatoes," said young Igor. "A triumph of modern igoring. They grow enormously."

"Only becauthe they vithiouthly attack all other vegetableth!" said his father. "But I'll thay thith for the lad, marthter, I've never known anyone like him for really *tiny* stitching."

"All right, all right, he sounds like the man I'm looking for," said Vimes. "Or close, at least. Take a seat, young man. I just hope there's going to be room in the coaches . . ."

The door to the yard swung open, blowing in a few snowflakes and Carrot, who stamped his feet.

"A bit of snow overnight, but the road looks open," he said. "They say there's a really big one due tonight, though, so we— Oh, good morning, sir."

"You're fit enough to travel?" said Vimes.

"We both are," said Angua. She crossed the hall and stood next to Carrot.

Once again, Vimes was aware of a lot of words that he hadn't heard. A wise man didn't make inquiries at a time like this. Besides, Vimes could feel the cold coming up through his feet.

He reached a decision.

"Give me your notebook, Captain," he said.

They watched him scribble a few lines.

"Stop at the clacks tower and send a message on to the Yard," he said, handing it back to Carrot. "Tell them you're on the way. Take young Igor here with you and get him settled in, okay? And make a report to His Lordship."

"Er . . . you're not coming?" said Carrot.

"Her Ladyship and I will take the other coach," said Vimes. "Or buy a sleigh. Very comfy things, sleighs. And we'll . . . we'll just take it a little easier. We'll see the sights. We'll dawdle along the way. Understand?"

He saw Angua smile, and wondered if Sybil had confided in her.

"Absolutely, sir," said Carrot.

"Oh, and . . . er . . . go along to Burleigh and Stronginthearm's, order a couple of dozen of everything off the top of their small arms catalogue, and get them onto the next mailcoach due to Bonk for the personal attention of Captain Tantony."

"The mail coach rate will be very expensive, sir . . ." Carrot began.

"I didn't want you to tell me that, Captain. I wanted you to say 'Yes, sir.'"

"Yes, sir."

"And ask at the gate about . . . three gloomy biddies who live in a big house near here. It's got a cherry orchard. Find out the address and when you get back send them three coach tickets to Ankh-Morpork."

"Right, sir."

"Well done. Travel safely. I'll see you in a week. Or two. Three at the outside. All right?"

A few minutes later he stood shivering on the steps, watching the coach disappear into the crisp morning.

He felt a pang of guilt, but it was only a little pang. He gave every day to the Watch and it was time, he thought, for it to give him a week. Or two. Three at the outside.

In fact, he realized, as pangs went it was barely a ping which was, he recalled, a dialect word for watermeadow. Right now he could see a future, which was more than he'd ever had before.

He locked the door and went back to bed.

On a clear day, from the right vantage point on the Ramtops, a watcher could see a very long way across the plains.

The dwarfs had harnessed mountain streams and built a staircase of locks that rose a mile up from the rolling grasslands, for the use of which they charged not just a pretty penny but a very handsome dollar. Barges were always ascending or descending, making their way down to the river Smarl and the cities of the plain. They carried coal, iron, fireclay, pig treacle* and fat, the dull ingredients of the pudding of civilization.

In the sharp, thin air they took several days to get out of sight. On a clear day, you could see next Wednesday.

The captain of one of the barges waiting for the top lock went to tip the dregs of his teapot over the side and saw a small dog sitting on the snowy bank. It sat up and begged, hopefully.

He turned to go back into the cabin when he thought: What a nice little doggie.

It was such a *clear* thought that it almost seemed to him that he was hearing it, but he looked around and there was no one else near him. And dogs certainly couldn't talk.

---

* The treacle mines below Ankh-Morpork had long been exhausted, leaving only a street name to remember them by. But the collision with the Fifth Elephant had buried thousands of acres of prehistoric sugar cane around the borders of Uberwald and the resulting dense crystalline sugar was the foundation of a large mining, confectionery and dentistry industry.

He heard himself think: "This little doggie would be very useful keepin' down rats that might attack the cargo, sort of fing."

It *must* have been him that thought it, he decided. There was no one else nearby, and everyone knew dogs didn't talk.

He said aloud, "But rats don't eat coal, do they?"

He thought, clear as day: "Ah, well, you never know when they might try, right? Anyway, it's such a sweet looking little doggie that's been strugglin' for days through deep snow, huh, not that anyone cares."

The bargeman gave up. There's only so long you can argue with yourself.

Ten minutes later the barge was on the long drop to the plains, with a small dog sitting at the prow, enjoying the breeze.

On the whole, thought Gaspode, it was always best to look to the future.

Nobby Nobbs had made himself a shelter up against the wall of the Watch House, and was gloomily warming his hands when a shadow loomed over him.

"What are you doing, Nobby?" said Carrot.

"Huh? *Captain?*"

"There's no one on the gates, there's no one on patrol . . . Didn't anyone get my message? What's happening?"

Nobby licked his lips.

"We-ell," he said. "There isn't . . . well, there isn't a Watch at the moment. Not *per say*." He flinched. He saw Angua behind Carrot. "Er . . . Mister Vimes with you, at all?"

"What is *happening*, Nobby?"

"Well . . . you *see* . . . Fred kind of . . . and then he got all sort of . . . then next thing you know he was setting for to . . . and then we . . .

and then he wouldn't come out . . . and then we . . . and he nailed up the door . . . and Mrs. Fred came and shouted at him through the letter box . . . and most of the lads have gone off and got other jobs . . . and now there's just me and Dorfl and Reg and Washpot, and we come here turn and turn about and we shove food through the letter box for him . . . and . . . that's it, really . . ."

"Can we have that again with the gaps filled in?" said Carrot.

This took considerably longer. There were still gaps. Carrot forced them open.

"I *see*," he said at last.

"Mister Vimes is going to go spare, isn't he," said Nobby miserably.

"I wouldn't worry about Mister Vimes," said Angua. "Not at the moment."

Carrot was looking up at the front door. It was thick oak. There were bars at all the windows.

"Go and fetch Constable Dorfl, Nobby," he said.

Ten minutes later the Watch House had a new doorway. Carrot stepped over the wreckage and led the way upstairs.

Fred Colon was hunched in the chair, staring fixedly at one solitary sugar lump.

"Be careful," whispered Angua. "He might be in a rather fragile mental state."

"That's very likely," said Carrot. He leaned down and whispered: "Fred?"

"Mm?" murmured Colon.

"*On your feet, Sergeant! Am I 'urtin' you? I ought to be, I'm standin' on your beard! You've got five minutes to wash and shave and be back here with shinin' mornin' face! On your feet! To the washroom! Abou-ut turn! At the double! One-two-one-two!*"

It seemed to Angua that no part of Fred Colon above the neck, except maybe for his ears, was involved in what happened next. Fred Colon *rose* at attention, executed a thudding about-turn and doubled out of the door.

Carrot spun around toward Nobby.

"You, too, Corporal!"

Nobby, trembling with shock, saluted with both hands at once and ran after Colon.

Carrot went over to the fireplace and poked at the ashes.

"Oh dear," he said.

"All burnt?" said Angua.

"I'm afraid so."

"Some of those heaps were like old friends."

"Well, we'll find out if we've missed anything important when it starts to smell," said Carrot.

Nobby and Colon appeared again, breathless and pink. There were a few bits of tissue stuck on Colon's face where the shaving had been too enthusiastic, but he was nevertheless looking better. He was a sergeant again. Someone was giving him orders. His brain was moving. The world was the right side up once again.

"Fred?" said Carrot.

"Yessir?"

"You've got a bit of bird doings on your shoulder."

"I'll see to that right now, sir!" said Nobby, leaping sideways. He dragged a handkerchief from his pocket, spat on it and rubbed hurriedly at Colon's temporary pip. "All gone now, Fred!" he said.

"Well done," said Carrot.

He got up and went over to the window. It did not, in fact, offer much in a way of a view. But he looked out of it as if he could see to the end of the world.

Colon and Nobby shifted uneasily. Right now, they did not like the sound of silence. When Carrot did speak, they blinked as if struck in the face by a cold flannel.

"What I believe there has been here," he said, "is a *confused situation.*"

"That's right, that's right," said Nobby quickly. "We was very confused. Fred?"

He jabbed Fred Colon with his elbow, waking him from a reverie of terror.

"Uh? Oh. Right. Oh yeah. Confusion," he mumbled.

"And I'm afraid I know where the blame ultimately lies," Carrot went on, still apparently engrossed in the spectacle of a man sweeping the Opera House steps.

In the silence, Nobby's lips moved in prayer. Only the whites of Fred Colon's eyes could be seen.

"It was *my* fault," said Carrot. "I blame myself. Mister Vimes left me in charge, and I rushed off with no thought of my duty and put everyone in an impossible position."

Fred and Nobby were both wearing the same expression. It was the face of a man who has seen the light at the end of the tunnel and it has turned out to be the twinkle of the Fairy of Hope.

"I feel almost embarrassed to ask you two to get me out of this pit I have dug for myself," said Carrot. "I can't imagine what Mister Vimes is going to say."

The light at the end of the tunnel winked out for Fred and Nobby. They *could* imagine what Mr. Vimes would say.

"However," said Carrot. He returned to the desk and pulled open the bottom drawer, extracting a few grubby pages that were clipped together.

They waited.

"*However*, each of these men took the King's Shilling and swore an oath to defend the King's Peace," said Carrot, tapping the paper. "An oath, in fact, to the king."

"Yeah, but that was only—aargh!" said Fred Colon.

"Sorry, sir," said Nobby. "I inadvertently trod heavily on Fred's toe while standing to attention."

There was a long drawn-out silken sound. Carrot was drawing his sword from its sheath. He laid it on the desk. Nobby and Colon leaned away from its accusatory point.

"They are all good lads," said Carrot softly. "I'm sure if the two of you call on each and every one of them and explain the situation, they will see where their duty lies. Tell them . . . tell them there is always an *easy* way, if you know where to look. And then we can get on with our jobs, and when Mister Vimes returns from his well-earned holiday the somewhat confused events of the past will be merely—"

"Confusin'?" suggested Nobby, hopefully.

"Exactly," said Carrot. "But I'm glad to see you made so much headway with the paperwork, Fred."

Colon stood nailed to the spot until Nobby, saluting desperately with the other hand, dragged him out of the office.

Angua could hear them arguing all the way down the stairs.

Carrot stood up, dusted off the chair and placed it carefully under the desk.

"Well, we're home," he said.

"Yes," said Angua, and she thought: You *do* know how to do nasty, don't you. But you use it like a claw; it slides out when you need it, and when you don't there's no sign that it's there.

He reached over and took her hand.

"Wolves never look back," he whispered.

The Discworld Novels

The Discworld novels can be read in any order, but
here they are in the order they were published.

Key

★ Wizards
♠ Witches
⚰ Death
† City Watch
✷ Moist von Lipwig
🧚 Tiffany Aching
● Standalones

About the Author

Terry Pratchett (1948–2015) is the acclaimed creator of the globally revered Discworld series, the first of which, *The Color of Magic*, was published in 1983. In all, he is the author of more than fifty bestselling books that have sold more than one hundred million copies worldwide. His novels have been widely adapted for stage and screen, and he was the winner of multiple prizes, including the Carnegie Medal. He was awarded a knighthood by Queen Elizabeth II for services to literature in 2009, although he always wryly maintained that his greatest service to literature was to avoid writing any.

WWW.TERRYPRATCHETTBOOKS.COM

WWW.TERRYPRATCHETT.COM

TERRY PRATCHETT'S DISCWORLD

THE WIZARDS SERIES

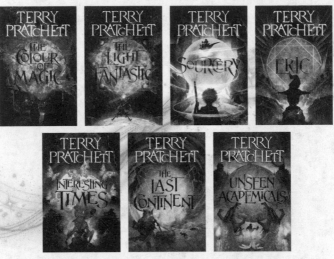

THE CITY WATCH SERIES

TERRY PRATCHETT'S DISCWORLD

THE ADVENTURES OF TIFFANY ACHING, WITCH-IN-TRAINING

"Exuberant and irresistible."
—*Washington Post Book World*

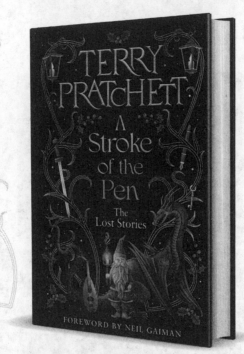